**Praise for John Gilstrap
and His Thrillers**

NICK OF TIME

"A page-turning thriller with strong characters,
exciting action, and a big heart."
—Heather Graham

AGAINST ALL ENEMIES

"Any John Gilstrap novel packs the punch of a
rocket-propelled grenade—on steroids! Tentacles of in-
trigue reach into FBI headquarters and military
hierarchy. Lines are crossed and new ones drawn.
The philosophy of killing to preserve life takes on new
meaning. Gilstrap grabs the reader's attention in a
literary vise grip. Each installment of the Jonathan
Grave series is a *force majeure* of covert incursions,
and a damn good read."
—BookReporter.com

"Tense, clever . . . series enthusiasts are bound to
enjoy this new thriller."
—*Library Journal*

AN AMAZON ... YEAR

"Gilstrap ... is
best novel ... able
bibliography. ... off explosively and keeps
on rolling. Gilstrap puts you in the moment as very few
authors can. And there are many vignettes that will stay
with you long after you have finished the book."
—Joe Hartlaub, BookReporter.com

DAMAGE CONTROL

"Powerful and explosive, an unforgettable journey into the dark side of the human soul. Gilstrap is a master of action and drama. If you like Vince Flynn and Brad Thor, you'll love John Gilstrap."
—**Gayle Lynds**

"Rousing . . . Readers will anxiously await the next installment."
—*Publishers Weekly*

"It's easy to see why John Gilstrap is the go-to guy among thriller writers, when it comes to weapons, ammunition, and explosives. His expertise is uncontested."
—**John Ramsey Miller**

"The best page-turning thriller I've grabbed in ages. Gilstrap is one of the very few writers who can position a set of characters in a situation, ramp up the tension, and—yes, keep it there, all the way through. There is no place you can put this book down."
—**Beth Kanell, Kingdom Books, Vermont**

"A page-turning, near-perfect thriller, with engaging and believable characters . . . unputdownable! Warning—if you must be up early the next morning, don't start the book."
—*Top Mystery Novels*

"Takes you full force right away and doesn't let go until the very last page . . . has enough full-bore action to take your breath away, barely giving you time to inhale. The action is nonstop. Gilstrap knows his technology and weaponry. *Damage Control* will blow you away."
—*Suspense Magazine*

THREAT WARNING

"If you are a fan of thriller novels, I hope you've been reading John Gilstrap's Jonathan Grave series. *Threat Warning* is a character-driven work where the vehicle has four on the floor and horsepower to burn. From beginning to end, it is dripping with excitement."
—**Joe Hartlaub, BookReporter.com**

"If you like Vince Flynn–style action, with a strong, incorruptible hero, this series deserves to be in your reading diet. *Threat Warning* reconfirms Gilstrap as a master of jaw-dropping action and heart-squeezing suspense."
—**Austin Camacho, *The Big Thrill***

HOSTAGE ZERO

"Jonathan Grave, my favorite freelance peacemaker, problem-solver, and tough guy hero, is back—and in particularly fine form. *Hostage Zero* is classic Gilstrap: the people are utterly real, the action's foot to the floor, and the writing's fluid as a well-oiled machine gun. A tour de force!"
—**Jeffery Deaver**

"An entertaining, fast-paced tale of violence and revenge."
—*Publishers Weekly*

"No other writer is better able to combine in a single novel both rocket-paced suspense and heartfelt looks at family and the human spirit. And what a pleasure to meet Jonathan Grave, a hero for our time . . . and for all time."
—**Jeffery Deaver**

AT ALL COSTS

"Riveting . . . combines a great plot and realistic, likable characters with look-over-your-shoulder tension. A page turner."
—*The Kansas City Star*

"Gilstrap builds tension . . . until the last page, a hallmark of great thriller writers. I almost called the paramedics before I finished *At All Costs*."
—*Tulsa World*

"Gilstrap has ingeniously twisted his simple premise six ways from Sunday."
—*Kirkus Reviews*

"Not to be missed."
—*Rocky Mountain News*

NATHAN'S RUN

ALSO BY JOHN GILSTRAP

FICTION

Friendly Fire

Against All Enemies

End Game

High Treason

Damage Control

Threat Warning

Hostage Zero

No Mercy

Scott Free

Even Steven

At All Costs

Nathan's Run

NONFICTION

Six Minutes to Freedom (with Kurt Muse)

COLLABORATION

Watchlist: A Serial Thriller

JOHN GILSTRAP

NICK OF TIME

PINNACLE BOOKS
Kensington Publishing Corp.
www.kensingtonbooks.com

PINNACLE BOOKS are published by

Kensington Publishing Corp.
119 West 40th Street
New York, NY 10018

All Kensington titles, imprints, and distributed lines are available at special quantity discounts for bulk purchases for sales promotions, premiums, fund-raising, educational, or institutional use.
Special book excerpts or customized printings can also be created to fit specific needs. For details, write or phone the office of the Kensington sales manager: Kensington Publishing Corp., 119 West 40th Street, New York, NY 10018, attn: Sales Department; phone 1-800-221-2647.

This book is a work of fiction. Names, characters, businesses, organizations, places, events, and incidents either are the product of the author's imagination or are used fictitiously. Any resemblance to actual persons, living or dead, events, or locales is entirely coincidental.

First printing: October 2016

10 9 8 7 6 5 4 3 2 1

ISBN-13: 978-0-7860-3295-2
ISBN-10: 0-7860-3295-2

Printed in the United States of America

The five parts of *Nick of Time* are available as separate e-books:
Time to Run: ISBN-13: 978-1-60183-698-4; ISBN-10: 1-60183-698-8
Time to Hide: ISBN-13: 978-1-60183-699-1; ISBN-10: 1-60183-699-6
Time to Steal: ISBN-13: 978-1-60183-700-4; ISBN-10: 1-60183-700-3
Time to Die: ISBN-13: 978-1-60183-701-1; ISBN-10: 1-60183-701-1
Time to Live: ISBN-13: 978-1-60183-702-8; ISBN-10: 1-60183-702-X

As always, for Joy.

CONTENTS

PART ONE
TIME TO RUN

Chapter One

Nicolette Janssen's hands trembled as she struggled back into her clothes. She was getting out of here. To hell with the consequences. She'd had it with the lies and the false hopes. This time she was leaving for real.

But she had to hurry. They'd be coming for her soon, and she'd need every second of a head start she could get. She prayed for a ten-minute lead, but doubted she had a chance for that.

Seven, then. Whatever.

As she fumbled with the button on her shorts, she tried not to see the deep purple bruises on her arms. *Ooh, sorry. We're almost there. You sure have tiny veins.* Sure, blame her veins. Forget about the railroad spikes they called needles.

Now there was a favor she'd like to return one day. When they yelled and cussed at her to be careful, she'd be sure to smile and tell them in that soft voice that it was really for their own good. See how they liked it.

Let somebody else be their chemistry set for a while.

With her pants on and fastened, and her T-shirt in

place, Nicki slung her purse over her shoulder and moved tentatively to the door, pausing a beat to thumb the TV remote that was part of the call button that was looped around the side rail of her bed. Oprah and the fears of pending Y2K crises disappeared. Nicki opened the door a crack, just to get a peek, and then stepped out into the wide hallway, standing tall and resisting the urge to run. *Just make like you belong,* she thought. And why not? With all the hours she'd logged, there ought to be a wing named after her. Her flip-flops squeaked on the tile floor as she turned right and started for the bank of elevators.

Jeez, what was she thinking? The elevators opened directly in front of the nurses' station. "Come on, Nicki, think, will you?" she mumbled. If a nurse or, God help her, her dad saw her out here, there'd be serious hell to pay. Patients weren't supposed to be up and around on their own. Hell, they weren't supposed to pee without telling someone. Prisons and hospitals had a lot in common, she imagined.

Oh, shit, there he is! Her dad—the famed prosecutor Carter Janssen—was standing right *at* the nurses' station, ranting at the phlebotomist who last dredged her arm. How typical of dear old dad: Better to yell at a stranger than to comfort a daughter.

An exit sign to her right showed the way to the stair well. As Nicki pushed the door open, she prayed that there wouldn't be an alarm. There wasn't. Score one for the home team. It would have been a short chase. She smiled at the thought of what it might have looked like: sprint fifty yards, fall down unconscious, wake up, run another fifty yards . . .

It turned out that the stairwell was the primary vertical thoroughfare for everyone who wore a lab coat. All of them moved at three times the speed that she could muster, and they were far too busy to notice her.

She had eight flights to go. That meant sixteen half-flights to the bottom, probably more than the total number of stairs she'd navigated in the last three months combined. *See, Dad?* she thought. *I'm not as fragile as you thought.*

If she made it, there'd be no turning back. Maybe now, finally, they would all understand that she meant what she said.

Carter Janssen knew that Priscilla, the phlebotomist, was the wrong target for his rage, but somebody had to answer for this atrocity, and she was the most available hospital employee. Nowhere near her thirtieth birthday, the technician looked close to tears.

"All I do is draw blood," she whined.

"But you're part of the *team*," Carter growled, leaning on the word he'd heard so often from the transplant crew. "We succeed or fail as a *team*, don't you remember?"

"You need to speak to the doctor," Priscilla said. She moved to step around him. "I have nothing to do with the decisions that are made."

"I'd love to speak to a doctor," Carter said, making a broad sweeping motion with both arms. "Do you see one here? All I see are people telling me that the doctors are all too busy to speak with me."

"Doctor Burkhammer is in surgery. I already told you that."

"That's not possible," Carter snapped. "He can't possibly be in surgery, because my *daughter* was next on his dance card, and she got stood up!" He yelled that last phrase, making Priscilla jump, and drawing uncomfortable glances from the nurses behind the glass. One nurse in particular, a broad-shouldered one in the back who carried herself with the posture of a boss, reached for a telephone. Carter had the distinct feeling that she was calling security.

"Can I help you?" a voice asked from behind.

Carter turned to see a chubby redheaded man who must have bought his clothes before going on a diet. He wore woefully out-of-date horn-rimmed glasses with lenses thick enough to start a fire if he looked the wrong way in sunlight. "Who are you?"

"I'm Dr. Cavanaugh," the man said, extending his hand. "We met a few months ago. I'm from the Heart-Lung Consortium."

Carter's jaw dropped. The last time he'd seen Dr. Cavanaugh, the guy had been the size of a boxcar. That he was now only thirty pounds overweight meant that he'd lost over a hundred. "I wouldn't have recognized you."

The doctor beamed and patted his stomach. "I decided to start taking some of my own advice. I'm terribly sorry about Nicolette. I don't mean to sound flippant, but such are the ups and downs of the transplant business."

"The ups and downs?" Carter repeated. The words tasted bitter on his tongue. "That's it? That's all you have to say to me?"

Dr. Cavanaugh gently grasped Carter's elbow with one hand and gestured to the collection of seats in the hallway. "Perhaps we should sit down and discuss this."

"No," Carter said. "I don't want to sit. I'm waiting for Nicki to get dressed, and I don't want her to step out and not see me."

"Well, let's keep our voices down, then."

"*Let's* keep *our* voices down? What are we, in fifth

grade? What the hell happened?" Carter reached under his suit jacket and pulled a pager from his belt. "We got the word," he said. "The message came through, we came down here just like we were supposed to, we went through all the pre-op bullshit, and then nothing. *Nothing.* A nurse told us it was just a false alarm, and that it was time for us to go home."

Cavanaugh showed Carter his palms in an effort to soothe the situation. "I understand that you're upset—"

"What the hell is going on?" That time, Carter's voice rolled like artillery fire down the hallway.

Cavanaugh jumped, and seemed conflicted as to whether he should answer. Finally, he said, "They changed their minds."

"Who?"

"The donor's family."

Carter wasn't sure what answer he was expecting, but this wasn't it. "They get a vote?" His tone betrayed his utter disbelief.

Cavanaugh sighed, clearly resigned to the fact that Carter would never understand. "They lost a child to suicide, Mr. Janssen. I know you think you've had a blow of bad news, but please don't ever—not for a moment—think that those poor people owed you anything. They made a decision and then they changed their mind."

The words rattled Carter. "I don't understand," he said. "They'd prefer that their child's organs be buried in the ground?"

"It's a problem we face with patients like Nicki," Cavanaugh explained. The rationality of his tone and his words belied the horror of his message. "There are a number of surgeons and patients alike who look at bilateral heart and lung transplants as the ultimate act of selfishness. A grieving parent has to decide, in the height of their grief, as they are being bombarded with one nightmare after another, whether their loved one's viscera should help only one person, or help many. The vast majority of transplant recipients need only a heart or one lung—"

"And Nicki needs all three." Carter closed his eyes against the pain of the revelation.

"Exactly."

"My God." Carter stared, searching for the next thing to say. He nodded toward that cluster of seats. "I think I'll sit down after all."

Dr. Cavanaugh took the seat directly opposite. "I don't know if this is a detail you want or need to know, but the reason Dr. Burkhammer couldn't meet with you and explain this himself is because he had to perform the heart transplant that the family made possible."

The enormity of it all was too much. So, this was how it was meant to be? At the whim of confused parents, one girl is condemned to death so that others might live? Carter had never allowed himself to understand that someone else would have to die to make that happen.

But those were concerns for another parent. Carter had a devastated child of his own to worry about. "Has this happened before?"

"Rarely, but it does happen. And before you ask why we don't make certain before we notify the recipient, the answer is, we try. We get a yes and a signature, and because time is of the essence, we make the phone calls."

"So, they *signed* an agreement and reneged?" Suddenly, Carter the lawyer felt his feet on more solid ground.

"We're not selling commodities, Mr. Janssen.

These are organs. Some might say that they're a part of the donor's soul. If grieving parents dig in their heels, we're not going to force a donation just because they spilled ink on a page. We're not ghouls."

But we had a deal, he didn't say. To give Nicki life and then to take it away seemed so horribly cruel. In Carter Janssen's world, everything was ordered and neat. Promises were met, and if they weren't then that was what courtrooms were for. This was all so . . . *unfair*.

"What can you tell me about the recipient?" Carter asked. The question came partly out of a need to fill the silence, but also from a need to know in his gut that whoever it was, was worth the price of Nicki's life.

"I can't say anything about that," Cavanaugh said. "I'm sure you understand."

"Man, woman, boy, girl? You can't tell me any of that?"

The doctor shook his head. "I know how devastating this news must be to you, and I caution both you and your daughter not to lose hope. Not only is there a chance that another donor might appear, but there are some fairly encouraging mid-term therapies for Nicki's condition—"

"She wants nothing to do with them."

Cavanaugh's head bobbed, but he clearly dismissed the relevance of that. "Of course she doesn't. She's a teenager. They frequently reject what is best for them. But as her father—"

Carter cut him off with a raised hand. "No lectures, okay? Not now. I'll do what I have to do. But it's such an onerous procedure."

Cavanaugh scowled. "Are we talking about the same procedure? We merely insert a pump into her chest—"

"And administer prostacyclin. Yes, I know. But it means hospital time."

"We have to monitor the condition carefully."

"Of course you do. Doctor, you don't have to justify any of this to me. Nor do you have to explain it to Nicki, but I've got to tell you, after watching her mother wither away in here, she's scared to death of hospitals."

"Well, then we have to set her mind at ease."

Carter closed his eyes to stave off the frustration. "That's not possible," he said. When he opened them again, they felt red. "Without the transplants she's got maybe nine months left, and of those only six are likely to be anything close to normal. The way she sees it, every hour she spends in a hospital is an hour she's not spending cramming life into every day."

"But it's necessary," Cavanaugh said.

"Of course it's necessary," Carter snapped. "Everything is so goddamned necessary. But it sucks."

Chapter Two

"Hi, this is Nicki. I'm either on the phone or I'm ignoring you. Leave a message, please."

"Nicolette, it's Dad. I don't know what's going on, but please give me a call. Like, yesterday."

She was gone. Poof. Without a trace. Carter could feel his face getting hot as his hands started to tremble. The hospital staff was falling all over themselves apologizing, but he was tired of hearing it. "Okay," he said, silencing the three nurses. "There are only so many ways out of here. Let's get security looking for her."

Okay. Absolutely. Brilliant idea. Clearly thrilled to have something productive to do, the nurses scurried off to put the plan into action. And the less face time they had with a lawyer, the better. There wasn't a hospital in the country that didn't look at lawyers as organisms only slightly less terrifying than Ebola.

Carter seethed. Nicki never would have dreamed of pulling a stunt like this if her mother were still alive. Jenny wouldn't have tolerated it. It had been her special gift to communicate with their daughter. In the quiet moments, he still wondered why God made the choices He had. Life would have been so much better for Nicki if He'd chosen Carter for His cancer games and left Jenny alone.

Carter kicked himself for not seeing the escape in the offing. It was exactly what she'd promised to do if he didn't agree to her terms. He just never thought she'd follow through. Her terms were the equivalent to suicide, for God's sake. He'd given her credit for being smarter than that.

He had to find her, and he had to get her therapy started as soon as possible. With the prostacyclin and a minor turn in their luck, she might be able to buy the time she needed to wait out the next donor.

So, where would she have gone? He spent a minute running through her options, but only came up with one: home. How sad was that? Ever since her grim prognosis was announced, Nicki's depression had manifested as an ugly rejection of all her friends and her hobbies, driving her instead to the impersonal interaction of the Internet and its endless chat rooms. God only knew what she talked about.

Carter called the house three times during his drive home, but to no avail. That meant one of two things: either she wasn't there, or she was dodging his calls.

Okay, there was one more possibility, but he refused to consider it. Suicide.

He pressed a little harder on the gas.

I don't care what happens to me anymore, she had told him a dozen times. *It's my life and I'm tired of it. Just let nature take its course.* Those damnable adolescent platitudes on fatalism drove him up the friggin' wall.

What the hell did a seventeen-year-old know about life or living? For her, life was exclusively about the comforts—junk food, freedom, and the right friends. There *was* no world outside of suburbia for her. It would be years before she could realize how thoroughly her limited horizon blocked any view of the future. What seemed so bleak to her now might well be the gateway to great things. Momentary discomfort was the price of long-term good health, period. Why couldn't he make her understand that? Why was she so much more impenetrable than a dozen juries?

God, he missed Jenny.

Carter slid the turn onto the parkway, past the landmark diner that told him he was exactly six point seven miles from home.

For some awful reason, his mind had seized on the image of Nicki slitting her wrists. If that was how she chose to do herself in, there'd be no stopping the bleeding. Not with the Coumadin on board.

"Stop it," he said aloud.

Nicki needed a mother, a confidante. He tried to fill those shoes, but every attempt at a father-daughter chat somehow turned into a cross-examination. His was a world of facts and logic, Nicki's was one of emotions and feelings. How was he supposed to deal with that? A couple of decades ago, when he'd signed on for this parenthood gig, he'd never in a million years thought that he might have to go it alone. With a daughter.

He sped past the Alabaster Dam on his right. Four point four miles to go.

It had been twenty months, almost to the day, since Jenny had been diagnosed with pancreatic cancer, thus beginning the longest, most relentlessly awful period of Carter's life. Two months later, just after Thanksgiving, she was dead. It felt like no time at all, the cancer equivalent of being hit by a truck, and whatever genius had devised the platitudes about grief diminishing with time had no clue what he was talking about.

Back in the happy days, Carter and Jenny used to chat glibly about what each of them would do in the event of the other's death. Jenny made him promise to let her go first, because she said she'd never be able to find another man, and he'd find a new wife in a heartbeat.

In a heartbeat. The irony brought a lump to his throat. There was only one heartbeat that he cared to hear again, and Carter prayed every night that she could somehow return to him. It was silly, he knew, but it was all he had.

He navigated the hairpin curve at Waples Mill. Three point eight miles to go.

In Nicolette's mind, she became an orphan when Jenny died. Those two were different sides of the same brain. They could think each other's thoughts, complete each other's sentences. Now, she found herself facing her own mortality without an ear she was willing to talk to. No wonder she was so depressed.

Nothing about Carter's relationship with Nicki had ever been easy, but it tore him apart to be shut out of her pain. The only person she was willing to open her heart to was the psychologist who charged a hundred twenty bucks an hour for the privilege.

He slowed for the stop sign at Clatterbuck Road, then gunned the engine. Three miles. He called her cell phone again, left another message.

In the clarity of 20/20 hindsight, Carter should have seen Nicki's impending illness long before he did. She'd had no stamina, no energy for anything but sleep. She'd allowed her grades to slip. Because it had started at the height of Jenny's illness, Carter had written it off to normal, ordinary depression. Besides, teenagers were *always* tired, right?

Working on the assumption that it was all about the depression, he didn't even take her to the doctor till February, almost three months after they'd buried Jenny. A diagnosis took four months: primary pulmonary hypertension, a gift from a pharmaceutical company that preyed on young women's desires to look like supermodels with physiques more suitable to the gulag than the runway. A death sentence.

Jenny had picked up on Nicki's binge-and-purge cycle four years ago and saved her life by whisking her off to a shrink. Carter had never had much tolerance for psychology or its practitioners—he'd always seen it as equal parts voodoo and bullshit—but God bless him, the doctor's counseling had turned her around. To Nicki's horror, she'd even put on a few pounds.

Then came Jenny's Cancer. The Big C. Within a month, between the chemo and the radiation, there was barely enough life left in Jenny to power a smile. A few weeks later, she was dead.

Suddenly, with the speed of half a finger-snap, Carter and Nicki were all alone together. Father-stranger, meet daughter-stranger. It was like trying to turn on a light when no one had connected the wires. All they shared between them was the desperate need for Jenny to somehow reenter their lives.

Carter took the bridge at Wilson's Creek way too fast. If there'd been a car coming the other way, there'd have been no survivors. As it was, he was only a mile from the house and accelerating even faster.

Nicki's relapse, it turned out, had been inevitable. In Nicki's mind, the doctor explained, recovery had been all about pleasing her mother. In the tangled non-logic that defined so much of psychology, Jenny's death had relieved Nicki's obligations to the get-well contract. "Surely you must have seen the warning signs," the doctor had observed. "Some kind of abnormal behavior."

Right. Nicki's behavior hadn't resembled normalcy since she was twelve. Besides, Carter would have been looking for all the wrong signs.

This time, instead of bingeing and purging, Nicki turned to diet drugs obtained from friends. Carter knew nothing about them, of course, but if he had, he might actually have approved. They'd have seemed like a good compromise: Nicki would eat *something* and keep it down for the whole day, even as the drugs reduced the size of her appetite. The diet drug was two drugs, actually, and taken together, according to the popular media—hell, according to the evening news— the results were truly amazing. People shed unwanted pounds, seemingly without side effects. Why wouldn't that have been a good thing to try? If it would have improved her consistently sour attitude, he'd have tried anything.

But there *were* side effects. Deadly ones. Primary pulmonary hypertension, PPH for short, thickened the tiny vessels in the lungs. This thickening, or "hardening," in turn caused the pressure in those vessels to increase, causing blood to back up in the rest of the body as the cells awaited their turn to pass through the narrowed passages. The biological chain reaction that resulted took a half hour for the doctor to explain, but the time would come when Nicki's lungs would no longer be able to sustain life.

The average life expectancy from diagnosis to death was eighteen months. The average waiting time for transplants was twenty-four to thirty months. Do the math.

At first, Carter had refused to believe it. Doctors were

a dime a dozen, for heaven's sake. He'd figured he could keep shopping till he found a physician who told him what he wanted to hear.

But the decision was unanimous: a bilateral heart-lung transplant was her only hope for long-term recovery. In the end, Carter decided on a multipronged approach. He'd wear the damn pager for the transplants, but he'd also keep pressure on the doctors to try something new.

No matter what the literature said, come hell or high water, he was not going to let Nicki die.

God forbid that Nicki might make it easier. She was so pissed off that her regularly scheduled teen years had been interrupted by illness that she'd turned downright recalcitrant. She just wanted it all to end, she'd said. Life wasn't worth living if it couldn't be lived on her terms, and long hospital stays for experimental procedures were not on her agenda. She wanted movies and pizza, not EKGs and intravenous drugs.

With five hundred yards to go before his street, Carter eased the Volvo down from eighty and hoped that he wouldn't spin out in the turn.

Carter's house on Berwick Place in the Westgate subdivision was identical to fifty percent of the homes in his neighborhood. The builder had designed exactly two interiors for his houses—both center-hall colonials, but one about $75,000 more expensive than the other—with half a dozen exterior elevations for each. The effect to the casual passerby was a wide variety of charming, 2,200-square-foot brick-and-siding homes. The homeowners' association saw to it that the lawns stayed trimmed and green, and that nobody dared to install chain-link fences.

Carter jerked the Volvo to a halt in the driveway,

nearly forgetting to turn off the ignition as he dashed to the front door. His heart sank when he found it locked. Nicki *never* locked the door when she was home, despite his repeated demands that she do so. Nobody would try to do harm to a prosecutor's daughter, she'd say with a smirk.

His key found the slot and he threw open the heavy door. "Nicki?" he called. "Nicki, where are you!"

No answer.

"Nicki! Are you here?"

Still, no answer.

Wheeling from the kitchen, he charged back through the foyer and up the stairs to her bedroom. "Please God," he prayed, "let her be okay."

Nicki made the one phone call she needed to make, then turned her phone off. She'd silenced the ringer while in the hospital room, so as she looked at the Nokia's display, she was surprised to see that she'd already missed five calls from her dad. So he knew. The clock was ticking.

She swung around in the backseat of the cab for the thousandth time to check out the back window to make sure no one was following her. As stupid as it sounded, this was the first time she'd ever been in a taxicab. It all felt so daring and adventurous. Now all she had to do was keep her cool. It wasn't the time to get jittery.

And no one was following. Duh. She hadn't broken any laws; why should anyone be following? She settled back into her seat in time to catch the taxi driver watching her in the rearview mirror. She smiled.

Now you've made him remember you, she thought—a violation of Brad's cardinal rule of evasion. How many times had he told her that? A hundred? No, five hundred. It was the keystone to her getaway plan: just blend in and always walk.

Wait till he found out that she'd actually put the plan into action. He'd be shocked.

Almost as shocked as her dad.

The first step in the plan was easiest to remember: cash. Not credit, not checks, but cold hard greenback money, the last nearly untraceable source of spending.

As they pulled into the center of Pitcairn Village—the chamber of commerce was lobbying to have the name changed to Olde Towne Pitcairn in hopes of spurring a tourist trade—Nicki leaned closer to the cabbie and pointed to a building up ahead on the right, past the Lewis and Clark memorial that marked the center of the square. "Could you pull in there for a minute, please?"

"Where? At the bank?"

"Yes, please."

Nicki had the door open a second after the vehicle pulled to a halt. "I'll just be a second," she said. "Do you mind waiting?"

"Are you going to pay me?"

"After I get some money, I will."

The cabbie was of some Middle Eastern descent, and his glare did not project trust.

She wasn't going to argue with him; he'd stay or he wouldn't. She crossed the sidewalk and entered the lobby, turning right to get to the ATM. She slipped in the card and entered her PIN with one finger while she kept another two fingers crossed that Dad hadn't yet found the card missing from his wallet and canceled it. It'd been two weeks, and she'd been counting on his inattention to anything but his work. She had him pegged as more of a check-cashing kind of guy than an ATM guy anyway, ever dedicated to anything that was out of date.

When the "Welcome, Carter Janssen" screen greeted her, Nicki smiled. "Time to milk the cash cow," she mumbled, smiling at the image her words conjured.

Her attempt to withdraw $5,000 choked the machine, prompting it to clatter and beep, finally displaying on the screen that $500 was the maximum she could take. So much for a turn of good luck. She'd had no idea that banks limited withdrawals. According to Brad, they needed a couple thousand, minimum, to make this work. As the machine spat out twenty-five $20 bills, Nicki tried to figure out how to make up the difference. She thought about running the card through a second time, but worried that the machine might sense a theft in progress and eat it.

She'd think of something later. As it was, she was spending way too much time in front of a security camera.

The driver was still waiting at the curb, the engine running, when Nicki walked up to his window and asked, "What's the fare so far?"

He pointed to the meter. "Twelve dollars and eighty cents."

She gave him a twenty. "Here. Is this enough to keep you waiting for a while longer?"

"How much longer?"

"Ten minutes, max."

"I will wait for seven minutes," he said.

Nicki rolled her eyes, knowing instantly that she'd misplayed that hand. If she wanted ten minutes, she should have asked for twelve. "Fine. Just don't leave me here."

"Where are you going?"

"To the coffee shop."

She walked across the street to the Square Cup and Saucer, a coffee bar/Internet lounge. Nicki had been a coffee fan for as long as she could remember. Even when she was a little girl, her mom would fix her a cup that was mostly sugar and milk, but she'd always loved the taste. Yet another favorite pastime crossed off the list by her death sentence. No caffeine, period.

But God, the aroma of the place. She wondered if this was how an ex-smoker felt when she sat in a bar.

Oh, what the hell. Brad said this was a whole new beginning. When the barista looked to her, Nicki ordered a large coffee to go.

It took a minute to figure out how the pay-for-computer-time thing worked, but only a minute. She paid her three dollars, slid into a booth, and clicked on her service provider. The page opened up in a blink, the wonders of a high-speed connection. Back home, Dad was too cheap to pay for a DSL connection, so she was stuck with a screechy modem. She logged on under her regular screen name and briefly scanned the headings of her incoming e-mail, finding nothing but junk, three of which were offers to make her penis longer. Go figure.

She still had three and a half minutes of the cabbie's time reserved when she opened the "Write Mail" window and tapped in Brad's address.

"Okay," she wrote. "You win. It's 2:37 now, and I'm on the next bus outta here. Don't stand me up. Luv, N."

She read it four times to make sure that it said all that it needed to, but not a word more, then clicked the Send button. Just like that, at the speed of light, her new life began.

Sipping her coffee, aglow with the feeling of guilt,

Nicki again concentrated on keeping her movements smooth and as normal-looking as possible. She ran the plan through her head one more time.

Looking back, it was probably a mistake to leave the message on the home phone so early. She just didn't want Dad to worry.

February 15

I got my work assignment, and it's the shittiest one. I'm in the kitchen, slogging pots. I've never seen so much stuck-on crap. And the roaches. There's a decent guy here named Derek Johnson who says the roaches own the place. We're only squatters.

I'm beginning to get the lay of the place. The Posse is the gang to stay away from. It's all white boys and they're sick bastards. If they want you they own you. That's what I've heard. So far, they haven't paid any attention to me. They're not afraid of anybody but Officer Georgen.

Lucas Georgen is a monster. He's 6' 4", probably, and I'm guessing three hundred pounds. He doesn't put up with nothing from anybody. He tells you the sky is green and you say yes, sir. I've seen him lay his stick against a guy's head, and it's good night, Nellie. Bastard hits the floor, and people step over him.

The Posse moves around this place like a pack of wolves. I don't know how many of them there are, but I think I know who the leaders are. In the World, they'd all be bikers. Skinheads, maybe. They've got tattoos on their tattoos. Derek says there's nothing to worry about from the Posse so long as you stay out of their way and never owe them anything.

I don't even look at them.

Chapter Three

Sitting on the edge of Nicki's bed, Carter listened to the message on the machine a dozen times before his mind shifted out of neutral.

"Hi, Daddy. I know how you think, so I'll tell you now that I haven't been kidnapped and I'm not doing any kind of suicide-y thing. I'm just being me, okay? And it's not about our argument last night. I just had to get away from everything. I'm not living my last months with tubes sticking out of me. You were there for Mom and I know you'd be there for me, but I don't want to go that way.

"By the time you hear this, I'll already be on my way to where I'm going. If I knew where that was, I'd tell you. There's a lot I would tell you if I could, but you'd never understand. I know you try to, but you just can't. And I don't say that to be mean.

"I can tell you that we'll be safe, though. And that I'll always love you."

It was almost two o'clock. God only knew what kind of head start she had. His heart hammered in his chest and his hands trembled as he tried to think logically. Nicki was a smart girl, a little impulsive, but very smart—the kind of smart you got from books, though; in the street smarts department, she was a zero. His mind whirled with possibilities. She wasn't suicidal and she hadn't been kidnapped. How reassuring.

Not.

Where would she go? How would she get there? He didn't keep any cash in the house, and she didn't have access to his credit or debit cards, so what could she possibly have been thinking?

Carter's head flooded with dozens of images he'd witnessed over the course of his career: the rapes, the mutilations, the murders. Didn't she ever listen to a thing he told her?

Think, Carter, he commanded himself.

It was useless. The very notion of seeing the world though her eyes made his head hurt.

Come on, think, goddammit. Nothing was ever hopeless.

As he sat there on the bed, awash in stuffed animals and a little unnerved by the come-hither look from Leonardo DiCaprio and the largely shirtless cast of *Dawson's Creek,* he tried to wade his way through what little information he had.

He rewound the tape and played it again. And again. One more time.

Then he heard a clue. It was near the end of her message: *I can tell you that we'll be safe, though.*

We.

So, at least she wasn't alone. He tried to think which of her friends might agree to something like this. Whom would she choose to run away with?

As he cast his glance toward the telephone on Nicki's

nightstand, he realized with a heaviness in his gut that he no longer knew who Nicki's friends were. Rachel Raty was a name that popped into his mind, but it was a name he hadn't heard in a long time. They were great buddies a while ago, but did they even talk to each other now? Carter knew how it was with teenage girls; he knew that a single transgression could separate best friends from worst enemies, and for the life of him, he didn't have a clue where Rachel currently stood in the hierarchy.

There *had* to be a name. Nicki was a terrific kid, and terrific kids all had friends. So, how come he couldn't come up with one?

Nothing on earth quite matched the odor of a Greyhound bus. The faint aroma of diesel combined with the sickening sweetness of the chemical toilet to form a mixture Nicki could almost see. It hung thickly in the air like humidity, made even worse by the two dozen varieties of perfume and aftershave that surrounded her.

For a while, she'd been able to keep the seat next to her empty by pretending to be asleep at every stop, but as they pulled into Baltimore, she knew that the charade would have to end. By her cursory count, there were only five seats left unoccupied, and at least that many people waiting to board. Unless a lot of people got off, some of the new arrivals would have to stand.

She moved her purse closer to her feet and tried to stuff it deeper under the seat in front of her. A black couple led the parade down the center aisle, each of them about a century old and hanging on to each other for balance that neither could provide. They doddered down three or four rows before a young guy wearing a Caterpillar baseball cap stood from his single window seat and joined a college kid who'd been trying to reserve a seat for his leg.

Caterpillar-man tossed a quick glance toward Nicki, but before she could return it with a flirty smile, he looked away and planted himself in his new digs.

She felt herself blush. Guys were always like that around her—something about her gaze made them uncomfortable. Her dad told her that she was crazy—that she was beautiful and everyone could see it for miles around—but she knew better. She was ugly. Born that way and getting uglier by the day.

Her suspicions were confirmed when a guy who looked more like Brad Pitt than Brad Pitt did refused to meet her eyes at all.

By the time it all settled out, Nicki's seatmate turned out to be somebody's grandmother, her thick body wrapped in a sundress the likes of which Nicki hadn't seen in years. She'd zeroed in on Nicki's seat the instant her head had cleared the door.

"Well, hello, young miss. May I sit here?" The woman's voice had a squeaky quality to it that put Nicki in mind of a man trying to impersonate a woman.

Nicki looked at the seat and shrugged.

"I'm Dora," the woman said, settling in. "I'm going all the way to Hattiesburg, Mississippi. I've got grandchildren down there."

Nicki smiled as politely as she could, and tried not to notice that the woman smelled vaguely like salami.

"How far are you going?" Dora pressed.

"Just to Brookfield." Nicki tried to sound abrupt and unfriendly, in hopes that Lorna Doone, or whatever her name was, would get the hint.

No such luck. "Brookfield, Virginia? Well, then you're almost home." She paused a beat then added, "You *are* going home, aren't you?"

Nicki shook her head. "No, I'm meeting a friend."

"How old are you?"

This time, Nicki's look exactly matched her tone. "How old are *you*?"

"Seventy-two." If Dora thought her seatmate was being rude, she didn't show it.

Nicki rolled her eyes. "I'm nineteen," she lied.

Dora clucked. "I'd have guessed seventeen and a half."

Jesus, she nailed it perfectly.

"Do you feel all right, dear? You don't look so good."

Nicki sighed dramatically. "Why, thank you so much. You, on the other hand, are the very picture of health and fashion."

The irony missed Dora by a mile. "I really don't mean to pry," she said. "Maybe I'm just a nervous traveler, but I always like to get to know my seatmates. It's one of the real pleasures of taking the bus. I just thought that if you were ill, then maybe—"

"I'm not ill, okay?" Nicki snapped. "I'm just dying. There's a difference."

Vinnie Campanella eyed the sweet rolls and tried to make temptation go away. He'd come into the shop for a cup of coffee, dammit—something to while away the ninety minutes that stood between him and the boarding call for his flight—not for a sweet roll. He'd had his diet shake for breakfast only two hours ago, and they were going to serve two meals on the plane, so he had no right to the snack-urge that haunted him. He'd promised Bets that he'd be strong this time, that this was finally the diet that was going to work.

But honest to God, that cinnamon spiral in the case just to the right of the cash register had a voice, and it was calling to him in that lovely, intoxicating way that only warm pastries could manage. How could such a tiny treat be harmful?

No! he commanded himself. This was only the second day of his new way of life, and he wasn't going to let himself be booby-trapped by an inanimate object, even if it *was* slathered in vanilla cream cheese frosting. If only the guy in front of him would move a little faster getting his wallet out, Vinnie could pay for his coffee and get the heck out of there. And wouldn't you know it? That asshole bought a chocolate chip cookie. The guy was only thirty years old, had a full head of hair and looked as if he could run ten miles without breaking a sweat, and he treated himself to a cookie! Where was the justice in the world?

Finally, it was Vinnie's turn. He ordered his grande coffee, proud of himself for stopping there.

"Is that all?" the clerk asked. At least that's what he thought she asked. It was hard to tell through the accent.

"No," he said. "I mean, yes. This is all. Just the coffee."

"No pastry?"

What was this, a conspiracy? "No, just the sweet roll. I mean, just the coffee." *Goddammit.*

The lady smiled at him. It was a friendly, knowing smile, entirely harmless, and he hated her for it. The smile only reminded him of the similar pitiful glances he'd gotten all his life from exotic-looking women.

They dared to be friendly because he was too fat to be a threat. Always was, and always would be.

Vinnie made a mental note to return to this very shop a year from now, after he'd dropped his seventy-five pounds. See what kind of smile he got from her then.

I can do this, he thought. *Keep your goddamn sweet rolls. I'll eat rabbit food for a year if I have to.* He pulled his wallet from his suit coat pocket and finger-walked through the bills till he found two singles and laid them on the counter. He didn't bother to wait for the change.

At the little kiosk where the half-and-half and the honey and the sugar beckoned him, Vinnie added a dollop of skim milk—it didn't even change the color from black to brown—and two packets of Equal. As he turned away and headed into the main traffic of Dulles Airport's C Concourse, he actually felt proud of himself. That was a lot of temptation coming in a short burst, and he'd withstood all of it. Maybe this really was—

The collision came from nowhere. One second, Vinnie was lost in his thoughts, and in the next he was lost in a fountain of scalding coffee. A guy—a kid, really, maybe twenty years old—moving too fast for the crowd hit him with the force of an NFL tackle. The impact knocked him off his feet entirely, and sent his coffee flying in an arc that somehow missed everyone and everything but the floor. Vinnie said "Oof" as he fell—actually formed the word—and closed his eyes as he anticipated the inevitable impact with the tile floor.

But the impact never came. His assailant caught him by the lapels in midair and kept him from hitting the floor at all. "I am so sorry," the boy gushed. "Are you all right?"

"What the hell are you doing?" Vinnie shouted.

"Really, I'm sorry."

"For God's sake, you could have killed me. Are you out of your mind, running like that through an airport?"

"I'm late for my flight." The young man seemed to know the emptiness of his words even as he said them. Vinnie could feel the strength in the kid's arms as he set him on his feet again and brushed him off. "Honest to God, sir, I am so, so sorry."

"You should be," Vinnie said.

"I am. Truly, I am. Are you hurt? Should I call an ambulance?"

The thought hadn't even occurred to Vinnie. "No, I'm not hurt. I'm fine. But great God almighty, you have to be more careful."

The young man nodded. "Yes, sir, you're right. I was stupid. I'm just glad you aren't hurt."

Vinnie scowled as he brushed himself off. It was hard to be angry at someone so genuinely apologetic. "No, really, I'm fine."

"Let me at least buy you another cup of coffee."

Vinnie shook his head. "No, that's all right."

But the kid was already on his way back into the coffee shop. "How do you take it?"

"A little skim milk," Vinnie said. "And two Equals." He had to smile at the ease with which the instructions came out.

Three minutes later, the matter was settled. Vinnie gratefully accepted his new coffee—this one a venti size as a form of compensation—and three times told linebacker-boy that everything was truly all right. Finally, they went their different ways.

As Vinnie headed toward his gate, it never occurred

to him to wonder why the kid who was in such a hurry to catch his flight was now on his way back to the main terminal.

Rachel Raty hadn't spoken to Nicki in over three months. In fact, according to her, no one in the old crowd had spoken to her. "I don't mean to be mean or anything, but Nicki's gotten kind of weird recently. I know she's sick and all, but sometimes, when she walks into class, she like just doesn't talk to anybody. Try to talk to her and she bites your head off. I don't think she hangs around with anyone anymore . . ."

Carter made an excuse and hung up. The clock was ticking too fast to waste time listening to some bitch dis his daughter. A second call, this one to Leslie Johnson, another name he pulled out of memory, brought essentially the same result. He stared at the phone after he hung up with her. Maybe Nicki really didn't have any friends anymore. Given the way she'd been behaving recently—the huge mood swings and the general nastiness—how difficult was that to imagine?

Okay, so if the "we" of her note wasn't someone from school, then who might it be?

Carter's eyes scanned the room and fell on her computer. Good God, that was it. The Internet.

Nicki's computer was an old IBM workhorse with few bells and no whistles, but it had nonetheless claimed that part of her existence once owned by the television. He couldn't count the number of nights he'd been on his way to bed at some ungodly hour and heard Nicki tapping away at her keyboard. Sometimes, he'd hear her laughing as somebody typed something back at her. Once or twice, he'd mentioned to her that it was getting late and that she should get to bed, but she'd re-

sponded with one of the withering glares that always
seemed to be in special reserve just for him.

Jenny used to lecture Carter on the importance of
choosing your battles when raising a teenager, and all
things considered, he'd decided to let the computer
fixation go. Score another home run for dear old dad.
His stomach knotted even tighter. The thought of running away with someone was horrifying in its own
right; that it would be with some predator she'd met
online was unthinkable.

Two years ago, Carter had worked a computer-
stalker case in which a teenage girl was lured out of
her house by some psycho posing as a sympathetic
ear. She'd been tortured and raped and ultimately left
to die, but turned out to be stronger than her attacker
had thought. She'd lived, only to wish every day that
she hadn't. Mercifully, the latticework of facial scars
were invisible to her slashed eyeballs. The police had
done a terrific job identifying a guy named Dickie Mene-
fee as the would-be murderer—a big-necked, washed-out
old gym teacher with the IQ of a seat cushion—but the girl,
Deni James, either couldn't or wouldn't make a positive
identification. Carter had never seen such terror on a witness. As a result, Little Dick, as Carter had come to call
him, got to walk. Last time he saw the son of a bitch,
Little Dick was holding court with others of his breed
in a little greasy spoon called the Pitcairn Inn, stuffing
his face with pancakes and beer, reveling in the fact
that the regulars still called him "Coach."

Carter made sure that Nicki heard the details of the
Deni James case, if only to drive home the point that
the Internet was a vast, unexplored frontier for psy-
chopaths. The anonymity of cyberspace made it poten-
tially more dangerous than the worst neighborhood in
the toughest city on earth. In the bricks-and-mortar

world, you at least had a chance to get a good read on people, to look them in the eye. In cyberspace, men could be women, friends could be predators. As her interest in computers grew, Nicki needed to understand that. He even showed her a few of the pictures of Deni's gruesome wounds.

After all of that, how could Nicki possibly run off with some guy from cyberspace? And he was certain it was a guy. Internet sickos were almost always guys.

Carter moved from the bed to her desk chair, where he pressed the button and waited for the machine to grind through its booting protocol. The monitor popped and crackled, and then he faced the computer wallpaper: yet another pop star, this one shirtless, with his pants unfastened to his pubic hair.

Carter guided the cursor to the swirly triangular logo for their Internet provider and clicked it. Since he didn't know her password, he didn't bother trying to sign on. It wasn't necessary, anyway; not for what he was looking for.

He clicked on her cyber file cabinet and searched his way through several menus until he found the one he wanted. Nicki changed her log-on password every other day, it seemed, but it never occurred to her to protect access to her files. Such a simple precaution wouldn't have prevented Carter from finding what he wanted, but it would certainly have slowed him down.

When he found the file marked Chat Logs, he clicked that, and there they were: a complete record of every chat his daughter had had since God knew when. After the Deni James case, one of the detectives he worked with had told him how to rig Nicki's computer software so that every website she visited and every chat and instant message she shared became a part of a permanent digital record, still around even after the user thought that the files had been erased. If the James family had had such a bug in their daughter's computer, they might have been able to get help before the permanent damage was done. Certainly, it would have left a trail that would have negated Deni's refusal to testify.

Carter gaped at the endless list of chats. He knew that she spent a lot of time online, but he had no idea that it was *this* much time! More surprising, he saw that the vast majority were time-stamped between midnight and three in the morning. No wonder she was always so tired.

Could it be that he was so hopelessly naïve, that Nicki was living a life he knew nothing about, hiding even more details from him than he'd thought?

Fifteen minutes later, he had his answer.

Chapter Four

Vinnie Campanella glanced nervously at the digital clock over the ticket taker's station. If everything were truly running on schedule, he had only fifteen minutes left before boarding, with thirty pages left to go in the novel he was reading. In it, a quadriplegic New York City detective was in grave danger, and Vinnie hated like hell to break up the action to board the airplane.

So engaged was he in the novel that he was surprised he even heard the page over the public address system: "Vincent Campanella, please go to the nearest white courtesy phone for a message."

The announcement caused his insides to tighten. He couldn't imagine that white courtesy phones carried much good news.

The nearest phone was mounted on a pillar two gates away. The other side was already ringing as he brought the receiver to his ear. "Customer service," said a pleasant voice on the other side.

"Um, hello, my name is Vincent Campanella. Did you just page me?"

He heard papers shuffling in the background. "Oh, yes, Mr. Campanella. Someone turned in a wallet here with your identification in it. Did you lose a wallet?"

Vinnie's right hand slapped his left hand suit coat pocket—a move fast enough to make passersby wonder if he might be in pain. Sure enough, his billfold was missing. How could that be?

"Someone found it on the floor near the coffee shop in Concourse C," she explained.

Of course, he thought. The collision in the hallway.

"I hope you didn't have any cash," she said, "because it was turned in empty."

"Yes, I had cash!" Vinnie boomed, drawing stares. "I had eleven hundred dollars!"

Ms. Customer Service made a clicking sound with her tongue. "Well, it's all gone now. In the future, you might want to consider traveler's checks."

Oh, how very helpful. It's always nice to know what you should have done after you've been caught not doing it. "What about my credit cards? There should be one Visa and one MasterCard in there."

The customer service lady hummed a little as she stalled for time. "Oh, okay, there they are. Yep, I see a Visa and a Master, plus a Costco card, and—"

"I don't care about the others," Vinnie said, cutting her off. "And I presume that you have my driver's license, or else you wouldn't have known to page me."

"Yes, sir, that's exactly right. We have a set of keys, as well."

Vinnie couldn't believe it; but sure enough, when he patted his pants pocket, they were gone, too. "Oh, my God," he said.

"I have one key that looks like it's a house key, and another that has the word *Ford* printed on it."

"My house and my car," Vinnie said. "Jesus, my pocket's been picked."

"Do you know when it happened?"

"Yes. A guy ran into me in the hallway here. It was a big collision, and in all the confusion, he must have lifted my stuff. He was good."

"You should file a police report," said Ms. Service. "I can page them, too, if you'd like."

Vinnie shook his head. What would be the point? With terrorism alerts and God only knew what other kinds of distractions, his pickpocketing incident wouldn't go to the top of anyone's priority list. Besides, he had a flight to catch. "No, the guy took the money, and that's my fault. The important stuff is still there."

"But sir, if he's still here at the airport, don't you want—"

"What I want is to catch my flight. In eight hours, I intend to be sitting in Paris, meeting with clients, and enjoying the sights. There's plenty of time for me to expense the cash I lost. Now, if you could just tell me where to go to get my property back . . ."

It felt great to be free again. For Brad Ward, it was the greatest feeling in the world. The fact that it was over a hundred degrees there in the long-term parking lot didn't bother him a bit, any more than it would have bothered him if it were thirty below zero or blowing like a hurricane. He didn't think it was possible for people who'd never been in prison to understand just how precious—how priceless—fresh air could be. Even if it was only as fresh as an airport on the outskirts of Washington, DC.

Simply seeing the sun without craning your neck

was life-affirming—or inhaling the aroma of freshly cut grass. Hell, even the smell of dog shit beat the stink of inmate shit.

He walked calmly down the wide aisles between cars, the slap of his flip-flops keeping time with a song that only he could hear. At the little bus stop where the shuttles took you to and from the terminal building, he stooped and reached under the trash can to recover the Leatherman tool he'd stashed there. Security in the airport might not be all that the government wanted you to believe, but there wasn't a chance in hell that he could have gotten the Leatherman through the checkpoint. Think Swiss Army knife on steroids. While he walked on, he slid the tool's leather pouch onto his belt.

In a perfect world, he'd have been in shorts instead of chinos, but he feared that the glaring whiteness of his flesh might cause people to ask questions. Institutional pallor was the tattoo of everyone who'd lived as Brad had lived these past two and a half years.

Soon, though, he'd be in Florida, and from there, if he could talk her into it, he and Nicki would be in the Caymans, out of the country and out of reach. Then, the entire world would belong to them. Three thousand miles would yield light-years of separation from everything that was ugly.

This was a big step, though, fraught with big risk. For the past six months, he'd lived by the baby step, moving no more than fifty or sixty miles in a day, laying low in campgrounds and flophouses and keeping in touch with the world via the Internet.

But now, the only part of the world he really cared about was coming to join him. Who would have believed the luck in that? Maybe the time really had come for life to settle out for him. It wouldn't be easy, of course—for him, nothing was ever easy—but if things could settle down just a little, he'd be better than fine with that.

So far, it was going even better than he'd hoped. The big guy in the airport was totally clueless about what happened, and Brad was particularly proud of the last-minute gambit to buy the second cup of coffee. It was the only way he could think of to keep the guy from reaching for his wallet.

What Vincent Anthony Campanella didn't realize was that he'd been Brad's sole target from the moment he'd driven into the parking lot. He met all of Brad's criteria: First of all, the car had to be a Ford, because that was the only key that Brad had with him. The model didn't matter all that much because all the Ford keys looked alike, and Fatso wasn't ever going to be driving his vehicle again. All that mattered was for the keys on the ring to *look* right if and when airport security returned them to him.

The second criterion Campanella met was his arrival in the long-term parking lot. That, combined with criterion number three—lots of luggage—made it a done deal. From there, it was just a matter of timing. Brad had followed him all the way to Concourse C, getting past the security station merely by showing the security guy a copy of an e-mail he'd sent himself this morning with an itinerary for some flights he had no intention of taking.

Once at the concourse, Brad had to wait for the mark to distract himself, and then it was time to move in. The wallet, of course, had been easy, but the keys were a work of art, if he did say so himself. It had been years since he'd pulled that particular gag.

The bright red Mustang lay dead ahead, nosed into the curb right where Campanella had left it. Brad paid cash to get out of the parking lot, then meandered his way to the eastbound lanes of the access road, which in turn led to the Braddock County Parkway. He figured it would take the better part of an hour to get to the Brookfield bus station, thanks to the 3.4 million traffic lights.

Before settling in for that commute, however, Brad had a couple of phone calls to make. As he was lifting the wallet from Vincent Campanella's pocket, his fingers had brushed the man's cell phone, but he'd decided to leave it there, lest the guy got the urge to make a call.

Brad pulled into the parking lot of the Giant Food store in Jefferson Farms, and went inside to the customer service desk to find the number he needed in the phone book. The manager was nice enough to offer the house phone to make a local call, but Brad declined, preferring instead to use the pay phone on the wall outside.

"Ritz-Carlton, Mason's Corner," said the accented voice on the other end of the line.

"Reservations, please," Brad said. As he waited for the call to be connected, he pulled from the pocket of his jeans the slip of paper he'd used to jot down Vincent Campanella's credit card numbers.

Detective Christopher Tu arrived within minutes of Carter's plea for assistance. He'd been the chief investigator on the Deni James case, and Carter knew him to be an unparalleled whiz at all things computerized. Thanks in large measure to a glowing letter that Carter had written for the younger man's file, Chris had only recently been bumped up to detective first class, and he was clearly anxious to give his friend a hand.

Carter met the detective at the door and ushered him into the foyer.

"Have you learned anything since we talked?" Chris asked. His body language showed that he fully appreciated the urgency. Born and raised in America as the only son of Chinese immigrants, Chris nonetheless spoke with a distinct accent.

"I haven't touched a thing," Carter said, leading the way upstairs. "I didn't want to screw anything up."

"What exactly are we looking for?" Carter had told him the essentials over the phone, but had not gotten into the details. Chris recoiled from the blast of pink as he entered Nicki's room.

"I loaded that security software you told me about, and I was able to find the chat logs where she talked about running off, but I don't know how to figure out the identity of the other party."

Chris helped himself to Nicki's desk chair. "Piece of cake," he said. He took a few seconds to review what was already on the screen. "So this is the guy you're worried about? This BW477?"

"That's him. I figure if I can find out where he lives, I'll know where Nicki went."

Chris went to work, his fingers flying on the keyboard. As the detective leaned forward for a closer look at the screen, Carter found himself leaning in right with him. When Chris leaned back again, they bumped heads.

Carter apologized.

"Why don't you go get me a soda or something?" Chris suggested.

Carter hesitated, then nodded. He'd seen Chris pull the "I'm thirsty" trick before, and recognized it as the detective's polite version of "Get lost." He took his time getting a Coke from the refrigerator and pouring it over a glass of ice, stalling to give the detective as much time alone as he could.

Seven minutes was the limit of Carter's endurance. He carried the drinks back upstairs. Chris didn't even turn around as he said, "She's on her way to someplace in Virginia called Brookfield."

Carter stopped, dumfounded. "You know that already?"

"Yep. She's going by bus to meet a guy named Brad. Give me a couple more minutes and I can get you a last name, too."

Carter froze. He felt the blood draining from his head and helped himself to the edge of Nicki's bed. "Ward," he said.

"Excuse me?" Chris took the soda from his host.

"His last name is Ward. Brad Ward."

Chris stopped typing and pivoted in his chair. "You know him?"

Carter closed his eyes against the realization. This was a terrible turn. "Keep looking, please, and pray that I'm wrong. The Brad Ward I used to know was bad news through and through."

The detective's eyebrows fused as he swung himself back to the keyboard.

Carter owed him an explanation. "Years ago, when Nicki was just a little girl, our neighbors next door were professional foster parents. Never really got to know them. My guess is, they knew what I did for a living and kept as low a profile as possible. They'd sometimes have four or five foster kids staying with them at a time. Brad Ward was one of them. He lived there for a couple of years, in fact, starting when Nicki was in fourth or fifth grade. He was a good-looking kid, athletic with a quick smile, but he was much older. In high school. And Nicki had an enormous crush on him."

"Puppy love," Chris offered.

Carter winced at the memory. "Well, you'd like to think that. Certainly, it was innocent enough on Nicki's part, but I was never quite sure about Brad. Seemed to me he was milking it. You know, strutting around the yard half naked. He always had time to talk to Nicki when she was outside—and she was *always* outside when he was."

"You think he's a perv?" Chris asked the question as he typed, and turned instantly apologetic for the lightness of his tone. "I'm sorry."

Carter waved him off. "Something about the kid bothered me. Made me nervous. He made Jenny nervous, too, and there was never a better personality barometer than she."

Chris scowled, leaned in closer to the monitor, then typed some more. "That's him," he proclaimed. "Brad Ward."

"Can you run his record from here?"

Chris looked wounded. "You're kidding, right? Do wild popes shit in the woods?" He typed some more then waited for the modem to finish screeching before he started up again. "This is a piece of shit computer, Counselor," he said. "You can go out and have dinner while the pages load."

"You need to go back to the office, then?"

Chris shook his head. "No, I can make it work. Just be happy that you're not paying by the hour."

In the silence that accompanied the detective's new concentration, Carter tried to figure out why Brookfield, Virginia, rang such a bell with him. He knew that he passed the signs south of Washington on I-95, but that didn't seem quite right. There was something more substantial in his memory, but he couldn't pull it up.

"So, what happened to this Brad kid?" Chris asked. His fingers didn't slow a lick while he spoke.

"He moved away."

"The whole family, or just him?"

"Just him. One day he was living there, and the next day he wasn't. There were lots of rumors about all of them, but like I said, I was never on the greatest terms with the Bensons themselves, so I don't know the details."

"What kind of rumors?"

"That it was an abusive household, that Brad was responsible for some local break-ins. That sort of thing."

"Did you ever get the department involved?"

"I'm not a prosecutor all the time, Chris," Carter said, noting the defensiveness of his tone. "Sometimes I'm just a neighbor."

The comment drew a look, but Chris said nothing.

"Ultimately, the Bensons traded the kid in for a later model," Carter said.

Chris shook his head. "I know you don't need me to make this any worse for you, buddy, but it's pretty twisted that he'd seek her out after all these years. Given the age difference and all."

Carter said nothing. What was there to say?

"Okay," Chris announced. "Brad Ward and Bradley Ward. Jesus, I've got over five hundred hits nationwide."

Carter gasped.

"Now, presumably, these are not all the same guy."

"Can you narrow it down to Virginia? Since that's where Nicki's headed, I guess it makes sense—"

"Twenty-six in Virginia," the detective announced. "I don't suppose you have a social security number or an address."

Carter gave him a look.

"No, I didn't think so." Chris pushed himself away from the desk. "That's about the last of it that we can do quickly," he said. "From here, I can get mug shots and individual criminal histories."

"Do that," Carter said. "That's a good idea. But I can't wait for it. I'm going to head toward Brookfield, Virginia, and see what I can dig up on my own. If nothing else, I'll be a little closer."

Christopher Tu shifted uneasily in his seat. "You're assuming that Brookfield was their final destination. Maybe it was just a bus stop. In the chat logs, all they said was that Brad would meet her there. There really was no discussion of where they'd go afterward."

Carter's face fell. "Nothing at all?"

Chris shook his head. "No. I mean nothing that jumped out in the five minutes I had a chance to go through it all. There was just some nonsense about him having a surprise ready for her when they got together. She was supposed to think about her greatest fantasy, and he'd have it ready for her."

"What kind of fantasy?"

Chris turned back to the keyboard and started typing again. A few seconds later, he pointed to the screen. "There it is. It's from their last chat, three days ago. That's how I found it so fast." He rolled his chair out of the way so Carter could see the screen more clearly.

Giggler: So, where would we go when I got there?

BW477: its a surprize

Giggler: would I like it???

BW477: ur gonna luv it. Think of ur wildest fantisy. U want $$? U want all the best their is? Queen Lizzy in britin will wish she was u.

Carter scowled and shook his head. "So, we don't have to look for them at any literary events."

"Hey, man, that's the best of Internet speak. Who needs grammar when your fingers are flying? But as you can see, it doesn't seem as if this Brookfield place is their last stop."

"Look at the tenses Nicki uses," Carter said, pointing at the screen. "Everything's conditional. It doesn't read as if there was a solid, established plan."

"A contingency," Chris surmised.

"Exactly. Waiting for Nicki to pull the cord. And, it's a place to start. There's a picture of Nicki on the refrigerator downstairs, her school picture from this year. If you don't mind doing me one more favor, could you get that out on the net up and down the East Coast? Maybe we can get other people looking for her, too."

Chris sighed and looked pained. "I can do that, yes," he said. "In fact, I will do it. But you know how it's going to be received, right?"

It took only a second for Carter to think it through all the way. "As just another runaway," he said.

Chris nodded glumly. "A seventeen-year-old runaway at that. They're a dime a dozen, I'm sorry to say. I'll pass the word along, but I think it's a mistake to expect much in the way of results."

"We can play up the sickness angle."

"I suppose we can try. I don't mean to be negative, but these are just the realities—"

Carter held up a hand to cut him off. "I understand. Just do what you can." Police department bulletin boards were papered with pictures of seventeen-year-old runaways.

Chris stood and walked with Carter back through the house to the front door. "I'll lock up for you when

I finish here," Chris said. "How long a drive is it, do you think, to this Brookfield place?"

Carter shrugged. "Five hours, maybe."

"Get started then. I'll run this Brad Ward for you and see if I can cough up a mug shot from somewhere. If he was bounced around foster homes, the chances are pretty good he's got a record. It's just a matter of finding the right one. I'll see what I can dig up and then e-mail everything to you. You'll have a laptop?"

"Always."

Carter was halfway to the stairs when Chris called from the room, "I hope this turns out fine, Carter." The prosecutor responded with a rueful smile. He was praying for fine, but he'd settle for anything short of disaster.

March 1

Derek Johnson got visitors yesterday. I don't know why that pisses me off, but it does. I guess I thought that we had lots in common. We're about the same age and like to talk about the same shit, but now it turns out he's got family and that pisses me off. He thinks he's like this great philosopher, giving me advice on how to make it through my stretch, telling me shit like, don't even think about the World. Think of this place as the World. If you don't know what you're missing, then you can't miss it. Made sense to me, too.

Then I find out that he's got family waiting for him. He's got people praying for him and thinking good things for him. I got nobody. Pisses me off.

Chapter Five

The bus nosed into its slot at an angle, one of a dozen identical vehicles. Together, they reminded Nicki of so many piglets nuzzled up to a sow. The rigors of the trip had wiped her out, and as always, the fatigue had brought on a bout of depression. It sucked to be her.

Nicki held on tightly to the aluminum guardrail as she eased herself down the stairs to the pavement below, where the steamy heat of the day took her breath away. People behind her buzzed with impatience as she took her time, apparently assuming that she moved slowly on purpose. So, this was Brookfield—or at least the bus-station section of Brookfield. Fetid and filthy, the station smelled little better than the vehicle that brought her there. Months-old trash jammed the gutters at the curb, and the sidewalk was nearly impassable, thanks to the horde of passengers hovering near the cargo bays of their motor coaches, clearly guarding their luggage from predators. She'd heard her dad wonder over the years if slums grew naturally in the shade of bus stations or if bus companies deliberately placed the points of arrival and departure in the worst parts of town. Now she understood the irony.

Nicki had no luggage other than her purse. Brad had told her that she needed nothing, and she took him at his word. She had her ID, the $500 from the ATM, and her meds. But for the shorts and T-shirt she wore, she had no earthly possessions.

Much to her surprise, that didn't bother her a bit.

Stepping through the double glass doors, Nicki entered the station itself. It had the look of a place that might have once been a train station; not one of the grand palaces from the big cities, but just another stop along the way. The ticket windows were arched, and decorative bars covered all but a little slot at the bottom. Behind those bars, the workers looked every bit as tired and neglected as the building. The yellowed tile and stained fluorescent light fixtures told her that the "No Smoking" signs went largely unheeded, as did the "No Loitering" signs. Some of the loiterers looked firmly enough encamped to call the place their home.

This was the most exciting thing Nicki had ever done. The most dangerous. The most stupid. With all the nut jobs and evil people her dad had prosecuted over the years, she had to be out of her mind to meet a guy in a bus station two hundred miles away from home. Why didn't she just put a gun to her head and blow her brains out?

She tried to tell herself that Brad wasn't like that. He was sweet, not evil. Still, it had been five years since she'd seen him, and now that she'd finally arrived at their designated meeting spot, she realized for the first time that she might not even recognize him anymore. She'd been twelve years old back then, all chubby and gap-toothed, with a hairstyle that more resembled a boy's than a girl's.

And he'd been a god.

Funny thing. Back then, she'd always thought that

he was older by only three years. Now, she realized
that it was a five-year gap. His boyish looks—and her
willingness to believe that he was even remotely more
attainable—had allowed him to pull off the lie, which
was itself created to cover for all the grades he'd had to
repeat in elementary school.

God, how she'd dreamed of him over the years. While
other girls in school drooled over the heartthrobs in the
teen magazines, she'd had one living in the flesh right
next door. Operative word: flesh. She'd loved to watch
him on summer afternoons as he mowed the lawn and
tended to his countless chores around the house, always shirtless, his hard muscles flexing under his taut,
tanned skin. But it was the smile that had melted her,
the gleaming teeth and piercing eyes so blue that you'd
swear they had to be contact lenses.

If only he had noticed her noticing him. The very
thought of it was laughable, of course. If he had, she'd
probably have just withered up and died. Gods did not
mingle with mere mortals, and Nicki had never known
anyone more merely mortal than she.

Then, one day, he was simply gone, and her dad told
her not to ask any questions. He was trouble, Dad said.
The neighborhood was better off without him. But Dad
didn't know the secret that they shared. He didn't
know about what happened the day before Brad disappeared. If he had, then he'd have known why she'd
never be able to stop thinking about him. Sometimes,
in her fantasies, Nicki saw herself with him still, traveling through life as his girlfriend. His mate for life.

It's funny how fate works. Over the years, Nicki
had lost track of the number of letters she'd written to
Brad, only to tear them up as soon as they were done.
She'd told him about school and about soccer and track
and about her mom's illness. She'd pretended that he

wrote back to her, his words sweet and understanding. In them, he would lie and tell her that she was beautiful.

Never in a million years did she think that such a crazy fantasy might actually come true.

He'd appeared out of nowhere as an IM—instant message—on her computer screen one night as she was cruising the chat rooms. His screen name was BW477. "My name is Brad," the message said. "I found your screen name through your website. Are you the same Nicolette Janssen who used to live on Berwick Place in Pitcairn County, New York?"

She remembered the rush of dizziness. "Oh, my God, yes!" she'd squealed, but she didn't dare commit that kind of enthusiasm to writing. She'd tried to calm herself as she typed, "Brad who?" Could it be? Could it possibly be?

"This is Brad Ward. How've you been?"

It was him! It really was him! God, could she possibly have been that lucky? She had to be sure. "How do I know it's really you?" she'd typed.

"Because I'm the only one who knows that you lent me your father's bathrobe," he replied.

That cinched it. That was their secret—at least, it was the end of their secret, and Nicki had never shared it with a soul—not a single solitary soul.

They'd chatted online for hours that first night, about everything, about nothing. They just caught up, and the longer he typed, the more she could hear his voice in her head. Honestly, if she hadn't had to get up for school the next morning, they probably never would have stopped.

That first encounter online was only the first of dozens, always begun late at night after her father had gone to bed. Brad was her confidant, her best friend. On the other end of all those miles of cables and telephone lines, he couldn't know how fat and ugly she was, and when she told him, he didn't care. Brad liked Nicki for herself, nothing more and nothing less. And he knew everything, too: about her illness and about the clock that was ticking down toward her last breath. She held nothing back and he absorbed it all.

And he was such a *bad* influence on her. It was only on their second or third conversation that he'd first suggested running away together. What did she have to lose? he'd asked. She had this terrible disease; she was looking at a tragically short life as it was, why waste those precious few hours in freaking history class? Why not tour the world, wander around as a nomad or a gypsy? Why not join a circus? And for God's sake, why worry so much about following the rules all the time?

At first, she'd thought that he was just pulling her chain; taking the role of the devil's advocate, tempting her with a wild lifestyle that they both knew she could never live. But after a few weeks of the recurring theme, she'd come to realize that he was serious. It was, she came to realize, the kind of life that Brad had chosen for himself—no fixed address, no responsibilities. Just a laptop, a few clothes, and a sense of adventure. A modern-day cowboy.

But she couldn't do that, she explained. Her dad needed her around; not just to make sure that there was food to eat at night, but also just to be there as company. Since Mom died, he needed company.

Brad thought she was crazy. Family was an anchor, he'd told her. To live—to *really live*—she needed to be out on her own. Brad offered to be her travel guide. It was fun to think about, but totally out of the question.

Until today. And maybe even today wouldn't have

pushed her over the edge if it hadn't been for last night. Yesterday afternoon, actually, after her doctor's appointment where they'd laid out a new torture they'd dreamed up for her. She was doing pretty well, they'd told her, all things considered, but to make sure that everything stayed on track, they had this nifty new technology they wanted her to play lab rat on: a pump that they would install in her gut to keep a constant flow of hormones into her system to keep the vessels in her lungs open. It was great, they told her; the next best thing to the transplants she needed, only there was one hitch—one little teensy detail that she probably should know about: It would mean a three-week hospital stay, hooked up to machines that would monitor every twitch of her heart and every squirt of her kidneys.

No flippin' way. Three *weeks*? In the *hospital*? What were they smoking? Oh, and to make it even more outrageous, there was no guarantee on the other end. The treatment might work wonders, or it might do nothing at all. The only constant—the only bet-your-ass guarantee—was that she'd lose three weeks of her fifty-two-week life span to somebody's chemistry experiment.

"Absolutely not," she'd told them. And when they looked stunned, she said it again. "Which part of 'no' confuses you?"

And dear old Dad, God bless him, was on *their* side. "Honey, it's for your own good," he told her. "We're only thinking of what's best for you."

Yeah, well, chemo was for Mom's own good, too. It was what was best for her, and look where it got her: she'd puked herself all the way to her grave. No one could explain to Nicki how slow poisoning in a hospital, surrounded by strangers, was a better way to die than just letting nature do her thing, surrounded by friends. Dead was dead, right?

The doctors had all kinds of euphemisms for it all—final decisions and terminal courses and God only knew what else—but when you cut through all the bullshit, it all added up the same: she had a year left in which to live a lifetime. She could do it her way and have fun, or she could do it her dad's way and be miserable. Did they think there was even a choice to be made?

The argument had continued all the way out of the doctor's office, all the way home, and all the way through the evening. It wasn't a discussion or a presentation of opinions, it was a real argument, and her father wasn't about to lose. "We're not discussing this, Nicolette," he'd said, his face red and his eyes redder. "I know you don't think this is fair, but you don't have a vote. You're a minor, and you'll do what I tell you."

"I won't," she'd countered. "You can't make me. If they hook me up, I'll just undo the leads. I'm not spending a twelfth of my remaining life in some stupid hospital!"

Her dad grew very serious with that, very quiet. Scary, almost, the way his eyes narrowed and his voice became barely audible. That's when he threatened to have her arrested. Unbelievable. And the thing of it is, he was *serious*. Either she'd do things his way or he'd have her put in irons and tied down to the hospital bed.

Then, the beeper had sounded, and for one brief *spectacular* moment, life had seemed fair.

Here you go, Nicki. Here are the organs that will save your life.

Ha! Only kidding!

God, she hated doctors. Minutes after they had taken her new heart and lungs back, Dad and the mad scientists were treating her like a chemistry experiment again.

And now she was cobbling together a new life.

"Adios, assholes," she muttered, drawing a look from a janitor old enough to have played soccer with Moses. When she fired off one of her patented "screw you" looks, the old man averted his eyes.

Brad would be proud. He'd given her step-by-step directions on exactly what she should do. He'd told her the place to go, and even how much the bus fare would be to get there. Now she'd just have to hang around long enough for him to get the e-mail she'd sent this morning and then come to pick her up. He was the man with the plan, the one who told her not to worry about a thing.

On paper, it had all sounded so *romantic,* but now that she was here, standing in a skanky bus station surrounded by so many strangers, so far away from home, the romance eluded her. Now that she thought about it—you know, *really* thought about it—how did she even know for sure that this guy who called himself Brad wasn't some twisted imposter who'd done some really good research? On the Internet, you could be anyone you wanted to be. How many times had her father told her that?

The familiar fluttery feeling tickled her stomach as a touch of panic gripped her, and she sat down in anticipation of the light-headedness that was never far behind when she got upset. By inhaling through her mouth, and then letting the breath go as a silent whistle, she could actually wrestle her heart rate down.

And nobody cared. Was that terrific, or what? Nobody rushed to her side, felt her wrist, or offered to get her a drink of water. Out here, no one knew anything about her. It was liberating as hell. As far as any of these strangers knew, she was just a regular teenager; maybe a runaway, maybe not. Maybe a fugitive from the law. Or, maybe just a girl waiting for her grand-mother to get in from Toledo.

It was as if she'd been given a chance to reinvent her-self, for as long as her body would let her. Keep your marijuana and your booze, baby. This freedom shit was the greatest high in the world.

"Nicolette Janssen?" The voice came from behind her, and sounded nothing like she'd remembered.

She whirled on her bench, and there he was, a fully grown, slightly bulkier version of the boy she remem-bered. He sported a beard now, albeit it a little scrag-gly, a darker brown than his yellow hair would have implied, and there was a certain pallor about him that led her to believe that he'd lost his passion for sun-bathing. There was no mistaking that smile, though—a flash of brilliant white. When he pulled the sunglasses off, she knew for sure.

"I hate that name," she said, wishing there was a way to control the heat that spread through her cheeks.

Brad tossed off a shrug. "I know. But I think it's pretty. I hear 'Nicolette' and I think 'class.'" He moved his shoulders to adjust the straps on his back-pack.

Nicki smiled in spite of herself and blushed even brighter. "When I hear it, all I think of is some fat French barmaid."

Brad laughed and came around to her side of the bench, where he held out his hand. "Come on, now, stand up. Let me see you."

This was the moment of truth—the moment when he'd see what he'd gotten himself into. *Stand and let me see you. Let me see how fat you really are.* She stood hesitantly, sheepishly, her face so hot that it nearly brought tears to her eyes.

"You look terrific," he said. "Even better than I'd imagined."

They stood there, looking at each other, neither knowing exactly what the next step should be. Brad made the move. He spread his arms wide, inviting a hug, and Nicki stepped closer. She moved haltingly, as if to keep from scaring him off, but when she was finally within reach, he enfolded her in a bear hug. Her face pressed against the muscles of his chest, still defined beneath the fabric of his T-shirt. He smelled . . . *rugged*. It wasn't the aftershave smell that she'd come to associate with men she'd met through her father. This was the smell of a man who knew what real work was. Not flowery, but certainly not unpleasant. When he didn't let go, she finally allowed herself to hug him back.

He eased her back out to arm's length, his hands still firmly on her shoulders. "God, it's great to see you again. Was your trip okay?"

"As good as it could be, I suppose."

He laughed. "Too important to ride the bus, eh?"

Nicki's instinct was to be defensive, but something told her to hold off—that he wasn't being critical.

"Are you ready for your adventure?" he asked.

Nicki made a face that said he was crazy. "You mean about who I want to pretend to be?"

"There's no pretending to it. Who do you want to be?"

Nicki waved him off. Surely, he hadn't been serious about that. Real was real. What was the point of this?

"Come on, now, tell me. Who do you want to be?"

"This is silly."

Brad shrugged. "Okay, it's silly. Now, tell me."

"I want to be me." Nicki wasn't sure why this conversation made her feel uncomfortable.

"Bullshit"

Nicki looked offended. "And what's wrong with being me?"

"Nothing's wrong with being you. I'm the one who's been telling you that for the last four months. But it's not about what I want; it's about what you want. Now come on, humor me. Who do you want to be? It can be anybody at all, real or imagined, present or past."

"I'm not good at these kinds of games." Nicki heard the whininess in her voice and it embarrassed her.

Brad planted his fists on his hips and cocked his head to the side. It was a gesture of good-humored frustration. He gestured to the bench and they sat down again. He tried to look at her, but Nicki couldn't tolerate the heat of his eyes. "Hey," he said. His voice was much softer now. Gentle, even. "Work with me here. This is supposed to be your escape."

Inexplicably, Nicki found herself close to tears. "I'm here," she said.

Brad laughed again. "Your *body* is here. Now, let your mind escape, too. Dream a little. Who do you want to be?"

The whole concept was just so foreign to her. The urge to cry grew stronger. She didn't know *how* to play this kind of game.

"Come on, Nicki," Brad urged. "Just this one time, loosen up. Give me a name."

Nicki sighed. He wasn't going to cut her a break. Brad Ward in person was exactly the same as Brad Ward on the computer: kind, always understanding, but never giving an inch. Not on the important stuff, not on the stuff that he wanted for her. "Okay," she said, finally surrendering to the ridiculous notion. "I want to go to a prom."

Brad beamed. "Perfect," he said.

"Perfect for what?"

"Perfect for both of us."

Nicki was confused.

"I get to be prom king."

Nicki loved the way his mind could just jump around like that, asking questions one second and then making proclamations the next. "What makes you think you wouldn't be runner-up?" she asked.

Brad didn't drop a beat: "Because of the arm candy I'll have with me." He stood and held out his hand. "Time to go."

"Where?"

He beckoned with his fingers and she took his hand.

"Are you going to tell me?" she pressed.

"To your fantasy," he said, and they started toward the door.

March 2

Okay, I'm not pissed anymore. Derek's mother made him a pound cake. The guards let him keep most of it, and what was left, he shared with me. Gave me half. Exactly half. And he said that his mother was going to pray for me. Next visiting day, she's going to ask to see me, too, so I can have someone to talk to.

It's hard to be pissed at someone who does something good for you.

Chapter Six

Deputy Sheriff Darla Sweet thumbed the button on the microphone. "Unit six-oh-four is ten-eight, leaving the Lion." She'd finished her dinner at the Shore Road Deli, and was back in service, leaving the Food Lion parking lot.

The dispatcher, George Sugrue, sounded bored as he responded, "Ten-four, six-oh-four, nineteen twenty-one hours."

Darla allowed herself to relax after the channel clicked dead, relieved that George hadn't pulled one of his adolescent radio pranks. He delighted in referring to Deputy Sweet as Darling or Sweet-cheeks on the radio. Darla had protested a dozen times to Sheriff Hines about it, but she'd never gotten through. In the Essex, North Carolina, Sheriff's Department, you were either part of the in-group, or you were not. She was not. The fact that she had a four-year degree in criminal justice, or that she could out-shoot, out-run, and out-think every other deputy in the department couldn't make up for the one qualification she neither had nor wanted: a penis. Not that they hadn't all offered to let her play with theirs from time to time.

Darla was living up to the commitment she'd made to herself to stick it out through two years. With that much experience under her Sam Browne belt, she'd be able to go anywhere in the country and get a job on a department where her skills would be appreciated. The good news was, at the ripe old age of twenty-four, Darla knew without doubt that no matter what lay ahead, she would be able to say that she'd already had the worst job in law enforcement.

Relief was on the horizon, though. In two weeks it would be Memorial Day and after that, Sheriff Hines would be free to hire in the supplemental force of summer deputies to help with the influx of tourists. For at least a few months, then, Darla would no longer be the only outsider to be shunned by the inner circle.

But two weeks was two weeks, and for the time being, it was Darla versus the department, with no reinforcements. Actually, she'd reached a certain peace with it. Let George Sugrue get his jollies calling her names, and let the rest of the department think that he was getting the best of her. Fact was, ten years from now, Darla Sweet would be a detective in a major police force somewhere, on her way to a command position, while those goobers were still yukking it up in Essex. Success was always the best revenge.

Darla piloted her cruiser through the parking lot, looking for trouble. Not to cause it, but to break it up when she saw it brewing. She learned last year that these middle two weeks in May were the toughest time for law enforcement here. The spring break hellions were gone, and the real-money tourists wouldn't start arriving till June, leaving great beachfront rental bargains to be scarfed up by college kids who then jammed thirty people into houses built to sleep ten, drinking themselves into oblivion. They'd get into fights and hurt themselves, or merely fall off the dune decks and hurt themselves, and every father in town would complain that their darling daughters had been asked by these pigs to do something unspeakable.

Not that far removed from the end-of-the-school-year party crowd herself, Darla understood how it all worked, and the partying, per se, wasn't what bugged her. What knotted her panties was the blatant way in which they flaunted their disobedience of the law, and Sheriff Hines's ready willingness to let them get away with it.

Right now, for example, in front of the Food Lion, three-quarters of the parking spaces were taken, and it was a pretty safe bet that the kiddies weren't shopping for vegetables. In fact, at this very moment, three boys who couldn't be older than sixteen hadn't even bothered to wrap their twelve-pack of Coors in a bag as they carried it to their car. They knew—as every tourist figured out after a season or two of visiting their fair town—that down here in Vacationland, you didn't need IDs or permission slips. Sheriff Hines knew as well as they did that the fastest way to get yourself unelected was to do anything to inhibit the flow of money into the pockets of the citizen-merchants. Essex businessmen tolerated five tons of bullshit from tourists every single day, thank you very much, and their only satisfaction was the cash left behind in their wake. So long as it didn't involve illegal drugs or violence against fellow tourists, Essex was an anything-goes oasis in the summertime. Kids could drink themselves into a stupor and fornicate themselves raw on the beaches. There was even an early-morning beach patrol to clean up the rubbers and other trash before the sun worshipers could hit the sand.

It was the job of the Essex County Sheriff's Department to walk a legal and political tightrope, making sure that the permanent residents of the community—the voters—remained unharrassed by the visitors, while at the same time making sure that the visitors enjoyed the sense of freedom that kept them coming back for more.

Darla had drawn duty on the north end of the county tonight—the sector with the most year-round residents. As she pulled into traffic, she checked her watch and sighed. It wasn't yet seven-thirty, and her tour went till midnight. This one had a long-and-boring feel to it.

Ahead and on the right, the sign for Surf's Up Amusements stood sentry over a field of weeds, marking the entrance to the dilapidated park. It looked like one of those rickety fairs that they used to set up in supermarket parking lots when she was a kid—the ones with the cheesy freak shows, and rides whose only real thrill came from the fear that the ancient Tilt-A-Whirl might disintegrate under the strain. Last season, she'd put even money on whether the Ferris wheel would finally spin itself off its axle.

Darla made a point of swinging through the closed park a couple of times every tour, recognizing it as an excellent place for criminals of every stripe to conduct business beyond the view of the public. Call her paranoid, but if there was one place in the world where she herself would be inclined to hide a body, the Surf's Up was it.

Darla stopped at the main gate long enough to pull the padlock off the chain that kept it closed, then climbed back into her cruiser. Weeds grew from cracks in the sidewalk, and the finish on the Go-Go-Go Carts sign was even dimmer and more chalky than last year. Flaking rust displayed the rot on every one of the metal rides, despite the owners' valiant effort to conceal it with a thick coating of red paint.

Darla drove slowly, weaving between the rides and behind the various buildings, doing everything she could to make as little noise as possible. What was the sense of going through this exercise, after all, if you were going to telegraph your every move to the bad guys?

Movement to her left drew Darla's eyes around to the Fun House. It was a flash of something, visible only for a fraction of an instant, but it registered as someone ducking quickly behind the corner. She coasted to a stop, then gently opened her door and walked in that direction, her hand instinctively resting on the grip of her Smith & Wesson .357 Magnum revolver. Essex hadn't yet made the switch to automatics as standard issue for their officers, and at $22K a year, she wasn't in a position to buy one of her own. Not if she was still going to pay for rent and groceries.

Merely being in the presence of the Fun House gave Darla the heebie-jeebies. She'd visited it once, shortly after she'd moved here, and what she saw still haunted her dreams: a two-headed fetus, floating in its amniotic formaldehyde. That, and a lamp shade supposedly made of human flesh from a Japanese prisoner-of-war camp, featuring the anchor-and-globe insignia from the United States Marine Corps.

Darla could smell the marijuana in the air even before she turned the corner, and the giggling gave the perpetrators away as a couple of kids.

They were trying to make themselves invisible behind some scrub pine, up against the eight-foot chain-link fence that eliminated any hope of bolting and getting away. Truth be told, if they *had* tried to run, she probably wouldn't have worked all that hard to stop them. What the hell else did teenagers have to do in a town like this but get high from time to time?

"All right, boys, this is the sheriff's department," she said, thumbing the strap off of her weapon, just to be on the safe side. "Show me your hands first, and then show me the rest of you. Step on out and let's not have any problems, okay?"

There was more giggling as one set of hands showed themselves, followed a second later by another pair. "You're gonna be sorry," someone laughed. "This is not going to look good on your record."

The other voice said, "Shut up, Peter."

"Sounds like good advice to me, Peter," Darla said. "Both of you show yourselves."

The two boys couldn't have been more than eighteen years old, and judging from the droopy, weepy look to their eyes, they'd been toking for quite some time. One of them—the taller of the two—had spiked, jet-black hair, while the other looked as if he just came off the golf course. Mr. Conservative's buttoned T-shirt bore the logo of the Essex High School Panthers' baseball team. Snorting through stifled giggles, they could barely put one foot in front of the other as they staggered out from behind the bush to present themselves to Deputy Sweet.

She couldn't help but laugh. "Let me see some ID."

From the body gyrations, you'd have thought the boys were on surfboards. Spike-head handed over his billfold, but Darla refused. "Take it out of the wallet for me," she said.

"But there's cash in there," the boy said.

She fixed him with a glare. "Maybe you ought to keep your mouth shut," she said.

"Jesus, Peter," his friend agreed. "Take it easy."

"Wiser words were never spoken," Darla said.

Peter fished his driver's license out of the billfold and handed it over. "Like she's going to arrest us?" he scoffed.

"I'd consider it an honor"—She looked at the license—"Peter Banks."

"My friends call me Peter."

"Potheads call me Deputy Sweet." Darla beckoned for the other boy's ID, which he'd already removed from his wallet. "You're next," she said.

"Look at that name closely now," Peter snorted.

The other boy exploded, "Goddammit, Peter, *shut up*!"

Darla looked first at the picture to make sure it matched the kid in front of her, and then glanced at his name. Whatever changed in her expression was apparently hysterical, because Peter busted out with a guffaw.

"Ain't that a kick in the ass?" he laughed.

Darla ignored him, keeping her eyes on the quiet one. "Jeremy Hines," she said, reading the license. "You Sheriff Hines's son?"

Where just a moment ago stood a stoned, defiant young man, a little boy had taken his place, his complexion gray with fear. She wondered if he might begin to cry. "Yes, ma'am."

Darla sighed. Things were suddenly a little trickier.

"I think this is where you tell us to behave ourselves and send us on our way," said Peter.

Ah, but therein lay the problem. If it were anyone else in the world, under any different circumstances, she might have done just that—almost certainly in the case of the quiet one, if only to show the loud one the price of being an asshole. "Both of you, have a seat there on the ground."

Peter looked stunned. "Yeah, right."

Darla glared. "Sit." Back home, her dog would have recognized the same tone of voice.

"Please don't call my father," Jeremy said. "He'll kill me."

Darla pointed at a spot on the sandy ground. "Don't make me use pepper spray and handcuffs, okay?"

Jeremy hesitated, then folded his legs beneath him to sit Indian-style in the sand.

Darla's eyes darted to Peter. "You, too, mouth," she said. "And if you want to guarantee a face full of spray, start flapping your gums again."

Peter clearly was confused. He thought about another smart-ass comment—Darla could see the words forming behind his eyes—but he thought better of it and sat on the ground next to his friend.

"Must be interesting growing up as the sheriff's kid," the deputy observed, her gaze boring straight through the sullen son. "My guess is, you must get away with quite a lot."

Jeremy shrugged, unable to make eye contact.

"It depends on who catches him," Peter offered. Darla's instinct was to tell him to shut up, but she sensed that the kid had finally rediscovered sincerity. "You guys—the deputies—are usually too scared to do anything. But if the sheriff catches him himself, there's hell to pay. For smoking weed, the dude's not exaggerating. His old man will kill him."

"Is that so?" Darla mused aloud, suppressing a smile. So much for sincerity. How terribly convenient that young Peter should show such heartfelt concern for his buddy at a time when that same concern served his own interests so well.

"These are things you should think about *before* you break the law," she said. Jeremy had begun to tremble, and while she couldn't see his face anymore, she could hear his snuffles.

Goddammit, she hated this shit. Crying women didn't bother her a bit, but there was something about a crying man—a crying *boy* in this case—that just tore her heart out. The kid was scared and clearly remorseful, even if his buddy was a class-A asshole, and she knew in her heart that the sheriff's reaction to this would be huge, especially in an election year. Jeez-o-peez, if it were anyone else in the world . . .

Screw it. At the end of the day, this was about choices, and the worst one made here was selected by Jeremy Hines when he lit up his joint. Maybe a hard lesson was the very thing he needed. Besides, either the kids in this community were going to respect her as a law enforcement officer or they weren't.

Come to think of it, the decision wasn't that hard at all. She brought the portable radio to her lips and keyed the mike.

Chapter Seven

Carter Janssen had just passed the Maryland House rest stop on I-95, heading south at eighty miles an hour, when his cell phone chirped. He flipped it open and brought it to his ear. "Janssen."

"Hey, Carter, it's Chris Tu."

"You've got news for me?"

"I do, but you might want to pull over before I give it to you."

"From the tone in your voice, it sounds like I'll want to drive faster."

The detective sighed deeply on the other end of the phone. "Okay, here it is. We had a tough time tracking down the right Bradley Ward, but I think we've got him."

"But you're not sure?"

Detective Tu hesitated. "Well, I guess we are sure. This is the Bradley Ward about whom you reached an agreement with his foster parents to have him removed from the household in return for dropped charges on some burglary thing."

Carter felt himself blushing. He'd forgotten that there was a letter in the file. Had he remembered, he would not have fudged his knowledge of how the boy came to disappear. "Okay, go ahead."

"After he left the Bensons' house, he pretty much fell off of the radar screen, mostly showing up in the occasional brawl at a homeless shelter here and there. It was enough to get him a record and get me a set of fingerprints to work with. Here's the part you're not going to want to know: two and a half years ago, he was sent up for murdering a bystander in the robbery of a little bodega in Lansing, Michigan. I don't know how he got to Michigan, but the way he got out was via the back door of his prison. In fact, he's a 'person of interest' in a couple of prison murders, too. He's been a fugitive for almost six months now."

Carter lifted the turn signal lever and moved into the right-hand lane, slowing down to the speed limit. Chris Tu was right; this was the sort of news for which one should stop the car. "So, that means that the FBI is after him, too. Interstate flight." He worked hard to keep the panic out of his voice.

The detective didn't bother to stifle his chuckle. "Yeah, and we know what kind of priority those cases are getting these days, right?"

Carter let a sigh escape. The FBI had been focused so exclusively on the fight against terror that sometimes it seemed as if those were the only laws on the books anymore. "I'm surprised that he's an escapee," Carter said, thinking out loud. "I get those bulletins every month, and would have thought for sure that the name would jump out at me."

"Ah, well, that's the point I neglected to tell you," Tu said. "He doesn't go by Bradley Ward anymore. He goes by Bradley Dougherty. I'm not sure what the origin of the name was, but it's strictly an alias. My guess is, he's got a whole new one by now."

Carter ran it all through his head, trying to decide on the best course from here. He checked his watch. Seven-thirty. "Have you put the announcement out on the wire yet?"

"I put it out on Dougherty, yes, but I wanted to wait to talk to you before I mentioned Nicki. What do you want me to do?"

It was a tougher decision than it might appear at first glance. "Clearly, we've got the best chance if we put pictures out there for both of them, but can you make it clear in the announcement that Nicki is not wanted for any crimes? Say that they're traveling together, but make it clear that they're not *actually* together. Can you do that?"

"Sure I can. And since you think that they're most likely to be headed toward the DC suburbs, we'll be sure to get their pictures to the media outlets in time for the eleven o'clock news, and then again for their morning broadcasts."

Carter nodded. "That's good. And if you can, make sure that all the police agencies east of the Mississippi get an alert in their morning updates."

"I can do that," said Detective Tu.

"I'm still heading to Brookfield," Carter said. "See what I can put together at the bus station."

"You holding up all right?"

Carter allowed himself a bitter laugh. "Chris, the way these past few years have gone, this just feels like any other day to me."

"I love your car," Nicki said. It was a Mustang GT convertible. Red. Most cool. He'd even held the door for her as she climbed inside.

"It's a pavement-eater all right," he agreed. He stuck a little too close to the line as he swung a turn, showing off the vehicle's suspension.

"How long have you had it?"

"It's new," he said. "Well, new to me. I got it for the trip."

"This trip?"

Brad bounced his eyebrows and smiled. "I promised you style, didn't I?"

Nicki giggled and sort of hugged herself, conscious of just how long it had been since she'd heard the sound of genuine delight coming from her own throat.

Brad laughed at the sound. "Now I understand why your screen name is Giggler."

She blushed. "When are you going to tell me where we're going?"

"Not very far," he said. "I figured you'd be tired. Besides, this is where your fantasy is set."

Nicki laughed again. "My *fantasy*? What do you know about my fantasies?"

"You said you wanted to go to a prom."

"Yeah, but you didn't know that."

He smirked. "I guessed a little. Okay, so tell me what you can't do."

"Excuse me?"

"This PPH thing you've got. What can't you do, other than climb Mount Everest, which fortunately is not on the agenda."

He was so *charming*. God, it was even better than she'd remembered. "I can do about anything," she said. "I just get tired doing it. If I push too hard, then I get short of breath, but then if I relax and take my rat poison, then everything turns out fine."

"Your rat poison?"

"Coumadin," she explained. "Blood thinner. It's the same stuff they put in mousetraps. The mice eat the Coumadin, and they bleed to death on the inside."

Brad was concentrating on the road as he wormed into traffic, but he shot her a quick look anyway. "Those are the humane traps, right?" He settled for the center lane. "Is bleeding to death a worry for you?" he asked. "Not that you look like a mouse, or anything."

Nicki laughed again. "Actually, I do have to wear this"—she waved her left hand to display her Medic-Alert bracelet—"in case I'm in an accident or something."

"So that's it?" Brad asked. "Shortness of breath and fatigue? Doesn't sound all that fatal to me. You look terrific."

Nicki knew that second part was a lie, but she appreciated the effort. "It's the way the disease works," she explained. "Today's a good day. Tomorrow might be really crappy. I never know. But I get way more crappy days than I used to get six months ago. In another six months, I'll have way more crappy days than good ones, and six months after that, I'll be worm food."

The worm-food comment drew an uncomfortable look, but Nicki smiled to show that it was okay. Along with pushing up daisies and the big dirt nap, worm food was her favorite for knocking people off balance. The one word she couldn't bring herself to say was *dead*.

"Well, at least we've got a year," Brad said. "Just you, me, the road, and adventure."

God, how she loved the sound of that. Adventure. *Real* adventure, free from prodding fingers and meddling know-it-alls. Free to die the way God intended her to.

"How are we going to support ourselves?" Nicki asked.

Her question sparked a guffaw from Brad. "You're too damned practical, Nicolette," he chided. "Do you worry about the little stuff all the time?"

"Every single moment," she said. It was the part of her personality that bugged her the most. There were days when she wondered if her mother's illness and then her own had just flat-out made her forget how to have any fun anymore. "Does this mean you're filthy rich or something?"

"Me?" Another guffaw. "Not hardly. I'm lucky to be able to afford McDonald's three times a week."

Nicki's features twisted into a scowl. This wasn't making any sense. "What about a job?"

Brad had a smirk in his arsenal that seemed designed purely for the dimples it produced in his cheeks. "I'm only twenty-two, Nicki. I've got a whole lifetime to have a job."

"Well, how do you—"

Brad held up his hand suddenly enough to startle her. "No more questions. Okay? For a little while, no more questions."

A warning bell sounded in her head. Out of nowhere, she remembered a story from her father about a girl who dared to meet someone from the Internet, only to wind up brutalized and left for dead.

"Uh-oh," Brad said. "I pissed you off. You're not talking."

"All I've got are questions," she said. "My father would tell me that you're probably a criminal and that I should be very careful."

"Your father's an asshole."

Nicki's jaw dropped.

Brad sensed her shock and turned his head to look at

her. "What, I'm telling you something you don't already know?"

"Well, no, I guess not . . ."

"Oh, it's one of those, 'I can say it but you can't' things?" Brad laughed. "Do you have any idea how many times you typed the word *asshole* during our chats online? Something like a million."

That sounded about right, actually. What was it about Brad that allowed him to say things that should have pissed her off, but in fact didn't? "At least I know firsthand."

Brad made a snorting sound. "Trust me. I have some firsthand knowledge myself."

"Sounds like a story I haven't heard yet."

"Nicolette Janssen, there's a thousand of those stories out there."

"Tell me."

"All in good time."

"Oh, come on. You know everything about me, and I don't know a thing about you. That's not fair." Nicki leaned forward in her seat to look around and see his face. "Come on, just one thing. One story."

"One's going to lead to ten, and then the mood will be ruined," Brad said. "I want today to be special."

"Just one," Nicki pressed. "I promise."

Brad let out a long sigh and smiled in spite of himself. "Just one, right?"

"Right."

"And then you'll stop?"

"I promise."

"Okay, then ask a question."

Suddenly, just one didn't seem like nearly enough. Ten, maybe, but not just one. "Okay, then, if you don't have a job, how can you afford this car?"

"I stole it," he said. Then he laughed at her gaping expression. "Sorry you asked?"

"You *stole* a car?"

"Not just *a* car. This one. A fire-engine-red Mustang convertible. I've wanted one of these all my life."

"But you can't just steal somebody's car!"

"Sure I can. It's not as difficult as you think."

Nicki was appalled, and couldn't understand why she was laughing. "But it's against the law."

"It must be tough being a lawyer's kid."

"Brad!"

"What?" He seemed both proud and amused.

"Suppose the police come after you?" She pivoted in her seat and looked behind them at the clutch of traffic.

"They won't," he said. He explained how things worked out at the airport.

"That's terrible!" she said when he was done.

"Oh, come on, Nicki, lighten up. I'm not hurting it. When I'm done with it, for all I know, somebody will find the car and return it. It's not like I'm running a chop shop here."

"A what?"

"Chop shop. That's a place where you take cars that have been stolen and you cut 'em up and sell 'em for parts."

Nicki couldn't believe they were talking about this. "Have you ever *been* part of a chop shop?"

Brad sighed and looked at her for longer than Nicki thought he should have had his eyes away from the road. He signaled right and pulled into a Giant Food shopping center, where he found a parking spot close to the road and pushed the transmission into Park. For a few seconds, Nicki thought that he was waiting for her to get out, to leave him alone, but then she realized that he was just gathering his thoughts.

"Nicolette, look—"

"Please don't call me that. It's Nicki. I won't even answer to that other one."

"Nicki, then." Brad turned sideways in his seat, curling one leg atop the center console. "I don't know what you think I am. I don't even know why you agreed to come on this crazy trip I planned. I think it's because you know it's your only shot at having a decent life, and you've got to live the whole damn thing in the next few months. This stupid disease is gonna take everything away from you, and you want to have something worth losing before it's gone. Am I close?"

His words made her feel somehow whole. Maybe he was just regurgitating what she'd written to him a thousand times, but it was wonderful to hear her own thoughts articulated by someone else. She smiled.

"Good. Great. I thought so. Well, I'm not like that, okay? I've seen plenty of this life, and there hasn't been a single day that I haven't wondered why I'm still doing the dance. If it all ended tomorrow, I honestly wouldn't give a damn. All life has handed me is one fistful of shit after another, and when I get a chance, I take it." While he spoke, Nicki watched his eyes darken as his voice grew thick. He wasn't about to cry—no tears could be found within a hundred miles of Brad Ward—but the hurt and the anger were all there. She could actually *see* those thousand stories flashing in his eyes.

"Don't tell me about laws, because I don't care. Obeying them gets me in as much trouble as breaking them does. And don't tell me about right and wrong and all that lofty church crap, because let me tell you, I've seen shit that 'wrong' doesn't even touch."

He was like an entirely different person right now. She wasn't sure exactly what triggered this diatribe, but she sensed that she'd hooked directly to his heart, bypassing the filters of his brain.

"I'm doing this trip as a kick, okay? As a treat. I thought we'd have some good times and a few adventures, but listen to me, Nicki, because this is very important. Are you listening?"

She nodded.

"Good. I only know how to be who I am. I tried being a thousand other things in my life, and I suck at all of them. I'm going to be *me*. You can think of me as a criminal, but I think of me as a pragmatist. You can think of me as a thief, but I think of myself as a provider. Am I making sense to you?"

Again, she nodded.

"Good. But I'm tired of providing just for myself. I wanted company, and from the very first moment that I started thinking about this, you were the only person I ever thought of asking. I know you don't believe that because you're all over that 'I'm not worth anything' bullshit, but I'm telling you like it is.

"Your father is going to tell people that I kidnapped you—or that somebody did. He's going to see only what the goddamn laws allow him to see, and when he does, he's gonna be pissed as shit that you went along with it. You need to decide if you're with me, or if you're going back to Bumfuck suburbia."

"I have to decide now?"

Brad shrugged. "For now you do, yeah. I mean, you can change your mind anytime you want. You say, 'stop the car,' and I'll stop it. But you need to know up front that I'm not going to get some job flopping burgers, and I'm not staying in no-tell motels. This is your swan song, and it may be mine, and I want it to have class and style. That means we're going to bend a few laws."

"You mean *break* a few laws."

Brad paused, correctly reading the signs that he hadn't run her off. He smiled. "It's hard to tell sometimes. They don't actually make a snapping noise or anything."

Nicki laughed. It was her nervous laugh, a little breathless, reflecting the fluttering of her stomach, the rush of adrenaline. Part of her was thrilled, but another part wished that she'd never asked her question. An even larger part of her worried about the other 999 untold stories.

This was decision time. As they sat there in the grocery store parking lot, invisible in the crowd of shoppers, Brad's eyes never left her, never eased the burden of her making a commitment one way or the other—a commitment for at least the time being.

Everything he said ran counter to everything she knew. Despite her adolescent attitude—yes, she knew she had it, and yes, she flaunted it every time she thought she could get a rise out of her father—she'd never broken *any* law, and now Brad was talking about a potential crime spree. She was riding in a stolen car, for crying out loud!

For all the potential danger, Brad was offering *real* living—real on-the-edge adventure. Maybe if somebody else had been sitting there with a better offer—someone else who liked her for who she was, and countered Brad's plan with a law-abiding alternative—then maybe she would have chosen differently. How could she know? But for the time being, the only alternative plan offered hospitals and doctors and the smell of disinfectant; a lifetime—literally—of worried looks and temperature-controlled environments and warnings to be careful.

"Okay," she said. "I'm in."

Brad beamed. "Outstanding." He pulled the transmission back into gear and headed for the exit from the parking lot.

"No violence, though," Nicki said.

He looked hurt. "We're not doing a Bonnie and Clyde thing, Nicki. We're not even doing a Thelma and Louise thing. This isn't *about* breaking the law, okay? That's not the point. The point is to have a good time. As it is, I've got plenty of cash to last for a while, and you brought some, too, right?"

"I could only get $500."

"That's fine. That's plenty." Suddenly, excitement returned to his voice, nudging aside that morose edge that had unnerved her before. He was once again the Brad whom she'd come to know so well in cyberspace. "And quit worrying about me being a sicko, okay? Because I'm not."

"I wasn't worrying about any such thing," she protested.

"You were too," he said, and he did the eyebrow thing again.

Nicki smiled at the windshield. "Maybe I thought about it a little."

"These days, you'd be nuts not to," he agreed.

"It's my dad. He keeps harping on me about all the crimes that he prosecutes—"

"Nicki?"

She stopped talking and turned to face him.

"Do me one favor, okay? Let's not talk about your father anymore."

His words hurt her feelings somehow, and he sensed it.

"He's the past," Brad explained. "He's what was. What used to be. Now, you and I, we're all about the future. We're all about finally having some fun!"

He punctuated that last sentence with a shot to the gas pedal that launched them back into traffic. "Can I see your cell phone?" he asked.

"Who are you going to call?"

"Does it matter?"

Nicki hesitated, but didn't really know why. Then she reached into her pocket and slid out her Nokia phone. She handed it to him.

"Thanks," he said. And then he threw it out of the car into traffic.

Nicki whirled in her seat. "What did you do? That was my phone!"

"It's cheap and old-fashioned," Brad said. "Motorola's Startac is way cooler."

"Brad! We have—"

"That's your old life, Nicki. That phone is your father and the doctors and everything else that sucks the life out of you. If you need a phone, we'll buy you a new one."

Nicki watched him for a long time while he continued to drive. God, he was hot.

Five minutes later, he slowed and pulled into another driveway. "There it is," he said. "Your fantasy castle."

Nicki saw it, but she didn't believe it. "Oh, my God," she breathed. It came out as a giggle. "Are you kidding?"

The smile blazed on Brad's face. No, he wasn't kidding.

PART TWO
TIME TO HIDE

Chapter Eight

Surf's Up Amusements was a terrible place to be under any circumstances, but in these off-season days it was particularly creepy—a playground for rats that doubled as a den of iniquity for druggies and horny teenagers. To be arrested in a place like this had to be particularly humiliating.

Jeremy Hines grew old before Darla's eyes, and as the minutes ticked by, she felt guilty that she hadn't looked the other way and saved these kids the humiliation that was barreling toward them. She'd turned her back on the opportunity to do a good deed.

Even Peter-the-mouth had settled down.

To make her point as vividly as possible, she'd cuffed them both, hands behind their backs. They sat in the sand with their legs folded, and the effects of the pot had dwindled to nearly nothing.

Peter cleared his throat to get Darla's attention. "I guess it's too late to apologize?"

She pruned up her face and gave a sarcastic nod. "Yeah, I think so."

"I notice you didn't tell the sheriff why you wanted him here."

"And I notice that you really don't know how to keep your lip zipped."

"How about if I tell you that this is Numb Nuts's first time doing weed?" Peter asked.

"Don't," Jeremy commanded.

"Why not? It's the truth."

Darla tried to see Jeremy's eyes, but he was busy studying his ankles. His pharmaceutical virginity seemed to be a source of embarrassment.

"Why today, then?" Darla asked.

Peter answered, "I talked him into it." He clearly knew that Darla didn't believe a word, so he added, "Him and his old man are at war, okay?"

"Shut up, Peter!" The vehemence of Jeremy's outburst convinced Darla that Peter was dancing perilously close to the truth.

"No, you shut up," Peter fired back. Then, to Darla, "Look, I'm the bad influence, okay? I'm the druggie. The homeless guy. The perpetual screwup. I figured that he needed a little weed, and I needed a little cover. This arrest'd be my third and a felony, and I figured there was no way they could lock me up and let him go, you know? Hell, the chances of getting caught in the first place are like, what? Nothing in a million? And I thought it was zero that you'd cut paper on the sheriff's kid."

"So you were using him," Darla concluded.

"We use each other. I take him places where he'd be afraid to go on his own."

"You better keep me cuffed, Deputy," Jeremy growled. "When you let me go, I'm gonna kill this asshole."

Peter laughed, but somehow he did it in a way that was free of derision. "He says that a lot. Fact is, he can't afford to kill me."

"How's that?" Darla asked.

"His scholarship. He's off to UNC next year on a baseball scholarship. Room, board, everything. That kind of shit goes on his record—or a drug conviction goes on his record—and he'll be cleaning condos next year instead."

One look at Jeremy told Darla that she was hearing fact. "So, why do you do this?" she asked. "Why would you take the chance?"

"Ask Peter," Jeremy mumbled. "He knows all the answers."

"I want to hear from you." When Jeremy still wouldn't answer, she turned back to Peter.

"He *hates* baseball," Peter said.

Darla didn't get it. "So, why—"

"He doesn't hate his teeth. Or his bones. All of which Sheriff Daddy is going to break when he gets here."

Darla tried to figure out the dynamic that was unfolding here. She couldn't tell if Peter was trying to be Jeremy's friend, or if he was just goading him on. Certainly, he seemed dialed in to the other boy's secrets. For his part, all Jeremy did was turn red.

Her portable radio broke squelch. "Unit six-oh-one's out at the Surf's Up." It was Sheriff Hines, and within seconds, Darla heard the sound of his tires crunching gravel. She turned to see the sheriff's specially outfitted Suburban pulling to a stop. A glance toward Jeremy made her wonder if the young man might pee in his pants.

Frank Hines had been sheriff of Essex County, North Carolina, for twenty-three years, and he carried himself with the arrogant grace of someone who not only enforced the law, but owned it as well. Not especially tall, he was nonetheless a big man, stocky and powerful. He wore his khaki uniform a bit too tight, highlighting a prominent gut that looked solid as stone. She could tell at a glance that he was angry.

"Deputy Sweet," he said, "in the future, when I ask you what a visit is in regard to, you by Jesus better answer up and tell me." His voice sounded half an octave too high for the size of his body.

"I'm sorry, Sheriff, but I thought that discretion might be the order of the day on this one."

Hines's scowl transformed from a mask of curiosity to one of fury. He saw his son on the ground in the classic pose of a perp under arrest, and then shifted his white-hot eyes to his deputy. "Speak," he said.

"They were doing drugs." Darla said the words as quickly as possible, with the intent of knocking the sheriff off balance. "Smoking weed. That one over there started running his mouth, and here we are."

Sheriff Frank Hines worked his jaw muscles hard. His gaze shifted to Peter Banks, whose face showed only contempt. There was history here that Darla didn't comprehend, but clearly the animosity ran deep between these two.

Without a word, Sheriff Hines moved toward Peter. As he closed to within two feet, he unleashed a brutal kick to the boy's thigh. Peter howled and rolled to his side, struggling, with his hands tethered behind him, to rise to his feet. A second kick had to break some ribs.

"Jesus, Sheriff!" Darla shouted. Jeremy winced at the sight and looked away.

"Stay outta this, Deputy," Hines growled. Then, to Peter: "I thought I told you to stay the hell away from my boy." A third kick was more like a shove with the sole of his shoe. Peter landed on his face, then curled up in a protective ball, sputtering and choking in search of a breath.

The sheriff turned to his son. "What do you have to say for yourself?"

Jeremy looked away.

"Talk to me, boy, before I break every tooth in your head."

Darla stepped forward, tried to get between them. "Come on, Sheriff, let's not—"

Hines froze her in her tracks with a forefinger aimed at her nose. His thumb was up, forming what looked like a pretend gun. "You've done your job," he said. "I can take it from here. This is a family affair."

Hines lifted his son by the hair, pulling him to his feet. Jeremy had to move quickly to keep his scalp from being torn from his skull.

"I asked you a question, boy. What the *hell* were you thinking, doing drugs in my county?"

"I wasn't thinking at all, sir." Jeremy's answer had monotonous quality of a memorized rejoinder.

Hines glared, as if trying to set the boy afire with his eyes. Then, his head turned, and he again focused on Peter. "Is this your doing, Peter?"

Peter didn't attempt to respond, struggling instead for his next breath.

"I'm calling for an ambulance," Darla said, reaching for her radio.

"No, you're not," the sheriff said.

"But he can't breathe."

"He's okay," the sheriff said. "He just had the wind knocked out of him." He turned to Peter. "Ain't that right, son?"

Peter managed a nod.

"See? What did I tell you?"

"You can't beat these boys, Sheriff," Darla said, trying to keep the tone of her voice steady.

Hines was trembling, his face red and hot. "Deputy Sweet, I want you to get in your cruiser and clear this scene immediately."

She stood her ground. "No, I don't believe I'll do that," she said. "I believe I'll stick around here as a witness."

The sheriff's eyes narrowed. "That wasn't a request, Deputy. I'm ordering you to clear this scene."

"And I'm telling you, I'm not going anywhere as long as you're this angry. If you want me to call the state police for backup, I can do that, too."

Sheriff Hines pivoted to face her full-on, his posture mimicking hers. "Are you disobeying a direct order, Deputy Sweet?"

Behind the sheriff, Peter caught his breath and worked himself back up to his knees, where he could watch the exchange between the cops. Jeremy's countenance had frozen itself into a giant O.

"I look at it as reasonable intervention to prevent the commission of a felony." Darla's racing heart made her words tremble in her throat.

Hines cocked his head. "A felony." Apparently, the words didn't taste quite right to him.

Darla stood a little taller. "Yes, sir, a felony. You're beating helpless, unarmed juveniles. That is a felony in this state."

"In Essex, we call it discipline," Hines said. He seemed amused by the conversation.

"Hit him again, and we'll see." To emphasize her point, she thumbed the button on her radio mike. "Unit six-oh-four to Central."

Hines's expression turned to one of concern. "Just what do you think you're doing?"

Her radio popped. "Go ahead, six-oh-four."

Darla arched her eyebrows. "You tell me, Sheriff.

You tell me if I'm calling for backup to have you arrested."

"Central to six-oh-four, go ahead."

The color of the sheriff's face intensified to something north of red, but still south of purple. He pressed his lips so tightly together that they nearly disappeared. "You're on dangerous ground, Deputy. This is a family matter."

Darla looked to the beaten boy on the ground. "This feel like a family matter to you, Peter?"

The boy smiled. "No, ma'am, it doesn't."

"Six-oh-four, do you have traffic?" The dispatcher's voice had a distinct edge on it now.

She thumbed the mike, and as she did, Hines jumped a little. "Ah, Central, stand by for a second." Then, to Hines: "Tell me what to do, boss."

Sheriff Hines faced the boys again. "You broke the law," he said.

Peter Banks winced as he straightened, but then smiled. He knew he'd won. "Cheer up, Sheriff. I'm sure it won't be my last time. You'll get another chance."

Sheriff Hines looked ready to kill the kid. He whirled to face Darla. "I suppose you want to just let him go with a warning."

"No, sir," Darla said. "I think that we should arrest them and prosecute them for possession of a controlled substance. I called you because of the presence of your son, and I thought a little deference might be in order."

The sheriff churned it all through his mind. A confirmed hothead, he was nobody's fool. He understood the corner he was in. When he took a step closer to his son, Darla moved to stay between them. "Do you know what you've done, Jeremy?" he growled.

His son stared at the ground.

"Answer me, boy."

"Yessir."

"Do you know how this makes me look? Do you understand what it can do to your future? A drug charge? Jesus."

"Won't make you look any too good, either, will it, Sheriff?" Peter said.

Darla wanted to kill him herself.

Peter continued, "Chief lawman of a little burg like this can't even keep his own son in line. For years and years, people'd be talking in the diner about how that Hines kid, boy, he really could've been something. Shame he lost that scholarship."

Sheriff Hines glowered at the Banks boy. "You're going to jail," he said.

"Not today, I'm not. Not without Jeremy coming with me. See? I choose my friends carefully, Sheriff."

Hines vibrated with anger. He wanted to do violence to something—some*one*—but that wasn't going to happen. Not today.

"Central to six-oh-four. Sweet cheeks, do you have traffic for me or not?"

Darla looked at the sheriff, waiting for a cue.

"Take those cuffs off," he said. "Let them go."

"I don't want you taking out your anger on Jeremy when he gets home," Darla said. "I'll be checking up, Sheriff, and I swear to God—"

"Know when to accept victory and back off, Deputy," Hines said.

Brad's surprise destination turned out to be the Ritz-Carlton Hotel, located in Mason's Corner on the western edge of Braddock County. A meaningless crossroads just thirty years ago, Mason's Corner was now the mecca of high-tech development in Northern Virginia, employing over 100,000 workers. Complete with its own traffic gridlock and distinctive skyline, this unincorporated city was center field for the computer technology game on the East Coast. In a few years, if things kept growing the way they had, Mason's Corner would make Silicon Valley look like a low-rent district.

The hotel was an opulent appendage to the Galleria at Mason's Corner, which itself appeared to be a freeze-dried version of Rodeo Drive, where Saks Fifth Avenue was the *low-end* store.

"This is beautiful," Nicki breathed.

"You ain't seen nothin' yet," Brad said with a wink.

Brad whipped the turn into the circular driveway, and the doorman walked with casual efficiency to Nicki's door and opened it. "Welcome to the Ritz-Carlton," he said. "Do you need help with your luggage?"

Brad answered before Nicki had a chance. "That's okay. I think we'll just leave it in the trunk for a while." He pulled a ten-dollar bill out of his pocket and handed it to the attendant. "I love this car," he said. "Please take good care of it."

The attendant's reaction made him think that it was the best tip of the day.

The doorman spun the revolving door for them, and then they were inside. Nicki gasped. "Oh. My. God."

"Close your mouth," Brad whispered. "You look like you've never been in a hotel before."

"I haven't. Not like this, anyway." The lush carpet looked like something out of a royal palace, boasting subdued splashes of burgundy and blue and green. In combination with the spectacular leather furniture and the polished mahogany walls, the lobby bore the ambience of a rich gentlemen's club.

Brad gestured to one of the wine-colored leather chairs.

"Have a seat. I need to work out some stuff with the front desk."

"I can't go with you?"

"I'd rather you not," he said.

Nicki's eyes said she wanted more details, but Brad walked away.

A man and a woman gave matching smiles in their matching gray suits as Brad approached. Neither was much older than he. "Hi," Brad said. "You have a reservation for Mr. Campanella? I believe it was made this morning."

The woman—Sam, according to her name tag—started typing in her computer while Patrick looked on. "Yes, I have it right here," she said. "You're part of the ASLO conference?"

Brad smiled. "Yes ma'am, that's right."

"Very good, I just need to see your credit card."

Brad winced. "Um, I think you need to read the rest of the record. My father made the reservation, and he doesn't like me to have a credit card."

Sam scrolled down through the record. "Okay," she said, "according to this, you're approved for room and miscellaneous expenses, but it also says something about a code word and asking for identification?"

Brad smiled sheepishly and reached for his wallet. "I don't believe he embarrasses me like this. One little misstep, and I have to be humiliated for the rest of my life. Rumpelstiltskin is the code word, by the way." He levered his Nevada driver's license out of his wallet. Thanks to some fast work at Kinko's, it identified him as Bradley Campanella. It was a calculated risk to include the identification in the ruse, but it worked well to put people at ease as they violated long-standing company policy.

From the brief glance that Sam gave the license, he might just as well have put Santa Claus's picture on it. Her fingers flew on the keyboard, and she read some more. Brad didn't like what he saw pass in front of her eyes, but he was in too deep to show paranoia now. He'd learned over the years that if you just kept your face passive and friendly, you could get away with anything.

"Okay, Mr. Campanella," Sam said at last, "how many keys do you need?"

"Two, please."

Sam pulled two plastic cards out of a slot at the front of her desk and did some more computer work to turn them into keys. Brad took the opportunity to scan the room. He didn't know squat about art, but the huge oil canvases on the walls all looked like originals. Very expensive ones at that.

"Here you go," Sam said, handing him the key. "Are you familiar with our hotel?"

"Actually, no, I'm not."

"Okay, then, well, you're in room 9000. I think you'll like it very much. If not, please let us know and we'll make sure that everything suits you. Whatever you need, charge it to the room. Can I have someone carry luggage for you?"

Brad pushed away from the counter. "No, we're fine, thanks."

"There's another note in your file about the Couture Shoppe?"

It took him a second, but then he remembered. "Oh, yes, of course."

Hailey read from her computer screen as she told him, "Pamela is waiting for your phone call, and she's very excited about what she's found."

Brad beamed. "Excellent. I'll tell you what. If it's not too much trouble, could you go ahead and call her and have her meet us in the room in say, ten minutes?"

Sam was already reaching for the telephone. "Of course," she said. "Enjoy your stay at the Ritz-Carlton."

Brad walked back toward Nicki, who was nearly dozing in her chair. "Okay, we're set. Are you all right?"

"I'm just tired," she said. "We've got a room?"

Brad fanned the two keys like so many playing cards. "The top floor," he said. "The Governor's Suite."

Nicki gasped and hissed, "Brad, you can't steal a hotel room."

He helped her out of her chair. "Who says I'm stealing? Just ask the folks at the front desk. My father is giving us this trip as a present."

March 16

Georgen tossed my cell three times this week. He still scares me.

I finally met Mrs. Johnson today. The way she smiled and squealed when she saw me, you'd have thought that I was really her son. She said that she'd heard a lot about me through Derek. She knew all about the robbery that got me here, and she said that she was going to talk to Derek's lawyer about appealing my case. I told her not to bother, but she said she's going to anyway.

The visiting area is just like you see in the movies. No physical contact. We talk through a telephone and look at each other through the thick glass. Mrs. Johnson told me all about a bunch of people I've never heard of. Cousin This and Uncle That, and about a family reunion. It was a look at the outside. It was good, but I'm not sure I ever want to do it again. I can't deal with hope right now.

Chapter Nine

The elevator car dinged as it glided to a halt, and the doors slid open to reveal even more opulence, every bit as posh as the lobby. A rich leather sofa greeted them on the opposite wall, and above it, Nicki could see their reflections in an enormous gilded mirror. The nap of the carpet nearly tripped her, and Brad struck like a snake to catch her.

"Be careful," he said. "Looks like they haven't mowed the rug in a while."

Clearly this was the special floor, the one designed for visiting dignitaries and movie stars. The hallways were wider than she'd seen in other hotels, and the doorways were widely separated. Brad led the way, scowling as he watched the room numbers pass.

"What number are you looking for?" Nicki asked.

"I told you. We're looking for the Governor's Suite. Room 9000."

It was at the far end of the hallway, the door staring straight back at them. "Governor's Suite" was etched in black letters on gleaming brass, the plaque mounted just above an ornate brass knocker. With his grin growing wider by the second, Brad slid the plastic key into the slot, and when the red light turned green, he pushed it open. "Welcome to your new hangout."

They both gasped at the splendor of the place. The gleaming walnut door swung in to reveal what Nicki imagined a Park Avenue apartment might look like. "Oh, my God," she said. Words were useless here.

A hardwood foyer gave way to a living room—easily twice the size of the one in Nicki's house on Berwick Place. The dining room table—yes, the dining room table, in the actual *dining room*—was set for six people, though it easily could have accommodated four more, and that led to a kind of mini-kitchen, with a fridge, a microwave, and a bar. Directly across from the front door, the living room curtains stretched the full twelve feet from the floor to the ceiling, and through them, she could see a glittering view of Mason's Corner.

"You like it?" Brad asked.

"We're going to jail," Nicki said, stifling a laugh. "And then we're going to hell."

"Where we'll find all of our friends," Brad said. "Come on, let's look around."

The bedroom was as grand as the living room, with a towering canopy bed and a fireplace that lit by remote control. Beyond that lay the bathroom, a symphony of rose-colored marble and solid brass fixtures. As she looked at the deep Jacuzzi tub, it was all Nicki could do to keep from pushing Brad out of the room.

"It's all too much," she said. "I can't imagine what all of this must cost."

"Keep worrying like that and you're gonna give yourself a health problem."

She laughed. Why could he say things like that to her and not offend her? She was dying, for God's sake, but Brad could talk about it as if it were just any other annoying detail in an otherwise normal life.

Nicki jumped when the doorbell rang. "Who's that?"

Brad's eyes grew even wider with mischief. "Wait till you see. This is the best part yet."

Nicki started laughing before she knew why. She let him take her hand and lead her back out to the living room. "What are you doing?"

When he reached the foyer, he stopped. "Oh, yeah, don't act surprised if they call me Mr. Campanella."

"Campanella?"

Brad beamed. "Yeah. And you might try to remember that we're here to attend the annual meeting of the ASLO."

"Ass-low?"

"The American Society of Law Enforcement Officials."

The doorbell rang again.

"The American Society of *what*?"

He laughed. "Don't worry about it. It was the only prom I could find."

Brad hurried to the door and pulled it open, revealing a forty-something woman and her assistant, wrangling a rack full of clothes.

Nicki's jaw dropped.

Brad caught the look of amazement and beamed. "Well, you can't go to a fancy dance dressed like that," he said.

Pamela and Simone brought only the best from the shop downstairs. Versace, Donna Karan, Nicole Miller, you name it. It was all evening wear, and all of it was size two, just as it was supposed to be. Obviously, Brad had been paying attention. They worked on her the way stylists work on a movie star, showing her one outfit even as she was trying on another.

Brad had asked to stay and watch the show, but that idea was dead on arrival. He was biding his time out in the living room, where he'd found a baseball game to watch.

In less than an hour, it was all done. She was the proud owner of a princess's wardrobe. When it came time for Pamela and Simone to leave, Brad called from the living room that it was his turn, that she had to stay in the bedroom for a while longer. Ten minutes later, she heard him bid good-bye to the visitors.

Over the years, Nicki had learned the art of looking at clothes in the mirror. If she did it right, she could see only the clothes, and nothing of herself. She thought of it as a survival skill—the talent that kept her from acting on that occasional suicidal urge. When she explained it to her shrink, the best analogy she'd been able to construct was to refer to one of those clear plastic mannequins you saw in store windows. You knew that something had to be holding the clothes up, but unless you really made an effort, the mannequins themselves remained invisible.

Intuitively, Nicki knew that the fat wasn't there, yet emotionally, if she allowed herself to look, it was all that she'd be able to see. Tonight, as she gazed at her reflection in the mirror, she saw a lovely gown and a terrific pair of shoes. And a necklace. It was a beautiful thing, floating there above the low neckline of the dress. It was a spectacular outfit, wasted on someone as uselessly unattractive as she.

The knock on the door startled her. "Nicki, are you ready?"

She went to the door, grateful to have an excuse to break away from the mirror. As she reached for the knob, she had a brief stab of panic. What would Brad say when he saw her? All of this, she knew, had as much to do with a fantasy of his as it did a fantasy of hers. What would happen if she so wildly missed the mark that he lost interest?

"Can I come in?" Brad asked through the door.

"No," she said, "I'm coming out. Are you ready?"

"When you are."

Steeling herself against the disappointment she knew she'd see in his face, Nicki turned the knob and pulled the door open. What she saw made her gasp: The Brad from the bus station had transformed into James Bond. He wore a jet-black tuxedo with black satin tie and cummerbund, with gold studs decorating the front panel of his crisply starched white shirt. And, as always, he wore that smile. He positively glimmered.

"You're gorgeous," he said. "The gown is perfect on you."

And then Nicolette Janssen positively glimmered as well.

Chapter Ten

Carter arrived at the bus station around nine-thirty and parked illegally in the bus lanes, leaving his blue Kojak light on the dash as a signal to any passing cops that he was due a little professional courtesy. As a matter of New York State law, he didn't really rate the light—truly there was no reason for a prosecutor to race to the scene of a crime—but it was the way things were done. He could only guess that the practice in Brookfield, Virginia, was similar.

As he stepped through the double doors, he winced at the stink of the place, a combination of body odor and institutional dirt. All the ticket windows but one were closed now, and the woman behind the glass read a paperback to pass the time. Carter wondered if Nicki had stood on this exact same spot, and if so, how long ago.

What must she have been thinking as she walked through here? Had she had a plan, beyond the musings in the chat room? As a girl raised in the comfort of upper-middle-class suburbia, how did she react to the plainness of a bus station? To the people who passed through it?

In the best case, Carter figured that he was only six hours behind her; the worst case was nine hours. Nicki had apparently been smart enough in her evasion tactics to pay for her ticket in cash and to travel under an assumed name. Such were the perks, he guessed, of having a father who spent his life working with criminals. Amazing what you teach your kids when you think you're teaching them something else. Had it occurred to her, even for a moment, that this guy might not show up? Or that he might not be the person she thought he was?

He'd asked himself that question dozens of times now, and every time, the answer came back, "Of course she didn't."

As he'd expected, he saw no local police on the lookout. Seventeen was a tricky age for runaways everywhere. Despite their legal status as minors and their emotional immaturity, most jurisdictions saw them as old enough to make decisions for themselves, and they tended not to commit shoe leather to a search until the kid had been missing for some prescribed period, usually forty-eight hours.

Chris Tu's discovery of Brad Ward's new name would certainly add some enthusiasm to the effort to find them, but that was a card he'd have to play carefully. Carter hadn't seen the sheet they were putting out yet, but he knew without question that as a murderer and escapee, the text would read "armed and extremely dangerous." That would mean guns drawn in any confrontation, and the very thought of Nicki being within a mile of a shoot-out made his stomach knot.

The clatter of a galvanized bucket drew Carter's attention around behind him, to a closet where a three-hundred-year-old janitor was wrestling with a mop and cleaning supplies. It was as good a place to start as any, he supposed. Carter waited until the old guy appeared to have things under control, then approached him softly. "Excuse me," he said.

When the janitor straightened, he appeared to be even older than before. His black skin had the texture of a well-ridden saddle, and the name tag over his shirt pocket read Stewart.

"My name is Carter Janssen. I'm a lawyer from New York, and I'm looking for this girl." He handed over a copy of Nicki's junior-year school picture.

Stewart gave it a cursory glance and shook his head. "Ain't seen nobody looks nothing like that," he said.

Carter offered it a second time. "Could you look at it again, please? This is my daughter and I need to find her. She's sick."

Stewart glanced again, even more briefly. "Nope, sorry."

Carter sighed as he felt himself flush. People like this were the reason for half the world's misery. No one wanted to get involved. "Anyone here that you can recommend I talk to? I figure she must have come through in the last four or five hours."

The old man pushed his wheeled bucket forward, using the handle of the mop as a rudder in a weird parody of a Venetian gondolier. "The ticket folks changed shifts two hours ago."

"What about the baggage handlers?"

Stewart's face folded into a smile, exposing a set of teeth that reminded Carter of a half-eaten ear of corn. "This is a bus station, young feller. The ticket folk do it all."

"What about you? How long you been on duty?"

The janitor bumped Carter's foot with his bucket and Carter stepped sideways to let him pass. "Hell, I never go home," he said. "Work twelve, fourteen hours a day just to keep the rent paid. Sometimes I wonder why I even bother since I ain't never there."

Carter reached for Stewart's arm and the old man cringed, as if expecting to be hit. "Look, I know you don't want to share information about the people who pass through here—especially with some lawyer from New York—but you have to believe me when I tell you that the girl in the picture is very sick. She's my only daughter—my only child—and she's run away." His instincts told him not to mention anything about Brad or his criminal record; he didn't want to scare the old man off. "Please," Carter pressed. "If you know anything at all—or if you know anyone else who might know something—please share it with me."

Stewart eyed him, considering his words before he spoke them. Just from the way the janitor's eyes narrowed, Carter thought that he was about to get a break.

"No, sorry," Stewart said. "I can't help you." He pointed to a pile of filthy clothes gathered in the far corner of the station. "Might want to talk to him, though. He's always here, though I can't say his mind is all that it oughtta be."

Carter never would have noticed the homeless guy if Stewart hadn't pointed him out. "What's his name?"

"People call him Lee."

Interesting way to put that, Carter thought. Was there a difference between the man's name and what people called him? "Thank you," he said. *For nothing,* he didn't say.

Carter crossed the lobby, past the half-dozen travelers crammed in plastic seats that were linked together for maximum discomfort. Off in the corner opposite the lump that was Lee, a bank of snack machines hummed and glowed against the stained walls and floor. He wondered how many cross-country travelers lived off a diet of Cheez-Its, Ding Dongs, and soft drinks as they hopped from one bus station to the next, without transportation to take them even to a Waffle House somewhere.

As he got closer to Lee, Carter realized that the bum was responsible for at least half of the station's offensive odor. One glance at the empty bottle of cheap cognac, and Carter gave him up as a lost cause.

"Hey," a voice called from behind, "Mr. Lawyerman." Carter turned. It was Stewart. He hadn't moved from where Carter had last spoken to him. "That true, what you said about her bein' sick?"

Carter fought the urge to step closer. "Yessir," he said.

"Swear to God?"

Carter made a slow approach. He crossed his heart with his fingers, a gesture he hadn't made in thirty years.

"It's important," Stewart said, "because half the people come through here got some kinda story to tell, you know? A lot of them is tryin' to get away from somethin', and it ain't none o' my business to—"

"I swear to God, Stewart. She's my daughter and she's sick. And I'm desperate."

The janitor stewed on it, and then sighed. "I had a daughter run away from me long time ago. Turned to the streets and got herself mixed up in drugs and whorin' an' all kinds of death." His eyes narrowed and grew hot. "I was a drinker and a hitter, I was. I drove her off and she got dead as a result. Prob'ly best, because I prob'ly woulda killed her myself sooner or later. You don't look like a drinker. You a hitter?"

Carter allowed himself a soft smile. "Do I look like one?"

"No, sir, you look like the lawyer you say you are. Thing is, I don't know what that's any better."

Now here's a guy with a thousand stories to tell, Carter thought. He assured Stewart, "I'm not a drunk and I'm definitely not a hitter. I'm just a worried dad."

Stewart bobbed his head. That was good enough for him. "She was here," the janitor said. "She's a pretty little thing. Tiny, though. Makes sense, now that you tell me she's sick."

"Was she by herself?"

Stewart scowled as he replayed the scene in his head. "I b'lieve she was, at least at first. I remember her sitting right over yonder and checking her watch."

"How long ago?"

"I b'lieve she was on the Zephyr from up north. That would've put her here round four o'clock. Like you said, five, six hours ago."

"Did somebody meet her?"

"Yessir, somebody did, after a few minutes. A nice-looking kid, dressed like he was goin' to Harvard or somethin'. They was happy to see each other, too."

"How do you mean?"

"How do I mean? I mean, they had this big hug, just like in the movies. He even twirled her around. You gotta smile at young love."

"That wasn't love," Carter snapped, but then he pulled back. The clothing detail interested him. "What did this guy look like? Other than like he was nice?"

Stewart gave that a hard thought. "That's a hard one, you know? I don't notice boys all that much, if you know what I mean. He just looked like any other kid. Tall, thin, big smile. Good lookin' boy."

"So you got the sense that the girl—my daughter—had been waiting for him?"

"Oh, yessir, without a doubt. One o' the best things about this shitty job I got is watchin' reunions. Lots o' happiness in a reunion, you know? Make up for all the sad good-byes I see. That girl and that boy, well, I kinda feel this ain't what you want to hear, but that there was a good reunion."

He was right; it wasn't what Carter wanted to hear. "How about luggage? Did you see any of that?"

"No, sir, I didn't, and I gotta tell you, that's one o' the things that drew my attention to the girl. You see somebody that size, that age hangin' around a bus station, and you gotta think maybe somethin' bad is happenin'. That's how my own daughter did her slide downhill. She was a bus-rider all the way. When I saw your little girl sittin' there on the bench by herself, I kinda kept an eye on her, just to make sure that she didn't do something stupid."

Carter smiled. Stewart the guardian angel. "And when you saw the boy come in for her?"

"Well, I just let them have their peace. If he was her pimp or some such, there'd've been a lot o' that awkward shit, but not there. I stopped lookin' because even in here, people deserve a little privacy."

"I don't suppose you saw the kind of car he was driving."

Stewart displayed his corn-teeth again in a big grin. "No, sir, and that's the God's honest truth. If it don't park out there into the stalls, or in here on the floor, I just plain don't see what people drive."

Carter tried to think of another relevant question.

"Oh, an' I got one other detail you prob'ly might like to know. I did overhear them talkin' a little, an' I heard him tell her he was gonna treat her like some queen. No, that he was gonna take her to a prom."

Carter scowled. "Prom, as in a high school dance?"

"That's it, yessir, he was gonna take her to a prom. Even named the place they was gonna go to. He was gonna take her to her fantasy."

Carter punched the numbers into his cell phone as he drove toward the Braddock County police headquarters, following the directions given to him by whoever was sitting on the watch desk. He'd been halfway through arguing with the watch officer about his need for police support when it hit him why the town of Brookfield rang such a strong bell in his mind. Four years ago, he'd done one hell of a favor for a detective in that department—a lieutenant—and once Carter put the pieces together in his mind, he knew exactly how to get the kind of help he needed. The watch officer refused to give out the lieutenant's number, even when Carter assured him that there'd be no repercussions.

After a call to Chris Tu, however, Carter got what he needed. He punched the number into his cell.

As the phone rang on the other end, Carter checked his watch. Eight-thirty was a little late to be calling anyone at home, but under the circumstances, he'd live with the guilt.

They picked up on the other end in the middle of the fourth ring. "Michaels residence, Nathan speaking," said a reedy voice.

Carter smiled. Last time he heard that voice, it belonged to a little boy. "Hello, Nathan, this is Carter Janssen, I don't know if you remember me, but I'm—"

"You're the lawyer from New York," Nathan said, and judging from the sudden weakness in his tone, the sound of the prosecutor's voice terrified him.

Carter felt bad for not having introduced himself more gently. He remembered that day on the square near the obelisk, just as most of the country remembered from the television news coverage. At the age of twelve, Nathan Bailey had been the object of a nationwide hunt as a suspected murderer, and had very nearly earned a sniper's bullet. Carter could have prosecuted the boy on dozens of charges, but when Warren Michaels and his wife stepped in to be his foster family, Carter had cut them a break.

"There's no problem for you to be concerned about," Carter assured him, "but I need to speak with Lieutenant Michaels. Is he home?"

The teenager hesitated. "Yes, sir, I'll get him."

On the other end of the line, Carter heard Nathan yell, "Papa! Telephone!" There was movement, and then intense, muffled talk that Carter couldn't understand.

A more familiar voice came on the line. "This is Lieutenant Michaels. Can I help you?"

"Hello, Warren, this is Carter Janssen. I'm sorry to have startled Nathan like that. This is nothing about him or those old problems. I need to talk to you about a favor."

"Name it and it's yours," Michaels said.

"Is there a place where we can meet, and where I can maybe get a bite to eat? I haven't had anything since lunch."

"You bet. Where are you now?"

They decided on a twenty-four-hour breakfast place near the bus station. Warren Michaels hadn't changed much in four years. Maybe a little grayer around the temples, but he still had the easygoing athletic grace that Carter remembered.

Carter stood and they shook hands before Warren slid into the padded bench on the other side of the table. "It's great to see you again," Warren said.

"I really am sorry about startling Nathan."

"Don't give it a thought. Keeping him a little off balance keeps him from thinking he rules the world."

"He sounds so old on the phone."

Warren nodded. "Sixteen. He sings bass in the choir, and he's a head taller than me. Wears size twelve shoes. It's amazing."

The small talk was killing Carter, but he understood that this was the way things were done in Virginia, and it only seemed polite. "So, is he living with you permanently?"

Warren explained, "He's officially my foster son, but it's as permanent an arrangement as you can get. After the . . . *incident*"—he leaned on the word—"I looked into adopting him, but what with his inheritance and all, it got too complicated. He knows where home is. He calls me his papa and I call him my son."

The explanation had the rhythm of a stump speech, details explained so many times that they'd become automatic. Such was the price of fame, Carter supposed.

"But you're not here to talk about Nathan," Warren said, reading the body language. "Still, before I turn over the floor, I want you to know yet again how much I appreciate everything you did to iron things out for him."

Carter waved it off as if it were nothing, but Warren didn't know the half of it. As the bright light of Nathan's

celebrity faded into memory, not everyone was so anxious to look the other way on the dozens of felonies the
boy had racked up. It took some major league arm-
twisting and more than a few official threats to get all
the signatures he needed to make it happen.

"Let me tell you my problem," Carter began. It took
the better part of ten minutes to tell the story, and by the
time he was done, Warren Michaels seemed moved.
"What I need is shoe leather," Carter concluded. "I can't
do all the canvassing I need by myself, so I thought
maybe you could get some of your guys on the street
for me."

"Consider it done. I'll make the calls right now.
Meanwhile, you look like crap. Do you have a place to
stay?"

Carter blushed. "I didn't think that far ahead."

"You're staying with us." The way he said it, there
was no room for argument. "Chez Michaels isn't the
fanciest B and B on the planet, but there's always a
spare bed."

Carter waved the offer away. "I can't take the time
to sleep."

"Actually, you can," Warren countered. "This is my
turf, not yours. Get some rest and I'll spin some wheels
for you. If my guys turn up anything, I'll be the first to
know, and you'll be next in line. Deal?"

Fact was, the vision of Brad Ward encountering
dozens of police officers scared the shit out of Carter.
"Just please be sure to make it clear to everyone that
Nicki is an innocent in all of this."

"You have my word."

"And to be careful in any arrest. There's no telling
what this Ward/Dougherty guy might do."

Warren reached over and grasped Carter's hand.

"Try to relax, Counselor. My cops are the best in the business. This isn't exactly new territory for me."

Carter considered that, considered his options. Maybe it *was* time for him to lie down and get some rest.

They shook on it.

April 5

Derek witnessed a murder yesterday. He's scared shitless about it. He said it was out in the yard in plain sight of the guards. Three of the Posse—Peter Chaney, Harold Letier, and Charley Samson—got a guy cornered back by the bleachers. The guy—I think it was a lifer named Raminowitz or something like that—started screaming even before they did him.

Chaney and Samson held him while Letier did it. They raped him with a knife blade, for Christ sake. Derek said he's never seen so much blood. I could hear the screaming from the other side of the yard. Sounded like an animal caught in a trap. He bled to death before the guards got to him.

Derek's terrified because Chaney and Samson looked right at him while it was all going on. Looked right at him. They didn't say anything, but now Derek's worried about being the only witness. He's afraid they're going to kill him, too.

Chapter Eleven

Brad hated this shit. He hated the penguin suit, the uncomfortable shoes, the finger foods that wouldn't fill you up if you stood at the table for a week, and the snotty people who swarmed all around him. To think that these assholes paid hundreds of dollars apiece to be here curdled his stomach. What a ridiculous waste of money. For what? An evening of gyrations on the dance floor, driven by music from a band that didn't have any idea what it wanted to be. Thus far, he'd listened to bad covers of Frank Sinatra, The Beatles, and—God help us—Cher.

But a formal ball was one of Nicki's dreams. She'd spoken of it three or four times in their cyber correspondence, listing it as one of the things that she'd never be able to do, thanks to her disease. If all he had to do was hang out in uncomfortable clothes and pretend to be interested in President Clinton's dallyings with Monica Lewinsky, then that wasn't such a high price to pay.

Many of the items on Nicki's list were beyond his power to obtain for her—going to college and raising a bunch of kids—but this one was easy. And tomorrow would begin the dream of spending a week at the beach.

Honest to God, Brad didn't get Carter Janssen. He knew from firsthand experience that the man could be a prick if he wanted to be, but why would he want to piss off the only remaining relative he had? His wife was dead and his daughter was dying and Carter couldn't pop his head out of his ass long enough to see the world through her eyes. She wanted to *live* before she died. Why was that so impossible for him to understand?

The man was irrelevant now, and Brad would be lying if he didn't admit to a twinge of ironic pleasure. But for Janssen's paranoia that Brad was diddling his daughter (which he could have done at any time if a) he'd been interested in diddling twelve-year-old girls, or b) asked), everything in Brad's life would have been different. There would have been no ejection from the Benson house, no caroming from one homeless shelter to the next, no robbery, no murder, and no jail time. Brad knew how that sounded—knew how it made him look like a whiner who blamed others for his own problems—but he'd thought this all through a thousand times, and that was just how it was.

He leaned closer to Nicki, so she could hear him over the Barry Manilow cover. "You having a good time?"

She smiled, but her eyes looked tired. "It's wonderful."

"You okay doing this? I don't want to wear you out."

"We can stay a while longer. I just want to hang out long enough to make sure I remember everything. Do I want to know how you got this invitation?"

"I called this morning and made it. They asked for my membership number or some such, but I told them that I was on the road and didn't have it."

Nicki couldn't believe it. This all came so naturally to him. "I suppose you charged this to the room, too?"

Brad shook his head. "Nah, I thought that might raise too much suspicion. So I charged it to his credit card."

Nicki laughed. She wanted to be horrified, but admiration won out. "You're amazing," she said.

Brad watched Nicki's eyes, and there was that look again: the one that said she adored him. Way back in the day, when she was just a little girl, that look was puppy love, but now it looked like the real thing, and it stirred some of the same in him.

"My father had something to do with you going away, didn't he?" Nicki asked, out of nowhere.

She'd brought it up before, during their cyber chats, but he'd always changed the subject—subtly, he'd thought, but apparently not. Despite being a creature who survived on his powers of deception, he couldn't bring himself to lie to her face. "Tell me what you know."

"I have."

Brad wouldn't let her get away with that. "If you'd told me everything you know, you wouldn't have just asked that question. Tell me *everything* you know." Before, when they were just talking on the computer and Nicki was still resisting his overtures to join him on an adventure, it had seemed cruel to turn her against her dad. That seemed less of an issue now, but he didn't want to be the one who started it.

"I heard people talk about a burglary," she said. "And I remember Daddy saying something about you being involved. We got in a big fight over it. Mom had to intervene. You never would have broken into a house."

If he opened this door, there'd be no closing it. Brad spotted two overstuffed chairs in the corner behind the registration table and gestured to them. "Let's go have a seat," he said.

Nicki's face fell. She understood that people only wanted you to sit down when there was bad news coming. Somehow, through some quirk of physics, the music was louder over here than closer to the dance floor. Brad moved his chair so he could sit knee to knee with Nicki.

He took her hand. "I promised you the truth," he said. "This is your last chance to change the subject."

Nicki refused. How could she do anything else?

"Okay," he said. "I *did* break into that house."

"Into the Premingers' house? He was a preacher!"

"He left his front door unlocked." Brad said that as if it explained something. "But that wasn't why I was sent away. I felt bad about it, and when I confessed to Mr. Benson, he went and told your dad, and the four of us—Reverend Preminger included—worked out a deal where I'd give back the stuff I took and then work off my penance scraping and painting his gutters."

"I remember that," Nicki said. "That was your punishment? I thought you were getting paid for that."

Brad scoffed, "There's not enough cash in the world to pay me for that kind of work. No, that was me coming to peace with God and the law. It was a done deal. Had nothing to do with me getting shipped off."

"What, then?"

Brad didn't want to close the loop for her; he wanted her to do that for herself. "What would piss your dad off more than anything?"

It was Nicki's turn to scoff. "There's no end to the list of what pisses my dad off."

"Think bigger," Brad said. "What *fear* would piss

him off so badly that he'd ruin a seventeen-year-old kid's life?"

Nicki knew her dad was a prick sometimes, and as square as a cinder block, but he wasn't vindictive. She couldn't imagine why he would *intentionally* make someone else's life difficult. Then she got it. Yes, she did know what would drive him to do just about anything. "Somebody told him our secret."

Brad bounced his eyebrows. "Remember Joey Benson, the oldest of the Benson spawn? Well, the oldest until I got there. He fought me on any day with a *y* in it."

"I remember you picking a few of those fights," Nicki said, recalling the brawls that would occasionally spill out into the yard.

"Yeah, well, I had underestimated that 'blood is thicker than water' thing. He knew that you and I used to talk a lot, and I made the mistake of telling him about the time you were feeling sorry for boys because they had to lift the toilet seat to sit on the pot."

Nicki blushed. "Oh, God." Naïveté did not come a lot more pure than hers back in those days. It had never occurred to her that boys could pee while standing.

"Anyway, he told your father that we talked about 'dirty stuff' and just for good measure told him that I made you play with my dick."

Nicki's jaw dropped. "He said *what*?" Her volume and tone drew looks from their fellow wallflowers, and she dialed it down. "I never did that."

"Your father didn't want to take the chance. He drew a line connecting the burglary thing to me being some sort of pervert, and he gave the Bensons an ultimatum. They could get rid of me, or he could make their life miserable. I mean, it happened like *that*." He punctuated the word with a finger snap.

"Why didn't you tell me?"

"I didn't get a chance to. I'm serious about the speed. Your dad called, and I was shipped back to social services within hours. It's not like I had a vote."

"But you didn't *do* anything."

This time, Brad's smile bore a patronizing edge. "You really think that matters when you've got no father and your mother's in prison? Even if the pervert thing didn't stick, he'd have had the burglary to fall back on. I was in no position to negotiate."

It all made sense, Nicki supposed. It wasn't entirely different than her own circumstances. She'd seen the futility of fighting her father, too. "So, why didn't you mention this before?"

Brad tossed off a shrug. "You'd already lost your mother. I didn't want you hating your father."

"And now?"

He gave a rueful chuckle. "Well, now that I'm telling the story, I'm hating him myself, so I guess I don't care." He didn't like the dejected look that invaded Nicki's face. "Do you want to talk about this anymore?"

"No."

"Good."

"You know what I would like to do?"

Something stirred in Brad's gut. "Tell me," he said.

"I want to go back to the room and soak in that gorgeous bathtub."

Brad had to be careful here.

Nicki squeezed his hand. "I had a wonderful time. But if I don't get some rest, there'll be hell to pay later. Really."

Brad stood and offered his arm, hoping that his erection didn't show. "Shall we?"

He escorted her out of the ballroom, overdoing it a bit with standing straight and tall. "Ever feel like you're about to turn into a pumpkin?" he asked under his breath.

Nicki thrust the point of her hip into him playfully. "As long as I'm with my Prince Charming, it doesn't matter."

Nicki had never seen so much polished marble. It was a deep rose color, with swirling veins of white and black.

She ran the water warm—just the other side of cool— and dumped in the contents of the tiny plastic bottle of bubble bath. She pressed the button that launched the Jacuzzi jets and thirty seconds later, the lather of thick bubbles was dense enough to walk on.

Nicki slipped out of her ball gown, draping it on the hook on the back of the door, and eased herself into the water. The hiss of the bubbles filled the room with white noise. One of the most disappointing complications of her disease was the need to avoid super-hot baths to keep her heart from racing too fast as it tried to slough off the heat. Keeping the heart rhythm normal was the rule of the day, every day. Don't get too excited, try not to exert too much, and the ever-thickening blood vessels in her lungs would be able to handle the load. For now, anyway.

The foam expanded all the way to her chin before she realized that she'd forgotten to take her rat poison. The thought made her groan aloud. The pills were all the way across the room, standing sentry next to the other prolonger-of-life, her Digoxin, a water pill that kept her tissues from absorbing the liquid from her blood and turning her into the Pillsbury Dough Boy.

The pills can wait, she thought, and she closed her eyes. If there really was a just God, then heaven would have lots of really big bathtubs.

You've got to take your meds. This was the part of her that bothered her the most: the part that wouldn't just let her relax. Ever.

There was no sense fighting it. Gathering herself, she rose out of the tub, quick-walking carefully on the marble floor over to the sink, where she snagged the two bottles and quick-walked back to the tub. The round-trip couldn't have taken more than ten seconds. She'd forgotten to grab a drinking glass, of course, but that wasn't such a big deal. She took her meds dry all the time. With her hands covered in white bubbly mittens, she expertly popped the caps off the pill bottles, dropped those little babies into her palm and tossed them back. They tasted a little like soap this time, but they went down. She laid the bottles on the wide edge of the tub, behind the Jacuzzi controls, so they couldn't fall into the bath, and she lay back and closed her eyes. She tried to imagine that the water was the way she used to like it, hot enough to make a good cup of tea.

The bubbles consumed her, concealed her, leaving her totally at ease. The day had been pure magic. To hell with the doctors. To hell with pagers and phone calls and disappointments. No schoolwork, no shrinks, no phone calls from supposed friends, no arguments with her dad. She'd just *lived.* Sure, the prom thing was hokey, and the room was over the top, and Brad was working too hard to impress her, but at least he was *trying.* And it all seemed so important to him. That she was *happy* was important to him. How could you not love someone who put you on such a pedestal?

She had to be careful, though, lest she think too much and start wondering why he was doing all of this for her. He *said* it was because he cared about her, and wanted her to be happy in her last months, and with all her heart, she wanted to believe that it really was that simple; but it was hard. Could it really be that he'd thought of her over the years as much as she'd thought of him? Was that even possible?

A brisk knock startled her off Memory Lane and back into the present. Before she could say anything, the bathroom door opened—first a crack and then all the way as Brad stepped inside, wearing only a pair of green paisley boxers.

Nicki made a squeaking sound and slipped farther under the bubbles. "What are you doing?" she demanded.

"I need a shower," Brad said as he walked to the glassed-in shower stall and pulled on the knob.

Nicki protested, "But I'm in here."

Brad's eyebrows did their dance. "I know. But I don't like baths." As the glass on the shower fogged from the heat, he turned his back to Nicki, then scooped his hands into the waistband of his shorts, which he let drop to the floor. "I'm a shower guy."

He stepped into the stall and closed the door, transforming himself into an apparition behind the glass. Nicki watched, mesmerized, as he turned this way and that to get his whole body wet, and she continued to watch as he lathered himself with soap, and she felt her pulse quickening.

Jesus, he was *naked*. Despite the fog and the water droplets clinging to the glass, she could see his whole body. His *whole* body. *Everything*. And while she knew what all the parts were, there was one in particular that she'd seen only in pictures.

* * *

Warren and Monique Michaels could not have been more gracious, serving up an impromptu snack of cheese and crackers. While Warren worked the phone from the family room, making call after call, Carter stayed in the kitchen and met the family. Kathleen and her younger sister, Shannon, were both stars in their local soccer league. They showed him their trophies. His interest was not entirely feigned, but as he listened to them prattle on about school and sports, it took real effort not to let their words worsen his melancholy over Nicki. It was a terrible thing to envy little girls for their carefree lives.

And, of course, there was Nathan, a taller, darker, yet still-slight version of the boy Carter remembered from four years ago. Unlike his sisters, the sixteen-year-old never grew comfortable around Carter—a living remnant of the boy's pitch-black past. Monique sensed it early on, and gave Nathan an excuse to make his leave. He disappeared upstairs, and she followed a moment later, returning to the kitchen after ten or fifteen minutes.

"He doesn't mean to be rude," she said. "He's just not completely over it all."

"I understand," Carter assured.

"Nathan says you wanted to throw him in jail," Shannon added. She drew sharp and simultaneous rebukes from her mother and sister. "Well, that's what he said!"

Carter held up a hand and tried his best to smile. "No, Monique, that's all right. I did try to put him in jail. That was my job."

"But you're also the one who got all the charges

dropped," Monique said. "And that was far more important."

Carter appreciated the spin. "True enough," he said. Then, to the girls: "But only after your father worked very, very hard to change my mind."

Warren appeared in the kitchen doorway. "So, have they talked your ear off yet?"

The girls groaned together, "Dad-dy!"

The burst of indignation made Carter laugh. He pulled on his ears just to make sure. "No, I think they're still attached."

Warren's entrance marked the end of the small talk. He announced that it was bedtime for the girls. They protested, but to no avail. Monique led the parade upstairs, leaving Warren and Carter alone in the kitchen.

"Here's where we stand," Warren said. "I've put word on the wire up and down the East Coast to keep an eye out for both Nicolette and her friend. Locally, we're sending patrol units to every hotel, motel, and flophouse to make sure that they have pictures available. Ditto the bus stations, train stations, and airports. One of my sergeants—you may remember him, Jed Hackner?"

Carter shrugged. Anymore, it seemed that every name rang a bell somewhere, but that particular one didn't clang very loudly.

"Anyway, at the suggestion of Sergeant Hackner, we're alerting the National Park Service, too, so that they can get word to their parks and campgrounds."

Carter had to chuckle. In New York, it would take hours to coordinate that many agencies.

"One last note," Warren went on. "The public information officer at our department has arranged for you to get some face time on the news tonight. Gather your thoughts, because they're coming here in about twenty minutes."

"God, you're good," Carter said.

"Just be thankful it's a slow news night," Warren replied.

Chapter Twelve

"I had a nice time tonight," Brad called over the rush of the water. "Better than I thought I would."

What was she supposed to say now? You can't just have a conversation with a naked person—a naked *man*. She sank lower into the tub, trying to disappear below the bubbles. She silently cursed herself for not having thought to lock the door.

"Are you still there?" Brad asked.

"Yes." But she wouldn't be for long. She had to get out of the tub and back into her bathrobe. She had to cover up before he had a chance to see what she really looked like.

Her father's dark stories invaded her thoughts. She knew where this was going, but Brad could have any girl he wanted—girls who at least would know what they were doing.

Nicki felt her chest thickening as the wild thoughts screamed though her brain.

She had to get out of here. Out of the bathroom, out of the hotel, out of this mess. She had to go somewhere. *Anywhere*. And this was the time.

Moving as quietly as she knew how, Nicki eased herself out of the tub, her body covered with a thick pelt of bubbles, and padded across the expanse of marble tile to lift the expensive terry cloth bathrobe off its hook and pull it on. If she hurried, she could get dressed and be out before Brad even knew that she was gone. She didn't know where she'd go, but that was a problem for later.

As she opened the bathroom door, Brad slapped the shower off. "Hey, where are you going?" he asked.

She moved faster, leaving a trail of wet footprints on the lush carpet as she hurried across the master bedroom toward the bed, where she'd left her travel clothes from earlier today, the clothes that were really her. The ones that had nothing to do with anybody's fantasies.

"What are you doing?"

She jumped at the sound of Brad's voice and whirled to see him standing in the open doorway to the bathroom, soaking wet, with a towel wrapped around his waist.

Keeping one hand on the waistband of the towel, he moved toward her, the other arm outstretched. "Jesus, are you okay?" He was at her side in two seconds, and she jumped back, as if shot with electricity.

"No, please don't," she said.

"Why? What's wrong?"

"I'm sorry," she said. "I'm really so sorry."

"For what? What's wrong?"

"I can't," Nicki said.

"What happened?" Was she having some kind of an attack? Had he said something or done something—

He saw it in her eyes, and then he understood. He became aware of his near-nakedness. He eased away from her. "Oh. I invaded your space, didn't I? I'm sorry."

The look on Brad's face was one that Nicki had never seen before. The confident, strutting raconteur now seemed like a little boy caught doing something bad in school. He hurried into the bathroom and reappeared a moment later wrapped in a robe identical to Nicki's. His blond hair was still matted and dripping and Nicki noticed that he still had soapsuds clustered behind one ear. He still looked uneasy and apologetic, and this time when he approached, he kept his distance.

"Are you feeling okay?" he asked.

Nicki nodded, despite the tightening in her chest and the light-headedness. That would all pass. It always did.

"I'm really sorry," Brad repeated.

She appreciated his words, but could see the confusion in his eyes still. He was sorry, but he had no idea what for. He thought it was for invading her space. How could she possibly make him understand? It was awkward. Neither of them knew where to look or what to say. Finally, she settled on his beautiful eyes. "Tell me why you're doing this," she said. "All of this. I mean, really. What's in this for you?"

"I already told you," he said. "I want an adventure. I thought this would be fun. A kick."

Nicki tried to read his mind. "That's only part of it. You could have any girl you wanted. Why me? Why hang out with a dying recovering anorexic?"

Brad wondered how in the world he was ever going to put it in words. "Can I sit on the bed?" he asked, stalling for time. "I promise I'll keep my hands to myself."

Nicki moved farther away. As he sat, his robe parted,

exposing his thigh, but he quickly covered himself back up. "You want the whole story, right?" he said.

"I just want things to make sense."

He gathered his thoughts, then took a deep breath. "Do you remember the day when I was edging the sidewalk out in front of the Bensons' house and you brought me a glass of chocolate milk?"

For a second, Nicki thought that he was making fun of her, but then she knew better. "Vaguely," she said.

"It was a hot, hot day, and Old Man Benson had me working like a mule. You just wandered up with a glass of chocolate milk."

"Was it bad or something?"

He laughed. "No, it wasn't bad. It was delicious. It was the first time I'd ever tasted chocolate milk. You know, the kind out of the carton. I thought it was wonderful."

Nicki's jaw dropped. "I don't believe that. You were fifteen."

"Seventeen," he corrected. "I've had it a thousand times since then, but that was a first."

Nicki didn't understand the connection. "So, this is all payback for a glass of milk."

Brad's ears turned red when he was embarrassed, and he could feel them heating up. "Maybe you can't understand if you didn't grow up in the system. You spend your whole life bouncing from one stranger's house to another. You're never part of a family, not really. I mean, if you happened to be there on Christmas, you'd get some presents, but they were like presents from the fire station or something. Sympathy presents. Every night, you sit at the dinner table and there's this forced small talk about what the kids did at school and stuff, but you always knew that they *en-*

dured your turn, waiting for the blood-kids to have their chance. Am I making any sense?"

Nicki said, "Not really."

Brad shifted again on the bed. "By the time I got into the system, I was too old to be cute and cuddly. I was what, ten, eleven years old when my mom went to prison, and I was pissed. I wasn't the kind of kid that people hurry to adopt. I pushed everybody away, and they were more than happy to stay away. Nobody cared about me, and I told myself that I liked it that way."

"But I cared," Nicki said, finally seeing the chocolate milk connection.

"Exactly." Brad shifted uncomfortably on the bed. "You brought me that glass and you had that look in your face."

"What was I, panting?" Nicki blushed.

"No." Brad's blush deepened. "Well, yeah, there was some of that, but there was more. It was a look I'd never seen before and it made me feel good."

"That was a long time ago," Nicki said.

"Not for me. Time kind of stops when you're in jail." As he spoke, he watched Nicki's eyes, trying to read her reaction. What he saw was empathy.

"You still haven't told me about any of that," Nicki said.

Brad smiled. "You're right."

"But I want to hear."

"No, you don't."

"Yes, I do. I'll tell you if I need you to stop."

Another deep breath, this one leaden with dread. "It's ugly, Nicki. It's embarrassing."

"It's who you are," Nicki said. "That's all I want. I just want to know who you are."

* * *

Of the four Washington broadcast stations, three sent camera crews. For the better part of an hour, all Carter did was talk. By eleven-thirty, it was over.

The Michaels house was a standard 2,000-square-foot suburban colonial, not all that different than the one Carter called home. They put him up in Nathan's room, having transferred its rightful owner to the floor of the little home office down the hall. "You don't have to put him out of his room," Carter said. "I can sleep on the sofa."

"Don't you worry about that," Warren scoffed. "That boy can sleep standing up. Really, he doesn't mind."

As Carter lay atop Nathan's bed staring at the ceiling, he felt guilty about the wasted sacrifice. Who did he think he was kidding? There'd be no sleep for him. His imagination kept taking him to the conclusion of this adventure, and no matter how he cut it, he had a hard time devising a happy ending.

He racked his brain trying to find one last *i* to dot or *t* to cross. There had to be something they were forgetting to do, and whatever that something was, it was bound to be the one thing that would mean the difference between success and failure.

But what was it? What hadn't they thought of? They'd gotten the pictures out to the media, they'd alerted all the police jurisdictions, they'd raised the awareness at all the transportation portals. What else was there?

Carter tried to think of a place that Nicki might want to go, but she'd never been to Virginia. Outside of seeing the sights in Washington, DC, what else was there? More to the point, what *wasn't* there? He'd spoken to Chris Tu on the phone in the car, and his review of all the e-mails and chat logs revealed that Brad and Nicki talked about everything and everyplace under the sun, from the beaches to the mountains, from Paris to Hong Kong. But according to Chris, the beach theme seemed to carry a lot of weight. When Brad Ward was putting on his hard sell to come this way, he'd talked a lot about the beaches in the Southeast, and Nicki had seemed impressed. That rang true with Carter. Back when Nicki was healthy, she used to beg to go to the beach with her friends, but Carter would never allow it.

So, why Brookfield, Virginia? Why not go to Miami or Fort Lauderdale? Or Nag's Head or Hilton Head or Myrtle Beach or Wilmington or Virginia Beach or Ocean City . . .

God, now that he thought about it, the list was virtually endless. For that matter, why wasn't Carter on his way to one of those places?

Because he didn't know for sure. He needed at least an inkling of where she might go. Otherwise, he'd merely be chasing shadows and hunches.

For the time being, he was powerless, completely neutered. And the clock continued to tick.

"They sent me up for murder."

There, he'd said it out loud. Led with it, so that she could wrap her mind around the worst part first. She flinched, but she didn't run.

"You know that I ran away from the shelter where they sent me, and from there, I never went back. I just stayed on the streets. I got to be a pretty good pickpocket, and you can always steal enough to live off of, but that shit's really intense, know what I mean? You're always having to come right up to someone and hope you don't get caught. It's fun. It's a kick, but it gets to you after a while. Your nerves start to get raw, and when that happens, you're doomed to get locked up.

"So I tried mule work for a while, carrying drug money back and forth, but that was even more intense. There are some crazy people into street drugs. Kill you just because it's Thursday, or because they don't like your name. That didn't last for more than a couple of weeks for me. I'm not built for that."

Nicki held up her hand to stem the flow of his words. "Did you ever think about just getting a regular job?"

"Sure, I thought about. I even tried it, but here's the thing: I don't have a high school diploma. What grades I got all sucked, and I didn't know how to do anything. It all came down to economics. I could make five dollars an hour your way, or ten, twenty times that doing it my way."

"But it was *against the law*," Nicki protested. The comment drew an impatient look.

"You are your father's daughter, aren't you?" He made sure to smile so she wouldn't take offense. "This legal/illegal shit is easy to talk about when you've got choices. For me, it was steal or starve."

Brad cringed as he heard himself playing the role of victim. He could hear the voice of the prison psychologist lecturing about the need to take *ownership* of his actions, how life was all about the choices we make. *Yeah, well, bite me.*

"Anyway, I hooked up with two buddies—Jamal and Barry—and we, like, hung out and shit. When we needed something, we'd pick a place, scope it out for a while, and then we'd do our thing. You know, mostly it was just petty shoplifting crap, or maybe boosting a purse out of a car."

"Or boosting the car itself," Nicki offered.

Brad smiled. "Yeah, that, too, sometimes. It wasn't any really serious stuff, but you know, it adds up over time. It was fun. I gotta tell you that much, it was a lot of fun."

"You said you were arrested for murder."

"I'm getting to that. One day, almost three years ago, we were taking down a gas station—you know, one of those places with the little grocery store attached? Anyway, I wasn't taking much. I think I had maybe a package of Twinkies or something. So, when I'm on my way to the door, the guy behind the counter sees me, and he starts yellin' and shit. 'You there! You! Stop!' So I stopped.

"But Barry, the idiot, brought a gun. He told the guy to stop shouting, but he just kept going on and on and on. So, Barry shot him. Right there. Right in the head. Jesus, blood flew everywhere, and the guy dropped to the floor, dead."

Nicki's jaw hung nearly to her chest. "So, what did you do?"

"What do you think we did? We ran. But the security cameras caught it all. I was arrested that night."

"But you didn't kill anybody."

Brad allowed himself a bitter chuckle as he shook his head. "That's not how it works. Because we were committing a crime when the shooting happened, *all* of us were guilty."

"Of *murder*?"

"Of capital murder. That's what they call it. Opens the door for the death penalty."

"So, you were convicted."

"The trial didn't even last a whole day. The prosecution showed the video, my jerk-off public defender made a speech, and I was sentenced to twenty-five-to-life. Just like that." He snapped his fingers.

"Then, it was just like you see in the movies. They cuff your wrists to your waist, and your legs to each other, and then they put you on the bus to Hell. You can't imagine anything as awful as the Michigan state prison. It was like being thrown into a damn lion's den. Maximum security. Anyway, it took eight months to figure out how to get out of there, and I did."

"How?"

He blushed. "You're not going to believe it."

"Tell me."

"Well, you know, I built up all these fancy plans on how I was going to get out. I thought about tunnels, and I was always looking for a hole in the fence or something where I could slip through, but nothing ever came of any of those. The place was just too tight."

"So, what did you do?"

"I hid in a laundry basket."

Nicki gaped.

"Yep, the biggest cliché of all, and I just did it on a whim. Nobody was tending this laundry cart, so I climbed in under a bunch of dirty underwear and uniforms, and they rolled me right out into the truck."

"They didn't see you when they unloaded it?"

"They don't unload it!" Brad laughed as he said it. "That was the biggest surprise of all. They just roll the cart into the back of the truck and drive off. How stupid is that?"

"What about security at the gate?"

"I heard the guard ask if they'd ever left the truck unattended, and the driver lied. It was amazing. After all that planning, all I had to do was lie down and they took me right out. That was five months ago."

Nicki closed her eyes tightly as she tried to process it all. "So, you really are a fugitive."

Another laugh. "Well, yeah."

"I just— Wow." She thought a moment more. "But you still haven't told me—"

"Oh," Brad interrupted, realizing that he'd never gotten to her question. "Through all the bad times in the joint, I swear to God, the image that I kept thinking about—the one that kept playing itself over and over again in my head—was of you and that stupid glass of milk. I know it sounds ridiculous, but that's the God's honest truth."

Nicki giggled.

"I think you had a crush on me."

Nicki's shade of red went beyond mere blush, to something closer to scarlet.

Brad leaned a little closer to her on the bed. "I think you wanted me to kiss you, didn't you?"

Nicki allowed herself to nod.

"Well, I wanted to kiss you, too."

"That's twisted," Nicki teased. "I was only twelve."

"You didn't think you were twelve," Brad laughed. "You thought you were twenty-three. But I kept my hands—and my lips—to myself."

He moved a little closer, and Nicki leaned in to meet him.

"So, you actually thought of me?" she baited.

"Every night."

"I probably don't want to know the details."

"I bet you can guess them."

Nicki saw the contour of his erection growing under his robe and looked away. The fluttery feeling returned, but it was somehow different.

"Would you mind if I kissed you now?" Brad asked.

Nicki thought she said yes, but she wasn't sure. This

was the fantasy. Right here, this was it. The kiss she'd been waiting for her whole life.

Their lips touched. A rush of heat raced from her head to the farthest reaches of her fingers and toes. It was a gentle kiss—her first—not the sloppy, tongue-tangled mess that she'd seen in the hallways of school, but rather a light, beautiful thing, exactly as she'd always dreamed that a kiss from Brad would be. He cupped her face in his hands as their tongues touched, and Nicki found herself being lowered gently backward onto the still-made king-size bed.

Nicki's mind reeled as her body surged with energy. She felt his hand move from her jaw, ever so gently tracing a line under her robe and toward her breast. She tensed.

"Relax," he whispered.

Her robe started to pull away from her body, and she realized that he was going to *see* her. All of her. He'd see the ugly body and then he'd know the truth of the mistake he'd made asking her here.

"I want the lights off," she said.

"But I want to see."

"Please."

Brad stood from the bed and glided to the light switch on the bedroom wall. He pressed it and the room went dark, save for the trapezoidal patch of light that spilled onto the carpet through the half-open bathroom door. Nicki watched as he walked back to her, a towering silhouette. He shrugged his shoulders and his bathrobe slipped away.

Then he was with her again on the bed, so close, kissing her mouth, her jaw, her neck. Nothing happened the way it did in the movies or in the trashy books she'd read. There was no grunting and fumbling, no tearing of fabric. His touch was like a breeze, barely palpable, but undeniable. Nicki's heart hammered a timpani beat as she allowed him to explore her, his eyes reflecting dim flashes of light as he looked at her.

"Relax," he said again, his voice barely audible. He caressed her left breast, and when his fingers found the nipple, her breath caught in her throat. It was as if he was somehow charged with electricity; his fingers introduced sparks that rewired her brain. She'd never felt like this before: confused, frightened, and oh, my God, so turned on. The mattress moved as he shifted his position and she closed her eyes. The terry cloth pulled away, and her breast felt the hotness of his breath. She gave a gentle yelp as he pulled it into her mouth.

"Are you okay?"

Nicki tried to control her breathing. "Yes," she whispered. *Oh, God, yes.*

Brad moved closer still, rolling his body just so, until the fullness of his erection was pressed against her thigh. The tip of his tongue drew circles around her nipple as his fingers found her hand and moved it south, past her belly and on down to his penis. It felt wet and slippery at first touch, and she pulled her hand away.

"It's okay," Brad whispered. There was amusement in his voice. "Just rest your hand there. You don't have to do anything."

Nicki relaxed and let him guide her hand back down. What she found surprised her. Certainly, she'd heard of hard-ons and boners and erections, even seen a few, although always in the form of distended trousers. From as early as junior high school, it was great sport to say things to boys that would make their dicks go stiff, just to see the lengths they'd go to hide the obvious. But bulging pants or even the pictures in the health books didn't prepare her for the reality of what things felt like.

Brad's penis felt smoother, more fragile, than she'd expected, and the testicles—the balls—weren't really balls at all, but more like, well, nuts. As she fondled him, Brad let out a little groan and his hips started to move in a kind of undulating, circular motion.

She yelped again as his finger found her belly button, and she could feel him smiling. His hand worked its way *down there* and she felt his fingers pressing against her. It was wonderful, and her hips began to match the swirling, grinding motion of his. As she counted the rhythm of her pounding heart, she realized that for this brief moment, it was no longer regulated by her disease, but by the passion that swelled inside her.

Brad's hand moved again . . .

"No!" she said, a little too loudly, and she rolled away from him and sat up.

"What's wrong?" he gasped. He might have been angry, or maybe only startled. It was hard to tell in the dark.

"I don't want to do this," she said. As she pulled her robe closed around her, she wiped the stickiness from her hand.

"Honest to God, I'll be gentle," Brad promised, and he moved closer again.

"No!" She said it more forcefully this time, and she stood. "I don't want to do this."

"Why not?"

"Because I don't want to."

"But *why*?"

Even in the darkness, she could tell that she'd hurt his feelings. She turned so that she could better see his silhouette in the blackness. "It's not you, okay? I swear to God, it's not you. Jesus, I can't count the number of times we've made love in my head."

"What, then?"

Nicki didn't want to answer. She knew how stupid it would sound. "It's my mother," she said, finally.

"Excuse me?" Brad's laugh came reflexively.

Nicki hugged herself and stood, stepping away from the bed. "I made her a promise, okay? It was probably a stupid thing to do, but when she was in the hospital, I promised her that I would save my virginity for just the right guy—the guy I love more than anyone else in the world."

"And I'm not him?" Brad's tone was hard to read without seeing his eyes.

"I don't know," Nicki confessed. "How can I know for sure?"

With a huge, frustrated sigh, Brad stood and gathered his robe from the floor.

"Are you mad?" Nicki asked.

He made a sound that might have been a growl. "Mad? No. Horny and frustrated, but not mad." He walked to her and kissed her on the forehead. "What's to be mad about?"

"I'm sorry I'm such a prude."

"We've got a long trip ahead of us, Nicki. All I have to do is convince you that I'm the guy." He took a step toward the door.

"Are you leaving?"

He looked back at her. She could see his smile, even in the dark. "You need your rest, and I think it's probably best if I sleep in the living room. I'll see you in the morning."

"I'm sorry," Nicki whined.

"No," he said, with a firmness in his voice that she hadn't heard before. "Don't apologize. I made assumptions that I shouldn't have. That's my fault, not yours.

I'm the one who should apologize." He walked as he spoke, heading for the bedroom door and the living room beyond. He paused at the threshold. "I'm sorry, Nicki," he said. "Really. Good night."

Nicki heard the door click as Brad closed it behind him.

April 11

He told! I don't believe it! Derek ratted out the Posse. He told Georgen. You're supposed to get transferred out if you rat out an inmate, but Georgen put him back into GP. Derek is terrified. When the Posse finds out, he's dead.

Christ, how could he have been so stupid? Everybody knows. Derek's begging Georgen for isolation, but I don't think he's going to give it to him. Georgen's having too much fun to give it to him.

Chapter Thirteen

Warren turned on the overhead light and smacked Carter's shoulder hard enough to hurt. "Carter, wake up. We've got a lead."

Carter didn't even know that he'd drifted off. He came awake groggy and confused. "What? Where?" He checked his watch. 3:04 A.M.

"The Ritz-Carlton at Mason's Corner." Carter's eyes cleared enough to see that Warren was wearing boxer shorts and a Nike T-shirt. "I just got the call from a patrol unit who got a hit off the picture we sent around."

"Nicki is there?" Carter asked. It seemed almost too simple.

"We're leaving in two minutes to find out."

Brad needed a drink. And a cold shower. Jesus, what had he been thinking? He never should have moved so far so quickly. But after such a long stretch without being close to a woman, nature was a tough beast to tame. He thought about that as he re-dressed in his khakis and polo shirt, being particularly careful as he zipped his trousers.

He hated the look he saw in her face after he walked into the bathroom. At first, it was shock—he'd expected that—but then it looked like fear, and that was when he should have left her alone. He'd thought that she would get a kick out of seeing him parade naked in front of her. In their e-mails, she'd told him how she used to fantasize about that when she was watching him mow the lawn.

A part of him wondered if it had been a mistake to tell her so much about his past. Maybe he should have made something up that wouldn't have made him look like such a criminal.

No, he decided, that would have been a mistake. There'd been too many lies in his life, told by too many people, and he had way too many sins on his soul as it was.

When Brad saw that clerk in the gas station fall with a bullet through his head, he knew that he'd crossed a line from which there was no return. He understood that every good thing he'd ever done in his life had become meaningless. It had all been wiped out at a muzzle velocity of a thousand feet per second. As he watched the lights go out in that kid's eyes, he realized that he really did care.

And because of what he'd done, nobody would ever care back.

Except for Nicki Janssen. She was the single exception. Back when he was in prison, lying on his bunk at night, listening to the sounds of men snoring and fighting and jerking off, he used to imagine what Nicki would look like as the years passed. In his mind, she'd become a cheerleader, or maybe even a model. So beautiful a girl had to grow up to be a beautiful woman. She *had* to.

After his escape, when he had five states under his

belt and he felt that the heat of the search had cooled a little, the first thing he set out to do was find Nicki. He never dreamed that the Internet would make it so simple. Once they started up their dialogue, he discovered the good deed that might balance the accounts for his soul.

He'd find a way to make her final days livable, while doing the same for himself. There was one certainty that they faced together: that neither of them would likely see another Christmas—Nicki because her body would kill her, and Brad because he knew how pitiful the odds were of staying ahead of the law in the long run. When they caught him, he would die; he would see to that. He'd never allow himself to be taken back to jail.

This knowledge of impending death was liberating in its own way. It took all the pressure off living. With a future that you could measure in a thimble, and a past that didn't matter anymore, he and Nicki were left with only the present, and the freedom that brought made his head swim.

When he was dressed, Brad stopped at the minibar long enough to slip two miniature bottles of scotch into his pocket. That done, he opened and closed the door to the suite as quietly as he could, and slipped out into the hallway, checking to make sure that he'd remembered the plastic card key.

What were the chances that the bar might still be open at this hour? At three-thirty in the morning, not likely. Still, he needed a walk in the fresh air. Ever since he'd stepped clear of those concrete walls, he couldn't get enough fresh air. Even the palatial digs of the Governor's Suite seemed too small and stuffy for him. And on top of all that, he had to do something to distract himself from the pressure in his crotch.

The elevator took him to the ground floor. As the door opened on the lobby, he stepped out onto the polished floor. The place seemed busier than he would have expected for so late an hour. Not crowded by any stretch, there were still six or seven people clustered near the front desk, and a couple more milling about the main entrance at street level. Two of the men near the front doors were cops, dressed in gray and black polyester uniforms. They didn't seem to be looking at anything in particular, yet they seemed to be a bit on edge.

Something wasn't right here. Of the people who weren't in uniforms, all were fully dressed in a way that didn't jibe with the hour. Three in the morning is the end of anybody's work day, yet these guys all looked fresh. One wore a well-tailored suit, and he stood with his hands on his hips, talking with someone behind the front desk. When he turned at just the right angle, Brad caught of flash of steel on the man's belt.

He was a cop, too.

Holy shit, they were all cops, and they were clearly waiting for something. Or some*one.*

Okay, don't panic, he told himself, but the panic didn't listen. They couldn't possibly have caught up with him this quickly. They couldn't have traced the credit card—not yet, anyway—nor could they have traced the car. It was too soon. Vinnie Campanella was just learning to find his way around a foreign country, for heaven's sake. He should be too busy to be worried about a robbery that happened the day before and an ocean away.

Nicki swore she'd followed the instructions he'd given her. She said she'd paid only cash and kept a low profile.

Yet, here they were, and what were the chances that

there'd be more than one cop-magnet staying in the hotel tonight?

The answer came a moment later, as activity beyond the glass doors drew everyone's attention to the front of the building. Just from the way people snapped to, Brad got the impression that the person they'd been waiting for had arrived. Maybe this was just the protection detail for some visiting dignitary.

One of the uniformed cops opened the door for a man who looked like he was probably a cop, but who walked like he needed rest. Two steps behind, he saw a face that looked vaguely familiar to him.

It took only a few seconds for him to recognize the second man as Carter Janssen.

Carter was impressed by the level of deference shown to Warren Michaels as he passed his troops. He sensed in them a great desire to please, tinged with just a touch of fear about getting on his wrong side. They hadn't taken five steps into the lobby when a well-dressed man stepped forward to greet them. Carter's first instinct told him that the guy had to be the manager of the hotel, but then he saw the badge clipped to his belt.

Warren took care of the brusque introductions. "Sergeant Jed Hackner, Counselor Carter Janssen." The men shook hands even as Warren continued to speak. "What do we know?"

Hackner said, "Not enough. The clerk says that he recognized the face on the news as a guest in the hotel, but that he doesn't know the guy's name."

"Are we talking about the eleven o'clock news?" Warren asked, incredulous. "Why are we just hearing about it now?"

"They rebroadcast the news at two-thirty. That's when the guy caught it."

Warren led the way to the front desk, where a clerk in a gray vest looked scared to death standing next to an older woman who bore a striking resemblance to Queen Elizabeth. "This is Missy Thompson, the night manager," Hackner said, introducing the woman. "And this is Gary Vaughan." Nodding to Warren, he added, "This is Lieutenant Michaels, my boss, and Carter Janssen, the father of one of the people we're looking for."

No one bothered to shake hands. "Which one of you saw our fugitives?" Warren asked.

Gary raised his hand sheepishly. "That was me," he said. "I just saw them for a few seconds. It was late. They were all dressed up."

"Dressed up?" Carter asked.

"Yeah, tuxedo and gown, like they'd been to a dance or something. I assumed they were at the big ball we had tonight. Some society of cops." For an instant, Gary looked worried that that last part might have offended someone.

Warren looked to Carter. "That make sense to you?"

"Not a lick."

"There are two Wards registered in the hotel," Jed Hackner explained, "and one Dougherty."

"Your storm troopers woke those people up," said Missy Thompson. "They were the wrong people, of course, but that didn't seem to bother any of you."

"You'd rather have a couple of murderers running loose in your hotel?" Jed asked, obviously not for the first time.

"My daughter is not a murderer," Carter said. "Let's not get that tidbit confused, okay?"

Jed looked embarrassed. "Of course. We did talk

with the Wards, though, and with Dougherty, and none of them were our guy."

"They must have registered under a pseudonym," Carter said. "How many Smiths and Joneses are registered?"

The night manager turned red. "You are *not* going to randomly interrupt people in their sleep on some wild goose chase. I agreed to cooperate, but this is ridiculous."

"He's a mur-der-er," Jed said, emphasizing the syllables as if she were hard of hearing.

"Then catch him," she said. "But do it without waking the whole hotel."

"We can get a warrant," Jed said.

"Then do it."

Warren stepped into the fray. "Look, folks, let's not get all pissy, okay? Ms. Thompson, we're not trying to make life difficult for you. Honestly, we're not. And Jed, we can't just go room to room, waking up everybody on the off chance that our guy is here." He turned to Gary. "On a scale of one to ten, ten being absolute certainty, how sure are you that the guy you saw is the guy on the news?"

Again, the attention made the kid shift from one foot to the other. "I don't know. Seven, maybe?"

Warren shook his head. "We need more than that. Who was working the desk this afternoon? Who would have checked them in?"

Pleased by her nominal victory over Jed Hackner, the night manager nearly smiled as she walked to the computer screen and tapped the keys. "What time are we talking about?"

"I'm guessing about five o'clock," Carter said.

"Okay, well, that shift started at four, and that would have been either Sam Shockley or Patrick Barney." She looked up for the screen and asked Warren, "Do you want to call them?"

Warren smiled. "You read my mind."

Carter noted with some amusement that the manager didn't think twice about waking fellow employees. What a peach. "There's got to be something we can do in the short term," Carter said. "How about people who paid with cash? Can you track that down through the computer?"

Missy Thompson returned her gaze to the computer screen and resumed her tapping. "I can pull up the information, but I'm not going to let you wake those people up, either. There are a thousand perfectly legitimate reasons why people pay in cash. You can't just assume—"

Warren showed his palm in a gesture for silence. "Ms. Thompson, please. I assure you that we don't want to bother people any more than they want to be bothered. But under the circumstances, we have a right to know who is here in the hotel, and we have the right to sort that information by whatever parameters we wish. It's your business if you wish to obstruct justice, but it's mine is to arrest you if that's your choice. Now, please. The clock is ticking. Decide which way you'd like it to be."

Missy Thompson looked as if she'd been slapped. Warren answered her look with a smile, and she went back to her keyboard.

Warren turned to Carter. "If push comes to shove, we can get officers stationed at all the exits in the morning, and watch every person who passes by. There are also security tapes."

Carter did his best to look interested, but this snail's pace was killing him. With his daughter's life in the balance, he really didn't give a rat's ass about constitutional protections. If he had to pound on every door himself, he was—

"Hey, now, this is interesting," said Missy Thompson.

All eyes turned toward her.

"Well, I can't actually sort by cash payments, per se, but I can separate out by different credit card companies, and then whatever is left would be cash, check, money order, that sort of thing."

Carter and Warren exchanged glances. How was this interesting?

"Well, here in the Visa accounts, I see a note in the file where a Vincent Campanella called to allow his son to check in without showing a credit card. Something about the boy not being trustworthy. But he did allow the son—named Bradley, here—to charge any and all expenses to his room."

Okay, so it was interesting, after all. Carter and Warren led a parade of cops around the end of the counter to get a look at the computer screen.

"Can you call up the file?" Carter asked.

Missy's fingers flew on the keys, and an instant later, there was the voluminous file. "Oh, wow," she said. "They *have* been busy. Goodness gracious, look at all the room charges."

Carter had to squint to see that far. He pointed to the screen. "Does that say tuxedo?"

Brad slapped every light switch he could find as he threw open the door to the Governor's Suite and charged through the foyer and living room and on into the bedroom. "Nicki, wake up!" he said, loudly enough to wake people in the next room.

She didn't move.

"Nicki, come on. Now. We've got to go."

She stirred and moaned something about going away.

Brad turned the switch on the nightstand light. "Seriously now, we've got to go. I saw your father downstairs. He knows we're here."

Nicki bolted upright in the bed. "What?"

"You heard me. He's downstairs in the lobby. I went down to take a walk, and there he was."

She was still sleep-addled. "My father is here in the hotel." She said it as if confirming that she wasn't stuck in a dream.

Brad gathered her clothes. "Yes, Nicki, he's here in the hotel. I don't know how he found us, but he's not alone. He's got a dozen cops with him."

"Cops?"

"For me. If we don't hurry, it's getting real ugly real fast. Now, are you coming or not?"

"Could I have a little privacy, please, to get dressed?"

He gaped at her, as if she'd grown another nose. "Nicki, we don't have time—"

But he didn't have time to argue, either. "Fine. But hurry." This was a complication he hadn't thought of. If he'd been traveling alone, he'd have been blocks away by now.

He stepped out into the living room and looked out the window at the Mason's Corner skyline. Nine floors below, he could make out the emergency beacons on police cars painting blue and white patterns on the street. In the distance, he could see more vehicles on the way.

They know. Dammit, how had he screwed up?

Forget that. How was he going to get out of here? Come to think of it, why hadn't they broken down the door already?

"Nicki, come *on*!"

"I'm right here." The voice came from just a few feet away. She was in her shorts and T-shirt again.

"Jesus, you scared me. Look at that. They're all over the place down there."

She pulled on his sleeve. "Let's go then."

He held her hand. "Maybe you should stay," he said. "They want you as a runaway. They want me as an escaped convict. There's a world of difference."

"I know. Let's go."

"I was serious when I said I wouldn't let them take me," Brad reminded.

"Then I guess you'd better not get caught." She tugged on his sleeve again. "Come on, let's get out of here."

Brad grabbed her hand and led the way out the door and down the hall toward the elevators. "I don't suppose you can handle the stairs?" he asked.

"I can if I have to."

"But would there be anything left of you?"

"Not much."

Well, there you go. "I can carry you if I have to," he offered.

Nicki smiled. "I don't think we're quite there yet."

In the ninth floor elevator lobby, Brad pushed the call button, then looked at their reflections in the polished brass doors. There really wasn't a lot to her, was there? He hadn't noticed it before, but Nicki looked positively fragile. He was out of his mind to be leading her on an adventure like this, and she was out of her mind to be following him.

"Okay, it's moving," he said, noticing the numbers on the digital readout next to the door. Two . . . three . . . and then it stopped. And started back down again. "Shit."

Standing here in the open like this, in front of the

giant window with its view of Northern Virginia, he felt like a target in a shooting gallery. This was crazy. On his own, he never would have trapped himself in an elevator, a piece of technology that could just as easily be disabled as made to work.

"Do you have a plan?" Nicki asked. The absence of fear in her voice baffled him.

"Actually, no," he said. "I'm winging it. I figure that an opportunity will show itself when I need it. That's kind of the way my life has been working these past few months."

She cast a doubtful glance, but didn't pursue it.

"You're not scared," Brad said.

"I'm dying. What's to be afraid of?" She pointed at the display on the wall. "It's moving again."

Brad tried not to tremble. Since his escape, he'd taken every step so carefully, with so much advance planning, that there'd never be any surprises. Now, on the one occasion when he stepped out and took a chance, this is what happened. *Dammit!*

He could do this. Hell, he had to. He glanced up at the digital readout and his blood froze. "Oh, shit. Look."

Nicki raised her eyes and let out a little gasp. The second elevator car was on its way, too.

"They're coming," he said.

"Which car?"

"I don't know. Maybe both."

Now she showed fear. "Oh, shit, Brad. Come on, let's use the stairs."

He tightened his grip on her hand. "No, there's no time. The stairs are all the way at the end of the hall. They'd be here and see us before we could get down. This is our only chance."

"But what if—"

"Then I'm screwed. But I think we've got a chance."
He pointed at the readout again. "See? The one on the
left is a floor ahead of the one on the right."

"What difference does that make?"

He smiled. "I have no idea. I just make this shit up
as I go along."

April 12

They got him. They got Derek.

I was asleep and I thought I heard a noise, but before I could open my eyes, they put a pillowcase over my head and hit me hard in the face and then harder in the nuts. I thought they ruptured something. I yelled and they hit me again. Told me to shut up and listen. It was Chaney's voice. There were others in the cell, I could hear them, but it was Chaney's voice in my ear.

He said, "I know that you're smart enough to know what's a lie and what you should believe. You choose right and you won't get the same as him. Choose bad, and you'll get worse."

They hit me again in the balls and they left. I've never been hit like that. I saw stars. I couldn't breathe. I rolled off of my cot onto the floor, and it was all wet. That's when I heard the moaning.

I pulled the pillowcase off of my head and there was Derek. They'd cut him bad. He was naked and was bleeding from everywhere. In the dark, I couldn't see anything but the blood. I started yelling, but nobody would come. I tried to see where he was hurt, but when I touched him he screamed. He was in agony. I didn't know what to do.

When he moved his mouth, I could see that they cut his cheeks all the way from the corners of his mouth back to his ears. They were just big flaps of skin. I could see his teeth from the outside. I don't know if he was trying to make words, or if he was just moaning from the pain, but I couldn't understand anything he was saying. When I saw his guts in his hand—he was trying to keep them from spilling out—I started puking. God, it was awful.

I screamed and screamed for help. Finally, Officer Georgen showed up at the door and told me to shut up, I was waking the other inmates. I screamed at him to help Derek, but he said that he looked okay to him. He said that maybe a night with some company was what he really wanted. He said that maybe company would help make him feel better.

It took Derek an hour to die. He'd just lay there on the floor of my cell gurgling and making moaning noises until the noises stopped.

They came and got him at around five-thirty the next morning. It was Georgen and Chaney and Letier. They all just looked at me. There was blood everywhere. All over the floor, all over me, all over the walls.

I guess you didn't sleep so good, Chaney said to me. I guess you had too much on your mind. Georgen laughed at that. Laughed like it was the funniest thing he'd ever heard. Then he told me to clean the place up before it starts to smell like a slaughterhouse. Then he smiled.

He's part of them. I don't understand why or how, but the Posse is in charge because Officer Georgen lets them have their own way. That's what this place is really all about.

I just stared at them. What else was I going to do? And I started cleaning my cell. It took all day. When I was done, they let me take a shower, but while I was there, so was Chaney, just standing there, watching me. He had this smile on his face. They're going to kill me, too. I know that now

Chapter Fourteen

Carter found himself trembling with anticipation as the elevator made its slow climb. The Governor's Suite, for Christ's sake. The kid was nothing if not ballsy. Nine-fifty a night, no less, plus another three grand in clothes and sundries. How in the world did either of them think that they were going to get away with this? He supposed it made sense for Brad—it was probably the way he was wired—but Nicki knew better.

This was grand larceny! Was she out of her mind? He was already planning her legal defense.

First things first, he told himself. Get her away from that killer boyfriend, and everything else will be negotiable.

Could the elevator ride possibly take any longer? They'd waited in the downstairs lobby just long enough for members of the Tactical Unit to arrive with their machine guns and battering rams. The air in the car reeked of sweat and gun oil. Carter felt woefully small and under-armed among these men.

"Please be careful when you go in," Carter begged. "She won't be armed."

The biggest man on the team—Brooks, according to

his embroidered name badge—said to Warren, "Lieutenant, I really wish we had not brought him along for this."

"He's on the job," Warren assured. "He'll stay out of the way. Won't you, Carter?"

There was so obviously a right answer that Carter didn't bother to articulate it.

Brooks said, "Mr. Janssen, if what you say is true, then you have nothing to worry about. We don't hurt people unless they try to hurt us first."

Carter pretended that the words calmed him, but he knew from experience what can happen when adrenaline and emotion mix with firearms in close quarters.

He reached around another cop and pressed the button for the ninth floor again.

Please, God, Carter prayed silently, *let her be safe.*

"When the elevator gets here, just duck in fast," Brad said. "If it's full of cops, we're done. If it's not, then we won't have much time before the other one arrives."

Nicki said nothing as she watched the numbers roll.

"Having fun yet?" Brad teased.

"Well, it's different," she confessed.

"If it gets rough, do exactly what they say, okay?" Brad said. "Just promise me that. If they say to get down, then get down like, right then. And don't hide your hands—"

"You worry about you," she said. "I can take care of myself."

Yeah, right, Brad didn't say. She had no idea what the world could throw at you when you weren't looking.

The digital readout for the car on the left read 8, the one on the right, 7.

"Here it comes," Brad said, and he nudged her closer to the doors.

The car dinged.

And nothing happened.

"Oh, shit, what's wrong?"

The car on the right read 8.

Nine.

It dinged, too.

"Shit!" Brad hissed, pounding the call button. "Open, open, open . . ."

Finally, the doors on their car rolled open. Brad shoved Nicki into the car, probably a little too hard, and pressed the button for the parking garage. The doors closed as leisurely as they'd opened, gliding with silent elegance on their tracks. Across the elevator lobby, he watched in the narrowing view of the mirror as the other elevator door opened, revealing a car filled with cops dressed as Delta Force.

They started filing out even before their door was completely open. The last face he saw belonged to Carter Janssen. Nicki gasped as she saw it, too.

"Oh, my God, that was him," she breathed as the car descended.

The tone of her voice drew Brad's head around. "You don't look so good," he said. Her lips had gone pale, and her breathing was labored.

"I'll be fine," she said. "What's next?"

Brad opened his mouth to answer, then realized that he didn't know. His instinct was to go to the garage and get their car and drive away, but now that seemed like a stupid idea. If they knew about the room, then they knew about Vincent Campanella, and that piece of information would take them right to the Mustang. Besides, they'd have all the garage exits covered. In fact, that probably explained the delay before the cops made their move. They wanted enough reinforcements to block any escape.

So, what did that leave? There had to be a way. There was *always* a way. And as crappy as their chances appeared to be, they were better now than they would ever be again. More cops were probably arriving by the minute, pulling the cordon tighter and tighter. His mind brought an image of the old *Star Trek* episodes where Kirk and Spock would just sparkle and disappear, rematerializing elsewhere. Yeah, that's what he needed, a transporter.

He rubbed his forehead, trying to rattle his brain, to get it thinking less-stupid thoughts. They were already passing the fifth floor, and in a few seconds, he was going to have one hell of a problem on his hands.

Then he looked at the buttons on the control board and he nearly knocked Nicki over diving to push the button for the second floor.

"What are you doing?" Nicki demanded, startled.

The elevator car slowed and opened on a hallway that seemed to stretch forever. Brad beamed. "I'm getting us out of here."

As soon as the door started to open, the attack force piled out of the elevator, their weapons up and ready. Carter felt like a fish caught in a current as the surge of manpower pulled him along. Movement on his right pulled his head around, and he swore that he saw the elevator door closing.

Sure enough, a glance at the readout told him that he was right. He started to say something to Lieutenant Michaels, but this simply was not the time to break anyone's concentration.

"You stay here," Warren ordered, putting his hand

on Carter's shoulder and pointing emphatically at the floor. "We'll come and get you when things are secure."

There was no room for discussion, no time for argument. Warren ran off with the rest of the team, his own weapon—an automatic pistol of some sort—drawn and ready. Considering the size of the force, they moved with impressive grace and stealth.

Carter watched as the cops swarmed down the hallway to the very end, where they formed up in a well-rehearsed cluster and then kicked in the door. The crash of the splintering wood shook the whole ninth floor, and the cacophonous chorus of shouted threats—"Police department! Nobody move! Everybody down!"—startled him.

Mere seconds later, he heard the chorus switch to individual pronouncements of "Living room clear . . . bedroom clear . . . bathroom clear," and he knew that they'd gotten away.

But how? This had to be the right place; the positive ID from the clerk and the crazy room charges proved that. He looked at his watch. Christ, at this hour of the morning, there was no way they wouldn't still be sleeping. Unless . . .

They got tipped off somehow. Maybe a phone call from a friend downstairs, or maybe just dumb luck, but something had clearly tipped them off that they were about to be busted. *Dammit.* Why couldn't Lady Luck show her good side just once?

Wait a second! There was a good side.

If the kids left because they'd been tipped off, that meant, by definition, that they couldn't have been gone long. Mere moments, perhaps. That meant that they were still catchable.

But how would they have gotten out of the hotel?

The cops had the place secured. Every door. At this hour of the morning, how difficult would it be to catch the only boy-girl combination on their way out of the hotel?

Carter found himself drawn to the huge window there in the elevator lobby, the one that overlooked the skyline of Mason's Corner. They were out there somewhere. He knew it. Just as he knew that Brad Ward was anticipating their moves and correcting for them on the fly. As the cops meticulously searched the hotel—what else could they do?—the kids would build another head start on them.

There'd be radio reports among the marauding cop cars out on the street, and there'd be BOLOs—be on the lookout—but without any idea what they were driving, or which direction they were headed, catching them would be more an act of luck than good police work. Carter closed his eyes and rested his forehead on the cool glass.

So, how *did* they get out?

This Ward character was resourceful and street smart; he'd proven that already, if not through his actions today, then through his ability to stay a fugitive these past months. There was a certain brazenness to his actions, too, which Carter found disturbing. On the one hand, bold moves increased the likelihood of his making a mistake, but on the other, they showed that he had a plan in mind if mistakes happened. *Armed and extremely dangerous.* He was not a man to be cornered.

But he *was* cornered, wasn't he? Sure, there were hundreds of rooms and thousands of hiding places, but sooner or later they would have to be found. Carter knew for a fact that all the exits were covered.

Unless, of course, they learned to fly.

Or exit on another floor.

Carter's eyes snapped open. Holy shit, that was it! Right there, seven, maybe eight floors below, there was the skyway that connected the hotel to the Galleria. It connected at the second floor, and from there, they'd have access to the rest of the world. They wouldn't get caught at the exits to the hotel, because they'd never pass through the exits of the hotel!

Pushing himself away from the window, Carter dashed back to the hallway, where the police were still mopping up their operation, and two other guests had gathered sleepily outside their doors to watch. From here, Carter could see Warren Michaels standing in the foyer of the suite, talking on his radio.

"Lieutenant Michaels!" Carter boomed.

Warren's head snapped around.

"I've got something."

Warren raised a finger to beg for a moment, and then went back to his radio.

"Screw this," Carter hissed. He could explain, or he could catch them himself. The clock was ticking. He waited a second longer, to see if Michaels would pay attention, and then he was off, sprinting directly toward the cops. The quick movement made the gawkers gasp, and at the suddenness of it, Warren Michaels instinctively reached for his weapon.

Carter made the sharp turn to the right and crashed through the stairwell door. As it rebounded off the concrete wall, Carter yelled, "Mall!" hoping that they might figure out what he'd already deduced.

He kept a tight grip on the tubular railing as his feet flew down the steel-edged concrete steps, jumping the last three stairs of every flight and the top three of the one that followed.

Man-size numerals painted in orange boldly announced every floor number. Eight. Seven.

Carter wasn't sure why, exactly, but he was confident that the skyway ran off of the second floor. Perhaps he'd noticed the button on the elevator panel, or perhaps he subconsciously counted floors while he was looking out the window, but somehow he *knew*. And the longer he ran, the farther away the second floor seemed to get.

Six. Five.

Finally, he hit the second floor. The stairwell reverberated from the sound of his feet hitting the landing. He barely slowed as he wrapped his hand around the doorknob and pulled.

It slipped right out of his hand. "Oh, no," he moaned. The goddamn thing was locked!

"Dammit!" The word rumbled as an echo. He should have waited for the elevator.

He should have listened more to Nicki when she was complaining.

He should have been a better father.

Later. Next time. Right now, he had to get her, wrestle her away from the clutches of a murderer.

He didn't wait an instant more. He had two more flights ahead of him.

Brad half-pushed, half-carried Nicki across the second-floor lobby, one flight above the main reception lobby, on the way to the double doors that would release them to the Galleria. He wanted to run, but he knew better. He needed to be as aware of his surroundings as possible, and he'd learned that it's impossible to run and think at the same time.

The door to the Galleria lay straight ahead: ornate wooden sculptures with intricately carved glass in the top halves. Off to the left, he made casual notice of the Couture Shoppe that had so kindly donated to his cause.

"Why no guards here?" Nicki asked, struggling to keep up.

"They're locked," Brad said. "They close these doors at twelve-thirty."

She shot him a panicked look.

When they stopped, Brad threw a look over his shoulder. So far, so good. "They're not *locked*-locked. They're just designed to keep people from wandering in from the mall after midnight."

"So how—"

Brad pointed to the sign that had been slipped into a mahogany-framed plaque on the strip of wood near the seam where the doors joined. EMERGENCY EXIT ONLY. ALARM WILL SOUND.

"They can't actually lock an exit," Brad explained. "In case of fire. They alarm them instead." He produced his Leatherman from his belt. "So, you just disconnect the alarm box." He folded out a pair of needle-nose pliers with wire cutters built into the jaws. "Best forty bucks I ever spent." Standing on tiptoe, he clipped two wires leading from the alarm box. "*Voilà.*"

"Are you sure it will work?"

"No," he said, and he pushed the right-hand door open. No alarm. He smiled. "But I was pretty sure."

Dimly lit and massive in its proportions, the inside of the Galleria was silent, save for the staccato slapping of their flip-flops as they hurried across the sky bridge toward the second-level entrance to the parking garage.

"Now we really need to hurry," Brad said. "We're probably on a lot of security cameras right now." Noticing the deep furrows of concern in Nicki's forehead, he smiled. "Like you said. Different."

Nicki didn't know how to respond.

"Relax," Brad said. "We'll do fine. I've come too far too fast to be stopped by some rent-a-cop."

At the doors, Brad pulled them to a stop, then scanned the edges of the doors themselves. "You see any alarm contacts?"

"I don't even know what an alarm contact looks like."

Brad crossed his fingers. "Here goes." He pushed the door open, and then they were outside, where the humid night air embraced them in a wet hug.

"Wait here," Brad said, grabbing Nicki by her shoulders and planting her on the curb. "I'll be right back."

"I can keep up," Nicki said, with barely enough air to manufacture a sound.

"I know you can, but there's no sense wearing you out. I've got to get some wheels."

Nicki scowled. "But our car is at the hotel." His look told her everything. "Oh," she said.

With the skills he'd honed over the years, he could grab any car that he wanted. It'd be slim pickings, though. At this hour, there were precious few to be borrowed from a mall parking lot. Still, Brad took off as if he knew what he was doing, running full tilt across the largely empty upper deck and disappearing down a ramp.

The night seemed awfully quiet. Sitting there on the curb, all alone, she felt vulnerable, and the ceaseless hammering of her heart didn't help. In her mind, she could see countless thousands of blood cells log-jamming in the hardened vessels of her lungs, waiting their turn to supply her ever-increasing demand for oxygen. Already, she could feel the swelling in her ankles. In a few more minutes, she'd be able to see it, too.

It was still too soon to take any more meds, but it wouldn't be long; just an hour or so. Meanwhile, she could just wait out the episode.

The irony of it all made her so angry: After seventeen years on the planet, without any semblance of a life to speak of, why did *real* living begin at the very time when her body was least able to handle it? She'd had enough trauma in her life, for God's sake. Why couldn't someone else take a turn?

Nicki leaned back against a light post and scanned the concrete horizon, resisting the urge to close her eyes. With so little time left, she found herself begrudging every second that her eyes were closed. There was just too much to see.

But until today, the vistas had never changed. Classrooms. Hospital rooms. Bedrooms. The same neighborhood with the same houses and the same cars and the same people she'd seen every day of her life. It was all so boring.

So terribly normal. That's not how Nicolette Janssen wanted to be remembered. She wanted people to think of her as anything *but* normal. As *better* than normal, whatever that meant. She knew it was stupid to think such thoughts, but when she died, she wanted it to be an event on the news.

Her shrink had told her that it was destructive to concentrate on the finality of her disease. "Quality of life," he'd said, "is more about what one feels in one's mind than what attacks one's heart." He'd looked proud when he'd said it.

"Let's trade places," Nicki had suggested. "I'll sit there saying important junk for two hundred bucks an hour, and you climb over here and handle a ticking bomb of your own."

Nicki understood the doctor's point. Intellectually, she understood *everything* the doctor told her. Who the hell wouldn't understand it? But *knowing* how you're supposed to think about something is a whole world away from ignoring the fact that you're sliding toward a big rectangular hole in the ground.

Now, though, for the first time, she thought she might have a handle on how to make intentions meet reality. The trick was to walk away from everyone who attempted to tell you what to do with your life, and to take a chance for once.

Look at where she was now: She thought she was heading off to hang out with a sweet guy, and now they were running from the cops. It was scary—scary as hell—but it was *real*. It was *different,* a *surprise*. Besides, Nicki hadn't done anything wrong. If the cops caught them, she'd go back to same ol' same ol', and that would stink, but man, the trip to get there would be epic.

She smiled as she thought about the look on Brad's face when he told her about the killing stuff and the jail stuff. He thought she was going to freak out, but when she just took it all in, he was surprised. She liked that look on him. That superconfident Mr. God mask had to be peeled away from time to time.

And she'd been the one to do it.

She could hear her father already, ranting on about the danger she'd caused herself by hanging out with a felon. She could see his red face and the distended veins at his collar. He wouldn't care that Brad had never hurt anyone, just as he'd never cared about what Nicki wanted for herself. In Daddy's mind, her worst offense of all would be her defiance of him.

But without the defiance, there'd be no living. That's what he couldn't see. It's why she could never go back, either.

Somewhere down below, the silence of the night rumbled with the sound of an engine turning over.

The stairwell door to the lobby was also locked.

"God*dammit*!"

So what the hell were people supposed to do in the event of a fire? Just pile up in the stairwells like ice floes in April?

Carter pounded with his fist on the locked door. "Let me in!"

No one answered. And then he understood. This was an emergency exit. If the building was burning, they'd want people to go all the way outside, not to cluster in the lobby. If it were any more obvious, it would have smacked him in the face: down another half-flight, the sign on another door read EMERGENCY EXIT ONLY/ALARM WILL SOUND.

He should have taken the elevator.

Carter charged at the door, hitting the panic bar with his hip and slamming the door open against the brick façade of the hotel. As promised, an alarm squealed, and he couldn't have cared less. Even the exit chutes were decorative, sporting colorful plants and bushes. He could see the portico circle at the top of the hill on the right. He took off at a run.

If his sense of direction did not betray him, the sky-way to the mall was past the main entrance, on the other side of the hotel. It occurred to Carter as he ran up the hill that he couldn't remember the last time he'd taken a quick step. Not exactly out of shape, he wasn't exactly *in* shape, either, and as sweat soaked his clothes, he could feel every one of his forty-five years.

Two uniformed police officers stood sentry at the front doors of the hotel, clearly stationed to watch anyone who might try to leave. The sight of a middle-aged man running straight at them put them on edge. In unison, their hands moved from behind their backs to rest on their Sam Browne belts.

"Come with me!" Carter yelled. "I know where they are!"

The cops exchanged glances that betrayed their assessment of Carter's mental stability. When Carter closed to within a few yards, the cop on the right shifted his hand from his belt to his weapon, holding the other hand out in a gesture that stopped Carter in his tracks. "Okay, mister," said the cop on the right. "Don't be stupid."

Carter knew what they must be thinking. "My name's Carter Janssen," he said breathlessly. "My daughter is with the man you're looking for—Brad Ward. They're not in the hotel anymore. They've fled to the mall over there. If we move fast, I think we can catch them."

The cop scowled. "I haven't heard anything about that."

"Of course you haven't. They don't know in there. But I'm telling you now."

The cop shook his head. "Sorry, sir, but I've got orders. If the lieutenant thought—"

Carter didn't wait for the rest. This was a waste of time. The officers did in fact have their orders, and they were not going to violate them on the whim of a complete stranger. His guys back in Pitcairn County, New York, would have done the same thing.

Without another word, he spun away from the cops

and headed for the Galleria parking garage. The two minutes it took for him to run the distance made his legs feel as if they'd hammered out a marathon.

He surveyed the layout of the garage with a single glance. It had been built into the side of a hill, with the mall itself blocking a second side. Nicki and Brad would face two options for escape: they could exit from the bottom level of the four-story parking structure, thus bringing them straight at him, or they could exit from the top level, which, thanks to the rolling hills of the surrounding countryside, was actually at ground level, with easiest access to the freeway.

Upstairs was it. The humidity pressed in on him as he paused to look up the seemingly endless flights, and then got down to business, taking them two at a time.

He was nearly to the third level when he skidded to a stop so abruptly that his momentum pitched him forward on the steps.

Off to his left, from somewhere in the middle of the dimly lit expanse of concrete, a starter switch ground, and an engine caught. From where he stood at the landing between parking levels, he couldn't tell if it came from the second floor or the third.

Then, from the floor above—the third—headlight beams swept the walls of the stairwell.

Carter dashed up the half-flight to the next level in time to see taillights disappearing up the ramp to the fourth floor.

This time, it was a Honda Accord.

Nicki stood as she saw the headlights painting the far wall, shocked at how much the effort took out of her.

The engine roared as Brad piloted the car around the curve, through a stop sign without slowing, finally skidding to a stop with the front passenger door positioned three feet in front of her. The window lowered itself, revealing a beaming Brad on the far side of the center console, leaning low over the steering wheel to make eye contact.

"Hey, good-lookin', want a ride?" he asked.

Nicki smiled in spite of it all. The guy never knew a serious moment. She lifted the handle and pulled the door open.

"Nicolette!"

Her head jerked up, not believing what she'd heard. Sure enough, there stood her father, fifty yards away, illuminated by the wash of a streetlight. He waved his arms over his head as if to divert an approaching aircraft. His chest heaved from the effort of his run.

"Nicolette Janssen, don't get in that car!"

She froze—having no idea what to do. Looking back through the window, she saw Brad's gaze shift from the front, where he could see and hear her father, and then back to her.

"Nicolette, please!" Carter yelled.

Nicki pleaded silently for Brad to tell her what to do.

"You've got to call this one yourself, hon," he said. "But do me a favor and do it fast."

"Do you want me to come along?" she asked him.

Up ahead, her father started walking quickly toward them. "Nicolette Janssen, I forbid you to get into that car!"

"Stay there!" she yelled back at him. She hated the airy sound of her voice, but there was enough emotion there to freeze her dad. She returned her gaze to Brad.

He looked back at her, his face showing nothing. "Nicki, you know what I want you to do, but that's not a reason to come, any more than what he wants you to do is a reason to stay. *You* decide."

"Nicolette, please don't go," Carter said. There was a new tone to his voice. A pleading tone. He sounded as if he might be ready to cry. "He's a killer, sweetheart. I don't know what he's told you, but I guarantee you that much is true. Please don't get into that car with him. Don't leave me."

Why did her father have to do this? Why couldn't he have just stayed away? Why did it have to be about staying with *him* or leaving *him*?

The clock had ticked down to nothing, and the whole world seemed to pause, waiting for her to make up her mind. In the end, the decision wasn't all that complicated. She could choose something new and alive, or something old and dying.

"My name is Nicki," she said.

She slipped into the seat, barely getting the door closed before Brad peeled rubber clearing the parking lot.

PART THREE
TIME TO STEAL

April 14

Derek's mom visited me again today. She cried and cried. They told her that Derek was killed in a fight, but she didn't believe it. She wanted to know if it was true. I told her I never wanted to see her again. I told her that Derek was a thief and he got what he deserved.

They monitor the conversations in there. What else could I say? She begged to hear something good but I just walked away. I'm a piece of shit. A goddamn coward.

Chapter Fifteen

Carter Janssen hadn't moved from the spot there in the parking lot, and when the police cars arrived, they came as a six-pack. Warren Michaels was first to step out onto the concrete.

"You missed them!" Carter shouted. He was furious.

Warren said, "I got a radio report from one of our men on the front door. He told me that you had tried to get them to come along."

"They wouldn't," Carter said.

"They should have," Warren said. "This is the only thing that made sense. Somehow they knew we were coming. Did you see them?"

"I talked to her," Carter said. He closed his eyes and saw that look of confusion in his daughter's face all over again. "I tried to convince her to stay, but she went with him anyway."

"What were they driving?" asked the lieutenant.

"A Honda," he said. "Red, I think, but it might have been blue. They were gone before I could get a tag number."

"Don't worry about it," Warren said, reading his

thoughts. He squeezed Carter's shoulder then let it go, a gesture of commiseration. "Besides, Ward is a smart guy. Chances are, he's already switched those plates out for someone else's."

"I tried to yell to you," Carter said, a little calmer. "There in the hallway, but I couldn't get your attention."

"I understand. The good news is, there can only be but so many Hondas out on the street tonight. We'll put the word out on the radio and stop every one of them if we have to. We'll get 'em."

Carter closed his eyes and tried to push away the approaching headache. *Please just let it be that simple.* "What did you find in the room?"

"They were definitely there," Warren said. "And they left quickly. All that formal wear and such, they left it all behind."

Carter sighed. "I guess that's good news."

"But there's bad news, too, I'm afraid."

The tone of the cop's voice caused a spear of pain to pierce Carter's body. As the cop reached into his suit coat pocket and pulled out its contents, the pain blossomed even more. "These bottles have Nicki's name on them. I suppose they're important?"

It was all of her meds. *All* of them. "Oh, my God," Carter said.

Nicki watched with amazement as Brad went to work.

The Honda lasted all of five miles, zigzagging from the highway off onto back streets, before he slowed to a crawl in a residential neighborhood.

"We need new wheels," he explained. "Your dad's probably got the license number, and even if he doesn't, at this hour, the cops'll be stopping anything that looks like a Honda."

"So you're just going to steal another car?"

Brad shrugged. "What difference does one more make?"

"So, when the owner wakes up in the morning, he's going to report his car missing, and when that happens, we're right back where we began."

Brad laughed, just a chuckle at first, and then a real laugh, like one you'd hear at a comedy club.

"What's so funny?" She wasn't sure why, but deep in her gut, Nicki felt offended.

"Think about it. You've got a fatal illness, you're wandering through the night with a convicted murderer, we're both probably gonna die in a hail of gunfire, and you're worried about getting caught stealing a car. It really is pretty funny."

Nicki was not amused. "Maybe I'm just too tired."

"Your head is in the right place, though. The trick is to find a car that no one will notice is missing."

"How do we do that?"

Brad stopped the Honda and pointed past Nicki at a house on their right. "Like this," he said. "Look at this place. The people aren't home." And sure enough, there was an old Toyota parked alongside the curb.

Nicki followed his finger, but couldn't follow the logic. "Brad, there's a light on in the house."

"Exactly," he said, pulling into the driveway. He killed the lights on the Honda. "What's the last thing your father does before he goes to bed at night?"

"How should I know?"

"Think about it. Before he goes upstairs for the last time, what's the last thing he does?"

Nicki pondered the question, but the answer wasn't there. An ember of anger started to burn.

"He turns out the lights, right?"

She thought about it. Yes, that *was* the last thing he did.

"It's the last thing *everybody* does," Brad explained. "But what does he do before he goes on vacation to make people think there's someone at home?"

Now she really did see it. She smiled. "He turns on a light."

He slapped his thigh triumphantly. "Exactly. Not just any light, mind you, but a light downstairs. I've broken into my share of houses, and I've got to tell you, at three in the morning, the ones with lights on are the ones that are empty."

"How do you know somebody's not sick?"

"If they were, then an upstairs light would be on, or maybe the foyer light. But look there. That's like a living room light. You can tell because of the bay window."

Nicki released a chuckle. "You know, there aren't any rules for that stuff. You could be wrong."

He flicked his hand in a dismissive gesture and made a face. "I'm never wrong." He opened the car door and got out, leaving the Honda running in the driveway.

Nicki followed. "What are you doing?"

"I'm making a trade," he said. As he approached the driver's side of the Toyota, he reached into his pocket and withdrew a ring of what might have been keys, but from what Nicki could see, they all had an odd shape about them.

"What are those?" Nicki asked.

Brad scowled and brought a finger to his lips. "One of the first lessons in thief school is not to shout, okay? We call it stealth." He stooped to the side of the door and stuck one of the thin black objects into the lock, while his other hand stuck a tiny Y-shaped strip of metal into the top and bottom of the key slot. "These are lock picks," Brad explained. His tone was that of a master explaining to an apprentice. "I stick the pick in the lock while holding tension on the cylinder with the tension bar." He raked the pick in and out of the slot, then withdrew the pick and reinserted it. "These older Toyotas aren't as hard as some of the other cars. This is a 1992, I'd guess. Beginning in '95, the lock technology got pretty tough."

"What are you scraping?" Nicki asked.

"The pin tumblers. There's a diamond-shaped point on the end of the pick, and as I push the tumblers out of the way, the cylinder turns a bit, and the tension keeps them from popping back in. When I get them all"— Nicki heard a distinctive *click*, and the lock turned all the way, raising the lock button just inside the window—"the lock opens." He stood and pulled the door open, triggering the dome light inside, which he extinguished by turning a knob on the dash.

Nicki's jaw dropped. "I don't believe you know how to do this stuff."

Brad beamed, clearly proud of his accomplishment. "But wait," he said in a strange announcer's voice, "there's more." He produced the Leatherman and again folded out the needle-nose pliers.

"First we have to unlock the steering wheel," Brad said. Slipping into the driver's seat, he grasped the steering wheel with both hands and wrenched it violently to the right.

A loud *crack!* made Nicki jump.

"It's just a pin," Brad explained. "A piece of plastic. Break that sucker off and you've got an unlocked steering wheel. Now, watch this." Manipulating the pliers with only one hand, he grasped the ignition cylinder with the tool's jaws, and again broke something with a mighty twist. Grinning widely, he pulled out the whole assembly and brandished it for Nicki to see.

"Did you break it?" she asked.

He shrugged. "Depends on what you mean by breaking."

Brad brought the pliers around to the ignition switch again, but with the steering column in the way, she couldn't see exactly what he did. Whatever it was, the engine turned and coughed to life.

"All you have to do is close the circuit," he explained. "All of this other crap is supposed to make you feel more secure."

Amazing, Nicki thought. Simply and utterly amazing. "So, what do we do with the Honda?"

"I need you to follow me in it," he said. "We'll dump it a couple of blocks from here and then take off."

Ten minutes later, they were done. It would have been even sooner, but Brad spotted a similar Toyota— later model but same color—parked down the street a ways, and he took an extra few minutes to swap the license plates.

"It's the little things that make the difference," Brad explained when they were on the road again. "To be on the run and stay alive means thinking three steps ahead all the time. When you steal, steal from someone who won't notice, but then plan that they might. This car here? We're gonna have to dump it and get another one before too long, probably tomorrow. Meanwhile, if someone does notice that we boosted the car and they report it, cops on the highway are going to be looking for those old plates. If they see us on the road, they'll call in the plates we've got and find out that they belong to a silver-gray Toyota, and we'll be in the clear. Pretty cool, huh?"

When Nicki didn't answer, he craned his neck to get a look at her.

She was sound asleep.

Carter sat on the sofa of the Governor's Suite, perusing the accumulated evidence. Somebody named Vincent Campanella had one hell of a surprise waiting for him when he got back from his vacation in France. His car had been stolen and over six thousand dollars had been racked up against his credit card without his knowledge. Carter wondered if the gendarme would break the news in person, or if it would merely be handled through a phone call.

The Braddock County cops had found the Mustang in the Ritz-Carlton garage, safe and sound, and even with a full tank of gas. There on the bed, Carter could see the assortment of clothes that his daughter had bought with money she didn't have.

"Under the circumstances, I think we can make a pretty good case for dropping any charges against your Nicki," Warren said. "They didn't keep anything they stole. That's a little bit of good news, anyway."

Carter forced a smile. "Somewhere under all that horseshit there has to be a pony, right?" he quipped, recalling the punch line from an old joke.

"We've got a BOLO out for their vehicle," Warren went on, "and we've got word going out to all the hotels and flophouses. We've narrowed their lead to virtually nothing, so I think there's a lot of reason to be hopeful."

Carter nodded because it was the thing to do, but he

sensed that Warren knew, just as he did, that things were not nearly as rosy as he was painting them to be. In the first place, Brad Ward was proving himself to be resourceful. Carter placed the likelihood that they were still in the same vehicle at just about zero.

"You've got to have some faith," Warren said. "Things have broken your way pretty well so far."

"You know what?" Carter said with a suddenness that turned heads. "I think I need to be reunited with my car and take off on my own."

"Where are you going?" Warren asked.

"South and east. Chris Tu, a detective on the force back home who's been working that end for me, told me that they talked in their e-mails about going to the beach."

Warren's eyebrows scaled his forehead. "Specifically? I mean, if you think they're headed for a particular beach—"

Carter shook his head. "No, it's nothing that overt. Apparently, they just talked about the beauty of the beach in their e-mails. That was one of the things she wanted to do before she . . . Well, it's one of the things she wants to do."

Carter eyed the brown pill bottles on the bed, the ones with his daughter's name on them. "I don't suppose you'd let me have those, would you?" he asked. "I know they're evidence, but if I happen to run into her—"

Warren scowled and shot Carter a look that said he was crazy. "Those aren't evidence at all, as far as I'm concerned." He scooped the bottles up with one hand and gave them to the worried father. "No, like I said, as far as I'm concerned, this isn't even a crime scene anymore. We've got everything we need."

Warren Michaels was doing Carter Janssen a huge favor here, turning away from Nicki's part in what clearly was grand larceny, if not worse. "Listen, Warren, I—"

"This doesn't begin to repay my debt to you, Carter. Nathan's debt to you. You just go and find Nicki, and be sure to give me a call if you need any help."

"I'll do that," Carter said. "Now how about a ride back to your house where I can get my car?"

May 3

Last night they got me. It was the Posse. There were five of them and it went on all night. It was after lights-out and they just appeared in my cell. I was asleep until they punched me in the face, and from there it was just one long nightmare. They threatened to cut my balls off if I yelled.

I didn't yell. I did what they told me to do. I couldn't stop them anyway. I don't know how long it went on. Maybe for hours. It even stopped hurting after a while. I think I stopped feeling anything. Until the next morning. This morning. I could barely walk. They promised me more. They said I was theirs for the taking whenever they want.

Georgen was there watching. He wasn't one of the rapists—at least I don't think he was—but he stood there and watched a long time.

Chapter Sixteen

Once they were past Stafford, the traffic on I-95 South was a breeze. The Toyota turned out to be a piece of crap, so Brad changed out cars one more time, this time taking a Chrysler Sebring—an old guy's convertible, but a convertible nonetheless. That was the one promise that Brad had made to himself. The less time he could spend cooped up with a roof over his head, the better. He missed the Mustang, though.

Nicki had fallen back to sleep, curled up on the passenger side with the seat tilted all the way back. As much as he craved her company to keep himself awake, he let her sleep on, envying her.

So, how *did* the cops catch up so quickly? He thought he'd been careful. It had to have something to do with the credit card, but for the life of him he couldn't put it all together.

Now that he'd put some miles on his escape, he needed to get off the interstate, and onto some thoroughfares where Virginia State Troopers didn't grow like bushes along the side of the road. In Fredericksburg, he slapped his turn signal and veered off onto Route 17. It would still take him south, and from there to his final destination, but it would take a lot longer, especially as he got into the nightmarish tangle of highways around Norfolk and Virginia Beach. Still, it was safer than the interstate. He just had to take extra care to watch the speed limit signs.

He hated this new paranoia. Until last night, he'd allowed himself to build up a sense of invulnerability, but the events at the Ritz had unnerved him. In one night, he'd undone months of evasion. Instead of having a whole world to scour in search for him, they were down to a hundred-mile radius. The pressure had increased a thousandfold.

The cops would flood news outlets with his picture, and they'd make it sound as if he was the worst criminal ever to walk the planet. They'd lace every report with warnings to consider him armed and dangerous.

Oh, that it were true. If he had the means to defend himself, maybe he could relax a little.

Nicki asked, "Do you know where we're going?"

He hadn't realized that she was awake. When he turned to look at her, he saw that her eyelids were still closed.

"South," he said. "All the way south. I've been thinking about it. My original plan was to hit the Outer Banks and just jump from place to place, but things are a little hotter than I'd hoped."

"I'm tired of being a prom queen anyway," she said, her eyes still closed. "Now I'm ready to be Bonnie Parker."

Brad smiled. "Turning tough, are you? How are you feeling? You don't look so good."

Nicki sat up straighter. "I think I'm gonna look worse before I look better, too. I left my meds back in the hotel room."

Brad's head shot around to look at her. "All of them?"

She nodded.

"We'll get you more, then."

Nicki smiled. "We've got time."

"How much?"

A shrug. "I don't know. I've never done this before. Everything is a matter of degree. I'll be okay, just a little slow until I get them."

Brad's head swam at the notion of finding a replacement prescription. Maybe he really was going to need that gun.

"Don't sound so panicky," Nicki said. "Honestly, it's not a huge deal for a couple of days. Maybe even a week. We really do have time."

"Then why do you look so bad?"

She laughed and opened her eyes. "Well, let's just say the last few hours have been more stressful than my average day. If I rest, things will right themselves eventually. The meds just speed things along."

She kept a careful eye on Brad's face. This was the part of being with her that he couldn't have thought about. She was a *cripple,* not the fun-loving travel companion he'd been looking forward to. She was holding him back—she had to be—and part of her wondered when he was going to just pull over and let her out of the car.

"Tell me what you're thinking," Nicki said. "I need to know."

Brad cleared his throat. "Well, if you really have a couple of days to work with, I was thinking that we could wait till we get down to the Florida Keys. There's a lady down there, the mother of a guy I knew from the joint. She moved there after her son was killed, but she promised me once that I'd always have a home. From there, I'll be able to find somebody who can help us. It's just not practical to go walking into a pharmacy and hold the place up for a prescription, you know? Especially not now, when we're trying so hard to disappear again. I go to a place like that, and ask for drugs like yours, and then all of a sudden they can track us on the map like we had a homing beacon on the car. I just don't think—"

"Brad, relax," she repeated. She hesitated before tossing out the Big Question. "Do you want to drop me off?"

This time, when he looked at her, there was pain in his eyes. Maybe even a little panic. "Why would I want to do that?"

"I don't want to slow you down. It's got to be easier for one person to hide than it is for two."

"Is that what you want?"

"I want to know what *you* want. It would be easier, wouldn't it?"

She was shocked to see that his feelings were hurt by her question. She thought she was doing the noble thing.

"Well, yeah, it's *easier,* but so what? I've done this by myself for a long time. I don't want to be alone anymore. I don't want to be without you anymore."

"But I'm sick."

"I know that. You gonna be less sick if you're by yourself?"

Nicki scowled. "You know what I mean. I'm worried that I'm going to keep you from getting away."

Brad shook his head in wonderment. "You really don't get it, do you? This is where I was going *to,* Nicki. *You* are where I was going to. I never in a million years thought you'd go along with this, but you did. I'm here now, and we're together, and I'm not going to let a little pressure from the cops change any of that. That's what I keep telling you. Why won't you believe me?"

Nicki heard the words but the message didn't make sense to her. He could have *anyone*.

"Unless you're anxious to get away," he said, mistaking her silence for uncertainty. "Unless you're scared."

Nicki scoffed, "I'm dying. I got past scared months ago. When you've got no future, I'm not sure what there is to be afraid of."

Brad smiled. "I couldn't have put it better myself," he said.

Deputy Darla Sweet stepped through the doorway to the Dairy Queen and adjusted her Sam Browne belt, trying to look confident even as she felt awkward as hell. Gisela Hines—the sheriff's wife—had called her at eight-thirty this morning to request this meeting, and now that she was here, Darla felt that she'd made a terrible mistake. Whatever was going on in the Hines house was strictly a family affair, and the less she knew about it, the happier she'd be.

All the way over here, Darla had recited the words she wanted to use to extricate herself from this mess, but as valiant and strong as they sounded in the car, she knew that she'd never be able to say them aloud. If she had a brain in her head, she would tell Gisela to talk to a counselor, not a cop.

Darla and Gisela had only met once before, at a courthouse Christmas party, but there'd be no problem recognizing her. Born and raised in Panama, Gisela

Hines had an exotic beauty about her that set her apart from the heavily cosmeticized locals of her age. Closing in on fifty, her olive skin had the smoothness of a teenager's, her eyes the dark intensity of a thoroughly lived life.

As Darla scanned the room, she saw Gisela waving from the back right-hand corner. She had a cardboard tray of food in front of her, but seemed not the least bit interested in eating.

"So, how is Jeremy?" Darla asked as she took the bench opposite Gisela. "Last time I saw him, he was expecting a pretty rough time at home."

Gisela toyed with her meal. "Frank was very angry. They had a terrible argument." The decades she had spent in this country had worn away all but the slightest trace of an accent.

"An argument or a fight?" Darla remembered the flash of rage.

"Do not think badly of him, please. It is not his fault. He is just a boy."

Darla was confused. "Don't think badly of Jeremy?"

"He is a good boy. Used to get good grades, but that Peter Banks, he is a bad influence. I don't know why he insists on hanging out with such trash. He knows what it must look like. He knows that his father must win elections to have a job."

Darla's jaw dropped without her realizing it. "Mrs. Hines, perhaps—"

"Call me Gisela, please."

"Gisela, are you aware of how close Sheriff Hines came to striking Jeremy yesterday?"

Gisela waved it off as if it were unimportant. "That's what I am telling you. That is the influence of Peter Banks. That is not Jeremy's fault."

"I'm not suggesting that it's Jeremy's fault, Gisela. I'm not even sure you and I are talking about the same things. Jeremy is only a boy."

Now it was Gisela's turn to look confused. She scoffed, "Jeremy is a young man. He is strong. There is no little boy left."

"Of course there is," Darla said, and then she lowered her voice. "He's only eighteen. Emotionally, he'll be a boy for another five years."

"But he knows right from wrong. He *should* know right from wrong, yet he smokes drugs with his friend. I'm telling you, before Peter Banks came into his life, Jeremy had no problems at all. Good grades, nothing but bright prospects for his baseball scholarship."

Darla opened her mouth to say something more, but stopped herself. "Mrs. Hines—*Gisela*—why did you ask me to meet you here?"

The other woman's gaze broke away from Darla's. Apparently, they had gotten to the part she wasn't comfortable with. She took a deep breath and talked to her hands. "Essex is a small town," she said. "People talk, and this thing that happened yesterday at the park, that is the kind of thing that can be very damaging." She raised her eyes. "Damaging to Frank, damaging to Jeremy, and even damaging to you."

An alarm went off in the back of Darla's head. Was it possible that this little woman with the charming accent was threatening her? She rattled her head, as if to fix a loose connection. "I don't think I follow what you're saying."

Gisela leaned into the table, lowering her voice even more. "I know how cops talk among themselves, how rumors spread a little at a time. You mention something to another deputy, and then he tells his wife, and pretty soon, everybody knows what is happening."

"You're afraid that I'm going to tell people about Jeremy?" Darla asked. "Is that what you're afraid of?"

"It is interesting to talk about, no? It is the kind of thing that might come up in the squad room. Certainly, it's the kind of thing that the newspapers would like to hear: Sheriff's son caught in drug ring. I would ask you not to spread that kind of rumor."

Darla allowed herself a wry chuckle, even though none of this was remotely funny. She leaned back in her seat, away from the table, and ran a hand through her hair. "I don't know where to begin," she said. "First of all, none of what happened yesterday could possibly be turned into a *rumor,* because it's all true. Jeremy did in fact get caught smoking pot—though I would hesitate to call that a drug ring—and he did in fact get a pass, courtesy of your husband. I presume that's what you're worried about, right? The fact that the people of Essex might draw the conclusion that there are different legal standards, depending on who you are?"

Gisela looked ashamed that she had ever brought it up.

"Okay, well, it's true," Darla said. "I've always known it's true within the department, but now I know that it's true on the streets, as well."

"It is the influence of that other boy," Gisela said again.

"Who cares, Mrs. Hines? I mean really, at the end of the day, who gives a flying shit why a teenager does something stupid? They all do stupid things. It's their job. No one cares."

The other woman looked around and lowered her voice. "My husband has enemies. They will care. They will try to ruin his job."

Darla wanted to argue the point, but sensed the fruit-lessness of it. It had been her experience over the years that parents in power think that their kids are under far more scrutiny than they truly are. "Let's not forget about the baseball scholarship," Darla baited. "That's very important, too."

"Yes, exactly." Gisela missed the irony completely.

"Why am I here? What do you want from me? Is it just to be quiet about what I saw yesterday?"

Gisela nodded triumphantly. "Yes, that's it exactly. I want you to be quiet. To not tell anyone what you saw."

"What did Sheriff Hines do to Jeremy last night?" Darla intended the question to catch Gisela off balance and it worked.

"What do you mean?"

"I mean, how badly did he beat him?"

Gisela squirmed in her seat. "My husband does not beat my son," she said.

"I don't believe you. I saw for myself how terrified Jeremy was of getting caught yesterday. I saw the fury in his father's eyes. Does he beat you as well?"

Gisela's jaw dropped, her face a mask of horror. "How dare you?"

"Tell you what," Darla said. "I'll keep quiet about what happened yesterday if you promise to go public about what happened afterward. Is that a deal?"

"I will do no such thing. You have no right to ask such a thing. What happens in our home is private business."

"I couldn't agree more. Yet, here we are in a public place, talking about it."

Gisela took a few beats to gather herself. "Look," she said, "my husband wants you to know that there are no hard feelings about yesterday."

Darla's eyebrows scaled her forehead. "Oh, he does."

"He wants you to know that there will be no, um, what's the word?"

"Retaliation?" Darla helped.

"Repercussions. He asked me to talk to you because he thought it would be, um—"

"Inappropriate? Morally wrong?"

"*Embarrassing,* to say so himself. He reminded me to remind you that he would do the same for you. He calls it professional courtesy."

"Oh, is that what he calls it?"

Gisela looked confused. "Why are you being so difficult about this?"

"I'm not being difficult," she said. "I'm being surprised. Aghast. I understand the part about professional courtesy, but to have you do his dirty work for him is appalling."

Gisela grew even more uncomfortable. "He has a favor to ask of you, also. You are free to say no if you wish—he made that very clear—but he would feel most indebted to you if you would think about it."

This should be interesting, Darla thought.

Gisela beckoned Darla to lean in closer to the center of the table. "He would appreciate it if you would keep an eye out for this Peter Banks boy. Watch him and wait for him to break the law."

Darla nodded, feigning a serious expression. "And then shoot him, right?"

There was that horrified look again. "Heavens no! Just arrest him. Take him off the streets, away from Jeremy. Away from other good boys he might lead astray."

Darla rattled her head again. "Isn't that a little over the top? Why not just tell Jeremy to stay away from him?"

"We have," Gisela said. The frustration raised her

voice louder than she wanted. "We have told him a thousand times, but he does not listen."

This was the moment when Darla should have gotten up and walked out of the Dairy Queen, but something drove her to stay. There was a point to be made here, and for whatever reason, she wasn't able to make the other woman understand. "Suppose I catch Jeremy breaking the law? Do you want me to arrest him, too?"

"That will not be a problem. He has promised."

"But you told me that he's promised a thousand times. What makes you think this time is any better?"

Gisela sat back in her bench and fiddled with a napkin, twisting it around her finger. "This time, he is frightened. This time, he understands what he faces if he breaks the law again."

At one level, this had started to become amusing, even while it remained largely tragic. "Why does it fall to me?" she asked. "There are a lot of deputies here who would do anything to kiss your husband's ass. Why does it come to Darling Sweetcheeks?"

From the smile, she could tell that Gisela had heard the epithet before. "They are not as loyal as you think," she said. "They talk too much about too many things. Many do not like my husband. Some might like to run against him one day. The less they know about this, the better."

"I see. And since I already know the details, I'm the natural choice to terrorize the young man who did nothing more than spend an afternoon with your son."

Gisela bristled. "He is a bad one, that Peter."

Darla suppressed a smile. "I keep forgetting. And why doesn't Sheriff Hines keep his own eye out for Peter?" The question was rhetorical; she already knew the answer. "Under the circumstances, he couldn't very well be the one to arrest him, could he? In fact, Peter Banks could commit just about any crime he wanted in this town, right under the sheriff's nose, and not have a problem, isn't that right? All Peter would have to do is open his mouth to one judge, and any charge would be thrown out. Is that what your husband was thinking?"

Gisela squirmed. "Something like that."

"But I was there, too."

"You wanted to arrest them," Gisela explained. "You do not have the same conflict of— What is the term?"

"Conflict of interest," Darla said. "And over the course of the last ten minutes, you've handed me one hell of a big one."

June 9

    Once I showed them how scared I was they knew they owned me. I'm Chaney's bitch now. A slave.

    I don't know how yet, but I'm going to kill him. I'm going to kill all of them.

    I've got to get out of here. One way or the other. I tried to hang myself night before last. Got the sheet tied up high around the bars, got the other end tied around my throat. Couldn't take the big step. I pussied out.

    I don't know how Chaney has the run of the place at night, but he does when Georgen is on duty. I don't know how he pays him, or what he pays him, but my cell door slides open and then he's got me. When he's done, he walks away and the door closes behind him and then I'm alone. Unless he's loaned me out.

    I'm disgusting.

Chapter Seventeen

By one-thirty, they were deep into North Carolina, feeling their way east and south, obeying every speed limit. They had the top down, and as the wind blew her hair into knots, Nicki thought for sure that she could feel her strength returning, nature's remedies taking care of nature's ills.

"I can smell the ocean," she said.

Brad craned his neck to look at the thickening sky. "Doesn't look like it's going to be much of a beach day."

"Did I ever tell you that I've never been to the beach?"

Brad laughed. "About a thousand times."

"Actually, I knew that," Nicki said. "That was my hint. Let's go to the beach."

"Don't you think we should get a few more miles behind us?"

"I'm seventeen years old and I've never once felt sand between my toes."

Brad rolled his eyes. "No sandboxes in upstate New York?"

"It's not the same. Or so I've heard. Wouldn't know myself, because I've never been to the beach."

He looked at her and made his dimples erupt in a smirk. "I can't believe you've never been. Didn't your friends just hop in a car and go?"

"You're kidding, right? My 'friends'"—finger quotes—"are all mindless idiots, and even if they weren't, there's no way my father would let me drive that far with other kids."

Brad regarded her with a scowl, as if he were confused. Then the smile returned. "Hey," he said. "Let's grab lunch at the beach."

"What a great idea!"

"Are we close to Nags Head? Kids at school used to go to Nags Head on spring break."

Brad shook his head. "We're close, but I don't want to go there. That's actually a pretty busy place. Too many cops. Besides, it's behind us, and this is a one-way trip."

"Where, then?"

"The beach is three thousand miles long, Nicki. I think we'll be able to find a place. There's a town called Sail Fish, where I went a hundred years ago. It's not touristy. Got a little drawbridge you've got to go over to get into the place. I think it's got maybe four restaurants altogether, and the people there don't particularly like visitors."

"That means they won't like us," Nicki said.

Brad laughed. "Nah, we don't look like visitors." He lifted one bare foot away from the clutch and showed it to her. "See? No sandals and knee socks. Oh, yeah, and no cameras. We definitely don't look like visitors."

Nicki laughed along with him. "How far is Sail Fish?"

He calculated. "Maybe an hour and a half. It's nearly at the South Carolina border."

"I've got to eat before then," she said. "Seriously, I'm starving. At least a snack."

"You okay?" His tone took on a note of concern.

"I'm fine," she said. "But until I get the meds thing worked out, food and fluids become even more important." It's amazing, she thought, how an illness like hers can make even a layman talk like a doctor.

Brad squinted as he tried to make out the writing on the sign up ahead. "Can you read that?"

Nicki squinted, too. It was a green highway sign with white letters on it. "It says, 'Essex, one mile.'"

Brad could see it now, too. "Let's find something to eat in Essex."

The scent of the ocean grew stronger as they turned left at the stop sign, but there was no sign of water. Dense woods surrounded them—mostly towering, skinny pines growing out of the sandy soil. What few houses they saw looked gloomy and unkempt.

Essex was the land of billboard advertising. Nothing particularly eye-catching or original—although she did get a giggle out of the sign for Dirty Dick's House of Crabs—most of the boards hawked mid-range motels.

"This is a charming community," Nicki said.

"Anything not built of steel and concrete looks right homey to me," Brad replied. "I guess this is all people can afford when they make money only five months out of the year." Brad kept the speedometer hovering around forty-five, just to be safe.

After another three miles, they found themselves approaching a T intersection with Shore Road. Directly in front, just beyond the dunes that frustrated any panoramic view, lay the ocean.

"You want to eat first or see the beach first?" Brad asked.

"Food," Nicki said. It wasn't even close.

Brad yanked the steering wheel, and then they were in the parking lot of a Quik Mart store.

"What are you doing?" Nicki asked.

"Stopping for a snack."

"But this isn't a restaurant."

"Because this isn't a meal." He perfectly mimicked her tone. He pulled the Sebring around the far corner of the store and stopped on the other side of a Dumpster, out of sight of the road. He wrenched the transmission lever into Park and turned sideways in his seat, drawing one foot under the opposite thigh, forming the figure *4*. "And let's talk about a big problem we have." He recapped his concerns about losing their new identities, and worse yet, their credit card. "From now on," he continued, "we're strictly on a cash basis, and we don't have a whole hell of a lot of that. Things are likely to be austere for a while until I can come up with more folding money."

"We're not stealing in here," Nicki said. "Okay? Promise that we're not shoplifting."

The comment startled a laugh out of Brad. "I don't think anyone's ever asked that of me before."

He opened his door, pausing to slip his sandals back on. "You're something else, Nicolette," he said. "You are something else."

She got out of the car, too, a little more slowly than he. Concern darkened Brad's face. "You okay?"

"I'm fine. And I'll kick your ass if you ever ask me that again. You're sounding like my father."

He clapped a hand over his heart and staggered back a step. He stopped her just as they got to the door. "Remember, no conversation with the clerk. Minimize eye contact, but always act normal."

Her scowl mocked his serious tone.

Brad smacked her on the backside and then walked through the glass door.

Funny how being a fugitive changes you. The first thing Nicki noticed as she stepped into the Quik Mart were the two security cameras, one behind the counter, where the clerk was no more interested in eye contact than she was, and one opposite the door. Maybe eighteen years old with a complexion that would benefit from more soap, the clerk was buried chin-deep in a *Star Wars* novel. He wouldn't have noticed if Tony Soprano himself walked through those doors. (Yet another thing her father didn't know was her obsession with the new HBO show about the mafia.)

The cameras unnerved her. That unblinking eye watched everything they did. She hurried to catch up with Brad, who'd gone straight to the refrigerated cases in the back of the store.

"Lunch meats," he explained, answering her look of curiosity. "Good nutritional value, quick, and cheap. That's my three basic food groups."

"Do you see the cameras up there?"

He didn't look up at them. "Don't stare."

"People will see us here."

"Not if they don't go looking for us," he said. "Nobody monitors cameras. They only look at the tapes if there's a problem and they want to see what happened. In a place this size, they probably record over the same tape day after day. After tomorrow, there won't even be a record."

That made sense. It took some of the edge off Nicki's concern. "Don't you wonder about fingerprints?"

He planted his fists on his hips. "Do you think we could talk about this later? What are you eating?"

"I want something salty."

"Up front," he said, pointing the way with a nod. "Opposite the register."

She started that way.

"Oh," Brad said, stopping her in her tracks.

She turned.

"Try not to look at the camera, okay?" He smiled, knowing that that was exactly what she was likely to do.

The Doritos called out to her. She hated the orange fingers and the rancid breath, but oh, boy, did she love Doritos. She couldn't remember the last time she'd had them. This dying thing was a hell of a cure for an eating disorder.

Outside, just beyond the doors, she saw movement. The suddenness of it startled her, causing her to whip her head around, fearful before she knew why. A man dressed in black pants and a red shirt approached the front door from the parking lot. His gait frightened her, the way he pivoted his head from side to side, as if worried that he might be seen. When the guy yanked down the front of a winter ski mask to conceal his face, she understood why. His other hand held a pistol. Before a scream could form in her throat, the door exploded open and the man brought his gun up and leveled it at Mr. Star Wars's face.

Nicki turned to run, but the assailant stiff-armed her, planting the heel of his hand into her breastbone, and sending her tumbling back into the Twinkies and Ho Hos.

"Stay the hell away from me!" he barked. The hand with the gun appeared to be trembling.

The clerk behind the counter didn't move. His jaw

dropped to his chest and his face paled as his eyes focused on the barrel of the gun.

"Don't look at me, you fucking moron," the robber growled. "Give me the cash from the drawer. You want to die?"

The clerk jumped as if poked with a cattle prod, dropping his novel to the floor and putting his hands in the air, high over his head, a parody of an old Western.

"Money," the attacker repeated. "Put your hands down and give me the fucking money."

"W-we don't have much," the clerk stammered. He looked scared to death.

"Stick your hand in the drawer, asshole. Grab what you've got, put it in a bag, and get down on the ground. If you even think of tripping an alarm I'll blow your head off."

Nicki had never been so terrified. She'd never seen the business end of a gun before, and she'd never seen anyone willing to commit murder. When she tried to get up from the mess of collapsed shelving and scattered groceries, the masked man unleashed a kick that nailed her in the ribs.

"I told you to stay the fuck where you are!" he spat.

The pain exploded through Nicki's chest, making her wonder if maybe he'd shot her anyway.

"Please don't," she sobbed. "Please don't hurt me."

But the robber had already turned his attention back to the clerk, who was frantically scooping money out of the drawer and stuffing it into a plastic shopping bag.

She'd forgotten all about Brad, thoughts of survival pushing everything else out of the way. So when she saw him moving up behind her assailant, it was all she could do to keep from yelling out his name. He moved like those ninja warriors she'd seen on television, slowly closing the distance.

The assailant sensed it, though. When Brad was still five feet away—a good two feet farther than he needed to be for a decisive strike—the gunman turned. Nicki screamed.

Brad rushed the attacker like a linebacker, hitting hard, somewhere in the midsection. An explosion rocked the Quik Mart as the gun discharged, triggering another scream from Nicki. She tried to roll out of the way of the fight, but the driving force of Brad's tackle sent both men hurling straight for her. She covered her head with her arms, and grunted as they fell on her hard.

Brad was yelling, too, and like Nicki's, his words didn't make sense. It was a roar of frenzied anger, and after the first two seconds, it became clear that the robber didn't have a chance.

Brad cocked his fist and fired it into the gunman's face. Nicki could feel the impact reverberate all the way down to her. "Drop the gun!" Brad commanded, and he leveled another bone-crushing blow to the face.

The gunman made a high-pitched squealing sound as the blows found their marks, and as he rolled away, across the white linoleum floor, Nicki noticed that he left a bloody smear. The gun clattered to the floor and Brad made a dive for it, executing a shoulder roll to come back to his knee, with the gun leveled at the attacker, who himself had found his feet.

"Freeze or you're dead," Brad commanded.

The attacker stood there, saying nothing, drooling blood through the tight weave of his woolen mask.

"Hands," Brad commanded. "I want to see hands." The gun looked different in Brad's hands than it did in the robber's.

The attacker made that high-pitched squeal again, then without a word, he spun and ran for the door, not even slowing as he charged out into the steadily darkening day.

"Stop, goddammit!" Brad yelled, and he threw the weapon at the door.

"What are you doing?" Nicki said. "Shoot him!"

"The goddamn thing is empty. He was robbing the place with an unloaded gun."

But it *wasn't* unloaded. She'd heard it fire. Her ears still rang from the noise of it. Movies and television couldn't come close to capturing the heavy percussion of a gunshot up close. Even firecrackers couldn't touch it, and she'd detonated some hellacious firecrackers in her time.

As her hearing returned, she watched Brad struggle with his temptation to chase after the gunman to get even with him. The look she saw in his face—in his eyes—was one that she'd never seen before, not in him, and not in anyone else. It was a look of sheer rage, the emotion raw and unfiltered. She saw it in the set of his jaw, too, and the way the ridge over his eye was bleeding, but he clearly had not yet noticed.

"Are you okay, Brad?"

"Son of a bitch is out of his mind. What the hell was he thinking? I shoulda broken his neck when I had a chance. I went for the gun instead. God*dammit!*"

The new Brad frightened her a little, and as he brought his gaze around to her, he seemed to realize it. "Oh, Jesus, Nicki, are you all right?" He hurried over to help her stand.

"I'm fine, I think," she said.

"I'm going after him," Brad said. He started for the door.

"No, don't. Please," Nicki said. "Just let it go. Nobody's hurt, so just—"

What was that?

It was an odd sound, a hissing, gurgling sound that made her skin pucker. Brad heard it too, and together they turned toward the cash register, where the young kid with the paperback was nowhere to be seen.

"Oh, shit," Brad breathed.

"What?"

He pulled on her arm. "Come on, we've got to get out of here."

She jerked away. "No. What is it?" She moved closer to the counter, frightened of what she might see, even as she knew that it could be nothing else.

"We don't have time for this," Brad said.

When she got close enough to the counter to see the horrors it concealed, she clapped a hand over her mouth to contain her scream.

The clerk—she could see now from his name tag that his name was Chas—lay sprawled on the white linoleum floor, half-sitting against the far wall of the clerk's space, a human island in a lake of blood that continued to spread at a horrifying rate from a gaping wound in his throat. "Oh, my God!" Nicki gasped. "Oh, Jesus, he's dead."

As if to prove her wrong, Chas tried to lift his hands to his wound, only to find that his arms were too heavy.

"Oh, Brad, what are we going to do?"

Brad pulled on her arm again. "We're getting the hell out of here."

"We can't," she said, again pulling away. "He's hurt. We have to call an ambulance."

"He's not hurt, Nicki, he's dead. He just doesn't know it yet."

Nicki couldn't believe he said that. She moved around

the end of the counter to enter the clerk's space and get closer. The metallic smell of his blood—redder and thicker than any blood she'd ever seen before—turned her stomach. She ignored the pain in her swollen knees as she leaned in close to him.

The boy's eyes—a brilliant green—were windows to his terror. "Brad, call 911," Nicki said.

"Are you out of your mind?" he hissed. "We can't do that."

"We *have* to. Look at him."

From a wound somewhere near Chas's collar, blood spewed in an irregular fan with each beat of his heart, cascading down his already-soaked shirt to get lost in the mess that was his pants. His eyes locked with Nicki's, even as the light in them faded. He reached for her, but again, the effort was just too much. His hand made a slapping sound when it landed in the lake of accumulating gore.

Without thinking, Nicki reached for it, enfolded it in her own. "I'm here, Chas," she said.

It wasn't the first time she'd watched someone die. In a strange, twisted way, it was easier to watch her mother slip away. At least then, the owner of the hand she held knew that it was a gesture of love. Here, Chas seemed to know that it was a gesture of pity, and that made all the difference in the world. His eyes begged for her to do something—anything—that would make things better.

"I'm so sorry," Nicki said. "I'm so, so sorry." She fought the urge to tell him that everything would be all right. It was what people who knew better liked to say, and she knew how much it pissed her off when people did it to her.

Panic sparked in those green eyes. Tears welled up. Nicki found herself back in the hospital room with her mother—or the emaciated shell that pretended to be her mother—begging her to stay, even as the electronic monitors and the gentle whispers from the nurses and doctors all told her that that was impossible. She remembered the uselessness of her mother's fight to stay with Nicki, to answer her prayers.

"It's a better place," she said softly to Chas. "There's no pain, and people are always nice to you. Just let yourself—"

"All y'all freeze right where you are!"

Nicki and Brad both jumped at the sound of the new voice and looked up to see an old man—probably all of eighty years old—staring down at her from the back of the counter, a huge automatic pistol gripped tightly in his fist.

"Leave that boy alone." Then he saw the carnage. "Oh, sweet mother of Jesus—"

This time, there was nothing stealthy or quiet about Brad's move. He just launched at the old man, pushing him hard with his left hand and then dropping him with a single punch to his face. Nicki yelled at the suddenness of it, the viciousness of it. "Brad! My God!"

Brad bent over and came up with the old man's gun, which he stuffed into the waistband of his chinos. "Come on, we gotta get outta here."

It was all happening too fast. Nicki didn't know what to do, what to think. All she knew was the panic welling up from somewhere deep inside.

"We've got to go now. He's probably already called the cops. Maybe set off an alarm."

"Where did he come from?"

Brad rolled his eyes, which were growing hotter by the second. "Who the hell cares? He came from the back room, okay? He must have been back there the whole time. Now, let's get out of here."

"But what about him?" she asked, pointing to Chas.

"Look at him," Brad said.

She did. The light in those green eyes had extinguished. They were dolls' eyes now, staring at forever.

"He's dead," Brad said. This time, his tone was softer.

"And him?" She gestured toward the old man, who lay somewhere out of her sight on the other side of the counter.

"I didn't hit him that hard. He'll be okay. Now, come on."

It was as if she were frozen in place. Should she stay or go?

"The cameras saw it all, Nicki," Brad said, reading her thoughts. "You've got no reason to stay. Nothing you say can add anything to what they'll be able to see on the tape. Decide now. Yes or no. I *can't* stay." He seemed to vibrate with anxiety to get the hell out of there.

It was too much. There were too many sides to consider all at once. This wasn't the kind of decision that you just made and walked away from. The ramifications were enormous. A boy was *killed,* for God's sake. This was all wrong. Wrong with a capital *W.* She'd somehow wandered through Alice's looking glass, and the whole world as she'd come to know it was all twisted and distorted.

Brad started for the door. "Bye, Nicki," he said. "I love you."

"Wait!" she called after him. "I'm coming!"

June 25

   Honest to God, I'm going to kill Chaney. Even if I die trying, I'm going to kill him. I've got a plan. I know a way to get a knife past the metal detectors. I've tried it twice—once leaving the kitchen and then on the way back in. Killing him will be the easy part. Living for more than thirty seconds afterward is a little tricky. That's okay, though, as long as Chaney's dead.

Chapter Eighteen

Darla Sweet was still a block away from the Quik Mart when she marked on the scene, speaking quickly and then tossing the mike onto the passenger seat. Heavy raindrops began to spatter the windshield of her cruiser.

Without dropping a beat, the dispatcher acknowledged, "On the scene, Unit six-oh-four at fourteen thirteen hours. Give us a situation report first chance you get."

No, I'm going to keep all the details to myself, Darla didn't say. A shooting! Part of her didn't believe it. Shootings didn't happen in Essex, at least not like this. Not in a robbery. Occasionally, a couple of goobers would get into an argument that blew out of proportion, but an armed robbery? That just didn't happen here.

Besides, this was old Ben Maestri's place. A nicer old man never walked the face of the planet. It was beyond her imagination that anyone would want to do him any harm. An alcoholic and a gambler, he'd fallen on hard times, Darla had been told, but even when the folks in town gossiped about that, it was always with a tone of pity, not disgust. She prayed silently that she wouldn't find him dead on the floor.

As she slid her cruiser to a halt outside the windows of the Quik Mart, she imagined the voices of her instructors at the academy. She knew all about waiting for backup and about tactical approaches, but this was *Essex,* where the nearest backup might be ten minutes away, and the nearest tactical unit was easily an hour beyond that. As her right hand threw the transmission into Park, she threw the door open with her left, leaving it gaping as she pulled her revolver and ran full-speed through the front doors.

"Sheriff's Office!" she yelled, her weapon extended at arm's length.

"Here!" someone yelled. "Oh, God, here, behind the counter!"

Her senses buzzing with premonitions of a trap, Darla eased forward far enough to peek over the counter to see the bloody mess on the floor behind. An old man and a teenager both sat on the linoleum, smeared with blood.

"Please help," the old man said. He seemed to be crying, even as his face showed emptiness of both color and expression. Besides the blood that coated the floor, another thin stream flowed from a gash just below the old man's eye.

Darla holstered her weapon and hurried around to the open end of the counter, nearly losing her balance when she hit the blood slick. She thumbed the mike on her epaulette. "Six-oh-four to Central, we have a confirmed critical GSW and another unidentified injury. Start two rescue units this way, and expedite backup. I'll be ten-seven rendering aid." Then, to the old man, she said, "Where are you hit?"

Old Ben just looked at her, uncomprehending. "How

could they do something like this?" The odor of booze wafted off him.

"I said, where are you hit?" Feeling for a pulse on Chas's neck, she found the gaping hole and realized instantly the seriousness of the boy's wound. It didn't matter what was wrong with the old man; the kid was worse off, and therefore first on her list. Pulling the kid away from the wall by his feet, she caused him to slip backward onto the floor, where his head impacted with a terrible thud. Darla keyed the mike one more time. "Six-oh-four to central, I'm beginning CPR."

With Chas now supine and staring, Darla lifted his jaw toward the ceiling, further exposing the gristly wound that gaped just above his collar. She pinched his nose shut while pressing her opened mouth onto his and blew. She'd recertified on this procedure six times now, and she still couldn't remember the sequence of events. She blew four quick breaths into his mouth, producing a terrible gurgling sound from the wound. At that instant, she realized that it was all a lost cause. With the trachea punctured, the air she blew would only make it as far as the hole, uselessly blowing a bloody fog against her cheek, but never reaching his lungs. Still, she had to try.

If she kept going, his chances rose to some tiny sliver of a percent above zero; if she stopped, he wouldn't even have that. Either way, she sensed that the taste of his blood would never go away.

Darla crossed her palms the way she'd been instructed, found the kid's xiphoid process, where the ribs came together just below the breastbone, and she started chest compressions. *One-and, two-and, three-and . . .* All the way to fifteen, and then she moved back up for another mouthful of blood. She didn't realize that a person could have so much blood.

"Do you think you can help me here?" she asked the old man, but he just continued to stare.

"I don't believe it," he whispered. "I just don't believe this is happening."

He was useless. Where the hell was the ambulance?

As the cycle switched from ventilations to compressions for the tenth or maybe fifteenth time, Darla paused long enough to vomit up the burger she'd had for lunch, adding a bit of herself to the unspeakable mess on the linoleum. It went like that forever, maybe minutes, maybe the better part of an hour. Ventilations, compressions, ventilations, compressions, puke.

Finally, in the distance, she heard the approach of sirens. The sound peaked, and then she heard the ping of the front door opening and the squeal of feedback as Sheriff Hines spoke into his radio. "Six-oh-one's on the scene."

"Sheriff!" Darla called. "Give me a hand!"

"What the hell are you doing, Deputy?"

The tone of the sheriff's voice startled her. She'd expecting something more urgent, something more congratulatory, perhaps. "CPR," she said. Like this wasn't obvious?

"Stop," Hines commanded.

Darla assumed she'd heard wrong and kept going. You don't stop CPR until you're exhausted or until the patient is pronounced dead. They'd said that a hundred times in the class.

"I said stop, goddammit," Hines growled. "Jesus, look what you're doing to the crime scene. What, did you miss the lecture on preserving evidence?"

Was he out of his mind? Darla stared at the sheriff in disbelief. "I'm supposed to let him die?"

"He's dead. Look at him. He's purple. He's got a

huge hole in his throat and he's bled out a gallon of blood. How dead do you want him to be?"

Darla understood the words, but the message eluded her. Why was the sheriff angry when he should have been writing up a citation for her heroic efforts?

"Come on, Deputy, enough already! Now! Stop."

She stopped. And for the first time, she got a good look at what the sheriff was seeing. Chas's mouth and nose were purple under the smear of gore, as were the tips of his fingers. She'd been so focused on saving his life that she'd lost sight of the fact that there was no life left to save. The futility of it all brought tears to her eyes.

The sheriff looked at her as if she smelled bad. He planted his fists on his hips and gestured toward the door with a jerk of his head. "Go on, get outta there. Step outside and get some air. Try not to step on more evidence than you have to." Outside, they could hear the approach of more sirens, and the distinctive rattle of a fire truck's Jake brake. Hines triggered another squeal of feedback as he told the dispatcher to put fire and rescue back in service. "We have a confirmed DOA here."

"What about him?" Darla asked, pointing to the mouse that was growing under Ben Maestri's eye.

"You need an ambulance, Ben?" the sheriff asked.

The old man shook his head. Neither his eyes nor his mind seemed able to focus.

"Bad day to be drunk, Ben," Hines said, his tone dripping with disgust. "Darla, take him out with you and see if you can get some information from him. I'll see what I can put together in here."

"They've got cameras," Darla said.

"Is that what those are? Come on, take custody of him."

Darla helped the old man to his feet and led him back around the corner. She was nearly to the door when the sheriff called her name.

"You *are* functional, aren't you?"

She took the question as an insult. "I assure you that I am fully *functional*." She leaned on the word to demonstrate her annoyance.

"Don't say yes if you mean no, Deputy. Tell me if you're too shaken up to do your job."

"I'm *fine*."

The sheriff seemed satisfied. "Okay, then I've got an order for you. I want you to keep *everybody* out of this place unless I say specifically that they can come in, you understand? The crime scene is already a mess, and I don't need any more tourists."

Anger boiled in her gut, causing her cheeks to flush. "What about the crime scene detectives from the State PD, can I let them in?"

Sheriff Hines's jaw set. "Don't be a wiseass, Deputy. You know what I meant. Now, get Ben the hell out of here."

Once outside, in the fresh air, the old man seemed to find himself again. They sat on the hood of Darla's cruiser, trying their best to ignore the bustle around them. Deputy Jackson Ryan arrived from the south end of town and made himself busy stretching crime-scene tape around the entire perimeter of the building.

The state boys had announced their interest in the case, and had promised to respond to the scene as soon as they had personnel available, but it was a pretty good bet that they'd take their sweet time. It was a robbery, after all, not a serial killing, and given the tumultuous nature of Sheriff Hines's past dealings with the

North Carolina State Police, Darla didn't expect anyone in that organization to put themselves out too much
on behalf of the Essex Sheriff's Department.

"Sheriff Hines won't be askin' nobody for nothin',"
Ryan said as he listened to the radio traffic. "If he
does, you'd best check to see how deep the snow is in
hell."

Ryan was a good man to have around if you needed
to arrest a drunken football player, but for anything re-
quiring more brain than brawn, he was the perfect
choice for stretching crime-scene tape.

"It was two kids," Ben repeated, sounding annoyed
as Darla kept pushing him for details. "That much I'm
sure of."

"You saw them?"

"I was as close to them as I am to you. I tried to stop
them, but they took my gun." He explained his encounter as well as he could, clearly trying to avoid the
mental image of the wounded boy.

"Did they say anything?" Darla asked.

"Honey, he coldcocked me the second he saw me. If
they said anything, I didn't hear it. Leastways, I didn't
pay attention." As he spoke, he rubbed the spot on his
cheek where the blood had already begun to scab over.

"But you actually saw them shoot your clerk."

"His name was Chas," Ben said. "He was a fine
young man. Wanted to go to Chapel Hill."

"That was the clerk?"

"Yes, ma'am."

"And did you actually see these robbers shoot him?"

Ben hesitated before answering. "Yes, ma'am, I as
much as saw them rob the store."

Darla cocked her head. "What does that mean, you
as much as saw them? Did you see them or not?"

"I saw them going through his pockets, trying to rob him, too."

The deputy tried to settle the wave of frustration. "Can you try not to get ahead of me, please, and just answer the question I've asked?"

"I'm trying to, Deputy." The old man looked close to tears.

She settled herself. "I know you are. Try not to think about what happened *after* the shots were fired. Tell me what happened *before* that."

Ben Maestri's gaze shifted again. He looked embarrassed.

"What's wrong?" Darla pressed.

"I was in the back room," he said. "I was in the restroom."

"Going to the bathroom?" Ordinarily, Darla would not have asked that as a follow-up, but the old man's hesitation told her that the location was about more than standard bodily functions.

"Life's been kinda stressful," Ben said. "The store's not doing so well, and even with a really terrific summer, I'm not sure that we can pull everything out."

Darla waited a couple of seconds for the rest of it, but he seemed to think that he was done. "Ben? What are you telling me?"

He closed his eyes and gave himself up to the detail that he hated to admit. "Sometimes, when life is just too much for me, I treat myself to a couple of drinks back there."

Darla wasn't sure she understood. "In the *bathroom*?"

"I'm supposed to be on the wagon," he said. His posture demonstrated his shame.

"You were in the bathroom so no one could see you."

He nodded. "Exactly."

"And how much have you treated yourself today?" Darla worked to stifle her smile. The way he smelled, everyone within a block of the old man would know that he'd been hitting the bottle. She'd been expecting something far more dramatic.

Another sigh. "More than I should have. Four drinks, maybe five."

"Whiskey?"

"Bourbon. I can handle it, though. I got a liver made of steel."

Soon to be concrete, she didn't say. This was disappointing news. Not because old Ben Maestri had fallen off the wagon, or even that he hadn't witnessed the shooting, but because every word of his testimony would be second-guessed later in a courtroom.

"So, what *did* you see?" Darla asked.

"I heard the gunshot," Ben said, "and I knew right away what was happening. I called 911 from the desk in the back room, and I grabbed my Sig from the drawer, and I went out there. I was surprised as hell to see that the robber was a little bitty thing of a girl. I told her to move away, and then *bam!* I got blindsided by the other one. A guy, but don't ask me what he looked like. Most of what I saw of him looked like a fist."

Ben's eyes drifted off again. "How can people do things like that? He was so young. Such a nice young man."

Darla agreed. Such a waste. The cash drawer was already open, for heaven's sake. Why did they have to kill the kid, too?

"Did you keep a gun out there at the register, Ben?" she asked. "Do you think maybe Chas tried to defend himself?"

Ben shook his head. "That boy never harmed a soul

in his whole life. God bless it, if I'd known that there was even a remote chance that something like this might happen, I'd have never—"

"Wait!" Darla exclaimed. Holy shit, could it be this easy? "Two teenagers, right? A boy and a girl?"

"I already told you, I didn't hear—"

Darla didn't wait for him to finish the thought. It didn't matter. She dashed around to the front seat of her cruiser and reached in for the clipboard that was forever propped in the center console. She had it in her hand when she came back to Ben. "We got word this morning on a couple of runaways," she explained. "Now I'm going to show you a picture, and I want you to look at it carefully. If you—"

"That's them!" Ben declared. He could see it already from his oblique angle on the clipboard. "That's them, I swear to God. Oh, Jesus, that's the two I saw."

The old man's outburst startled her. "I know you're anxious for the killers to be caught," she said, hoping to settle him down, "but it's important for you to take your time with this."

"I don't have to take my goddamn time, missy. I know who I saw, and this is them."

Darla thought of asking him one more time, but the look of exasperation told her that he was as sure as anyone could be.

"We got this on the wire this morning," Darla explained. "We're halfway home." As she spoke, she walked toward the front doors.

Jackson Ryan yelled, "Hey! You can't go in there!" But she'd already pulled it open.

The door pinged as she walked through, and she was surprised to see the sheriff leaning against the counter, his expression vacant, clearly unnerved. He looked up at the sound of the bell and growled, "I thought I told you to stay out of here."

"Are you okay, Sheriff?"

He glared at her. "Don't try to mother me, Deputy. Even my mother didn't enjoy the experience."

"You just look kinda—"

"There's no videotape in the recorder, okay?" It sounded as if he'd intended to shout the words, but couldn't muster the energy. "I got a dead boy on my hands, and the one good shot we had at catching his killer was screwed up because a drunk old man was too lazy to load his damn security machine."

"We won't need it." Darla started to take a step closer as she announced the news, but stopped as Chas Delphin's corpse came into view. "I got a positive ID from Ben. It's those runaway kids who came over the wire this morning." She checked the clipboard again. "Brad Ward, aka Brad Dougherty, and Nicolette Janssen. She's from upstate New York, he's from Michigan."

Sheriff Hines looked confused as he processed the information through his head. "That's awfully fast, Deputy. Are you sure that Ben knows what he's talking about?"

"I showed him the pictures, and he was certain. Aggressively certain. I think these are our perps, Sheriff."

Hines still did not seem convinced. In fact, he seemed kind of lost, as if he'd checked out of reality.

Darla continued, "Ben told me that the killers were rifling through Chas's pockets. Maybe they left some prints behind. If we can get a positive hit from that, then we're home free. We don't even need the video."

Sheriff Hines considered that, and a smile blossomed on his face. "You're right," he said. "If we can put some known fugitives here on the scene, then we've got all the evidence we need, don't we?"

"Exactly."

"Yes," he said. "That's really very good, isn't it? That's excellent, in fact." The smile became a grin. "Okay, Darla, here's what I want you to do. Get the information out on the net that these escapees are murderers and that they're expected to be in the area. Have Deputy Jackson bring me the fingerprint kit out of the trunk of my cruiser and we'll get to work on that part of it."

"You want me to put in a request for the State PD crime lab?"

Hines gave her a look. "This one's ours, Deputy," he said. "Even a hick backwoods sheriff like me knows how to lift a fingerprint."

Darla understood the subtext: This was an election year, and given the events of the past couple of days—not to mention the faltering economy, the drop-off in tourist dollars, and all the other crap that led voters to seek changes in November—it wouldn't harm Sheriff Frank Hines one bit to have a solid success on his record.

"Okay," Darla said. "I figure they've got a twenty-, thirty-minute head start at best. There's a good chance we can close this one today."

The sheriff smiled. "Good work, Deputy," he said. "Damn good work."

Those were words that Darla Sweet never thought she'd hear, uttered by a man who did not speak them easily. The warmth they brought surprised her. "Oh, and listen, Sheriff," she said, stopping when she was halfway to the door and turning to face him. "I spoke to your wife this morning—"

Hines waved her off. "I'm sorry about that. It never should have happened."

"That's okay, really. I just wanted you to know that there's nothing for you to worry about."

The sheriff gave a tired smile. "Darla, I've got a son experimenting with drugs in an election year. He's been gifted with a pitching arm that he's not interested in using, and he's solidly on the path that's going to keep him from ever escaping this little burg. I've got plenty to worry about. But it's my problem, not yours. I just panicked a little, is all."

She didn't know what to say. Suddenly, she'd become one of the sheriff's confidants. "I think anyone would, under the circumstances. I put myself in your circumstance and—"

"Don't," he interrupted. "Don't put yourself in my head, Deputy. I don't want you there. What I want is for you to get your ass out on the street and find the bastards who did this."

She'd pushed too hard. "You got it," she said. "I'll get right on it." She ignored the urge to apologize.

"And Deputy? Make it clear that these are heartless killers, okay? Make it clear that they shot and killed an unarmed teenager just to get a few dollars out of the till. Make sure that responding officers react accordingly."

Darla scowled. "Accordingly?"

"If there's more blood to be spilled, I want it to be theirs."

Chapter Nineteen

On its best day, Interstate 95 was ugly. Parts of it were less ugly than others, but from origin to terminus, it was thousands of miles of monotony broken only by the occasional view of open road. In this weather, with the rain falling in sheets, it was an exercise in white-knuckle driving. The worst problem was the spray from the tractor trailers, which rendered Carter's windshield nearly opaque.

Carter hoped he wasn't being foolish driving all this distance without knowing where he was going. How did he know he wasn't heading in exactly the wrong direction? Sure, the smart money said that Brad and Nicki were probably heading for the beach, but who was to say that the terrible weather hadn't scared them off toward an entirely different compass point? Who was to say that they weren't still hanging around Brookfield, waiting for the heat to disappear?

No one could say anything for sure, but motion was better than sitting still. Carter wondered when the pressure would make him implode.

When he was a younger man, Carter harbored dreams

of suburban contentment. Unlike so many in the office of the district attorney, he had no designs on wealth or fame or political advancement. He was what he'd come to realize was the last of a dying breed—a public servant whose chief sense of gratification came from serving the public. He took pride in putting bad guys behind bars.

The whole idea was to have a plain vanilla life, sweet but ordinary. The linchpin, though, was always the family. God knew he loved Jenny, and Jenny knew it, too. In retrospect, he wasn't at all sure that he could say the same about Nicki. He'd left far too many of the child-rearing chores to her mother, always promising to make it right just as soon as he crossed the next hurdle.

But the hurdles never ended. Somehow, in mere moments, seventeen years had passed, and he was all alone, struggling to temper bonds with his daughter that should have been forged when she was a toddler.

Every time he thought that life had gotten as bad as it possibly could, he discovered that there was no bottom to the well of badness. Honest to God, he just didn't know how much more of this he could take.

"Get a grip," he told himself, embarrassed that he'd spoken aloud. Who was he to feel sorry for himself, when Nicki was staring down the tunnel at her own death? It was terrible, he knew, but more and more he'd come to think of Jenny and Nicki as the lucky ones. For them, the pain had stopped, or soon would. For Carter, the misery and loneliness had no foreseeable expiration date.

The bungled transplant call was the end of the line for Carter. It was the goal for which he and Nicki had focused everything for so long, and when the call finally came, he'd allowed himself to smile.

Then, when the heart and lungs were ripped from

their hands, it was as if his soul had been ripped from his body. There was nothing left anymore. There was no hope. When he replayed the details of last night's argument in his head—no, wait, that was two nights ago, wasn't it?—he found that the specific words were gone, evaporated from his mind into the cloud of so many similar screaming matches. But the desperation in Nicki's voice remained etched forever in every synapse: All she wanted was to be normal.

Even in the panicky, giddy ride to the hospital for her transplants, her nervous chatter had dealt not with life in its metaphysical form, but in terms of being able to go to college next year, with a specific eye on spring break. This, from a girl who'd never attended anything close to a spring break.

Carter hated himself for never having taken his daughter to the beach himself. She had in fact seen it several times, en route to Italy one year and to Disney World another, but she'd never touched it. Neither Carter nor Jenny were all that fond of the water, and together, they'd justified their dismissal of a beach vacation by telling Nicki that she had a whole lifetime in which to make up for lost time at the beach.

A whole lifetime. *My ass*.

The ring of his cell phone brought Carter back to the here and now. He pulled it from the clip on his belt and flipped it open. "Janssen."

"Hello, Carter, this is Warren Michaels. I've got some troubling news for you."

As he listened, it was all Carter could do to keep his vehicle on the road.

The sky was the color of lead. Brad and Nicki didn't make it five miles down Shore Road before heavy drops started to hammer the windshield. Three minutes after that, the skies erupted. Rain fell in torrents. They had no choice but to pull to the side of the road and stretch the fabric top over the Sebring. It was time they could ill afford, but necessary. Brad told himself that the rain gave them a reason to have the windows up, and therefore be less noticeable.

"I know what you're thinking," he said when they were on the road again. Nicki hadn't said three words since they'd left the Quik Mart, and the silence made the whole nightmare even worse. His comment drew a numb gaze. "A boy was *killed*," he said, "and we witnessed it, and we need to do something about it. Is that close?"

He was right on the money.

"Well, listen. That's not our problem. If we'd come into that place ten minutes sooner or ten minutes later, we wouldn't even be giving it a second thought. That poor bastard would still be dead, and we'd still be on our way to Florida. It was a coincidence, okay? A random happening. You can't sacrifice your future because some asshole you never met fired a gun."

"But he's dead," Nicki said. No matter how many times she tried to wrap her mind around it, the concept seemed too large. Dead was forever.

"We're all gonna die sooner or later." Brad looked at Nicki, a long enough take that she began to worry about him seeing the road. "We're in the sooner category, know what I mean? So was the kid in the store. Christ, I don't even know his name."

"Chas," Nicki said. "Short for Charles, I guess."

Brad brought his eyes back around to the road. "Well, Chas just drew a low number. That sucks, but I wasn't holding the hat he drew from. Us staying free for a while won't bring him back. All it will do is keep us free."

Nicki couldn't believe what she was hearing. "Don't you even care?"

"Of course I care."

Nicki pounded her thigh with her palm. "We should have done something!"

Brad flashed anger, and then his features softened. "You did do something, Nicki. You held his hand and stroked his head and made sure that he didn't die alone. You made sure that somebody noticed his pain, and you eased him over to whatever lies on the other side. You did everything that could have been done."

Nicki looked at him, shocked.

"I care, Nicki. I really do. But he'd be no less dead if we'd hung around there. Don't you understand that? It'd be different if we were patching his wound, or keeping him from bleeding to death or doing CPR or something. But dead plus one minute is the same as dead plus fifty years. We *had* to leave."

"What about the old guy?" Nicki asked.

"What about him?"

"He thinks that we did the shooting."

"All the more reason to get the hell out of there," Brad said. "The tape will show it wasn't us. That'll be the first thing the cops look at, and when they see what happened, you'll be off the hook. I, on the other hand, will be one giant step closer to getting nailed again."

They fell silent. Nicki couldn't clear the image of the dead boy out of her mind.

"Do you want me to drop you off and go it alone?" Brad asked.

Nicki looked at him, surprised. "No."

"It's getting a lot hotter than you signed on for," he

added. "I just thought— Well, I want you to know there's no hard feelings if you want to just bag it. For you, this is like spring break. For me, it's life and death. If they get too close—" He cut himself off before he said something he might regret.

The spring break line pissed her off. "Jesus, Brad, I'm dying. That's not exactly a vacation."

"I didn't mean it that way," he said. "I just meant that the stakes are different for you. If this all goes to shit, you get to go home. I don't exactly have that option."

Nicki's gut seized with the tone of his voice. There was a finality to it, a subtext that terrified her. "What are you saying?"

Brad returned his eyes to the road. "Forget it."

"No, I won't forget it. What are you telling me?"

"I'm telling you exactly what I said. I'm not going back to prison."

"Neither am I."

Brad kept his eyes on the road as he said, "It's not the same."

There it was again. "So, what, you're going to kill yourself if the cops get too close?"

He didn't answer.

"That's crazy, Brad. That's totally insane."

She saw the muscles in his jaw flex as he worked to swallow anger. "You haven't been there, Nicki. You don't know."

"Oh, I think I have a pretty good idea."

"Well, you're wrong," he snapped. "You think that because you're sick, you've got the shittiest deal in the world. Trust me. It can get a lot worse than that."

"Spoken like somebody who has a life ahead of him," Nicki said. It was one of the most powerful lines in her repertoire, guaranteed to shut down an argument, the one verbal thrust for which there was no parry.

But Brad didn't back down. "Oh, for Christ's sake, I'm already dead. Don't you get it? My clock started ticking the second I walked out of prison. It's just a matter of time. There *is* no transplant that can prolong anything for me. Today, tomorrow, next week, one way or the other, I'm dead."

"But you can't do that," Nicki argued. "It's too . . ." She struggled for the right word. "Easy."

Brad laughed. "If it were easy, I'd have done it by now. I'd have done it after my first week in the joint. Killing yourself might be a lot of things, but easy isn't one of them."

Nicki opened her mouth to speak, then shut it again. What was there to say?

"And you're a fine one to talk about easy. If you believed the crap you're slinging you'd be in a hospital, squeezing out every drop of hope. Yet, here you are."

The words hit Nicki hard. She'd never thought about this adventure with Brad being a weird kind of extended suicide pact. Now that she did think about it, she didn't like it at all. "It doesn't matter for me," she said. "I've got a year. Maybe. At best. It might as well be a week or a second. You could have another fifty, seventy-five years ahead of you."

Brad scowled. "I think you really think that's a good thing." He looked at her. "I'm twenty-two years old, Nicki. Do you realize that if the State of Michigan has its way, I'll be forty-six before I even get my first parole hearing? And nobody ever gets out on their first hearing. I can't do that. I *can't*."

"Won't," Nicki corrected.

He shrugged. "Okay, I *won't* spend the rest of my

life in prison, just as I *won't* sit here and argue the point with you. That's not to piss you off, that's just the way it is. You've never lived with that kind of violence, and until you have, there's no way for you to understand."

Nicki could tell from his body language that this discussion was over. Maybe the smart play for her really would be to just walk away. Brad was a *criminal,* for God's sake. A cute criminal, and sweet and mostly kind, but everything about him was criminal. He stole cars, he lashed out at old men. He participated in armed robberies where people were killed. Having seen for herself how horrendous a thing that was to do, how could she possibly continue this way?

They were barely moving. All she had to do was open the door, and it would be all over. She wasn't a prisoner. Pull the handle, open the door, take a step, and there you go. There was no way this could turn out well, not for either of them. If Nicki had a brain in her head, she'd get as far away from Brad as she could, and head on back to—

What?

What was there for her to return to? A hospital room and a pump in her gut? Slow death in a sterile room. Just like Mom.

"What are you thinking?" Brad asked, breaking the silence.

Nicki forced herself to look right at him as she answered. "You never laughed at me," she said.

"Huh?"

She felt the heat rising in her cheeks. "I was trying to figure out a reason to stay here, a reason not to run back like a scared little girl."

Confusion etched Brad's brow. "When didn't I laugh?"

"You know, back then. Back in the old days, when you lived next door and I was drooling over you. When I pretended to be so worldly, talking about things I thought would impress you, you never laughed. You could have. I was always afraid that you would, but it would have destroyed me."

"This is a high-price reward for showing a little restraint."

Nicki was getting to the difficult part. "That's just part of it. You were the boy of my dreams."

Brad grew uncomfortable, shifting in his seat.

She went on, "I used to do those crazy things, like writing my name as Nicolette Ward, and I used to hate myself for it, because I knew that nobody as gorgeous as you would ever think twice about me."

He groaned, "Oh, God."

"I know. It was puppy love. But even after you left, I used to dream that we'd get married and we'd go on long drives, just the two of us."

He shifted uncomfortably again.

"This is the dream," she said. "Silly, huh?"

Brad didn't know what to say.

"Too much information?" Nicki ventured.

He answered, "No! I guess maybe I'm just not all that comfortable with the idea of being 'gorgeous.'"

They shared a laugh. "Your turn," Nicki said. "What happened to your parents?" The question seemed to startle him, so she added, "I know your mother's in jail, but I don't know anything else."

He quipped, "I guess that jail thing is the family business."

"What did she do?"

"She sold drugs to the wrong guy. Sold a lot of them, in fact, got hit on a federal beef and sent up for like, forever."

"Oh, that's awful."

"Last time I saw her, I was eight. I never did know who my dad was. I don't think my mother did, either. At least she couldn't narrow it down to one paying customer."

Nicki gasped. "You mean she was a pros . . ." She couldn't bring herself to say the word.

"Prostitute? No, she was a whore. A crack whore at that. I don't remember a single day when I could look in her face and not see her stoned. She decided to keep me around for the welfare money. She got a check every month to take care of me." He scoffed. "Now, there was money well spent."

"She spent it on drugs instead?"

"I don't know what the hell she spent it on." As he mined deeper into the memories, Brad's tone hardened, and the muscles in his jaw flexed. "But it wasn't on dinners and birthday cakes, I can tell you that. Neighbors were the only reason I didn't starve to death. They fed me and the other stray cats. All of us alive because nobody got around to putting us in a sack and drowning us in the river."

It was an image that hit Nicki hard. No wonder Brad had learned how to hot-wire cars. No wonder he could compartmentalize his thoughts so well.

"When they first arrested her, I was scared to death," Brad continued. "I didn't know what would become of me. I didn't know where I would live, or how I was going to do anything. I mean, my mom wasn't good for anything useful, but at least she was *there,* you know? At least there was another heartbeat in the room at night. But then this nice social worker—her name was Alice—took me away from our apartment, and put me in this group home, just for one night. She actually stayed in the room with me.

"Alice settled me down by telling me how they'd get help for Mom, and how they'd get all the drugs out of her system so she could be healthy again. And in the meantime, I would be sent to live with some other really nice people. You know? Like, I was going to be taken in by the Brady Bunch or something. I had these images in my head—I mean, really, this is how I thought—I had these images in my head of me tossing a ball around in some front yard somewhere, hanging out in the neighborhoods where kids like me never had a chance in hell of living. It was like I'd get this really big jump start on my life. And then, after Mom was healthy again, she'd join us, and everything would be just like it was on television.

"Then I hit the first foster home. Nice enough people—I mean, they fed me and didn't scream at me—but they were both four hundred years old and smelled like dirty underwear. That's what I remember most about them, seriously. They smelled like dirty underwear."

Nicki laughed. "How pleasant."

"No, it wasn't. I stayed there for a few days, I guess, maybe a few weeks, they all run together after a while. They drove me to a new school where I'd never been before, with kids who only knew that I was somebody's foster. That meant I was fair game for anything anyone wanted to do. Who's gonna complain to the principal, right?"

"What, did they beat you up and stuff?"

"Only at the beginning. This 'nobody cares' shit cuts both way, you know? It wasn't like I was gonna get in trouble at home if I got expelled from school. There's nothing like getting beat up a few times yourself to teach you how to beat the shit out of others. I was never in one school long enough to have any friends, so it was fine with me to have only enemies. Just so long as they were all scared shitless of me. In the long run, it's easiest to have one really nasty, nose-crushing, ball-busting fight at the beginning, so that everybody knows to stay the hell away from you. When you're the new kid and you're nice, people just think you're a pussy."

"So, how many fights did you get into?"

Brad launched a bitter laugh. "Hundreds. Thousands, maybe. How many days are there in a school year? Times how many years in school. I was the baddest guy in the building, all the time. It was the way I survived."

A station wagon on their left was pacing the Sebring as the traffic crept along, its turn signal blinking relentlessly. When Brad paused to let a space open up in front, the guy behind them blasted them with his horn. Nicki spun in her seat and gave the guy the finger.

"Way to go," Brad laughed.

"Fastest finger in New York." She let a moment pass before pressing for more. "What happened to you after you left the Bensons?"

Brad didn't want to go there. "You want the first day or the second?"

"There's a difference?"

Brad considered changing the subject, and then just went for it. What the hell. "The Bensons were fed up with me. All of the foster families got fed up with me. It's my special gift. But giving the devil his due, they did keep me for almost two years. That was, like, eight months longer than anyone else. Anyway, the burglary beef was the final straw, I guess, and your father's never-ending desire to make his house a convent. Since I was seventeen then, just a few months from official sorry-pal-you're-on-your-own emancipation, the social workers didn't want to endanger another family by putting me in with them, so they sent me to another group home."

"A detention center?"

"Not really, but it might as well have been. Nasty-ass place. One thing for sure, I wasn't the baddest guy in the house anymore. There, I wasn't even in the top ten. So, after one night, I said screw it. I packed my stuff into my school backpack, walked out the door in the morning, and never checked back in. I lived on the streets after that."

Nicki looked horrified.

"It's not that bad," he said, shooting her a smile. Then he had to hit his brakes hard to keep from hitting that station wagon, whose driver had finally decided to move over.

"It has to be scary," Nicki said.

Brad shrugged. "You learn who to stay away from, and who you can trust. I'll tell you what surprised the hell out of me is that there really is a homeless community. Just like you get to know people in your neighborhood because you go to the same clubs or the same church, us street bums do okay taking care of each other."

"How did you live? On handouts?"

"I wish. You see, that's what the smart ones do. You can make a pretty decent living panhandling if you're not one of the drooling crazies. My age kinda worked against me there. People look at a homeless guy who's sixty and they feel sorry for him. Try that when you're a teenager, and you just get a lot of lectures about your work ethic."

He intercepted the look that flashed across Nicki's face.

"You're one of them, aren't you?" He laughed. "You're one of the lecturers."

"Well, why should you get handouts when you're perfectly capable of working?"

"What was I going to do? I couldn't put my hands on a school transcript if I had to, so I can't even qualify as a high school graduate. If you pick the right street corner, you can get double minimum wage, and you don't have to clean baby vomit off the fast food booth."

"What about your dignity?"

This time, the smile erupted into a laugh. "Okay, well, there are early casualties to certain lifestyles. My dignity stopped being important around the time when my mother started screwing strangers in our living room."

"God, that's awful. So, how did the prison thing happen?"

"I was stupid. Begging bored me. It might keep food in my belly, and a buzz in my head from time to time, but I gotta tell you: It's really freaking boring. I needed a business to get into. Something I knew how to do." He glanced over at Nicki and waited for her to connect the dots for herself.

"Drugs?"

"Bingo. The family business. You know what they say. Do what you know. So, I did."

"You're lucky you weren't killed."

"I was in the game for precisely one day."

"You're kidding. Why?"

"My very first customer was a cop."

"No way."

"I swear. I walked right up to this guy, offered him a nickel bag, took his money, and then every cop on the planet swooped down on me."

"You were in Michigan then?"

"No, that was in New York. Rikers country. Anyway, I didn't have to do much time. A few months, and then a long probation, which I promptly ducked, but nobody seemed to care."

"Getting away seems to be another one of your special gifts."

"Well, I certainly hope so. I never want to do anybody harm. I never really want to get in trouble. It's just that whenever I see an opportunity, I somehow get involved only on the dark side of it. Everybody dreams of being an entrepreneur, right? I just chose a bad product."

"That happened to be illegal."

His eyebrows climbed his forehead. "Look who's sounding like a prosecutor."

Nicki blushed.

"All the really profitable stuff is either already taken, or it's illegal. And I didn't have a lot of seed capital, as they say."

"You don't even sound repentant," Nicki said. Her tone was leaden with accusation.

"About what? Surviving?"

"About being irresponsible."

Brad laughed. "Oh, *responsibility*. And who are we supposed to be responsible for? Do you think that old Chas back there felt responsible for earning money for college or for a new car, and then ended up bleeding to death on a cold floor? Life isn't about responsibility, Nicki. Life is about *living*, and doing whatever it takes to make sure you end the day the way you want to end it. It's why I'll never go back to prison. You own nothing in that place, not even your life. Every day in prison is just another routine, highlighted by psychos who want to stick you with either a knife or a dick."

Nicki listened to his rant, mesmerized not so much by his message as by his commitment to it. It's what she liked most about him; *loved* most about him. He lived in a world where there was no doubt. You decided what you were going to do, and then you did it; if that pissed people off, then too bad for the pissed-off people. She marveled how anyone could talk about things that were so clearly wrong, yet make them sound so right. Every time she tried to form an argument in her head, it ended up sounding like an empty platitude.

"So, now you know what an asshole I am," Brad said, breaking yet another thoughtful silence. "You still up for the weird adventure?"

She looked at him long and hard, searching for the hint that he was something other than what he portrayed himself to be. What she saw was a little boy in a man's body, a kid who never discovered his own childhood and instead constructed a world where breaking laws was fine so long as you broke them for the right reason. He was Robin Hood meets Peter Pan. She had no business staying here with him. This was the road to ruin, the road to hell.

"I'm up for it all," she said.

But she was looking sicker and sicker. Maybe not so bad that strangers would notice, but Brad could see it around her eyes.

Chapter Twenty

Carter didn't even slow his stride as he showed his badge to the cop out front and ducked under the crime-scene tape. The name tag over the deputy's pocket read Ryan, and he seemed to be pissed that he'd drawn guard duty.

"Whoa," Ryan said. "Just where do you think you're going?"

"I'm with the district attorney's office," he said.

The deputy scowled and took a closer look at the badge. "That says you're from New York."

Carter didn't argue. "That's right. My daughter was allegedly involved in this crime, and I understand that you people think she killed someone." On the other side of the door, Carter could just barely make out the sounds of an ongoing argument.

"What's your name?"

"Carter Janssen. I'm Nicolette Janssen's father." In his first stroke of positive luck, Carter had been only thirty-five minutes away when he'd gotten the call from Michaels.

"I see." Jackson Ryan looked at the identification wallet one more time, as if to assure himself that he was talking to the right guy. "You'll need to speak with Sheriff Hines."

"I'd love to. Is that him there?" He nodded to the thickset man in the khaki uniform.

"Yes, but he's busy."

"Don't you think he'd want to talk to me?"

Deputy Ryan considered that. "Wait here."

"Thank you."

The deputy walked through the front doors. Carter followed two steps behind.

The old man locked in verbal combat with the sheriff looked like hell, red-faced and madder than a hornet. His left eye was black and swollen. Spittle flew from the old man's mouth as he spoke. "I swear to God, Frank, if you accuse me of being senile one more time, I'm gonna punch you in the nose."

Sheriff Hines seemed amused as he held out his palms to ward off the old man's attack. "I'm not saying you're senile, Ben. I'm saying you're drunk."

"And I'm telling you there was a tape in that machine this morning!"

"Okay, then. What happened to it?"

"I don't know!"

Another uniformed officer, this one a woman in her twenties who hadn't quite found the right combination of macho and feminine to really be attractive, joined the conversation. "Mr. Maestri," she said.

The old man turned away from the sheriff to face the deputy.

"Is it possible that the robbers went back there and took the tape?"

"Absolutely not," he said. "I'd have seen that. The only person who could've taken the tape is the sheriff here."

Behind the old man, a team of four uniformed cops

sifted through debris and photographed the scene. They all stopped working at Ben Maestri's comment and looked up, clearly expecting an emotional show from the sheriff. Carter thought he saw the cop's back stiffen, but otherwise, he seemed to take it in stride.

Carter asked, "Is there a back door?"

All eyes turned toward the newcomer. "Who the hell is this?" the sheriff demanded.

Deputy Ryan jumped a little. "Oh. Uh, excuse me, Sheriff, but this man here says that he's the father of one of the perpetrators."

"Alleged perpetrators," Carter corrected. "There's no way she did any of this."

"What's he doing here?"

"I can speak for myself," Carter said. He produced his badge again, and handed it to Hines. "I'm Assistant District Attorney Carter Janssen, from Pitcairn County, New York."

The lady cop tried to get a look at the credentials, but Hines snapped the case shut before she had a chance, and handed it back to Carter. "What are you doing here?"

Carter passed the badge case to Darla Sweet. "My daughter is a runaway," he explained. "I was on my way south when I got a call from a colleague in Virginia that you had put out a multistate BOLO for her."

"So, you just happened to be in the neighborhood?" Hines asked, looking skeptical.

"Something like that. But I'm here to tell you that you're barking up the wrong tree." He accepted Darla's return of his badge case.

"And why is that?" Hines asked.

"She'd never hurt a soul, Sheriff. She's a model student." Carter recognized how naïve that sounded, but it was the truth.

"A model student *and* a runaway?" the sheriff baited. "Unusual combination."

Carter had been expecting a little professional deference here, or at least a moderate show of sympathy, but he got none of it from Sheriff Hines. The temper regulator in the back of his brain began to twitch. "There are extenuating circumstances," he said.

"Extenuating enough to justify murder?" There was a hardness to Hines's eyes that boiled Carter's blood. He'd dealt with dozens of these God-complex cops over the years, and there wasn't a single one of them he didn't hate.

Carter didn't rise to the bait. "You have a witness?"

"Right here," said the old man.

Carter offered his hand. "Carter Janssen."

"Ben Maestri." He smelled like a dirty rug.

"Tell me what you saw," Carter said. His tone carried an implied "please."

"The hell are you doing?" the sheriff said. "This ain't New York, Counselor. You got no jurisdiction here."

"And if this is your only witness, you've got no case. I heard you say yourself that he's drunk."

"That don't mean I didn't see what I saw," Ben said. "There's a videotape of it, too, 'cept Barney Fife here lost it."

Hines ignored Ben, while Darla touched the old man's arm. The gesture said that this was neither the time nor the place for aggression.

Carter's stomach flipped at the thought. "You've got a video of my daughter shooting the clerk?" It was beyond rationality that such could be the case.

"Apparently he never loaded the machine," Darla said.

"Don't you start, too!" Ben yelled.

Everyone ignored him. The sheriff said, "Mr. Janssen, I know this is difficult for you, and you know that you have no right to be here. You're interfering. Still, you need to know that it's more than what Ben saw or didn't see. I've also got fingerprints belonging to Nicolette Janssen and to Bradley Ward—"

"You can't possibly have fingerprints on Nicki. She's never been fingerprinted."

The sheriff glanced to Darla, who opened the plastic cover on her clipboard and found the applicable notation. "Big Top Elementary School. Looks like she was in the sixth grade."

That was ridiculous. Nicki had never been involved in the justice system. Then he remembered. He'd had her fingerprinted as part of the frenzy a few years back about kids being kidnapped. The police sold the program to the community as a way to keep kids safe, when in fact its real purpose was to facilitate identification of human remains. It had been Jenny's idea; Carter had never been comfortable with the whole notion. "Those records aren't in any database."

Darla answered this one. "No, sir, they're not. But since we already had word to be on the lookout for these two in particular, and since I already got a positive ID on the photos that went out on the wire this morning, it was merely a matter of confirming."

It just was not possible. "Maybe they just stopped in for a soda or something, and they left their prints," Carter offered. "There must be thousands of fingerprints in a place like this."

"The fingerprints were in blood, Mr. Janssen." Darla delivered the news softly.

Carter opened his mouth to argue, but he had nothing to say. He just stared, his mind unable to grasp it all.

"I'll have to ask you to step outside now, sir," Hines said, and he motioned to Deputy Ryan.

The deputy from outside put his hand on Carter's arm. Carter didn't resist, but he didn't move, either. He looked around the ravaged room at the toppled racks and the blood on the floor. Mercifully, the body had already been removed. "Nicki could not have done this," he said. "She's not capable of this kind of violence."

"We don't suspect otherwise, sir," Hines said. Carter's eyes lit up at what he thought might be a glimmer of hope, but it snuffed itself when the sheriff said, "But she's an accessory for sure. In an aggravated capital murder. If you have any idea where she is, you'd be wise to help us find her before this really spirals out of control."

Carter knew the implications. For the difference in penalty between capital murder and accessory before the fact, Nicki might have pulled the trigger herself.

"Sheriff," he said, "if I knew where she was, none of this would have happened."

"This isn't good," Brad said.

Nicki stirred at the sound of his words, unaware that she had fallen asleep. They'd just rounded a sand dune and were approaching the Matoaka Fishing Pier when they got a good look at what was causing the traffic backup. A hundred yards ahead, a frenetic display of blue lights blocked the roadway.

"An accident?" Nicki asked.

Brad squinted to see. "I don't know. Looks more like a roadblock to me."

"Searching for us?"

"What do you think?" That sharpness had returned to his voice. Brad slapped the turn signal and turned into the parking lot of the fishing pier. The wind-ravaged sign boasted the best crab cakes and onion rings in the Outer Banks.

"What are you going to do?"

"I don't know. Something. Ask me what we're *not* going to do. I have a better answer for that."

Attached to the fishing pier was modern-looking video rental store. Not a national chain, but the neon sign announced that tourists were welcome.

"We need current information," Brad said. "I'm gonna chat up the folks inside. You still hungry?"

It was nearly four o'clock by Nicki's watch, and at the mention of food, she remembered how famished she'd been before the incident at the Quik Mart. "I'm starving," she said, and then she felt guilty for even thinking about something as mundane as food.

As they walked up the ramp to the front door of the fishing pier restaurant, Nicki couldn't decide if the combined aromas of salt air and fish were appetizing or repulsive. The rain drenched her clothing, but without the capacity to run, she just endured. Brad made no comment as he matched her slow gait.

The floor tiles popped under their feet as they crossed the sagging lobby, past the ancient Pac-Man machine in the corner on the right, and the racks of fishing supplies on the left, toward the door with the sign, EAT HERE.

Ceiling fans churned in a futile attempt to draw cooler air into the dingy dining room. Given the hour, precious few people were eating. In fact, of the half-dozen patrons bellied up to the bar, not a single one was munching anything but alcohol.

A busty woman in a BEAT ARMY T-shirt shot them a

snaggletoothed grin as they entered. "You gonna want food?" she asked.

"Yes, please," Nicki said. She added a smile as an afterthought.

"I'm Mandy," the woman said. "Just sit anywhere and I'll be out to take your order in a shake."

The walk and the stress had taken a worse toll than Nicki had feared. She felt utterly wiped by the time they got to the first table, but Brad didn't want to sit there. "Let's go where we can watch out the front window," he said. Now that they were inside, he moved quickly, leaving Nicki to fend for herself.

By the time she joined him, fifteen seconds later, he was watching the traffic. "This is gonna be tough," he said. "They're gonna have pictures of me, and with the traffic moving this slow, they must be looking inside every vehicle. I don't know how—"

He clipped off his words as Mandy approached with two menus. "That's some storm, ain't it?" she said. Between the water on the outside of the windows and the condensation on the inside, it was tough to see anything out there.

"That's some traffic," Brad countered. "Looks like there's a big accident up the road."

Mandy flipped the menus on the table as if she were dealing a couple of cards. "That ain't an accident. That's a roadblock. We got us a manhunt for a couple of killers. Robbed a convenience store up in Essex, killed the clerk. Terrible thing."

Nicki gasped before she could stop it. *What about the videotape?*

The gasp brought a look from Brad, but Mandy didn't seem to notice. "I heard they was looking for two kids. A couple. A boy and a girl." She paused and her eyes narrowed. "Couldn't be you two, could it?"

The inside of Nicki's mouth turned to chalk.

Brad smiled. He rubbed his chin dramatically and pretended to think it through. "Let's see, what's today, Saturday? The kidnapping was on Monday, the arson on Tuesday, the bank robbery on Wednesday . . . Nope, we're not scheduled to rob the convenience store till next Thursday."

If Mandy saw the horror in Nicki's eyes, she didn't show it. What she did show was genuine amusement. "Okay, smarty, do you know what you want?"

"Are they really the best crab cakes in the Outer Banks?"

The waitress winked. "Guaranteed to be the best in the restaurant, anyway."

"Sold," Brad said.

The waitress wrote something on her pad, then turned to Nicki. "Are you all right, missy? You don't look so good."

Nicki forced a smile. "Summer flu," she said. She'd never been any good at lying and she knew that Mandy must have seen right through her. "How about just a Diet Coke and an extra fork for his crab cakes?"

Mandy shook her head. "They're not big enough to share," she said.

"That's okay. I'm not very hungry."

The waitress made a clucking sound. "Missy, a girl your size needs to eat. With the winds that are comin', your boyfriend's gonna have to tie a string to your ankle and fly you like a kite." She waited for Nicki to change her mind.

"Bring a second order for her," Brad said.

He waited till Mandy walked away then leaned

into the table and hissed, "Jesus, Nicki, that was . . . not smart." He stumbled over the word *stupid,* knowing that it would piss her off. "Now she has a reason to remember you."

"Me!" She knew it was too loud, and she cranked it down. "What about you? Talking about the traffic, getting her to ask if we're the ones."

"Now she thinks we're not. At least not until they start flashing pictures around."

Fear and anger turned Nicki's face into an unsettling mask. She lowered her voice even further. "What happened? I thought the video was going to show that we're innocent."

She was getting better at reading his eyes, and despite his calm façade, she saw the fear. "I don't know," he said. "Maybe the tape didn't work. Maybe the cops are running false rumors so people will be scared enough to look for us. I just don't know."

"Well, now's a pretty shitty time to be ignorant," Nicki snapped. "When I wanted to stay at the scene, you were a hundred percent positive that there was no reason. What are we supposed to do now?"

Brad shot a glance over his shoulder to make sure no one was watching them. "Will you please settle down?" he hissed. "We're good for now. For the next few minutes. That gives us time to plan. I'll think of something."

"What?"

"Nicki, are you deaf? I don't know, okay? Give me some time."

Nicki threw herself into the back of her chair and crossed her arms. It was the same gesture of pouty frustration that she'd perfected when she was three years old. "I don't believe this is happening," she groused.

"Hey. You can just walk away anytime you want, remember?" He turned away from her and looked out the window again.

Nicki pushed away from the table and stood.

"Where are you going?" There was an edge of panic to his voice.

"To the bathroom. Is that okay?"

Brad hesitated. "Okay." As she walked away, he said her name and she turned again. "Don't be too long. If I see an opportunity, it'll probably happen fast. We can't stay here long."

Nicki turned and headed off to find the ladies room. She made eye contact with Mandy, who read her mind and pointed to the back corner. "Over there, dear. Be sure to hook the door because the latch doesn't work."

Nicki felt her chest tightening. Her heart was pounding at 140 beats per minute, and that was too fast. When you had this kind of condition, you became very adept at counting your pulse at a subconscious level. Without her meds, the stress was going to trigger an episode for sure.

In the galaxy of people who suffered from primary pulmonary hypertension, Nicki had been one of the luckier ones. She remained largely asymptomatic, even as the disease progressed with alarming speed. Fatigue was the chief complaint, which likewise rendered the disease difficult to diagnose before too much damage was done.

When the disease did flare up for her—Nicki called them her episodes—the telltale sign was the fluttery feeling in her chest, not entirely different than the feeling brought on by routine anxiety. Without quick intervention, the fluids would back up in her bloodstream, and then the real problems would start. Coumadin kept the backed-up fluids from clotting, while the Digoxin got rid of the fluid altogether.

The restroom had to be a hundred degrees, a hundred ten maybe. Stifling. And it reeked of sweat and fish guts. Nicki slipped the door hook into the eye that would keep it from drifting open, did her business, flushed, and washed her hands. She started to reach into her bag for her pills, but stopped herself. How could she have left them behind?

She tried to settle her heart down with a deep breath. "You can't think about the bad stuff," she whispered. "You can't panic."

But the panic was there, anyway. So was the sadness. A wave of it took her breath away. A sob choked her, and then it just started to flow from her soul. She sat on the rickety toilet, covering her mouth to keep the sound from escaping.

You can't lose it. Not now. It's too late for that.

But what else was there? What more could she do than cry?

She needed to get her breathing under control and do something to slow her heart rate or there'd be hell to pay, and very soon. She could almost feel the vessels in her chest starting to close.

By forcing herself to take long, deep breaths, Nicki was able to kill the sobs, and as they died away, she wrestled control of her breathing. It took five minutes, but the episode never fully bloomed.

Brad would be getting pissed that she was taking so long.

Nicki hadn't seen the pay phone on the wall as she'd entered the restroom, but there it was now, a dilapidated old thing that looked like it had been installed before she'd been born. The wall surrounding the phone bore dozens of names and numbers drawn in pencil, ink, and crayon. God only knew how many romances those names launched, how many arguments. She thought it poignant that each of the scrawled numbers reflected a moment in the writers' lives. There was something terribly romantic about it all.

She wondered if the phone was a sign. The same phone that had played so important a role in so many lives could end this entire nightmare. All it would take was a single call to her dad, and he could fly down and have her back at home in just a few hours. Through him, her doctor could phone in a prescription to the nearest pharmacy, and the flutteriness would go away. It was really just that simple.

It was really just that complicated.

And what about Brad? What would he do? Obviously, he'd continue running. He had a *reason* to run, and it would be so much easier without the burden of caring for her. He'd so much as said so himself. Without her meds, who knew what lay ahead?

It all made sense when she thought about it. Really, making the phone call was the only rational thing for her to do. Or it *would* be if the alternative nightmare were any less bleak. She conjured shadows of what her future would look like after the phone call: the hospital rooms, the needles, the doctors who spoke in her presence as if she weren't there. Was that what she really wanted?

Please, no. Still, no. A million times no.

But neither was this.

A boy was dead. She had to do something about that. No matter what Brad said, they had to do something. People needed to hear the real story of what happened.

Otherwise, all of this manpower being invested in tracking Brad and her was being completely wasted. The police needed to be looking for the *real* killer. If nothing else, at least Nicki knew what he was wearing.

It wasn't about her, she told herself. It wasn't about Brad. It was about justice for that kid in the store. Justice for Chas.

Chapter Twenty-one

Carter sat in his car in front of the Quik Mart, trying to force it all to make sense. He had the engine running for the air conditioner, but he wouldn't be going anywhere. Not until he got some of this madness sorted out. He sat there with his forearms resting on the steering wheel, staring without seeing through the opaque wall of water that cascaded down the windshield.

The case against Nicki, as wildly off base as it had to be, felt frighteningly strong. Ironclad. They had fingerprints, a positive identification from a witness, and a perpetrator with a past record of armed robbery and murder.

He wanted it to be impossible, but it was *entirely* feasible that Brad Ward could have done this. If Nicki had even been in the same car, that would mean an accessory charge at minimum.

It was all too big to wrap his mind around: his daughter—his only child—sentenced for a crime committed by a boy she hardly knew. Surely, a jury would show leniency under those circumstances. Maybe not. Would it matter? If the North Carolina courtrooms were as packed as their New York counterparts, it could take a year or longer for the case even to arrive on the docket. Given Nicki's out-of-state status and the seriousness of the crime, the prosecutor would undoubtedly oppose bail. Carter would have if the roles were reversed.

For Nicki, every scenario equated to life without parole.

Carter tried to think of the right thing to do. The kids were bound to be caught. If not today, then certainly this week. The search was just too hot for it to be otherwise. People might not care about teenage runaways, but they cared a whole hell of a lot about teenage murderers.

He needed to talk to her, counsel her on what her next move should be. As if he had any clue what that was.

The right thing would be to turn herself in and hope for the best. But was it the reasonable thing? If he were in her position, is that what he would do, or would he try to preserve every moment of freedom?

How was a person supposed to wade through such terrible options and come up with any kind of rational—

The chirp of his cell phone interrupted his thoughts. Reaching into his suit coat pocket, he checked the number on the display, and when he didn't recognize it, he nearly ignored it, but then pushed the connect button anyway. "Carter Janssen."

"Daddy, it's me."

The sound of Nicki's voice startled him. He shot a panicked look to all compass points to see who might be listening. "Nicki, are you okay?" He settled his tone. This was a time to be cool, a time to chat as if he were hearing from an old friend. "Where are you, honey?"

"Daddy, I'm in so much trouble. You need to help me." She was crying, but not hysterical.

"I know, sweetie," Carter said. "Just tell me where you are and I'll come right there and get you."

"I'm so sorry, Daddy. I didn't mean to . . . I'm so sorry."

"That's all right, honey. Whatever happened, there's a way to fix it. Just tell me where you are, and I'll be there as fast as I can."

"You don't understand, Daddy. Somebody's been killed. In a little town in North Carolina—"

"Essex. Yes, I know. I'm there now. I know what happened. I know who you're with, and I know that you never would have been the one to pull the trigger. Your friend Brad did that. I know. But if you—"

"No, Daddy, it's not like that. He—"

"Listen to me, Nicki. I think there's a deal to be made here. If you cooperate and turn Brad in—just tell me where you are—then I think a judge would be swayed—"

"No, Daddy!" This time, the urgency in her voice cut him off in mid-sentence. "We didn't shoot anyone. Someone else did. He wore a mask and he had a red shirt on. A sports shirt with a number on it. He came into the store, pulled a gun, and when Brad tried to stop him, the guy shot the clerk. He shot Chas."

Carter wasn't buying it. "Honey, I know you think you love this boy, and I know that you're trying to cover for him—"

"No, Daddy! Listen to me! He didn't do anything."

"Nicki, your fingerprints are all over that store. Bloody fingerprints, at that. You can't—"

"Of course they are. We tried to save him. Brad and I. We tried to stop the bleeding in his neck, but we couldn't."

"There's an eyewitness, Nicki."

"There can't be! Oh, wait. That old man? He didn't walk out till way after the shooting. He saw us trying to help, and then pointed a gun at us. That's when we ran."

Carter felt the air escaping from his lungs. This sounded like a very well-rehearsed alibi, one he'd love to buy, but his bullshit-o-meter was pinging. "Nicki, you're not making any sense. If you didn't do anything, why would you run away?" He heard himself cross-examining her and he hated himself for it. "Look, none of that matters—"

"It *does* matter, Daddy. We didn't do anything. They think we did."

"It's not his first time, Nicki." There. He put it right out there for her to see. "He's committed this same crime before."

"He only drove the car before. He never shot anybody. He's never killed *anybody*."

Carter couldn't believe what he was hearing. "You *know* about his record? You know about the robbery and his escape from prison, and you're still with him?"

"I love him, Daddy."

Carter was ready to do battle. She did *not* love him. She was seventeen years old. She wouldn't know what love was if it hit her with a rock.

But he restrained himself. This was neither the time nor the place. "I know you do," he said. The words tasted like sour milk. "And I know that you're trying to run away from the life you think is awful, but honey, you can't do it this way. It's too dangerous. Every moment you're on the run makes it that much more difficult to prove your innocence."

"There was supposed to be a video," Nicki said. "There are cameras all over the store, and we thought that the video would show that we didn't do anything but try to help."

"You thought wrong, Nicki. The cameras are there, but the man who owns the place has a drinking problem. He forgot to load the machines with videotape. Which to me is a good thing under the circumstances, because he swears that he saw your friend Brad shoot the clerk."

"That's a lie!" He could tell that Nicki was in a place where she could be overheard by the way she dialed down her tone. "He couldn't have seen that."

Carter was growing impatient. "Nicki, he's an eyewitness. He knows what he saw."

"That's just the point," Nicki said. "Even if we'd done the shooting—which we didn't—he couldn't have seen it because he wasn't there. He was in the back room. He didn't come out until Brad and I were on the floor behind the counter trying to help Chas."

Carter drummed his fingers on the steering wheel. He was beginning to see an early ray of light here. "Maybe he saw it on the monitor in the back," he offered, testing the strength of Nicki's argument.

"Then why did he stay back so long? Why didn't he come out shooting earlier?"

"Maybe he was frightened."

"Then why did he come out at all? Why didn't he wait till we were gone? Or call the police from back in the back room? Come on, Daddy, that doesn't make sense."

Carter started to say something, but stopped. She asked a very good question, one that was not adequately answered by what old Ben Maestri was saying. "But why would he lie?" he wondered aloud.

"Why would I?" Nicki responded. The question knocked him off balance. It was perhaps the most important question of all, and it hadn't even passed through his head. "I'm not a murderer, Daddy."

"I know that—"

"And I wouldn't stay with someone who is. You have to know that."

Up ahead, through the rain, Carter noticed that the female cop from inside the Quik Mart was watching him through the front window. "But you *are* with a murderer."

"Says you."

"Says a jury of his peers."

"Who convicted him on a technicality. He didn't *shoot,* Daddy, he *drove.* The law might see it as the same, but you know as well as me that it's different."

"What about the prison murder?" Carter asked. "How does he explain that?"

"What?"

He could tell just from the sound of her voice that he'd blindsided her. "So, he didn't tell you about that one?" he baited. "Maybe he's not being as forthright as you give him credit for."

"I don't believe you," Nicki said.

"He killed a fellow inmate," Carter said, recalling the brief details sent on to him by both Chris Tu and Warren Michaels. "He was about to be arrested for that when he bolted from the prison."

She was stunned. He could tell from the depth of her silence. "So, he hasn't been tried on that, then," she said. She was fishing for anything that looked like hope.

"Nicki—"

"No, he must have had a good reason. He's not a violent man. He couldn't hurt anyone. He just *couldn't.*"

The circularity of her logic made his head swim. "Look, Nicki, I know it's important for you to believe—"

"I'm not leaving him," she said. "I'm *not.*"

"Then why are you calling me?"

Again, she was flustered. "I, uh, I just thought . . . I wanted . . ."

"You wanted me to come and get you." He said this gently. He had to be careful. If he pushed her too hard, she'd hang up on him. "Just tell me where you are, sweetie. Give me the address, and I can be there in just a few minutes. Or, I can send the police." The instant that word—the *p* word—left his lips, he knew he'd blown it.

"Dammit, Daddy, it's always the same with you. You don't understand anything."

He cursed himself. In the heat of the moment, he'd said exactly what was on his mind. He *knew* better than to do that. *Dammit!* "Okay, then, no police," he said. "I won't call anyone. I promise." He spoke quickly, fearful that she'd hang up on him. "Just let me come and get you. Let me pick you up."

"And then what?" she asked.

The question caught him unprepared. "What do you mean?"

"You pick me up and then what? You said that they want to arrest me for that killing. If they really believe that I did it, then what happens after you pick me up?"

A sense of dread invaded Carter's soul. He hadn't thought it through this far yet. "Then we'll get it straightened out. Somehow."

Nicki sneaked a glance around the corner to look at Brad. The food had arrived, and he was eating. She ducked her head back before he could see her.

"Nicki, are you there? Pay attention to me."

"I'm here, Daddy. You haven't answered my question. I ran away in the first place because I didn't want to spend my last months in a hospital. I sure as heck don't want to spend them in jail." Past the rain-spattered glass on this end of the restaurant, the fishing pier extended out a hundred yards over the churning sea. She envied the few remaining holdouts whose lives allowed them the luxury of fishing in the rain.

Her father's tone lost some of its edge. "We'll show that you're innocent. We'll show that he's the one with the record of killing, and that you're deserving of mercy, under the circumstances."

"There *are* no circumstances!" It came out as a whispered shout, but a shout nonetheless, too loud for the tight surroundings. "He didn't kill anyone. I didn't and *he* didn't. Why won't you believe me?"

"But he did, sweetheart. If not at the Quik Mart this afternoon, then twice before. At *least* twice before. You can't pretend that those just go away."

Nicki's head reeled with the revelation of this second killing. Her father would do a lot to get her back, but she didn't think he'd lie. "He's gentle, Daddy. And he's sweet. He's taking care of me."

"This is taking care of you?"

"Brad saved my life. If he hadn't been there, I might have been the second victim. It's not our fault that the guy chose that moment to rob the store."

"You shouldn't have run."

"I shouldn't have had to." Nicki found herself startled by the defiance in her own voice. "Daddy, you know what's going to happen if I turn myself in. You've told me a thousand times how cops like to prove their own theories. If I step out, they're going to arrest me, and then they're not going to believe me any more than you do. I'll die in jail." That last sentence caught in her throat, and she realized that she was crying.

Something softened in her father's voice. "Dammit,"

he growled, but it wasn't a sound of anger as much as it was one of defeat. "Tell me again that he's treating you well," he said.

The tears continued to flow. "Like a princess," she said, but even she could barely hear her words.

"And promise me that the minute that changes—the *instant* it changes—you'll be on the phone to me or to the police. No second chances for him. No talking you out of it."

Nicki's voice was thick. "I promise."

She could see the expression in his face, his eyes closed, the muscles in his jaw flexing as he clenched his teeth. "Tell me again what happened. Every detail."

It took another five minutes, but she told him everything about the robbery. When she left something out, he prodded her to fill in the blanks. She swore again that she was safe, but lied when he asked how she was feeling.

"How are you going to get more meds?" he asked.

She realized that he'd probably seen the bottles she'd left behind. "We don't know," she said. "We haven't thought that far ahead. It's not a problem yet, though."

"Yes, it is. I can hear it in your voice. I can hear it in your breathing."

Nicki smiled. "Okay, it's not a *big* problem yet."

"I have the bottles," Carter said. "Maybe we could meet somewhere and I could hand them off to you."

Nicki sensed a scam. She was probably a terrible person for thinking such a thing, but her mind conjured a picture of a trap: her dad handing over her meds while a hundred cops lay hidden in the shadows, watching.

Carter interpreted her silence for what it was. "Keep

it in mind," he said. "It's an option. I don't mean to push. I just want you to know that I'm always a phone call away."

There was a tenderness in her dad's voice that Nicki had rarely heard. In the past, there'd been orders and occasional grunts. Now he sounded like . . . a father. "I love you, Daddy," she said, and the tears returned.

"I love you, too," he rasped back. "More than that, I miss you." He cleared his throat. "You be careful."

"I will," she said. "I promise."

As she hung up the phone she sensed the shadow that was Brad. When she turned to face him, his expression was plain, entirely neutral. "That your dad?" he asked.

She nodded. The emotions from the call were still too raw to reduce into words.

He put his hands into his pockets. "So, what's the deal? Are you staying or going?"

Looking at him standing there in the shadows of the little phone alcove, Nicki felt her gaze grow hot. "You lied to me," she said.

He looked shocked. "What are you talking about?"

She pushed past him, heading out toward the pier. "Hey," he called, hurrying after her. "Where are you going? What's wrong? What did he say?"

After the stifling heat of the restaurant, the chill of the torrential rain made Nicki gasp. She didn't *know* where she was going, but anyplace indoors had become too crowded. She needed space, fresh air.

Brad kept with her step for step as they hurried out onto the pier. Their clothes became saturated within seconds. "Nicki, come on. Talk to me. What happened? What did your father tell you?"

She stopped short, causing a collision. "Don't ask me what he told me," she spat. "Cough up what you *didn't* tell me."

Brad was oblivious to the water cascading down his face. His eyes narrowed as he tried to figure out what Nicki was talking about. "Give me a hint," he said. "Give me a place to start."

"Well, you could start with the other murder," she said.

Chapter Twenty-two

Brad's eyes launched sparks of fear. Then it was gone, leaving just Brad again, back in full control of his emotions. "I didn't lie," he said.

"Bullshit." She turned away.

He grabbed her shoulder and pulled her back around. "I never lied to you," he said. "You never asked, and I never told, but that's not the same."

"You said you never killed anyone!" But for the rain, the loudness of her voice would have stopped traffic.

"This isn't the same," Brad said. "This isn't what we were talking about."

Nicki looked amazed, her brows scrunched as she grunted out something that might have been a laugh or a cough. "So, what, I have to itemize things now? Have you murdered so many people that we have to talk about them one at a time?"

"I'm telling you it's not like that," Brad said, his voice more forceful. "In the world, it's murder. In prison, murder is different. In this case, murder did the world a favor. It was about me staying alive."

Nicki laughed again. "Oh, you're a piece of work," she said. "Always the victim, right? It's not your fault—"

"No, it's not," Brad said. He was angry now, and he cut her off in mid-sentence. "It's not my fault. I did it, and I admit I did it. Hell, the whole prison knows I did it, and there's not a soul alive who would want it a different way."

This time, Nicki's laugh was less dismissive. She wanted to punish him for hiding details of his life, but she could see from the heat of his expression that she'd trod on private ground.

"You want to hear the story?" he said. "Is that what you want? You really want to hear the details? Because if you do, I can sure as shit share them with you."

No, she didn't want to know. She didn't want to know any of this. Hell, she didn't even want to *be* here; certainly not like this, not with all the crap that was swirling around them. But she nodded anyway. "I think I have a right to know," she said.

"I think you're right." Brad held out his hand. "Let's take a walk."

"In the rain?" No sooner had she asked the question than she realized what an idiotic one it was.

"What, you're afraid of getting wet?" Already, they couldn't get any more soaked if they dove off the end of the pier.

Brad led the way back toward the restaurant, his hand gripped around hers. It was as if he wasn't going to let her go. Before they reached the doors to go inside, though, he veered off to the left, and from there, it was a steep climb through scrub grass and rocks down to the beach below. So near the pier, the air smelled of creosote.

"Where are we going?" Nicki wanted to know.

"We're going where we can have some privacy," Brad said.

In rain like this, no place without a wall could be dry, but at least the space under the towering pier was a little less unpleasant. Brad led the way to one of the pilings, where he leaned his back against the splintery wood and examined his toes as he collected his thoughts. Nicki helped herself to a seat atop a rock.

"I don't know what you've heard about prison life," Brad began, "but whatever it is, reality is worse. I was mainstream general population from day one. Guys who can afford good lawyers to lose their cases for them can at least draw isolation for a few weeks till they figure out how the place works, but not my public defender dickwad. I was GP from the very first day. You can't believe how much violence there can be till you're locked inside with it. There was one guy, his name was Chaney. He led a group called the Posse. It was a gang of killers. There was no limit to what they were capable of." His voice trailed off as he remembered the details.

Brad relayed the details of Derek Johnson's murder and the way that Lucas Georgen just allowed it all to happen. It took the better part of fifteen minutes to tell the whole story, and with each additional word, Nicki edged ever closer to asking him to stop.

"After Derek was dead, and I denied him to his mother—to the one person in the world who seemed interested in pushing a little kindness my way—I hit bottom. I just didn't give a shit anymore about anything. And then they came after *me*."

Nicki's eyes grew wide. "Were you . . . Did they . . ."

Brad chuckled. "It's the first thing people always

want to know, and it the one thing that the media has right. You take it wherever they want to put it or they cut your throat. Sometimes, they cut your throat anyway. There's no sense fighting. All it does is make everything hurt more for a longer time.

"But then they think they own you. They think that you're their property to lend out or to sell however they want."

"Sell?"

"For cigarettes, mostly. That's another thing the movies have right. Inside, cigarettes are cash. Even if you don't smoke."

Nicki screwed up her face. "But why would they sell you? What were people buying?"

Brad gave her a look that said, "Duh."

"Oh," she said.

"But I knew after that first attack and that monster Georgen just stood there and watched—I swore that they were going to die. I knew I couldn't get them all, so I targeted Chaney. He was the leader, and he was the one I hated most. If I'd had time, Georgen would've been next. Looking back, I wish I'd done it the other way around."

"So you killed Chaney?" Nicki said.

Brad didn't answer at first, retreating to that place in his mind where she'd seen him go before.

"Brad?"

"I waited in the same corner where the Posse liked to wait for people. It was like one of two spots in the whole place that nobody could see unless they were looking for it. Chaney used to work in the prison library, and his thing was to take the rolling cart of books all over the place, and in the process, he'd collect his protection money. Thing is, it was the one time when he used to travel alone. I waited for probably fifteen minutes. A couple of people saw me there, and they had to know what I was up to, but nobody squealed me out.

"My boss thought I was going to the infirmary to get my hand stitched." He displayed a ragged scar on his palm. "I told them that I'd cut myself, but if I didn't show up soon, they were gonna come looking for me.

"I waited and waited, and then I heard the sound of the book cart. It had these crazy wheels that always rattled and squeaked whenever you pushed it along. Nothing else in the world sounded like that cart. So, I heard it coming, and I just waited.

"I saw the cart first, and then I made my move. Chaney tried to step back, but he wasn't fast enough. I stuck the knife in his belly right at his belt line, pushed it all the way to the hilt."

Nicki could tell by his expression that Brad was back there again, reliving the moment in vivid detail. The expression on his face was anything but the revulsion she felt at hearing the story. His expression was all pleasure.

"He tried to fight me for maybe two seconds, but then I guess the pain got the better of him. I started sawing with the blade, in and out, a full thrust every time. It was a goddamn sharp knife, too. I spent hours putting the edge on that thing. Christ, you should have seen the blood. It spilled out of his gut like I'd burst a water balloon. He tried to fall, but I wouldn't let him. I pulled him closer and kept sawing until I hit the underside of his ribs. I had no idea how hot blood is when it comes out of a person. It's like spilling coffee down the front of you when it pumps out like that.

"I think he died then, standing up, with me supporting his weight. I was looking right at him, too. Right into his eyes, and it's like this light just goes out. It's there one second and then it's gone."

Brad looked up, saw Nicki's expression of revulsion, but beyond it, lying under the surface the way cake sometimes peeks out from under the layer of icing, he thought he saw a glimmer of understanding.

"He deserved it," Nicki said. From her tone, Brad couldn't tell if she was reassuring him or herself.

"Yeah, he did," Brad agreed. "When it was over, I looked up and there were all these people staring at me. Inmates, all over the place. They weren't cheering the way they normally do in a fight like this, and nobody was coming in to break it up. They just stood there, watching. It was like they were afraid of me. Like I was back in middle school, where people were afraid to step on my shadow. Then somebody said, 'You're toast, dude,' and I knew that he was right. Way too many witnesses. If the Posse didn't kill me before dinner, then the state would get to it in a couple of years. Prisons don't mind letting the violence escalate to the point where you have to kill, but when you do it, they call it murder, just the same as if I'd gone to some school yard and shot the place up.

"So, I'd had all these ridiculous plans to break out of there through tunnels and shit—stuff that I'd never in a million years have been able to do—and there I was, with a need to get out of right-by-God now, and I had no idea what I was gonna do. I just ran. Had no idea where I was going, and there was the laundry cart. It was just sitting there on the loading dock. I dove into it and pulled clothes over top of me. I knew I'd be caught. I mean, really, who'd have thought it could be that easy?

"I was gone before anybody even moved the son of a bitch's body. I just wish I'd taken the extra time to hunt down Georgen. That would've made it all worthwhile."

"They'd have killed you," Nicki said.

"They're gonna kill me anyway. At least then, the books would be settled."

He stopped talking. There it was, out in the open, just the way Nicki said she wanted it. "Sorry you asked?"

Nicki reached out and took his hand. "Yes."

"So, what are you going to do?"

Nicki looked at him hard. For the first time, she sensed that he'd shed all the masks. She was seeing the *real* Brad. There was more to this man than kindness and love. There was violence, too. And pain.

She loved him even more.

"There wasn't any tape in the security recorders," she said. "Daddy told me. They're looking for us as the killers, just like she said in there."

Brad winced.

She forced a smile. "How are you coming with those getaway plans?"

As if lifting a veil, the pain evaporated from Brad's face, replaced by one of his patented smiles. "I've got a good one, I think," he said, "but I don't want to tell you about it till it's done."

Nicki cocked her head, wondering.

"It means breaking some more laws," he explained. "Some big ones. And you don't want to be part of it till it's over."

PART FOUR
TIME TO DIE

Chapter Twenty-three

Carter stared at the phone after he hung up. If he was wrong about Nicki, or if she was wrong about Brad, he'd just made himself an accessory to murder. Worse, he'd just granted tacit approval for his daughter to remain in the company of a convicted killer.

What the hell was he thinking?

It occurred to him as he sat in his car contemplating his own stupidity that he'd inadvertently started a clock for everyone involved. He needed to find this kid in the red shirt, and he'd end up doing it alone. Nicki was dead-on about the mind-set of cops. They already knew who their suspects were, and whatever Carter told them would be discounted as the frantic rantings of a worried father.

He jumped a foot as the front passenger door opened. Before he could say a word, the female deputy he'd seen inside the Quik Mart slid into the seat next to him and closed the door. She smelled of wet hair. "Couple days of this and we'll have to build an ark," she said. When she saw the look of confusion in Carter's face, she extended her hand. "Darla Sweet. We met inside."

A little stunned, he took her hand. "I remember," he said. "Can I help you?"

"I was watching you through the window," she said, nodding to the front of the store. "That was a long chat. You looked pretty animated. I presume you were talking to your daughter?"

Carter tried his best to look unfazed, but he didn't think he pulled it off. "If I were, it would be none of your business," he said. "Attorney-client privilege."

"That's a good one," Darla said. "I was thinking misprision of a felony."

Carter felt trapped. He didn't know what to say, and his silence told the deputy that she was correct.

Darla let him off the hook. "If you did speak to her, I hope that you had the good sense to advise her to turn herself in."

"It wouldn't be that simple," he said. "She's innocent."

"Evidence to the contrary notwithstanding."

Carter looked past the deputy and saw through the front windows of the Quik Mart that the crime scene technicians were still bustling. "You're not searching for exculpatory evidence," he said. "I wouldn't expect you to find it."

She didn't bite. "Evidence is evidence. Prosecution and defense have equal access."

Carter allowed himself a bitter chuckle. "I *am* a prosecutor, Deputy. I know better. The good news is, I can take your case apart in court."

"All the more reason for you to tell her to come on in," Darla observed.

"You mean if I speak to her?"

"Of course. Let her stand trial and humiliate us all."

Carter had learned a long time ago to trust his instincts about people, and he liked something about Deputy

Sweet. She had the look of an idealist. On a different day, he'd have called it naïveté, but not on a day when he needed her help. "Suppose I did talk to her," he said. "Hypothetically, of course, and suppose she told me that she and her friend only witnessed the killing, and tried to help the victim after he was shot? Suppose all those fingerprints were as a result of that?"

"Then I think that she'd need to step up and say so."

Carter wondered how much he should share with her. "Like I said, it's not that simple. Not for Nicki. I don't give a shit about the guy she's with. If I had spoken with her, I think she would have said that the robbery was committed by someone else, a man wearing a red jersey of some sort. A sports jersey. I think she might tell you that Brad Ward—"

"Dougherty."

"Whatever. I'm guessing that she might tell you that he actually tried to stop the robbery, but couldn't before shots were fired. She might tell you that given Brad's record, and her desire to stay on the run, they'd panicked and left the scene only after they'd seen that the victim was already dead."

"That would be after they'd disarmed Ben Maestri."

"Who approached them with a gun and threatened to shoot."

Darla said, "We keep coming back to the strong argument in favor of them turning themselves in and letting the justice system grind its gears. It is a pretty good system, you know."

"Not for my daughter, it's not. In the amount of time it would take for the case to come to trial, she'd already be dead. That's not how I want her to spend her last months."

Darla looked confused. "Mr. Janssen, prison is not an easy place, but it is certainly survivable."

"It's not the prison," Carter said. "She's sick." He explained the nature of the disease. "I need to find the exculpatory evidence before you arrest her. I need to find the *real* bad guy. And you need to keep your crime scene open and operating until I do."

Darla seemed moved by Carter's predicament. "Don't you understand how dangerous it is out there for her if she doesn't turn herself in? The whole state of North Carolina is on the lookout for a pair of murderers. That's a lot of guns."

"Of course I know that." Christ, how could she think that he *didn't* know that? "That means my clock is ticking. My question to you is, are you going to help, or am I going to go this alone?"

Darla recoiled. "We've done our investigation. I don't see how—"

"I don't see how it could hurt to take a look at the other side of the equation," he interrupted. "Assume for the sake of argument that I'm right. You can prevent a terrible miscarriage of justice. If I'm wrong, you might actually strengthen your case. It's a win-win."

Darla smiled as if he'd just told a joke. "I'll run it by the sheriff and see what he thinks."

It wasn't what Carter wanted to hear. "You really think there's a chance that he might go along with that?" he asked. The sheriff was a hard-ass through and through. He wouldn't take kindly to being second-guessed.

Darla gave an incredulous chuckle. "What, are you suggesting that I open up a separate investigation without telling him?"

"It's not a separate investigation," Carter said. "It's a different angle on the *same* investigation."

Darla looked at him as if he'd suggested that the earth was flat. "You're talking career suicide," she said. "The sheriff's very excited about closing this case. He's got elections coming up soon."

"So, to hell with justice?"

Darla didn't sniff the bait. "Justice and windmill jousting are two entirely different things."

Carter felt his face flush. "You heard the old man. What's his name, Ben? You heard him swear that he put a tape in the machine."

"Ben Maestri is a drunk," she said. "He's been a drunk for as long as anyone can remember."

"Yet, he's the eyewitness on whom you want to hang your entire case," Carter said. "You can't have it both ways."

"So, what are you suggesting happened to the tape?"

"You tell me," Carter said. "Let's find out. It's not wrong, is it, to actually *test* the theory that you hold so dear?"

Darla scowled. She seemed to be debating whether or not to say what was on her mind.

"Do you want me to ask him?" Carter pressed.

She said, "If you had talked to your daughter—"

"Nicolette," Carter said quickly. It was always best to put a name on a suspect. Even better when the suspect was young. "She prefers Nicki."

"If you had talked to Nicki and she had offered the details you passed along, I confess that I would be intrigued. Frankly, between you and me, the fingerprints in the blood have been troubling me."

Carter waited for it.

Darla watched the investigators as she spoke. "Why would they check his pulse if they were the shooters? Why would they care? You pull the trigger, somebody dies. It's the way it works."

Carter allowed himself a smile. "Deputy Sweet, I think I might like you after all."

"Don't," Darla snapped. "I don't give a shit about your daughter. I'd arrest her in a heartbeat. And I'd sure as hell take down her boyfriend."

"I already told you I don't care about him."

"And I don't care that you don't care."

He acknowledged her with a nod.

"And then there's the gun itself," Darla went on.

"You've got the murder weapon?"

"We think so. It's the right caliber, but we have to do the ballistics tests to be sure. Problem is, there are no prints and there are no bullets. It was freshly fired, but with evidence of only one bullet expended."

Carter's eyes narrowed as he tried to see where she was going. "What are you saying?"

For the first time Darla seemed sympathetic. "I don't think the shooter intended to shoot."

Carter didn't understand.

"The weapon we recovered is a Glock," she explained. "I was thinking—"

He saw the answer for himself. "There was a round in the chamber," Carter said, finishing the thought for her. The Glock was respected the world over as a weapon for law enforcers, but it had a well-known downside in the hands of amateurs: it remained forever cocked. Even after the magazine was dropped out of the grip, a bullet remained in the chamber, and from there, it was a matter of a slight trigger pull and the thing would fire.

"Exactly," Darla said. She seemed impressed that he could catch on so fast. "I figure he got a little anxious and squeezed too hard."

"Or, he was tackled by an innocent bystander," Carter offered.

"One who happened to be wanted for murder in Michigan?"

Carter let her connect her own dots.

"It's a hell of a coincidence," Darla said. "But it holds up."

"It's a hell of a lot more believable than a shooter who pulls off his gloves to check a pulse," Carter said. "And what about those tipped-over racks and stuff in front of the counter? What are your investigators hypothesizing about that?"

"Ben said that they were already tipped over when he came out."

Carter's stomach tightened. Eyewitness testimony was hard as hell to beat in court. "Did Ben actually *say* that he saw Nicki and Brad shoot the boy? I mean, did he ever say something as direct as, 'I saw them pull the trigger'?"

Darla started to answer then stopped herself. "Actually, no. In fact, he said he was in the back room when the shots were fired."

"*Shot,*" Carter corrected. "Singular. So that adds even more credence to Nicki's version of events."

"No, it doesn't," Darla said. "Gives you a barrelful of reasonable doubt, but it's non-data; doesn't support your theory any more than it supports ours."

Carter felt his frustration mount. "*Justice,* Deputy. It's not your theory versus mine. It's about *justice.*"

"Sounds to me like it's about protecting your daughter," Darla said. The words might have sounded harsh coming from someone else, but from her, they sounded nearly sympathetic.

The rain continued to pound. "Fair enough," he said, "so long as you remember that she's an innocent."

"Despite the company she keeps."

Carter did not respond. What could he say?

"Maybe we could speak with Ben again," Darla mused. "We sent him home, but I have his address."

Carter felt something jump inside of him as he realized that he might have an ally here. "I'd like to come along."

Darla scowled. Clearly, it was as inappropriate in Essex, North Carolina, as it would have been in Pitcairn County, New York. "I'll drive," she said.

Nicki had never seen so much rain. It fell in torrents, flooding the parking lot and transforming the afternoon into perpetual dusk. As they sat waiting in the Sebring, the radio informed them that a developing low pressure system was stalled off the Carolina coast. If the winds picked up another ten miles an hour, the unnamed tropical depression would become Tropical Storm Carlena.

"Are you going to tell me what we're up to?" Nicki asked.

"Not yet. Soon." They'd been watching the cars in the parking lot for ten minutes. Nicki had figured that Brad planned to hot-wire one of the diners' vehicles, but he'd ruled that out on the outset. "We wouldn't get a half mile before someone reported it," he'd said.

When she pressed for more, he ignored her. Now they sat in silence. It was all Nicki could do to keep her eyes open.

When a well-traveled Ford Bronco pulled into the parking lot on the video store side, Brad sat up straighter in his seat. "Okay," he said. "I think this one might be it."

Nicki pulled herself closer to the windshield to see through the distortion of the cascading water. She watched as a woman and a boy exited the truck. Clearly the grandmother, the woman opened an umbrella in a vain attempt to deflect the pelting rain, while the boy basked in the downpour and made a point of stomping in every puddle.

"This is it," Brad said. "Are you ready?"

Before she could even open her mouth to respond, he'd already opened his door.

At Gramma's insistence, Scotty Boyd pulled off his sneakers and socks and left them outside the door of the video store. It was a compromise to not being allowed to enter at all. Good boys didn't soak themselves in rain puddles.

Come to think of it, good boys didn't do any of the things that Scotty liked to do. They didn't drink milk out of the carton, they didn't watch cartoons, they didn't piss in the grass, and they didn't shoot at anthills with BB guns. And that was just today. What good boys did do was behave themselves twenty-four hours a day without ever complaining.

Living with Gramma brought a lot of rules into the twelve-year-old's life; certainly a lot more than he'd had to live with before Mama died. Still, even though Gramma smelled funny and went to bed at nine o'clock, she was good on her word. He'd finished picking up the front yard, and she hadn't let a little rain keep her away from the video store. The deal was, after he'd picked up the blown-in trash from the front yard and swept the sand off the front and rear decks, he could get one movie and one video game. And here they were.

The game was a no-brainer: *Spiderman.* His real first choice would have been *Grand Theft Auto,* but Gramma would have had a stroke if she saw it. She wasn't all that wild about his Xbox in the first place; between *GTA*'s whores and the exploding blood, she'd have had him sweeping the porches with a toothbrush. No, Spidey was a fine compromise.

Compromise. Funny how many times that word

came up in his life these days. Two months ago, he didn't even know what the word meant. Now, since his address had changed, it ran his life.

With the game chosen, he was left with the conundrum of choosing a movie. (*Conundrum* was another new word; Scotty liked the way it sounded.) It was hard to find the compromise between the singing-animal Disney crap that Gramma wanted him to watch and the Bruce Willis flick he was hoping for. Gramma wouldn't even let him watch a PG-13 movie until he was actually thirteen years old, to hell with the fact that he'd been watching Rs for as long as he could remember.

Still, it wasn't worth the fight. Singing fish were the price he had to pay to get his game.

As they approached the checkout counter, the teenage clerk looked at Scotty and laughed. "You look like a drowned rat," he said.

Scotty caught Gramma's don't-you-dare glare before he had a chance to form his reply. Good thing, too. Pizza-faces should think twice before calling someone a drowned rat. Of all the adjustments the last eight weeks had brought into his life, the language thing had been the hardest. In the end, the boy just smiled.

"Try to stay dry," the clerk said.

Gramma carried the plastic bag with the goodies and held the door for the boy. "I don't like him," Scotty mumbled as he passed.

"You don't even know him," Gramma scolded. "You can't dislike people you don't know."

With Gramma, life was a lot simpler when you just went along. Slipups brought a thousand extra chores followed by solitary confinement in his bedroom. Scotty had thought about breaking out a couple of times—just climbing out the window and taking off—but out where they lived, there was no place to run to.

Back in Richmond, before the Big Move, there'd been plenty of places to visit after he'd sneaked out of the window, but here in Buttscratch, North Carolina—that's what his mama had liked to call it—there was nothing but sand and bugs and water. Lots and lots of water, enough to make him wish that he'd spent those afternoons at the YMCA learning how to swim instead of perfecting moves on a basketball court that he'd probably never see again.

On his way back out to the truck, Scotty stopped to pick up his footwear, pointing out gleefully that his socks now weighed more than his shoes, thanks to the water.

Gramma made a huffing noise and snatched the shoes away from him. "You'll get these back when you learn to appreciate owning good things," she said.

Fine, he thought. *I didn't want to wear the dumb things anyway.*

"Hurry now and buckle in," Gramma called from under her umbrella. "I want to be back at the house before the roads flood."

Scotty stopped near the front fender. "Can I sit in the front?" he asked.

"You may not."

"Please, Gramma? We don't even *have* an air bag. That's what kills people, not the seat itself."

"It's hardly worth the risk, do you think?" Gramma replied.

Scotty rolled his eyes. How was he going to get through six years of this? That's what the judge had told him: he'd be stuck with Gramma until he was eighteen. *God help me.*

"I don't think it's so dangerous," he muttered, just loudly enough to be heard, but not enough for her to make out the words.

"You have something to say, young man, you just say it right out where I can hear it."

Scotty didn't bother to reply. He climbed behind the death-inducing passenger seat into the back of the truck, reaching forward again to close the heavy door.

"Remember your—"

"—seat belt." He finished the sentence for her. He saw the stranger in the back, in the cargo bed behind the backseat, the instant he turned around, and he yelled. It was an involuntary thing, a loud "Ooooh!" Gramma whirled in her seat.

"Now, darn it, Scotty—" She saw him, too. The man had a gun.

Brad leveled Ben Maestri's pistol at Gramma. "Don't say anything. Don't do anything, and nobody'll get hurt, okay?"

A young woman popped up out of the back as well. She looked as terrified as Scotty felt. "Brad, don't—"

As the man with the gun scaled the seat next to Scotty, the boy considered diving for the door and bailing out, but a hand planted in his chest, accompanied by a hard glare, convinced him otherwise.

"Don't even think about it," Brad warned. "Buckle up like your grandmother told you."

Scotty did exactly that, his hands trembling. Suddenly, there was a very good chance that he might throw up.

Brad redirected his attention toward Gramma. "I want you to start the car and back out of this place just as if it were an ordinary day. Honest, nobody needs to get hurt."

"W-what are you going to do?" Gramma stammered. "I don't have any money. Not enough to be worth stealing."

Brad beckoned with the muzzle of his gun. "I'll take that purse, please," he said.

Scotty shifted his eyes to the girl, who looked as if she might throw up, too. There were tears in her eyes. She tried to say something. "Brad—"

But the guy cut her off. "Not now, Nicki," he said. Then to Gramma, "The purse, please."

"There's nothing in it," Gramma whined.

"Hand it to me, anyway," Brad insisted. There was a growl in his voice that reminded Scotty of an animal. The boy fought off tears of his own.

The girl with the boy's name put her hand on his shoulder. "You'll be just fine," she said. "He won't hurt anyone."

"I'll kill him if he does," Scotty heard himself say.

The comment drew a swift response. Brad brought the muzzle to within an inch of the boy's eye. "Don't push me, kid."

Gramma lifted her purse from the seat and handed it back to Brad. "Here," she said. "Take it. Take whatever you want."

"I'm not interested in your money, lady," Brad said. He handed the bag over to Nicki. "Search through there and find her driver's license," he said. "I need her address."

"Why?" Nicki asked.

"Just do it," he said. After that, he leaned in close to Gramma and whispered in her ear. Scotty couldn't hear the words, but he knew it was about him just from the way Gramma stole glances his way.

Gramma started to cry. Her hands trembled. "Please don't do this," she whimpered.

"I have to," Brad said. "I'm caught in a crack, and you happen to be my only way out. It sucks, but welcome to my world."

"I don't think I can," she whined.

Scotty felt his face and ears turning red with rage. Who did this guy think he was, making Gramma cry?

Brad said, "You think about it, Gramma. Ask yourself what you asked the kid: is it worth taking the chance?"

"Please don't," she said again.

Brad gave her a poisonous smile. "You're in the driver's seat. Get us out of here safely, and your troubles are nearly over."

Gramma made her decision. Scotty felt a surge of pride as he saw the sniveling weakness drain from her face, then to be replaced by the angry set of her jaw that Scotty had become so used to seeing. "Where are we going?" she asked.

"Out of the parking lot and hang a right. Join that line of cars." The rain had slackened a bit, but there was plenty left in the clouds.

Gramma backed out of the parking space, then pulled the transmission into Drive and whirled the wheel to the left to clear the back of the car that had parked next to her. That done, she straightened the vehicle out and headed for the driveway, beyond which the traffic was barely moving.

Brad climbed back over the seat to join Nicki in the back. "When they stop you, they're going to ask if you've seen us, and that's when you need to put in an Oscar-winning performance. If they want to know where you're going or where you've been, you just tell them that you took your grandson out to get a movie."

"And a video game," Scotty corrected. He shrank from the heat of Brad's glare.

"Just get us through this," Brad continued, to Gramma, "and everything will be fine. Screw it up and you'll regret it forever." He faded farther back into the shadows, pausing to whisper in Scotty's ear. "Listen here, little man, I'll tell you what I told your grandmother. If something happens so these cops find out that we're here, there's going to be shooting. When that happens, the very first bullet kills your Gramma. The second one kills you. Think about that."

Brad turned to Nicki. "Did you find the driver's license?"

Actually, she'd forgotten completely about it. With trembling hands, she turned her attention to the mammoth purse. Glancing at the flashing lights of the roadblock, she asked, "Are you really going to shoot if we get stopped up there?" she asked.

Brad gave her a hard look. "I told you that I'm not going back to prison. You just keep your head down."

"But Brad, what about them?" she asked with a sweeping gesture. "They didn't do anything."

He turned away to face front again. "Not yet they haven't," he said.

Chapter Twenty-four

North Carolina State Trooper Matt Hayes would not have been more soaked if someone had stood on a ladder and poured buckets of water over his head. On typical wet days, his plastic rain slicker kept most of the rain out, but today he might as well not have worn it.

He handed Hector Nunez back his license and waved him through the roadblock, beckoning the next in line to stop. He'd chosen this spot for the checkpoint because it was only a few hundred yards from the place where the road from Essex split in three. A similar checkpoint had been set up on the northern end of the same road, some thirty miles from here. Getting in and out of Essex required passage on this road, period. If the murderers were traveling by car, their escape route was sealed off. They were either holed up or trapped. Matt couldn't see a third option.

Now that he'd been here for three hours, though, things seemed a hell of a lot less sure.

A battered green Bronco without hubcaps was next in line, complete with a little old lady behind the steering wheel. Matt whirled his fingers in the air to motion her to lower her window. The height of the vehicle allowed him to look her straight in the eye rather than tilting his head and dumping a torrent of water from the wide flat rim of his plastic-covered hat. "Hello, ma'am," he said. "Are you keeping dry?"

The woman seemed nervous as she shot him only a cursory look and then returned her eyes to the road. "I'm trying," she said. "I'm taking my grandson to get a video and a game."

Matt's curiosity was piqued by her behavior. "Are you okay?" he asked. "You look nervous."

"No," she said. "I'm fine. Just tired of the weather."

Matt wiped the cascade of water from his mouth. "Could I see your driver's license, please?"

This time, the look in the woman's face was something close to panic.

Brad felt his insides seize. Why hadn't he thought of that? Of course, they were going to want to see her license, but Nicki still held the bulky purse on her lap, hugging it to her chest and trying not to let her breathing run away from her. Up front, Gramma clearly didn't know what to say.

"Are you okay, ma'am?" the cop repeated. "You don't look so good."

In his mind, Brad could see the cop slipping his pistol out of its holster. His hand tightened around the grip of his own.

"I've got your purse here, Gramma," Scotty said, and he unhooked his seat belt. Reaching over the edge of his seat, he grabbed the bag from Nicki and lifted it over to his grandmother. "I was looking for some gum while you were inside getting the movie," he explained. "Then you came back and I was scared that you might get mad about me going through your stuff."

Corporal Hayes smiled as a waterlogged boy leaned forward with the purse gripped in his fist.

The grandmother accepted her bag, and at the moment of the handoff they exchanged a significant glance that Matt didn't quite know how to interpret. When the boy caught him watching, it grew awkward, and then the kid smiled at him.

Gramma still avoided eye contact as she fished through the junk in her bag for her wallet, and from there she started fishing for her license. She riffled through all of the picture sleeves in the wallet—past a couple of credit cards and a photo of what could only be a younger version of the boy in the backseat.

"I know it has to be here somewhere," she said.

"Ma'am, you look nervous," Matt said. *Scared to death* actually came closer to it.

"Do I?" she said. "I just can't— Oh, there it is!" She looked past her wallet into the cavern of the purse itself and pulled out the plastic card. "It must have fallen out." She dared a flash of eye contact as she handed it over.

Matt looked at it, compared the picture to the face in front of him, and was reassured. It was her, all right. But there was something wrong here. "Give me just a minute, will you?" he said. He stepped away from the truck just far enough that the occupants wouldn't be able to hear what he was about to say on the radio.

* * *

In the back of the Bronco, Brad seethed. How could he have been so stupid? Jesus, he should have thought of the license. As it was, he was lucky to snatch it away from Nicki in time to dump it in the purse. The kid was one smooth liar, though. Brilliant.

Brad dared a peek over the boy's seat, out toward the window. What was happening? Why were they still sitting there?

"The cop took her license," Scotty whispered, making Brad wonder if he'd spoken his thoughts aloud.

Brad touched a finger to his lips.

"It's not her fault," Scotty said. "She's trying, she really is. She's just not very good at this stuff."

"Be quiet," Brad hissed. "And quit looking at me. It doesn't matter whose fault it is."

"Brad, you can't shoot them," Nicki said.

"You be quiet, too," he snapped. Brad had no idea what he was he was going to do if things got ugly, but it sure as hell didn't involve shooting an old woman and a kid. He had to threaten them, though, or else they wouldn't be frightened into doing what he wanted. And he had to be equally hard on Nicki simply because she didn't have it in her to *be* frightening. That left only one effective option: she had to look as frightened as the others. People on edge were pliable. It was a skill he'd learned a long time ago. Intimidation wasn't about *being* tough so much as it was about *sounding* tough.

He liked to call it the Big Bluff. It was how he'd survived on the street. Sure, you had to duke it out a few times to keep it credible, but if you chose your opponents properly, even the fight could be part of the ruse. Pick on the weaker ones and only hit them hard enough to maybe break a nose. He didn't care what

people saw in the movies, a fight always ended once
you broke somebody's nose.

What the hell was taking the cop so long? Brad had
been watching the guy. Every other car that approached
the roadblock was stopped only for a few seconds—
long enough to show their identification—and then they
were motioned through. This was trouble for sure.

Brad tried to think of some way that Gramma might
have communicated with the cop. Maybe she'd sent
him a note, or blinked out an SOS. There were a thousand ways she could have sent a silent signal. After
he'd promised to kill the boy, though, if anything went
wrong, he didn't think she'd risk it.

But what else could it be? The cop was taking forever on the radio. The whole damn plan was unravel-
ing right in front of him. There had to be something for
him to do. There was *always* one more option.

Running wasn't a choice. The act of rushing the driver
alone would make the cop draw down, and nobody here
needed that kind of madness.

Think, Brad. Think . . .

"What's he doing now?" he whispered to the boy.

"He's still talking on the radio," Scotty said. "Oh,
no. He's not anymore. He's coming back to the window."

Brad ducked back down, lying faceup on the floor,
his weapon ready in his hand.

Killing a cop wasn't on the agenda, but it looked as
if the agenda might be changing. His grip tightened.

It was a good ruse, Matt thought as he finished his
discussion on the radio. He never would have suspected
the Bronco, and certainly not the old lady. According to
her license, she was June Parker, from one of the off-

road neighborhoods in Lincolntown. When he returned to the window, he did so carefully. At least he understood why the woman was acting so crazy.

"You didn't tell me the truth, did you, ma'am?" Corporal Hayes asked.

There was that terrified look. She seemed to be close to tears.

"I was wondering why you were shaking like that," the cop went on. "You've got two outstanding warrants for speeding on the interstate, did you know that?"

The news seemed to startle her, and something changed behind her eyes. "Yes, sir, I do."

"You've got over five hundred dollars in outstanding fines. I'm supposed to arrest you and take you in for that kind of money. You're in very serious trouble."

"Are you taking me to jail?" she asked.

Matt looked at her and sighed. The answer here should have been a resounding yes. *Should* have been. "I'll tell you what. If you promise me right here and now that you'll bring yourself to the courthouse first thing Monday morning and set this all straight, then I won't take you in. The weather is miserable, and they don't arraign on the weekends anyway. With that boy and all, it doesn't make a lot of sense for you to sit in a cell for forty-eight hours."

She stared at him, as if she didn't comprehend.

"You need to say something, ma'am," Matt prompted.

"Oh, yes," she said. "Yes, of course. Monday morning, first thing."

Matt leveled his forefinger at her nose. "This is a gift, Ms. Parker. My favor to you in deference to your situation. But don't think that I won't be checking up on you. If I hear that you haven't been by the courthouse by, say, two o'clock on Monday, I'll come out to your house and cuff you myself. Do we have a deal?"

"Yes, we have a deal," she said. Again, there was something leaden in her tone.

Matt chalked it up to the fact that her kid had over-heard that his grandmother was a criminal. "For what it's worth," he said, more for the benefit of the kid than for the driver, "if you can write a check right there at the courthouse, or show proof of some kind of pay-ment plan, they'll vacate the warrant, and you'll be able to go on home. I'll make sure that it's noted as such in the file. But if you don't show—"

"I know," she said. "You'll cart me off yourself."

Matt sealed the deal with an abrupt nod. "Done," he said. "Now, you can be on your way." He started to turn away, then stopped himself. "Oh, I almost forgot. Keep an eye out for a couple teenage kids, a boy and a girl. They're wanted for a murder up the road, and we've got this checkpoint set up to look for them. If you see any strangers fitting that description, please give us a call."

"I will," said the driver. "I'll be sure to do just that."

She drove off, and Matt beckoned for the next vehi-cle in the line.

"She was just nervous," Scotty said once they were moving again. "She wasn't trying to shit on your plan."

"Scotty!" Gramma hated crude language.

"What? Oh, Jesus." This language crap was going to kill him.

"Scotty!"

Brad stood as tall as he could in the confines of the truck. "Both of you, be quiet," he barked. He again climbed over the seat and helped himself to the spot next to the boy. "Scotty, watch your mouth. Gramma—do you mind if I call you Gramma?"

"Fine," she said.

"Okay, Gramma, I want you just to drive home. You're going to have some guests for a while."

"What are you going to do to us?"

"Not a thing if you do exactly what I tell you. You heard what that cop said about me. One murder or three, the penalty's the same." He made a deliberate effort not to look at Nicki, who'd stretched out on the floor in the back. "I looked at your driver's license, so I know where you live. If you don't drive straight there, I'll know."

He settled into his seat and pivoted so he could keep an eye on both of them.

Chapter Twenty-five

When Ben Maestri's wife opened the front door, Carter wondered whether he should have brought a doctor instead of a cop. She looked to be about seventy years old, and a grayness around her eyes spoke of some imminent health problem. She cracked the door and peered out at her visitors, her hands poised to slam it shut in an instant. She said nothing.

Deputy Sweet did the talking. "Hello," she said, her tone light. "Is this the Maestri home?"

The woman glared.

Carter gave it a try. "We're looking for Ben Maestri, owner of the Quik Mart on Shore Road."

"Who are you?" the woman asked. The question was leveled at Carter.

Carter produced a business card from the pocket of his suit coat. "I'm Carter Janssen. I'm a lawyer from upstate New York, and I was wondering if Mr. Maestri might have a moment to speak with me."

"Us," Darla corrected. "Speak with us."

The woman regarded them both with a look that hovered between contempt and fear. Then she closed the door.

"Well, that was friendly," Carter said to Darla.

Darla arched her eyebrows. "Do you suppose she's going to get Ben, or was that our signal to leave?"

Carter took a few steps back to the edge of the porch and craned his neck to catch a peek into a window. Behind them, the rain continued to pour.

They waited a full minute before knocking again. This time, Ben answered. He glared.

Carter decided to go first, extending his hand. "I'm Carter Janssen," he said. "I'm—"

"I know who you are," the man said. He displayed Carter's card, holding it like a cigarette between his first and second fingers. He squinted at Darla. "Deputy. What do you want?"

"Can we come in?" Carter asked.

"No."

The bluntness of the answer caught Carter off guard. "It'll only be for a few minutes," Darla said.

"Just say what you need to say from there."

Carter scowled. The attitude confused him. A wild thought shot through his brain, and he let it fly. "Are you frightened, Mr. Maestri?"

The question drew a startled glance from Darla, but she didn't say anything.

"Your clock is ticking, folks. Unless you want to talk to the door, you'd best get on with it."

"We're getting soaked," Carter said.

"And you won't get any dryer standing there."

In the car, they'd agreed in deference to his personal stake in this that Carter could take the lead in the questioning. He began, "I know you've had a very difficult day, sir. It's a terrible thing that you went through, and if there were any way for me to—"

"I know everything I need to know about myself, Mr. Janssen. Try talking about *you*."

Carter cleared his throat. "Yes, of course. Well, sir, you seem to think that my daughter was involved in that unpleasantness this afternoon."

"Oh, really?" the man said. "Is that what you call murder up in New York City? Unpleasantness?"

"It's New York State, sir—"

"I don't give a goddamn what it is, state, city, or country. Murder is murder. And if your daughter was one of them that killed Chas, then I'm probably gonna feel sorry for you one day. It'd be a shame to have a girl on death row."

"My daughter didn't kill that boy," Carter said. "That's what I want to talk to you about."

"I already told them everything I know." He glared at Darla. "And Deputy, I don't much appreciate you bringin' him here. This is not the day for social chats."

Carter started to speak, but Darla placed a hand on his arm to stop him. "There's nothing social about this, Ben. You're upset and I understand that. But I've got a murder to investigate, and Mr. Janssen has some pertinent questions to ask."

Ben shifted his glare to Carter. "Say what's on your mind."

"You didn't see the shooting, is that correct?" Carter asked.

"Never said I did. But I sure as hell saw the kids who did it." He gingerly touched his bruised eye. "Got the trophy to show for it."

"But you never saw them *shoot,*" Carter pressed.

Ben's eyes narrowed. If he were a younger man, it was a look that would have spelled impending violence. "You *are* a lawyer, ain't ya? Always huntin' for the technicality. Well, let me put it this way for you: if I wake up tomorrow morning and the ground is dry,

I'll assume that it stopped raining even if I never saw it stop."

"It's an important distinction, Ben," Darla added. "Mr. Janssen has a theory that someone else did the shooting, then fled before you stepped out from the back. From what you told me earlier, I don't see a way to tell him that he's necessarily wrong."

"But the sheriff said that that boy was a murderer," Ben said. His faith in his own assumptions appeared to be weakening.

"He is," Darla said. "But from another state. Michigan. That doesn't necessarily mean he's our man for this."

"My daughter's never hurt a soul in her life," Carter added. "I think that what you saw—I mean what you *really saw*—were actually two witnesses to the crime whom you caught in the act of trying to help."

Ben started to close the door again. "I'm calling the sheriff," he said. "I want to talk to Frank Hines himself on this."

"He thinks you're senile." Carter stopped the closing door with a few inches left in its arc. "You know for a fact that you loaded the security recorders, yet he says that you're just too old to remember."

Ben allowed the door to open again, his expression more wary than ever. "What's y'all's game, anyway?"

"I have no game, sir. What I have is a crisis. I'm trying to save my daughter from a murder charge, and you're the only person in the world who can help me."

"What makes you think I want to?"

"Because the law requires it," Darla said. "We don't get many murders around here, Ben. You don't want to be on the wrong side of this one. At the end of the day, we all want the same thing—justice." Carter cast her a grateful glance, but she didn't acknowledge it.

Ben scoffed and tossed a thumb at Carter. "He don't give a whit about justice. All he wants is to protect his baby girl. I heard what he had to say in the shop this afternoon."

"Of course I want to protect her," Carter said, "but only because I know she's innocent. That means there's a real killer out on the streets somewhere who needs to be arrested."

Ben looked to Darla for confirmation.

"It's complicated, okay, Ben? It's just really very complicated. Now, are you going to let us in or not?"

"I'm not supposed to be talking to you," Ben said as he led them inside. "Either one of you."

Darla recoiled. "Says who?" Once inside, she removed her Smokey the Bear hat and dangled it by her side. Water dripped onto the floor.

Ben's tone made it seem obvious. "Sheriff Hines. He doesn't want you or anyone else messing up my memory. I already told him everything I know, and he said that he doesn't want me to get confused."

Darla scowled. "He mentioned me by name?"

"Not you. Him." Another thumb at Carter. "Once he heard you were a lawyer *and* the murderer's father, he predicted you'd come."

Carter braced at the continued use of the *m* word. "She's not a murderer," he said again, trying to push from his mind the number of times he'd heard the parents of ruthless killers utter the same words.

Ben led the way into the living room, where everything was slipcovered and doilied. The gloom of the day, filtered through heavy blinds, bathed everything in the sepia tones of an old photograph. He gestured to the woman on the couch, whom Carter recognized as the initial gatekeeper. "I believe you've already met my wife, Carol," he said.

Carter smiled. "Hello again."

Carol's frown didn't loosen a bit. "You're crazy inviting him in here like this," she growled. It was as if Darla wasn't even there. "Sheriff told you not to, but you do it anyway, you're likely to end up in jail yourself." For a lady who looked like everybody's grandmother, with her hair tied into a tight bun and an apron tucked up under her ample breasts, Carol Maestri had a tough edge.

Ben gestured to the chairs. "I ain't never been much for following orders," he said. "Have a seat. You've got the floor."

Carter stalled by clearing his throat. The moment of truth had arrived. In order to get Ben Maestri's cooperation, Carter was going to have to confess to a blizzard of felonies. For starters, there was misprision of a felony—the fallout from his conversation with Nicki—followed by accessory after the fact to murder. God only knew what an aggressive North Carolina prosecutor could dream up to go along with them. Even if he stayed out of jail, he'd probably never be permitted to practice law again.

Actually, that particular prospect didn't seem so bad.

Carol Maestri used the brief silence as her own invitation to speak. "Chas Delphin was a good boy," she said. "Fifteen years old, lives just down the road a bit. I used to babysit for him years ago, and every holiday, he used to come by just to say hello."

Ben looked uncomfortable. "Carol, sweetheart, I don't think you need to—"

"I do so need to," she snapped. "I want this fellow to know what a terrible thing has happened. I want him to know why his pain don't mean nothing to me. Chas was a good boy, Mr. Janssen. He wanted to be a writer. Science fiction. He knew more about nothin' than any ten boys his age, and now he won't never become anything because somebody wanted the money in his till." As she spoke, Carol's lip started to quiver, but her eyes stayed dry. "It hurts to live in a world where that sort of thing can happen."

Carter hadn't prepared himself for this. Through all the machinations of trying to get Nicki back home, he'd never allowed himself to think about the boy who was killed—about the parents who would suffer the unspeakable agony his death. Hearing her talk about Chas's dreams to be a writer, he thought about the millions of words that would never be written, the stories that would never be told, all because some asshole with a gun took his life with a simple flick of a finger on a trigger. Carol was right. It did hurt to live in such a world.

"Mrs. Maestri," he said softly. "You might not believe it, but you and I are on the exact same side of this issue."

Carol scoffed and looked away. "Innocent people don't run away, Mr. Janssen."

Carter told Nicki's story one more time. When he was finished, no one said anything as they grappled with the dilemma faced by a desperate young lady.

"So, you've spoken to your daughter," Ben said.

Carter couldn't deny it. "The details she gave me were vivid. The kids bet everything that the video would prove their story. Without it, they're stuck."

Something transpired between Carol and Ben that Carter caught only because he was wired into such things. It was a shared glance, and a shift of position.

They seemed to be waiting for the other to speak first. "What is it?" Carter asked.

Ben seemed to be sifting through the images in his mind. "When I heard the shot, I knew right away that it was a robbery. And I think I knew that Chas had to be dead." His voice caught in his throat, and Carol reached over and tapped his hand. "I didn't do anything. I cracked the door just a little and peeked out. Isn't that terrible? A boy not even old enough to shave is shot in my store, and I don't have the guts to step out without peeking."

Darla took a breath to console the old man, but Carter stopped her with a brief twitch of his hand. Ben had tapped into his emotional memory, and Carter didn't want anything to break his train of thought.

As if reading each other's thoughts, Ben and Carol clasped hands. "I just stood there, watching, wondering what the hell I was supposed to do. I mean, my God, they'd just killed my clerk. I'd have been a fool to rush out into something like that."

Carter said nothing, silently urging the old man to continue.

"At first, all I saw was the boy. Your boy. Your daughter's boy. He was by the front door, looking out, anxious to get going, I think, because he was looking for something outside. Then I saw him look toward the counter, and that's when I first saw the girl, your daughter." Ben raised the fist of his free hand to his forehead.

"No, that's not right, either," he corrected himself. "I guess I couldn't really see her. Not all of her anyway, because that view is blocked from the door."

"Could you hear what they were saying?"

"No, sir, I couldn't. My hearing ain't all that it used to be. I mean, I probably could have if I'd really con-

centrated on it, but I was just too blamed scared to pay
attention. Then I remembered the security monitor. I
remembered that if I wanted to see what was going on
out there, all I had to do was look into the TV screen."

"Why didn't you do that before?"

"Never thought of it. I just heard the sound of that
shot, and I went right to the door. When I did get to
looking at that screen, that's when I saw them both
with Chas. Your boy was nervous as a cat. He couldn't
get out of there fast enough."

"What was Nicki doing?"

Ben seemed to age five years as his mind replayed
whatever he was looking at. His eyes grew red as he
shot a look to his wife.

"What is it, Benny?" Carol asked. She leaned in
close, as if worried that he might be sick.

"I thought she was trying to rob him," Ben said. "I
swear to God, that's what I thought." He shifted his
eyes toward Carter. "But she was trying to help him,
wasn't she?"

Carter just held his gaze, letting him close the loop
for himself.

"I'm so sorry," Ben said. "I just assumed."

"I understand," Carter assured him.

"How many lives can one afternoon ruin?" Carol
asked no one in particular.

Where Carter came from, lives were ruined every
hour. "How different was the story that you just told
me from what you initially told the police?"

"They didn't even ask the same questions." He looked
to Darla. "You know that."

Darla clasped her hands. "We all made assumptions."

Carter didn't want to travel that road again. It was
all asked and answered. "Think hard on this, Ben: Do

you have any idea who might be inclined to rob your store? Or, perhaps more to the point, to kill Chas Delphin?"

"Absolutely not," Ben said.

"We have our toughs and our hoodlums just like any other community," Carol added, "but we don't have murderers in Essex."

Evidence to the contrary notwithstanding, Carter didn't say. He decided to change tacks. "Tell me about the tapes in the security recorder."

"They're not there."

"But you thought they were."

The old man frowned. "I'd have sworn on a stack of Bibles that I'd loaded it just this morning."

"But you're sure it's empty now?"

"It's the first place the sheriff went when he arrived on the scene," Darla reported.

"I can't understand," Ben said. "Changing the tapes is the first thing I do every morning. I don't know how I possibly could have forgotten it."

Something stirred in the back of Carter's brain. It was rare in his experience for nondelusional, healthy people to claim that they had done something so recently only to find that they in fact had not. It was much more common in the reverse—that people would go to do something twice, forgetting about the first iteration.

"Is it possible that the shooter was aware of the cameras and took the tapes on the way out?"

"I don't see how. There's no way someone could have passed without me seeing."

"How about a back door?" Carter pressed. "A separate entrance where they could have slipped in after the fact, while you were tending to Chas?"

"There's a back door, but that's locked, all the time. I got a iron bar that needs a key to pull it away. The fire marshal don't like it, but I don't care. I'm tired of having stuff stolen from back there."

Carter tried to make the pieces fit. "Have you looked at the tape deck yourself, Ben? I mean, since the shooting?"

"I haven't been back in the office at all," Ben said. "They wouldn't let me. I don't think anyone's been back there except the sheriff. They've got it all roped off."

It made sense, Carter thought. As long as the Quik Mart was an active crime scene, it would have been inappropriate to let anyone enter.

The shadowy outline of an idea began to form. Carter hesitated, then went for it: "Is there a chance that the sheriff made off with the tape?"

Darla nearly launched out of her chair. "Whoa, whoa. Where did that come from?"

Carter raised his hand to calm her down. "Take it easy, Deputy. It's just a question."

"Well, I don't like what you're suggesting."

"I'm not suggesting anything," Carter said. "I'm just following a lead. If Ben is certain that he put the tape in the machine, and the sheriff is the only other person to walk into the back office, what's left?"

"Why on earth would he want to do that?" Ben asked.

"One question at a time," Carter said. "I'm trying to balance both sides of the equation."

"That doesn't even make sense," Carol huffed. "Why would the sheriff want to destroy evidence?"

Carter shrugged. "To keep anyone else from seeing it."

Darla stood, ready to walk out. "Oh, for God's sake."

"But *why*?" Ben asked again.

"You tell me." Darla was clearly upset by the mere hint that the sheriff might have been involved, but Ben seemed only intrigued.

Ben's scowl deepened. "I suppose just about anything is possible, but I don't see how he could have smuggled them out, either. I was standing out front, and I already told you that the door in the back is barred. And before you ask, I don't think he could have snuck it past everybody in the front, either. You already seen how he fills out his uniform shirt. It ain't like he could stuff it under there."

Darla had had enough. "I can't sit here and listen to this."

"Then leave," Ben said. Coming from him, the words startled everyone.

Carter spoke up to keep Darla from having to respond. "Look, Deputy, I know it's startling, and maybe we're way out of line, but at this stage, the only dangerous question is the one we don't ask. There's a long list of those in this case. Have you been listening to Ben?"

"Why would Sheriff Hines do such a thing?" Darla asked. "Surely, you're not suggesting that he's the killer."

Carter waved that off as preposterous. "Of course not. Maybe he's covering for someone else."

"Who?"

"You tell me."

"How about his boy?" Carol asked.

Ben and Darla answered together: "Impossible."

Ben expounded, "That boy's never done a wrong thing in his life. He's the local baseball star. He's got a bright future ahead of him. His father's the *sheriff,* for God's sake. That's just not possible."

Carter turned to Darla, expecting more confirmation. Instead, he found her staring at infinity. "Deputy?" He broke the trance, got her attention. "You disagree?"

"Huh?" she grunted. "Oh, about Jeremy Hines? Absolutely not. He's not capable of something like this."

Ben jumped as if someone had poked him. "Wait a second!" he proclaimed. "There *is* someone you need to talk to. Oh, goddamn, why didn't I think of this before? There's a kid, a troublemaker, been in and out of my store a lot the past couple of months. Tall kid. Dark hair."

Darla's head whipped around. She knew exactly. "Peter Banks?" she asked.

"That's him," Ben said. "He and Chas had a big fight a couple of weeks ago."

"They did?"

"Okay, not a fight, I guess, but words. Angry words. Chas caught him tryin' to steal and made him give it back."

"Did you call the police?" Darla asked.

Ben waved away the idea. "Nah, the kid put it all back, so I figured no harm, no foul. I was right proud of Chas for that, though. He told the kid that he was banned for life from the store."

Carter thought it seemed thin. It was a place to start, but—

"It don't fit with your theory of the sheriff coverin' for somebody," Ben said. From his tone, it was hard to tell if he was relieved or sorry.

"Don't be so sure," Darla said.

Carter shot her a curious look and she responded with a little shake of her head that said, "Not now."

She asked, "Do you remember if Peter came to your store alone, or was he with someone else?"

Ben had to think on that one. When he remembered, his eyes grew large.

"It was Jeremy Hines, wasn't it?"

Ben looked like a man who'd had an epiphany. "Yes, it was. And he was as angry at Peter as Chas was. I remember that. He told him to give it all back and went on and on about getting him in trouble with his dad."

Carter arched his eyebrows. "Time to pick up Peter Banks?"

"Gotta find him first," Darla said. "I know exactly where to go to start looking."

Chapter Twenty-six

"**C**'mon, Nicki, wake up. We're here."

The words startled her. She didn't realize she'd fallen asleep. When she sat up and looked around, it occurred to her that maybe she'd pulled a Rip van Winkle. The whole world had changed. The beach road had given way to just a beach with a house in the middle of it. Dunes surrounded them on three sides, with the front door facing the fourth.

"Where are we?" she asked. Her mouth was so dry that her tongue felt swollen.

"The end of the line," Brad said.

Scotty correctly interpreted her confused look. "This is where we live," he said.

Nicki wondered if they were playing a joke on her. The place wasn't even a house, at least not in the classic sense of the word. Roofing shingles doubled for siding on all the vertical surfaces, separated from the roof itself only by a difference in color. The wall tiles were gray, the roof brown. The driveway brought them in on an angle, and on the side of the house closest to them, the most prominent feature was a red-stained heating oil tank listing on rusted legs. Next to it rose a twenty-foot steel tower, capped at the top by an elaborate antenna of some sort. The place had the feel of a wartime military outpost erected in a hurry and designed to last only a day or two. Most remarkable of all were the heavy steel bars over all the windows.

"What is this," Nicki asked, "a converted jail?"

"Shitty neighborhood," Scotty mumbled, just loudly enough for Nicki to hear. When she looked at him, the boy rolled his eyes, clearly embarrassed to call this place home.

She was about to say something vapid like "Be it ever so humble," but Brad interrupted her thoughts with a command: "Nicki, I want you to get out with Scotty and make sure he doesn't run off."

"Where would I go?" the boy protested. "We're in the middle of freakin' nowhere." He offered the comment as bait to his Gramma, but when she didn't rise to it, he realized again how frightened she was.

The boy opened the door of the Bronco and they climbed out into the rain. Nicki's legs and ankles were swollen and throbbing. After only a few steps, she was ready to go back to sleep.

The rain had let up a little, settling into a steady mist. "What is this place?" she asked. "Where are we?"

"We're off the road," Brad explained. "I don't know how you slept through the ride." His face darkened. "You look awful."

Nicki forced a smile. "I feel worse." She worried that she'd passed the point of no return.

"Are you going to be okay?"

She looked at him. What could she say?

"We'll get you some meds," Brad said. "That's the very next thing on the agenda."

"What's wrong with her?" Scotty wanted to know.

Brad changed back to badass. "Mind your own

business and get inside," he said. He gave the kid a little shove, and when he did, Scotty jerked away and whirled on Brad, who met him with the pistol pointed at his face. "You think you're tough, kid, but do yourself a favor and don't mess with me."

Gramma looked horrified. "Please don't hurt him."

"It's his choice," Brad said. "Pain or kindness. It's all up to Scotty." He let the words settle on the boy, who'd already taken two giant steps backward. "Let's get inside."

Gramma led, with Scotty close behind and Brad helping Nicki.

The inside of the house belied the destitute appearance of the exterior. The furniture—a chair and a sofa, arranged in front of a television—was worn but not worn out, and the television and DVD player couldn't have been more than a couple of years old. There was a faint old-person odor to the place, but on balance it seemed clean enough.

"How long have you lived here?" Nicki asked.

Gramma gave her a contemptuous look. When Scotty opened his mouth to speak, her withering glare froze his words in his throat.

Brad gestured with his gun toward the chair. "Have a seat, Gramma."

"Let the boy go," she said. "He's got nothing to offer you. I can be your hostage."

Brad gestured one more time. "I don't do hostages," he said. "And if I did, I guarantee that two is always better than one." He turned to Scotty. "Okay, kid, you take a seat on the floor next to your grandmother."

The boy did as he was told as Brad helped Nicki onto the sofa. "We're going to stick around here long enough for the weather to break."

"I'm hungry," Scotty said. He sat Indian style on the floor to the side of Gramma's chair.

"Suck it up," Brad snapped.

Nicki had had enough. "Why are you being such a shit to them? They're doing everything you tell them to do."

He ignored Nicki and asked Gramma, "How far away is your nearest neighbor?"

"The Mellings," Gramma said, pleasing Brad by answering right away. *That* was why he was being such a shit. "They're about a quarter mile south of here. We passed them on the way here."

"They friends of yours?"

Gramma made a noncommittal motion with her head. "I suppose."

"Cathy Melling is hot," Scotty said. "She showed me her father's *Playboy* collection."

Gramma's jaw dropped at that, and her head whipped around. "She did *what*?"

"Day before yesterday," Scotty said. "Out on their dune."

Gramma swatted the boy on the back of the head.

Scotty smiled and bounced his eyebrows. To Nicki's eye, he looked small for twelve, but she had always been a bad judge of boys' ages. Handsome and lean and capped with a mop of brown hair that hadn't seen a comb in way too long, he had struck her as the kind of boy who mercilessly teased girls like her.

Gramma caught the expression and swatted him again.

"Ow! You can't do that! You're not my mother!"

"Hey!" Brad boomed, startling everyone. He leveled a finger at Scotty. "You show some respect."

"Tell *her*," Scotty snapped.

"I'm telling *you*." The silence that followed made Brad uncomfortable. "Sorry," he said.

Gramma rubbed Scotty's hair. "You're just fine," she cooed. "You're a good boy. Don't listen to him."

The boy jerked his head free. "What's wrong with *her*?" he asked with a nod toward Nicki. Her face had lost most of its color. "She looks like crap."

Brad growled, "Shut up."

"I've got a bad heart," Nicki said.

"So, you're dying?"

"Scotty!" Gramma couldn't believe he'd just said that.

Nicki allowed herself a smile. "Yes, I am. Not today, though. At least, I hope not."

"Nobody's dying today," Brad snapped. "Or tomorrow or the next day. We're getting out of here, we're getting you your medicine, and we're letting these people get their lives back."

Chapter Twenty-seven

Darla slowed her cruiser and checked house numbers on the mailboxes. In the seat next to her, Carter stewed over the story he'd just heard. "So you think this is all about a guy named Peter Banks?" he said.

"I'm saying that if the sheriff is involved, it's all about an election year. If Peter Banks is our shooter and he's arrested, he's going to go public with the bit about smoking dope with Hines's kid. In a county like this, that's plenty to get you thrown out of office."

"So he suborns *murder*? Jesus, what kind of animal is this guy?"

Darla took her time answering. "Let's just say the sheriff likes his job."

Carter rubbed his forehead as he ran all the facts. "And to keep his badge, you honestly believe he'd send my daughter to prison on bogus charges?"

"I've been thinking about that," Darla said. "Just for the sake of argument, let's assume that I'm right in his motivation. Even in the best of circumstances, he has to know that his case against Nicki is purely circum-stantial, and weak as hell. She'd never be convicted. Maybe he thinks that he can have it all ways. In the worst case, he's recaptured a fugitive from out of state—a Yankee state, no less. That'll give him bragging rights and front-page coverage."

Carter thought about it, trying to find holes. "I like it," he said.

"I don't like it at all," Darla countered. "It's ugly and it's frightening, and it would put this town on its ear. But it's not that far from what people like you do every day."

"People like me?"

"Prosecutors. You pile on dubious charges all the time in hopes of leveraging testimony."

The characterization pissed him off. "There's a difference when you're working with the certifiable bad guys."

"Which you can't *really* know until after they're tried and convicted," Darla said. "I don't mean to be insulting. I'm just showing that it's not that far of a stretch in logic." She slowed the cruiser nearly to a stop, trying to make out the house numbers.

"You don't know which house is his?" Carter asked.

"He's my boss, not my buddy," she replied, squinting to read the numbers. "We're looking for four-seventeen."

The houses in the Sea Pines neighborhood were at least thirty years old. All of them bore that self-consciously woodsy look that was so popular in the 1970s—appropriate, Carter thought, given their location in the middle of a forest. They were bigger than the houses in the Maestris' neighborhood, and no doubt more expensive. The woodland setting gave the feeling of a place where laundry left outside would mildew before it dried.

"There it is," Darla said, pointing. She pulled into the driveway. Clearly, someone in the house was a gardener—not just the kind who plants a few flowers in the spring and keeps them watered, but a *real* gardener, whose creative eye saw a patch of land the way a sculptor sees a lump of clay. Carter saw grasses and flowers and bushes, none of whose names he cared to know, but which nonetheless turned an otherwise unremarkable yard into a work of art. A meandering trail of crushed seashells doubled for a front walk, leading all the way to the front door. As they hurried from the car to the shelter of the tiny front porch, Carter smiled at the little statues of frogs and bunny rabbits mingled among the flowers.

As before, Darla led the way. From the top of the porch, they could hear muffled conversation on the other side of the door, which stopped the instant she rapped with her knuckle. Fifteen seconds later, the door opened to reveal an attractive Latina woman clad in jeans and a red-and-white-striped shirt. Call it paranoia, but Carter could have sworn from her posture that she was trying to block their view of the inside.

"Hello, Mrs. Hines," Darla said. Carter noted that there was no extension of a friendly hand in greeting.

The woman nodded. "Deputy. Is there a problem?" Her voice quavered a bit as she spoke.

"This is Carter Janssen. Is Jeremy home?"

"What do you want to speak to him about?"

Without making too big a deal, Carter craned his neck to see past the gatekeeper. Behind her, a spider-web of imploded Sheetrock spoke of recent violence.

"Can we come in?" Carter asked. As the words left his mouth, he slid past Gisela into the foyer.

"Hey!" she protested.

"Carter, what are you doing?" Darla demanded. Once the door was all the way open, she saw the fractured wall, too. To Gisela, she said, "Is everyone okay in here?"

"Everyone is fine, and you have no right to be in my house."

Carter would have none of it. "Actually, once you opened the door and I saw the damage to the wall there, I think we had probable cause."

"And who are you?" Gisela's accent wasn't one that Carter had heard before. Hispanic in origin, it had a softness that would have been sexy on a different day.

"I'm a prosecutor from New York," he explained. He fought the urge to produce his business card. "Deputy Sweet and I are investigating the murder down at the Quik Mart this afternoon."

Gisela's eyes burned white-hot as they bored through Darla's head. "Does my husband know that you're here?"

Darla returned the glare. "That's really not relevant. May we see Jeremy, please?"

"Is he a suspect?"

"We need to speak with *him,*" Darla stressed, "not with you."

"He's not here."

Darla exchanged glances with Carter. "We heard you talking as we knocked on the door, ma'am. Please don't make this difficult."

"It's okay, Mom," said a voice from off to their left. They all turned to see the lanky form of Jeremy Hines standing in the open door to his bedroom. His left eye was a purple mass, and nearly swollen shut.

"Oh, my God," Darla said, moving a step closer to him. "What happened?"

Jeremy forced a smile. "I fell," he said.

Darla's jaw set as she put the hole in the wall together with the bruise on the teenager's face. "Your father did that to you, didn't he?" she said. "My God, you said he would and then it happened." She turned to Gisela. "Did your husband do this?"

Gisela stood frozen in place, her arms folded across her chest, staring at the floor. "You heard him," she said. "Jeremy fell."

"Against what?"

Jeremy looked at Gisela as best he could through the wounded eye, his face a blank. "It's not against the law to slip and fall, is it?"

"You don't have to tolerate this kind of abuse, Jeremy. All you have to do is say the word, and I can get you out of this." She turned again to Gisela. "You should be ashamed."

This time, when Gisela looked up, her eyes were again fierce. "You don't know what you're talking about," she said.

"He's your *son,* for God's sake," Darla shouted. "Your only child! How can you allow this to happen?"

Carter watched the eruption as one might watch a tennis match. "Excuse me," he said, interrupting them. "Can I remind you that we have a murder to solve?"

"We'll get to that," Darla spat. "There's a more immediate concern."

Jeremy zeroed in on Carter's comment. "I thought they caught the people who did the murder."

"No," Carter said, "they haven't."

"We're following up on some loose ends," Darla said. "Mr. Janssen here is the father of one of the kids who Ben Maestri identified as a killer."

Carter sensed that there was nothing accidental in Darla's misstatement of the facts.

"What do you want from Jeremy?" Gisela asked.

"I need to know where to find Peter Banks," Darla said.

Jeremy flinched. "Why?"

"Do you know where he is?"

"It's not my turn to watch him," Jeremy said. The old defiance had returned.

Each tick of the clock was a liability, and now they were engaging in verbal swordplay. "Look," Carter said. "This is way too complicated to go into right now, but we think that this Peter Banks might have had something to do with that killing. We just need to ask him a few questions. You either know where he is or you don't."

"So you can get your kid off the hook," Jeremy said.

Carter surrendered the point. "Yes. So I can get my daughter off the hook for a crime she didn't commit."

Darla said, "Tell me about the fight Peter Banks had with Chas Delphin."

Jeremy blanched. "What fight?"

They waited.

"It wasn't a fight," he said, caving to the silence. "It was a little yelling."

"About shoplifting."

Jeremy's eyes shifted to his mother and then back. "I didn't steal anything," he said.

"I didn't say you did," Darla said. "I just want to know where we might find Peter so we can talk to him."

Chapter Twenty-eight

Scotty stood, startling them all. "I'm hungry," he said for the fourth time, and he walked toward the kitchen.

Brad jumped to his feet to stop him, then pulled back. What the hell? They were all hungry. Maybe with food in their bellies, everybody would feel less edgy. He followed. "Don't even think about pulling a knife on me," Brad said.

Scotty didn't bother to acknowledge him; he just kept on into the kitchen. That's when Brad thought of the back door. "Wait!" he commanded, his booming voice making everybody jump. He quickstepped past the boy into the kitchen.

"What's wrong?" Scotty asked.

Brad checked out the door in the back. Only the storm door was closed, the solid wooden door wide open and inviting. "Nice try," Brad said. He walked past Scotty and pushed the door shut, leaning on it until he heard the tongue find its keeper.

"I wasn't going to run away," Scotty said.

Brad rolled his eyes and turned the key in the dead bolt above the knob, double-locking the door. He placed the key itself on top of the refrigerator, out of reach.

"Not now, anyway," he said. He watched as Scotty dragged his chair from the table over to the sink. "What are you doing now?"

"Getting the bread," Scotty said. "I want to make a sandwich."

Brad pointed to the open loaf that was already on the table. "What's wrong with that?"

The boy seemed startled by the sight of the open package. "I don't like that bread," he said. He climbed up on the chair. "We've got fresher stuff up here." He opened the cabinet.

Brad stepped up to join him. "Here, then, let me get it for you."

"I can do it myself!" Scotty barked.

Gramma appeared in the doorway to the kitchen. "What on earth are you two doing?"

Brad whirled at the sound of her voice, leading with his weapon. "I thought I told you to stay in the living room."

Gramma blanched at the sight of the gun and took a step back, warding him off with her hands. "Put that down," she said. "If I was going to run off, I'd have done it. Your friend is in there sound asleep. She's getting worse, you know."

Brad didn't like the way people had stopped obeying his commands. If the tide didn't turn, he was going to have to hurt someone just to restore order. He needed to keep them *scared*.

"I know she is," Brad said. "You don't have to tell me. Now, please go back into the other room."

"Don't you want to look at her?" Gramma asked.

With that question Brad knew something was up; he knew that he was at a disadvantage, even if he didn't know the specifics. He raised his weapon higher. "Let's go, Gramma, I don't want to have to tell you again."

The old woman's eyes shifted a little, focusing on Scotty just long enough for Brad to understand. Goddammit, they'd hidden something in the cabinet. He turned in time to see the pistol clutched in Scotty's hand.

Brad lunged for the weapon, but not before he saw the tiny muzzle flash.

Scotty had been thinking about the pistol since they'd been in the car. Gramma didn't think he knew about it, hidden the way it was, in the cabinet he was never to open, but he'd known about it for a week.

It was a little .22 revolver—a piece of shit that no one in his old neighborhood would dream of carrying—but it was loaded. All he needed was an excuse to climb up into the cupboard and get it. That's when he came up with the gambit of being hungry. Truth be told, he'd never even thought about dashing out the back door.

He thought he was dead in the water, though, the instant he saw Gramma in the doorway. He expected her to blow a gasket seeing him reaching into the Forbidden Cabinet. For the longest time, he just stood there on the chair, frozen in place, waiting for the tirade. Then he realized that she was actually *helping* him, running interference, distracting the kidnapper so he could snatch the gun out and shoot.

They were talking about Nicki, about her illness, and Scotty could tell that Brad was pissed that Gramma hadn't done exactly what he had told her to do.

Even standing on the chair, he had to raise himself on tiptoe to reach far enough in to find the weapon. Usually, it was right there near the front, and when he couldn't feel it on his first try, he wondered if maybe Gramma had moved it.

Then the tip of his middle finger—his bird-flipping finger—touched the hard plastic of the grip, and he knew he was home free.

His heart pounded hard enough for him to hear it as he wrapped his fist around the grip and pulled it from the cabinet.

There was no time to look or to think, no time to check to see if it was loaded. There was only time to turn, aim, and fire. In that second when he was turning, he caught a glimpse of Brad's gun coming around—a cannon compared to his. Scotty didn't know much about guns, but he knew the monster in Brad's hand would blow him apart if the kidnapper fired first.

There was no time for hesitation. No time for a mistake. He pointed the .22 at Brad's midsection and pulled the trigger.

The water on Shore Road was ankle-deep, and Trooper Matt Hayes was ready to move on. They'd been at this for nearly four and a half hours, and the north end roadblock hadn't turned up anymore than his at the south end. When the word came from the duty commander, Maury Donnelly, to stand down and let traffic pass, he was thrilled. Back at the barracks, a hot shower and dry uniform were calling his name.

All things considered, Matt admired the drivers' patience. Once they understood the stakes, they mostly tucked their frustrations away and went with the flow.

Even though they had failed to capture the killers, Matt felt confident that they'd trapped them. By reopening the road, though, they were about to lose their edge. Didn't it make sense that once the bad guys saw the stopped traffic, they'd hole up someplace? That's certainly what Matt would have done.

Matt took a last look at the road, drearier than ever under the gray skies. His was not to reason why, his was but to stand in the middle of a friggin' rainstorm and catch pneumonia. They had cops in white shirts to devise strategy.

Slogging his way back to his cruiser, he smiled as he thought back on the number of drivers who'd assumed that he was running a sobriety checkpoint and had contorted themselves accordingly to keep him from smelling their breath. As the faces flashed through his mind, he couldn't help but wonder if he'd somehow missed the big catch. How difficult would it be, he wondered, to sneak through the line? If they'd hijacked a car and driver, all they'd have had to do was crouch low in the backseat.

Trooper Hayes had just turned the ignition of his cruiser when he thought of the old lady in the big old Ford. He remembered that odd look in her face as she was talking with him. Why was that?

Oh, that's right. She was the one with the outstanding warrants. She had a grandson in the car with her, and was jumpy about being discovered. He remembered the kid's smile, and the way his soaked hair and clothing stuck to him as he confessed to messing around with his grandmother's purse. Jeez, if Matt had done that with his own mother's purse at the same age, there'd have been ten kinds of hell to pay. Matt's wife was the same way about her purse. It was as if all the secrets in the world—

A thought formed out of nowhere that made him freeze.

The kid was wet.

The boy had made a point of explaining that he'd been killing time searching though his grandmother's purse while she shopped for the videos, but if that had been the case, how did he get soaked? Besides, no kid that age would wait in the car while his grandmother chose videos.

Wait a second! If the kid had the purse, then how did Granny pay for the movies in the first place?

Holy crap, that was them. He'd been *this close*.

If only he could remember the woman's name. He could see her clearly enough in his head, and he could certainly make out the big green Ford, but what the hell was her name? He'd threatened to arrest her for unpaid summonses. It had been a bluff, so he hadn't written the name down.

They had an odd address. Lincolntown, as he re-called, down on the numbered lots. The old fishing community. He remembered because he used to spend time in one of those little shanties as a kid, back when his uncle would invite him down for a week in the summer. Very little to do, but lots of adventures to be found. Only a couple of hundred feet from water's edge during high tide, those were the first places to be evacuated when a hurricane blasted through.

What the heck were those people's names? Peters? Parnell? Something like that. Something that began with a *P*. Parker! That was it. June Parker. Don't ask him how he remembered that sort of detail, but it was the way his mind worked; the quirk to his personality that he hoped would one day earn him a detective's badge.

June Parker from Lincolntown. That should be easy enough to find. Pivoting the computer screen in his pa-trol car till he could see it better, Trooper Matt Hayes started typing.

* * *

Brad knew he was dead the instant he saw the gun. He lunged at Scotty without thinking, the instant the tiny gun fired. It popped twice and miraculously, impossibly, he missed! Brad didn't know how, not at point-blank range like this, but sometimes God just steps in on your side at exactly the right time.

Brad grabbed the revolver with his left hand and lurched it up and back, doubling Scotty over at the waist, while his right hand brought the barrel of the Sig down in a glancing blow across the top of the boy's head. Scotty yelled as a gout of blood burst from his scalp. The kid wouldn't let go of the gun. His forearm flexed and the tiny revolver fired again, this time launching a bullet within inches of Brad's eye on its way to drill into the ceiling.

Scotty's strength surprised Brad. He fought like an animal, wriggling and kicking and cussing as he tried to break free and finish the job he'd started. To break the boy's grip, Brad brought the heel of the Sig down hard on Scotty's knuckles.

Then the real screaming started. Gramma launched herself into the fray, her eyes red and wild. It was an animal sound, pure rage. She hit Brad with stunning force, leading with the heel of her hand into the tip of his nose. He heard a crunch, and his vision disappeared in a fog of tears and blood. There was another pained shriek as all three of them tumbled to the linoleum floor. He heard a clatter, and as he blinked his vision clear, he saw the little .22 skitter across the floor toward the locked back door.

"Run, Scotty!" Gramma yelled. "Run as fast as you can!"

The boy found his feet and Brad saw him staggering toward the door that led to the living room. "Stop!" he yelled, but the words only seemed to make the boy move faster.

Gramma clawed at Brad's face, her fingernails digging into the flesh of his cheeks as they searched for his eyes. He pushed her away with his gun hand, and delivered a half-powered punch with his left. Gramma grunted and rolled off him onto the crimson-smeared floor.

He had to stop the boy. Their only chance of survival was to stop him from running for help. Pausing long enough to snatch the .22 off the floor, Brad struggled to his feet and dashed for the living room. As he stepped over Gramma, she caught his ankle with her hand, and brought him hard back onto the floor.

"Leave him alone!" she shouted. "If you hurt him, I swear to God I'll kill you!"

Brad rolled to his side, avoiding the anemic punch she tried to throw, and scrambled through the entryway into the living room, where Nicki was struggling to rise from the sofa.

"Oh, my God," she gasped. "What happened?"

Brad didn't stop to explain. He ran to the door, where he saw Scotty lingering in the front yard. When he saw Brad at the door, he ran.

"Scotty, stop!" Brad commanded, and for an instant, Scotty did just that. He stopped and stared, his chest heaving from the effort, his face a crimson mask from the cut on his head. He listed a little to one side and holding his right arm as if it hurt, he looked to be all of eight years old. "Don't make me shoot you," Brad said. "I don't want to have to do that. Come on inside."

"Scotty, run!" Gramma yelled.

Brad turned to see the old woman approaching from

behind, and he raised the .22 in his left hand to point at her, even as he aimed the cannon in his right at the boy. "You stay right where you are," Brad said to Gramma. "Don't move, or I'll kill you both."

Gramma stopped, but there was no fear left in her face; it was all anger now. Her eyes never left Brad as she yelled, "Run, Scotty! Run now!"

Brad spat a curse as his head whipped around in time to see the boy inching backward. "I'll kill you, kid," he said. "I promise, I will." He raised the pistol higher. He whipped his head back to his left to keep tabs on Gramma, and then returned his gaze to the boy, who again seemed frozen in place. "Come on back inside, kid."

Something touched Brad's shoulder, causing him to jump. It was Nicki. She looked exhausted after her trek to the front door. "Let him go," she whispered.

"Leave me alone," he growled. "I don't want to do this."

"Then don't," she said.

"I don't have a choice."

"Sure you do. Just lower the gun and let him go."

Behind them, Gramma yelled again, "Please, Scotty, run!"

"Do you *want* me to kill him?" Brad boomed. "Do you *want* me to blow a hole through your boy?"

"He doesn't belong here," Gramma said. "He's not part of this. You've still got me. Look, I'll go and sit down if you'd like."

Brad's eyes were red, and the blood from his bludgeoned nose dripped from his chin. He looked back outside and spat a crimson spray. "Die an old man," he said to Scotty, "not a little boy."

It seemed like an eternity that they stood there, separated by twenty feet, staring at each other. Neither knew what the next move would be. Finally, Scotty pivoted and took off running.

"No!" Brad yelled. "Goddammit, no!" He took two steps forward and centered the gun sights on the fleeing boy. He had time for maybe three shots before he disappeared around the dune. The idiot kid wasn't even trying to zigzag as he ran. It was the simplest shot there was.

Brad tightened his finger. He had to do it. There was no choice.

But he couldn't.

Chapter Twenty-nine

When the electronic hardware on his belt chirped, Carter jumped, startling Deputy Sweet. "What?" she said.

Carter's first instinct was to reach for his cell phone, but by the time it chirped a second time, he realized that it wasn't the phone that he was hearing. It was his pager.

The pager. The one that he'd carried in silence for so long that he'd often wondered if it even worked anymore. The one that had brought false hope nearly thirty-six hours ago. Even as Carter read the LCD display, he was reaching for his cell phone. He dialed the number from memory, ignoring Darla's inquiry about what was going on.

"New York Heart-Lung Consortium. May I help you?"

Carter couldn't believe the ease with which they answered their phone, as if it were just any other business. "This is Carter Janssen. I received a page from you." He leaned against the door as he spoke, in part to steady his trembling hand.

"Have you been awaiting word on a donor?" It was the voice of an ageless female, very efficient.

"Yes, ma'am. In fact, we've been waiting for some time. My daughter's name is—"

"Can you hold, please? I'll put you in touch with the person you need to speak to."

He heard a *click* and then synthesized pop music. This was impossible, he told himself. It couldn't be happening.

"What is it?" Darla inquired yet again. There was real concern in her tone. "You look awful."

"It's the donor center," he explained.

Darla gasped, "Oh, my God. Do they have the transplants ready?"

Carter responded with a shrug, not trusting his voice.

He had no idea how long he sat on hold. *Not now,* he prayed. *Please don't let them be ready now.* He needed a week. A day. Donor organs had to be transplanted within hours, and they were so far out of the area—

After a click, a pleasant male voice said, "Hello, this is Dr. Cavanaugh. Is this Mr. Janssen?" It was exactly how he had begun the phone call two days ago.

"Yes, it is."

"Father of Nicolette Janssen?" The doctor read off his address and phone number from the computer. Had he forgotten that they'd done this same drill last time?

"Yes, it's me." He heard the frustration in his own voice and made a point to settle himself down.

"All right, and I just need you to answer the question you gave us on the application as a means of verifying your identity over the phone. What was your mother's maiden name?"

"Fox." Jesus, would he ever get to the point? And

while we're at it, where the hell was the groveling apology they owed him?

"Very good," said Dr. Cavanaugh, and Carter heard papers shuffling on the other end of the line. "I have some very good news for you."

"Again?" Carter felt dizzy as he pressed his head against the cool glass of the side window.

"A sixteen-year-old boy was killed tonight in an auto accident in Towanda County, blood type AB positive, and his parents have approved him as a heart-lung donor. You need to get Nicolette to the Pitcairn General Hospital as soon as possible so that we may begin the procedure. Congratulations."

Carter felt the panic blossom in his belly. "How much time do we have?" There had to be a way. There had to be time. He knew in his heart that Nicki had floated back up to the top of the list because the last screwup was no fault of her own. This time, the Janssens had broken all the rules; if it didn't work, she'd fall right back to the end of the line, another eighteen months. A death sentence.

"Well, sooner is always better than later," Dr. Cavanaugh explained, "but you don't have to panic. It will take an hour or so to harvest the organs, and probably another hour to get them to the hospital, so you've got plenty of time."

Carter's mind raced through his options. Bilateral heart-lung donors were impossibly rare, once-in-a-lifetime gifts. Literally once-in-a-lifetime. If he were to tell the consortium that—

"Mr. Janssen, are you there?" The silence had triggered a touch of alarm in the doctor's voice.

"I'm here," Carter said. "What's the longest you can hold on to the organs before there's a problem?"

"As I said, sooner is always best. Is there a problem? If there is, I need to know about it. These organs are precious and the last thing—"

"No, it's not a problem. I just have to pick Nicki up from school and take care of some housekeeping stuff. No real big problems." Carter closed his eyes as he spoke, feeling terrible about the lie.

Dr. Cavanaugh's voice took on a very sharp edge. "It's Saturday," he said.

Shit! This was why Carter never told lies. He sucked at the details.

"Mr. Janssen, if there's a problem, you need to be up front with me. These gifts are far too valuable to play games. Is there a reason why Nicolette can't get to the hospital in the next few hours?"

"Can I have eight hours?" he asked.

"Eight!" The doctor's incredulity came through the earpiece clearly enough to draw a look from Darla, who quickly returned her eyes to the road. "Why on earth would you need eight hours?"

And even that might not be long enough, he didn't say. In pondering his answer, he lost the opportunity for Dr. Cavanaugh to trust his words.

"Once more, Mr. Janssen," he said. "I cannot overstate the importance of you being forthcoming with me. I'm on the feather edge of withdrawing my offer and moving to the next name on the list."

"Please don't do that," Carter said. "Please." He decided to try the direct approach. "Okay, here's the truth of it, okay? I don't know where she is, exactly. I'm sure I can find her, but I don't know precisely how long that will take."

All traces of friendliness evaporated from the doctor's tone. "Were the instructions not clear enough for you, sir? We made it very clear that any form of travel out of the area would jeopardize any gift. What were you thinking?"

"I was thinking that we'd crossed this bridge two days ago!" Carter yelled, then he found the handle for his temper. Why did doctors presume the right to speak to you as if you were a child? "She was upset and she ran away. If you'd come through with your end of the promise on Thursday, we wouldn't have this problem now, okay? So how about cutting me a break and telling me how much goddamn time I have?"

Carter could hear papers moving on the other end. "I'm going to move to the next name on the list—"

"Oh, God, please don't do that," Carter begged. "Not now. Not yet. Give me some time. Any time. You owe me that. Hell, just tell me what my criteria are. If I blow it, I blow it, but at least give me a chance here."

"When can you let me know?" the doctor pressed. "People wait years for donor organs to become available—"

"Like I don't know that?" Carter boomed. "This is my daughter's life we're talking about. We've been waiting nine months ourselves. I'm desperate here. I just need to know how much time I have to work with."

For fifteen seconds, silence echoed from the other end of the line. Carter wondered if maybe the doctor had hung up on him. When Dr. Cavanaugh spoke, he dealt his words as if they were individual sentences, very slow and very measured. "We need to be in the OR within six hours of the time of harvest," he said. "Assuming that they've begun the harvest already, that means that I need you here within five hours. But I'll need a commitment from you within the hour to verify that you'll be here."

"And if we can't make it, where does she go on the list?"

"It's not like that, Mr. Janssen. There are too many factors. Nicolette is in the good position of having a universal-recipient blood type. On the other hand, if the next donor turns up with a rare blood type that is difficult to match, and we have a recipient waiting for that rare blood type, then obviously, we have to lean toward them. It would not be unreasonable to expect another ten- to fifteen-month wait."

The air rushed out of Carter's lungs. He needed to say something, to negotiate more, but there was nothing left to say. "Okay," he said. "I'll be back in touch in an hour."

"If I don't hear from you," the doctor said, "I will go to the next name on the list, and that decision will be unalterable, you understand?"

"Yes, sir, I do. And—"

"Let's say forty-five minutes, then," Cavanaugh said. "That's forty-four minutes and sixty seconds. At forty-four sixty-one, the offer is off the table."

Carter opened his mouth to acknowledge him, but the line was already dead. As he folded the phone closed, he laid his head against the back of the seat and closed his eyes. "On any other day of my life, that would have been the best news possible."

"Her transplants are ready?"

Carter nodded. "Somewhere in Towanda County, New York, parents are grieving the death of their son in an auto accident, and in the midst of all that grief, they had the decency to offer up his body parts to the living." He opened his eyes and rocked his head to face the deputy. "How macabre is that?"

"I think it's beautiful," Darla said.

"And after all the shit that two families have gone through, walking the tightrope between life and death, it's all going to mean nothing because I can't get Nicki there in time for the operation."

"How long did they give you?"

"I have to call them in forty-five minutes." He checked his watch. "Make that forty-four."

"You can't get her there in that amount of time," Darla said. "Even if your theories are correct, and everything goes right, there's no way you can have her on her way in less than an hour."

Carter closed his eyes again. "We've got six hours total."

"That's still not enough time."

His eyes opened and he lifted his head again. "Just whose side are you on?" he said.

Darla felt uncomfortable knowing that she'd wandered into territory where she did not belong. "Partly on your daughter's side," she said, but there was no commitment to the words.

Carter scowled. "Only partly?"

Darla shifted in her seat. "Well, mostly, I guess I'm on the side of the parents who are trying to build something good out of tragedy."

"The donors' parents."

"Exactly. If you delay, doesn't that lessen the success of the surgery?"

Carter couldn't deny it. "The game is fraught with risk. All I need is one small miracle. Everybody is owed one of those in their lifetime."

The crowd in Billy Yards's pool hall was a little thin, given the weather and the time of day. Carter and

Darla allowed their eyes to adjust to the darkness before stepping beyond the entryway and the abandoned bouncer's stand. This front room of Billy Yards's was arranged in a large horseshoe, with the main entrance and the bar on the closed end, and the parquet dance floor on the open end. A cluttered stage spoke of a house band, which hadn't yet arrived.

In the late afternoon, it turned out, the real action hummed in a dimly lit room just beyond the dance floor, where half a dozen college-age kids were knocking balls around three of six pool tables. Darla led the way to the back, and as the two of them crossed the threshold, five of the six stopped playing, while one merely noted the cop's presence with a crooked smile. Carter knew without asking that Mr. Cool was the one they were looking for.

"Why, good afternoon, Deputy Sweet," Peter Banks said. He sank an impossible shot into the side pocket, then moved on to his next.

"We need to talk with you for a minute, Peter," Darla said.

To Carter's eye, all of Peter's remaining plays were scratch shots, but the kid seemed intent on a combination to sink the four ball. "*We* need to talk to me?" Peter mocked. He lined up the shot. "Who's the suit?"

"Now would be a good time," Darla said. "Let's keep it friendly, okay?"

With a stroke so smooth that it could have been in slow motion, Peter's stick kissed the cue ball, which in turn kissed the two, which sank the four. He allowed himself a grin. "Have I done something wrong?" he asked. Compared to the nervousness around the room, Peter Banks seemed to be the only innocent party here.

"That's what we need to talk to you about."

Peter resumed sizing up the table. "Sounds like maybe I need a lawyer," he said.

"Only the guilty need lawyers," Darla said, drawing a look from Carter.

Peter laughed. "Oh, is that a fact? I didn't realize that the Court was so specific in the Miranda ruling." He decided on the one ball into the far corner and lined himself up. "Why don't you just say what's on your mind, Deputy, and I'll decide from there whether or not I should talk with you."

"It's about the murder at the Quik Mart this afternoon," she said.

Peter let the words just hang there as he took his shot. Perfect. He looked up again. "And?"

"And we want to talk to you about it."

Peter came around to their side of the table and offered his hand to Carter. "Peter Banks," he said.

"Carter Janssen. Mr. Banks, this is really very important."

Peter made a show of recoiling from his words. "*Mister* Banks? You must be from out of town."

"New York," Carter said.

The next shot was a gimme. All Peter had to do was breeze the three ball into the corner. He flubbed it, sending the three into the cushion instead. He held his posture and shook his head. "I suck," he said to himself. To one of the others in the room he added, "Your turn, Georgie."

He motioned with his head for them to follow him to a cocktail table just inside the threshold of the pool room. "I didn't have anything to do with that shooting."

"I heard that you had words with Chas Delphin a couple of days ago," Darla said.

Peter's eyes narrowed as he stewed on that. "Okay. But it was a couple of weeks, not days. He busted my balls for buying some beer without an ID. That's not exactly murder."

"What about the candy you stole?"

Peter looked at her as if she were crazy. "They were cupcakes. And I *didn't* steal them. I *tried* to steal them. Dudley Do-Right behind the counter wouldn't let me."

"That's not exactly respectful for the dead, Peter," Carter offered.

Peter laughed. "That a crime in New York, Counselor? Chas Delphin was a pansy-assed dickhead. I didn't respect him in life. Why the hell would I respect him after he's dead?"

Carter didn't know what to make of the aggression, and judging from her scowl, neither did the deputy.

Peter caught the look. "What, you want me to lie to you? I'm not a violent guy. Why the hell would I go there and shoot him today? That doesn't make sense."

"Because you didn't go in there to kill him," Carter said. "Because you didn't even think the gun was loaded. You just wanted to scare Chas and then you got tackled from behind and the gun went off."

Peter recoiled. "Is that what happened in there?"

"Where were you, exactly, at around two this afternoon?" Darla asked.

"Right here. I been here all day. Couldn't buy a break on the table till just before you guys got here."

"Will these people testify to that?" Carter asked.

Peter snorted a laugh. "You kidding? These guys are my friends. They'll tell you I was in Tahiti if I ask them to." When he saw that no one else was smiling, he dialed it down. "Yeah, sure. They'll vouch for me."

He turned to Carter again. "You think the gun was unloaded?"

"I didn't say that. I said I think *you* thought it was unloaded."

"I don't even own a gun." The magnitude of the problem Peter faced was dawning on him, and there was a new hint of desperation in his voice. "You can't possibly think I did this," he said.

"Do you own a red baseball jersey?" Carter asked.

"No."

"How about a red T-shirt?"

Peter started to deny it, but then opted for honesty. "Yes," he said. "And I own a blue one, two green ones, and God knows how many white ones."

"We're talking about an Essex High School jersey, probably," Darla prompted.

"What, like the ones Hines wears? Hell, no."

"Like the ones half this county wears," Darla corrected. "And why not?"

Peter's scowl deepened. "You mean because of all my rah-rah school spirit?" His tone dripped sarcasm. "I wouldn't let any part of that shithole school touch my body."

"Is that a fact?" Darla said. She stood from her chair and pulled a set of handcuffs from the pouch on her belt. "I need you to come along with me."

Peter couldn't believe this was happening. "You're *arresting* me?" Carter was a little stunned himself.

"No, I'm taking you into custody as a material witness."

"To *what*?" Peter protested. "I told you that I had nothing to do with that murder. You've got no evidence."

"I don't need evidence to treat you as a witness," Darla said. "Please put your hands behind your back."

Carter found himself surprised that Peter did as he was told. Apparently, the mouth worked independently from his spirit. "Hey, Mr. Lawyer, can she do this?"

Carter shrugged. "If she considers you to be a material witness, and she believes that you constitute a flight risk, then yeah, she can."

The panic didn't enter the young man's eyes until the bracelets ratcheted closed, but when it came, it came in a rush. "I didn't kill anybody," he protested. It was hard to tell, but he might have been crying. "Honest to God, I wasn't anywhere near that store today." He struggled, and Darla pulled once on his arm, bringing him to a stop.

When she spoke, her voice was soft, almost soothing. "Look, Peter, you've got nothing to be afraid of if you haven't done anything. I'm just taking you in to keep you at arm's reach while we look into this."

Peter tossed a quick look back at his buddies in the pool room, all of whom were gaping at the scene.

"Think of them," Darla continued, her voice even softer. "Today or tomorrow, if everything works out, you'll be back with them. Be a man now, and it won't come back to haunt you."

The act of getting off the sofa exhausted Nicki. She'd never had a spell this severe, and as her heart raced even faster, she had the sense that everything would soon get worse. She felt as if her head weighed fifty pounds, her arms and legs a hundred pounds each. She imagined that this was the way Superman felt in the presence of kryptonite, as if someone had found the valve to her body's strength reservoir and cranked it all the way open, until all that was left were the dregs on the bottom. All that, and the sensation that there wasn't enough air in the world.

She needed her meds.

With Scotty gone, Brad turned his rage to Gramma. "Sit down!" he commanded, gesturing with the Sig to a padded wooden chair in the corner.

She did as she was told, her face showing that she'd resigned herself to dying today.

He helped Nicki back into the corner of the sofa and handed her the .22. "Keep an eye on her," he said, "while I find something to tie her up with."

"Oh, Brad," Nicki moaned.

"Please don't do that," Gramma begged, but Brad seemed not to hear as he moved to the window and checked behind the drapes. He gave a satisfied nod when he saw the cord strung vertically between pulleys. Tucking his weapon under his arm, he fished his Leatherman out of its tiny holster on his belt, folded out the blade, and cut the cord into two six-foot lengths.

When he turned around again, Gramma's eyes were red as tears spilled down her cheeks. "Please don't tie me up," she said. "You don't have to do that. You can trust me. I swear."

Brad chuckled, then winced against a cramp in his belly. "I tried trusting," he said. "Just rest your hands on the arms of the chair."

"I'm claustrophobic." She was stalling for time, but the panic in her eyes was genuine.

"Please don't make this into a fight, okay? I'm tired of fighting." As if to emphasize the point, his belly cramped again, bringing a grunt. "You won't be here all that long anyway. Scotty will bring the police soon enough."

Gramma did not fight. She placed her hands on the arms of the chair just as she had been asked, and she didn't move as Brad lashed her in place with loop after loop of the cord.

"We're just going to take your truck and see what we can do to get away. I'm not going to hurt you."

"Why bother to tying me up at all, then?"

"In case you have a machine gun in here." Brad smiled as he finished the last knot. "I don't need you shooting me on my way out, know what I mean?"

"Looks to me like you've already been shot," Gramma said. She nodded at some smears of blood on his shirt.

Brad's hand went to the spot, and as it did, the cramp fired up again. When he lifted the front of his shirt he saw a larger smear of blood and a purple bruise. "Shit."

"Let me see," Nicki said from the sofa. Sitting up was difficult, but there was nothing wrong with her vision.

Brad pulled his shirt off over his head and took a couple of steps closer to Nicki. She saw what might have been a big bee sting, just a half inch up and to the right of Brad's navel. She started to touch it, but Brad recoiled, and stepped away.

"There's a hole, Brad. No shit, there's a hole right next to your belly button."

He made a sound that might have been a grunt or a chuckle "I don't believe it," he said. "I thought the little shit missed me. I wondered how it was possible, but I thought for sure that he missed me. *Damn* it!"

"Doesn't it hurt?" Nicki didn't understand. She'd

seen the damage done to Chas. This hardly looked like anything.

"Shit, shit, *shit.*" He looked at Gramma, whose expression was a study in intentional passiveness. "Look what he did!"

"What did you expect him to do?" Gramma asked.

Brad looked again at his bloody fingers. "I expected him to be a scared little kid."

"You disgust me," Gramma said.

Yeah, well, I disgust myself sometimes, he didn't say. He picked up Gramma's car keys from the table where she'd dropped them and turned to Nicki. "You're looking pretty bad," he said. "Can you still walk?"

Nicki looked sad. And exhausted. "It's over, Brad," she said. "Don't you see? With my spell and you being shot, it's over."

"Not yet it's not," Brad said.

"There's no way we can get away," Nicki argued.

"Not if we stay here. Now, I'm leaving in that truck. Are you coming with me?" When she didn't answer in two seconds, he started for the door.

"Wait!" Nicki called. "Just help me up."

He hesitated. "You sure?"

"Somebody's got to keep you out of trouble," she said with a little smile.

Brad took back the .22 and stuffed both it and the Sig into the back of his waistband, then paused just long enough to put his shirt back on before holding out both hands as an invitation to help her out of the deep, soft cushions of the sofa.

It was a struggle, but he got her to her feet, and together they limped toward the door. Nicki paused and looked back toward Gramma. The old woman looked helpless. "I'm sorry," Nicki said. "Honestly, you'll never know how sorry I am to have put you through this."

"Come on," Brad said, and he pulled on her arm. "We don't have time." When they were on the stoop, he closed the door behind them.

"Where are we going?"

"Away. The plan's the same as it's always been. When we get some miles between us and the cops, we'll switch out cars again."

"What about that?" Nicki pointed to his blood stain.

"I can make it," he said. "It's a tiny bullet, but a hospital would still have to report it. We'll figure something out on the way. Can *you* hold out?"

"If you can, I can," she said. Fact was, she was probably going to sleep through most of it. Brad was the one in the most pain.

"Good," he said. "That's very, very—"

He froze in mid-step. The hood of the Bronco was open. "What did that little shit do?" He left Nicki and moved to the truck. As he crossed the back side of the vehicle, he saw the long-handled bolt cutters lying in the sand, and he knew exactly what he was going to find.

"Shit!" He shouted the word to the gray-black sky, turning his face up to the pounding rain. "God *damn* it!" In a rage, he picked up the bolt cutters, holding one of the handles as if it were a baseball bat, and swung it as hard as he could into the driver's side door, over and over again. "You. Son of a bitch. I. Should've shot you. When I had the chance." To punctuate the last phrase, he threw the cutters through the window in the door, launching a shower of glass pebbles.

Nicki stood there, stunned, watching as Brad melted down in front of her. When he was done, the bloodstain on his soaked shirt was three times the size it had been before, and the look she saw in his face was one of utter defeat.

"You don't get it, do you?" he said, listing to one side and struggling to catch his breath.

"What is it?" Nicki asked.

"He was still out here when I came after him. He'd had a good half minute to run away, but when I stepped out, he was still here." He said this as if it would somehow explain his outburst. Nicki just waited for the rest.

"He cut the damn battery cable, Nicki! He took those bolt cutters and he cut the cable in two. We're screwed. We're totally, hopelessly screwed."

Of the things that Nicki understood, cars were nowhere on the list. "Can't you hot-wire it, like you did with the others?"

Brad looked at her as if she'd grown a new eye. "No! It's the fucking battery! The little shit did the one thing that irreversibly cripples a car. When you hot-wire, you just bypass the ignition. You still need the goddamn battery."

When he was done, there seemed to be nothing left. He breathed hard, waiting for someone to cough up an idea. Nothing came but darkness and harder rain.

"What are we going to do?" Nicki asked.

Brad snorted a chuckle, and his shoulders sagged. "I guess we go back inside and wait," he said.

"But the police will be here."

He nodded. "And soon."

Nicki was confused. "What happens then?"

"Let's go inside," Brad said. "You'll catch your death out here." He tried to smile, but there was no humor left.

Nicki started to move, but Brad didn't. "Are you coming?"

"I'll be there. I just have one more thing to do." He pulled the Sig from his waistband.

"Brad, no!"

He raised the weapon and fired one shot through the Bronco's radiator.

PART FIVE
TIME TO LIVE

Chapter Thirty

Peter Banks protested bitterly about being treated like a prisoner, cursing Darla Sweet and her entire family tree. Darla tried shutting him up by telling him that his belligerence was only hurting his own case, and Carter told him that he was a fool to say anything from now on without his lawyer being present. Neither approach worked, so by the time Carter was dropped back at his car, he was relieved to be free of them both.

Something about Darla's conclusions vis-à-vis Peter didn't sit right with him. First of all, Carter had a hard time seeing that kid in the role of a murderer—even an accidental one. His shock at being accused seemed too genuine, as did his calm demeanor when they arrived at the pool hall. Guilty people ran away, or at least tried to.

Just as Nicki and Brad had.

This Banks kid never seemed even close to bolting. His eyes didn't shift, he didn't seem to calculate distances to the exits. Instead, he played a damn fine game of pool. Perhaps Deputy Sweet was not an aficionado of the game, but Carter knew from personal experience that when nerves got edgy, pool shots paid the price. Peter Banks was threading needles with the cue ball.

But if Peter wasn't their man, Carter was no closer to saving Nicki than he was when he spoke to her on the phone three hours ago.

He had to find that tape. There'd be no arguing with a video. Standing there in the parking lot with his key poised at the lock, he cast his gaze back at the façade of the Quik Mart. Crime scene tape sealed the opening of the doors, but all of the investigating personnel had left. In their minds, he supposed, the case was closed.

Wiping the mask of rainwater from his face, Carter ran his options through his mind. The one that made the most sense involved calling the state police and playing out his new theory to the powers that be. To do that, though—to accuse the senior cop in any community of this level of malfeasance—a person had better have his shit together in a watertight bag. Circumstantial evidence wouldn't be enough. Which meant that Carter didn't yet have what he needed.

It all came back to the damn videotape. *That* was the single piece of evidence that would get everybody off Nicki's case.

Suppose the tape was still in the store. That was possible, wasn't it? If Hines couldn't have smuggled the tape out under his shirt, and the place had been crawling with investigators ever since, then maybe he'd hidden it somewhere in a back room. Surely not. Maybe. Carter considered prying open a door and combing through the Quik Mart himself, but he dismissed the thought. He wouldn't know where to look, and it would hardly help Nicki's case for him to be arrested on a burglary rap.

The more he thought about it, the more he fumed. How could one father put another through this kind of anguish? What would drive Hines to do such a thing?

Surely, the sheriff's own instincts as a parent should have triggered some measure of mercy.

It just didn't add up. At a visceral level, Carter couldn't buy the motivation inherent to Darla Sweet's theory of the cover-up. It would take a beast with no heart to inflict this kind of distress and pain on innocent people merely for the sake of protecting one's career, or even a son's future as a professional athlete. The motivation just seemed too light. Add to that the apparent innocence of Darla's prime suspect, and that left one huge mystery.

Not only would the sheriff have had to stash the video, but he also would have had to wipe the murder weapon free of fingerprints. Surely, the killer didn't stick around to do that, and for Hines to go to those ends to protect the son of a bitch—

"Oh, my God," Carter breathed. The answer flashed into his head with such brilliance and clarity that it *had* to be the right one. Sheriff Hines was covering for his son, Jeremy. That explained everything. It never did make sense for Sheriff Hines to go through all of this for the sake of a ne'er-do-well dropout, but it was the least he could do to protect his own flesh and blood.

Carter thought about the look on Gisela Hines's face when they'd first arrived, and about that huge bruise on Jeremy's eye. Darla had been quick to conclude that the bruise came from a beating from his father, and maybe some of it was, but it was equally feasible—even *more* feasible in Carter's mind—that Jeremy Hines's black eye was the result of one hell of a punch delivered by someone trying to foil a robbery.

He thought back to his telephone conversation with Nicki. She'd told him that Brad had tackled the robber from behind and hit him hard in the face.

But why would Jeremy Hines rob a store? What

could he possibly hope to gain by sticking a gun in a store clerk's face? Surely, in a town this size he didn't think that he could get away with it.

As he felt himself running away with this new take on events, Carter forced himself to put on the breaks. To convince anyone—even himself—that this theory had merit, he needed means, motive, and opportunity. Right now all he had was a wild hare of an idea.

And a bruised eye.

And a gun wiped clean.

And a million questions.

It was time to pay another visit to the Hines residence.

Scotty had never bled like this before. About the worst was a gash in his knee when he'd slipped at the swimming pool. Back then, he could see the flash of white bone smiling back at him from behind the torn skin. That had hurt like crazy.

This thing on his head didn't hurt all that much, but it bled like he was in a horror movie. The rain probably made it look worse than it was, but the blood had turned his T-shirt crimson. He could even see little red rivers flowing down his legs. He wondered if maybe his brains were hanging out. That was the fear that kept him from touching the wound. The very thought of brain tissue under his fingernails made him feel queasy.

He picked up the pace and ran again. He had to get to the Mellings'. From there he could call the cops and then they could rescue Gramma.

Did you see the way she swung into action to fight Brad? She was like an animal, flying through the air and nailing the son of a bitch like a linebacker. Who'd've thought? She saved Scotty's life. He never in a million years thought anyone would risk their own life for his. With Mama, it had been just the opposite. In Scotty's world, people existed for themselves.

After all, Gramma barely even knew him. That was because she'd thrown Mama out of the house for getting knocked up with him, and they never talked to each other. In fact, if it hadn't been for Scotty, none of the bad shit that tracked his mama through life would have happened.

No surprise there. Scotty knew he was a pain in the ass. It was his mouth that got him into trouble. He didn't have that little switch inside that other people had to cut off thoughts before they could become words. Sometimes, he found himself saying shit that he hadn't even known he'd been thinking.

It was only natural that Gramma got so pissed off at him. *Everybody* got pissed at him. Just last week, he'd promised Gramma that he'd move out the instant he turned sixteen—as soon that he could get the e-constipation paper signed. E-constipation was the process by which kids could be treated as adults under the law. Kathy Melling had told him all about it.

Gramma laughed when he told her the plan; he'd never heard her laugh so hard. "Honey," she'd said, "I wouldn't sign your e-constipation papers on a bet." He hadn't thought that the idea was all that ridiculous.

But he *had* begun to think that maybe she was beginning to like him a little. They laughed a lot when they weren't screaming and being mad at each other.

Now she was alone with a couple of killers. And that one—that Brad—was plenty pissed off.

If something happened to Gramma, Scotty would have nowhere to go. Those first nights after Mama's murder, when no one was sure what to do with him, were the most frightening of his life. If Gramma got murdered too, where would he go?

Now that he thought about it, maybe cutting the battery cable hadn't been such a good idea. Maybe if he hadn't, they'd be gone now. He'd done it on an impulse, really, inspired by seeing the long-handled bolt cutters leaning against the wall of the garage. He was worried that they might try to kidnap Gramma and drive her off and do something terrible. Rape her, maybe—which Scotty had only recently learned meant a lot more than the when-a-man-beats-up-a-woman explanation that his mama had given him.

In the heat of the moment, Scotty had reasoned that if the killers couldn't drive off anywhere, they'd be easier to catch. Now, as it was taking him for-freaking-ever to get to the Mellings', he wondered if he hadn't just pushed Brad over the edge. Everybody knew that a trapped animal was more dangerous than a roaming one, and Scotty wondered if the same thing applied to people.

If they did hurt Gramma, or if they killed her, it would be all his fault. He picked up the pace even more.

Up ahead, a flash of something blue caught his eye. Through the rain, in the lingering early twilight, he could barely make it out. It looked like a car.

Not just any car, but a police car.

And it was heading right for him.

Trooper Hayes blinked twice. When he first saw the speck in the distance, he didn't know what to make of it through the fog of the rain. It took him all of three seconds to connect the dots.

He pulled the microphone from its clip and spoke the words that would bring cops from all over the state to this little corner of Lincolntown.

Chapter Thirty-one

Carter Janssen didn't bother to knock this time. Blocking the space between the boxwoods with his vehicle lest someone try to get away, he strode up the walk, across the porch, and into the Hines's living room. In New York, they called it "home invasion."

Gisela rushed in from the dining room, her features set in a mask of fear. She struggled with the weight of an over-and-under shotgun, the stock tucked under her arm, the muzzle pointed at him.

"Get out of my house," she said.

"I need to speak with Jeremy," Carter said. "Where is he?"

"Get out."

The shotgun told him much of what he needed to know. "I'll leave right after I have a talk with your son."

"I'll count to three," Gisela said. "Then I'll pull the trigger. One."

"Go right to three," Carter said. The sight of the muzzle stirred his insides, but the look in the woman's eyes screamed bluff. "I need to speak with him now."

"About what?"

"I think you know," he said.

"You can't take him away," Gisela said. She started to cry. "He's too young. It was all a mistake."

"I know," Carter said. "He thought the gun was unloaded, didn't he?"

Her grief turned to shock. "How did you know?"

"Mrs. Hines, honestly, I'm not concerned about what he did or why. I just need to exonerate my daughter. She had nothing to do with this. It isn't right for her to suffer. There's a transplant waiting for her. Heart and lungs. We're about to miss the deadline, and unless I get the truth from Jeremy, that one bullet will have killed yet another child."

The pressure seemed more than Gisela could bear. The muzzle drifted downward. "Please don't let them take my baby away," she cried.

Carter took a hesitant step forward, hoping perhaps to comfort the woman, but a noise from behind made him spin on his heel. It was a distinct *thump,* and it came from the room where Jeremy had emerged last time. It was the sound of a window opening. Dammit, the kid was getting away!

Carter lunged toward the bedroom.

"Don't!" Gisela screamed from behind. "Leave him be!"

Carter tried to ignore the leaden feeling in his stomach, the tingling in his back as his skin tightened to receive buckshot. The bedroom door was locked. Stepping back, he threw his shoulder into it, cracking it down the middle. The flash of pain in his shoulder made him wonder what exactly had broken.

"I'll shoot!" Gisela yelled.

He ignored her. She'd do what she thought she had to do; he had no control over that. But he wasn't about to let his only hope disappear. He took a step back and fired a kick with the flat of his foot, landing a blow just above the knob. The jamb splintered in an explosion of wood and hardware.

Gisela screamed.

At a glance, Carter saw that this was not the first violence done in the confines of the bedroom. Near a little student desk, shelves had been toppled, their contents strewn across the floor. Near the bed, he could almost make out the outline of a head and a pair of shoulders where someone had been tossed into the wall, puncturing the drywall. A two-by-three-foot picture frame lay on its side near the bed, its glass shattered, and if Carter wasn't mistaken, the stains on the carpet looked like blood.

Gisela flung herself into Carter, knocking him off balance, but he stayed on his feet. She was punching him now, all over his back and shoulders, but he didn't feel the blows. He didn't care. He ran to the wide-open window, where a tattered screen hung by a corner. In the distance, he could see a lanky young man in shorts and a T-shirt disappearing into the trees.

Carter ducked low as he stepped through, dropping four feet to the soft, sandy ground. He hopped three times in a struggle to keep his balance, then found his feet and took off at a run.

"Jeremy!" he yelled. "Wait up! I need to talk to you!"

The kid had vanished into the trees. How did he do that? The woods didn't seem *that* thick out here. Most of the trees were so scrawny, with foliage that didn't thicken till waist height, that he'd have thought it impossible to hide. But Jeremy was nowhere to be seen.

So, where was he? Could it be that he was just that freaking fast, that he could build insurmountable distance between them in just a few seconds? Carter knew that he wasn't in the shape that he once was, but really.

Carter slowed to a jog. Running made sense only when you knew where you were going.

He called out to the woods, "Jeremy? Running doesn't make it any easier. Come on out. I'm not a cop, I'm not here to arrest you. I just need to talk. When we're done, you go your way and I'll go mine."

A new wave of rain arrived, a thunderous roar of water made louder by the acoustical tricks of the woods. He shouted again, but it was hard to tell if his voice would carry for miles or inches. Certainly, it would be a simple matter to sneak up on somebody in weather like this, and that was a thought that made him move more slowly.

There was no mistaking the sound of a gunshot, though, and the one that rocked Carter's world seemed to come from only a few feet away.

Chapter Thirty-two

Nicki lay back on the sofa, trying her best to fight off the fatigue.

"I'm stumped," Brad said. He'd pulled a straight-back chair into the living room from the kitchen and allowed himself a brief rest. "Honest to God, I just don't have a clue what to do next. I should have shot the kid."

"You couldn't have," Nicki said.

Brad snorted. "Yeah, I could. And this is why I should."

Nicki closed her eyes. "You're not like that. You couldn't hurt a child."

"What makes you think so?"

"You were hurt too many times yourself." She glanced at him in time to catch the roll of his eyes. She smiled. "You want to be tougher than you are," she said. "You want to be a bad guy, but it's not in you."

He started to argue, but he let it go. What was the point? Nicki's universe played by the rules. In it, good things came to good people, and good people never did bad things. Having never met animals like Peter Chaney and Lucas Georgen, she'd never understand that sometimes it was necessary to kill. Even here, in this god-forsaken little house, she couldn't wrap her mind around the fact that it was *important* for Gramma and Scotty to be afraid of him. Fear was what kept him from having to hurt them worse than he did.

If they'd been even more frightened, Scotty never would have risked going for the gun.

If there were, in fact, rules, no one in Brad's universe played by them. Wasn't there a rule, for example, that you don't get chased down for crimes you didn't commit? The irony made him dizzy. It wasn't even his real crimes that were going to bring him down; it was the one accusation that *wasn't* true that was going to kill him.

For the first time since this whole adventure began, he felt a tug of panic. There'd been stress and fear before, certainly a sense of danger, but over the past few years, he'd gotten used to that. He'd come to live with it as surely as a wounded veteran lives with his limp. Sometimes he told himself that a pervasive sense of danger was what kept him sharp, prevented him from becoming complacent.

But this panic thing was new to him. He'd subsisted for so long on hope and luck that he'd allowed himself to believe he had some measure of control. What an idiot.

He and Nicki were screwed: stuck in the middle of nowhere, without wheels, and neither one of them in any condition to walk. What the hell were they supposed to do now? When he glanced to Nicki for advice, all he got in return was that expectant look. She was counting on him to have the answers.

"Are you all right?" Nicki asked.

Brad realized that he'd been completely lost in his thoughts. "Huh?"

"You're bleeding pretty badly. Are you all right?"

He forced a smile. "I guess that question pretty much answers itself, doesn't it?" It was a weeping wound, not a pumping one, but leaking enough volume to soak the lower part of his T-shirt and the upper part of his trousers.

"What are we going to do, Brad?" Maybe she thought that asking enough times would produce an answer.

He heard the fear in her voice, saw it in her eyes. "We could always take a nap," he said.

"How long before they come?"

Brad looked out the window. "Out here? Hard to say. Ten minutes, maybe. I wouldn't think any more than twenty. They won't storm the place as long as we've got her with us." He nodded toward Gramma.

"Let's let her go," Nicki said.

"What?"

"Look at her." As Nicki spoke, Gramma seemed to grow older in her chair. "She didn't do anything."

Brad dismissed the notion out of hand. "No way. She's the only insurance we've got."

"Against what?"

Brad gave her a look.

"I don't want hostages," Nicki said. "I don't want anybody getting hurt for me. All I want is peace. I want all of this to end happily."

Brad scowled. "Do you really think that's possible? With the way our luck's been running, you can't possibly think there's a happy end."

Nicki offered up a wan smile. "I guess it all depends on what makes you happy. If getting out of here is key, then no, probably not."

Brad didn't get it. Actually, he feared that he did, but didn't want to jump to conclusions. "What are you talking about?"

"You said it yourself," Nicki said. "Sometimes it's

just a matter of setting your own terms." A wave of pain surged through her chest, and Nicki winced. Brad saw the deep furrows in her brow as she fought off whatever was attacking her insides. The sound of her breathing reminded him incongruously of someone petting a piece of sandpaper. It hurt to listen.

When he turned back to Gramma, he saw her watching, an expectant look in her face. "You're not going anywhere," Brad said. Just to make sure, he rose from his chair and checked to make sure that she was still securely bound. Gramma asked if he could loosen the rope a little, but Brad didn't bother to answer.

When he was done, he offered the .22 to Nicki. "Keep an eye on her," he said.

"Where are you going?"

"To piss." Ask a direct question and you get a direct answer.

"I don't want the gun," Nicki said.

"Look, we can't afford—"

"I don't want it."

He let the pistol hover, then shoved it back into his bloody waistband. "Fine."

Things inside his gut didn't feel right at all. The pain was a constant, a dull ache that stabbed him every time he moved, and sometimes when he didn't, but it wasn't crippling. No worse than the aftermath of most of his beatings in prison, and not nearly as bad as some.

When he pissed a solid stream of blood, though, Brad knew that he'd been kidding himself. This wasn't that pink-tinged stream that he'd come to expect after a night with the boys in the joint, the gift of pummeled kidneys; this was a dark crimson that turned the toilet water scarlet. So, being gut-shot wasn't about unspeakable pain after all.

It was about bleeding to death on the inside.

In the distance, through the frosted open window, he could hear the sound of approaching sirens. Taking a long pull of air through his nose, he held it then let it go through pursed lips. So this was it. They were coming. Now was the time for all the tough choices.

He had to get ready. Once the cops heard that this was a hostage situation, the first thing they'd do was call in a tactical unit. Out here in the boonies, that might mean just a couple of good old boys with shotguns, but the one constant to tactical units everywhere was a sniper with a long gun and the temperament to use it. Starting with what was closest, he shut the bathroom window and locked it. The frosted glass would obscure them enough to keep the shooter from getting a good view.

Nicki called from the other room, her voice trembling. "Brad, I hear sirens!"

He flushed the toilet and opened the door. "They're faster than I had hoped," he said. The next stop was the living room, where he pulled the draperies closed. "Listen to me," he said to Nicki. "This is very important. Stay away from the windows. If they see you, they're likely to shoot."

"Oh, my God," she gasped.

His belly hurt. He was feeling light-headed, too. The cops' first steps when they got on the scene would be driven by whatever the kid had told him. If the responding officer came to the door, Brad would have no choice but to shoot. In his current condition, he couldn't fend anyone off in a fight.

He needed to stop the cops from leading off with the wrong move. His brain wasn't working all that well right now, but in the seconds he had to plow through his available options, he came up with only one, and it righteously sucked.

He limped to the phone and picked up the receiver. Then he dialed 911.

Carter cowered behind a tree, trying to make himself invisible. Where the hell was the shooter?

"Show yourself," a voice said from the woods. It was a young voice, and stress made it crack.

Carter didn't respond. The gun changed everything. It wasn't what he'd been expecting.

"I could shoot you now if I wanted you dead," the voice said. "I can see you."

Carter's skin crawled as if covered with ants. Laying on his belly in the saturated mulch of the forest floor, he was shivering.

Two more shots shattered the afternoon and chips flew from his tree, just inches above his head.

"The next ones will kill you," the voice said. "Now, stand up where I can see you."

Carter's mind raced. What were his options here? He could stand and be shot, or he could lie on his belly and be shot. He decided to go for the greater dignity and he raised himself to his knees. When he wasn't shot down immediately, he thought that he might actually have a chance.

"Okay," Carter said to the forest. "Now it's your turn."

"Put your hands where I can see them," the kid said.

Carter made a shrugging gesture. "They *are* where you can see them. I'm not armed."

"Put them up in the air, then."

Carter thought about that. It was time to piss on a

new fire hydrant. Someone was going to be in control of this situation, and in a perfect world, that person was never the one with the gun. "No," he said.

"Excuse me?" The incredulity in his voice nearly made Carter laugh.

"I said no," Carter repeated. "Not until you show *your*self."

Some bushes rustled up ahead. Out stepped Jeremy Hines, a pistol clutched in both hands. It looked like a World War Two–vintage .45, with a muzzle the size of a manhole.

"You can put that down," Carter said. "I'm not armed. I'm not here to hurt you."

The boy looked confused. As he cocked his head to think, a stream of rainwater dripped from his nose.

"Why'd you shoot Chas Delphin, Jeremy?"

"Who said I did? I thought you were looking for Peter Banks on that."

"We got Peter Banks," Carter said. "But then we got more evidence. It was you. You were wearing a red jersey, and you nearly got away with it, except someone else startled you and beat the shit out of you."

Jeremy's jaw dropped. "You don't know that."

"Come on, Jeremy," Carter snorted. "You left evidence all over the place." That last part was a lie, of course. He wanted the boy to feel as if everything from this moment forward led to his inevitable confession.

"What kind of evidence?"

Carter's eyes narrowed as he pretended to formulate an answer, but ultimately, he just shook his head. "No, I don't think I'll share that with you. Not just now. All I want to know is why you did it. How did you think you could get away with it?"

Jeremy's eyes darted some more, scanning the woods

for any reinforcements. "If you're talking about your daughter and her friend—if you're talking about the *real* murderers—nobody's gonna believe a word they say."

"Oh, I think they will," Carter said. He took a step forward but stopped when Jeremy raised the pistol higher. He showed the boy his palms as a peace offering. "This doesn't help."

"Nobody will believe them," Jeremy repeated.

Carter decided to probe a little deeper. "I've got the security video," he bluffed.

"You *couldn't*!" The kid knew his mistake as soon as he heard himself.

Carter smiled. "Couldn't? And how would you know that?"

Jeremy trembled. "Y-you don't know what you're talking about."

"Yeah, I do," Carter said. "And so do you. Let's drop the charade and set the record straight, okay?"

The boy raised the gun higher again. "I could shoot you."

For an instant, Carter thought that was exactly what he was going to do. He flinched, but he didn't back off. "Who would you blame that one on? There's no hiding secrets like this, Jeremy. People try all the time, but murder is just too big a crime."

"I didn't murder anyone." His voice broke again.

"I believe you," Carter said. Clearly, it wasn't what Jeremy was expecting to hear. "I think you believed that the gun was empty."

The kid's eyes got huge and he nodded enthusiastically. "Yes!" he said. He nearly shouted it. "That's right. I didn't think it was loaded. I just wanted to scare him." He paused as the inevitability of it all settled in on him. "It wasn't my fault," he said. "If that guy hadn't hit me, the gun never would have gone off. It wasn't my fault."

Carter said nothing. What was the sense in pointing out the fallacy of his reasoning now? As the world closed in on him, legal technicalities would be of little interest. "Can you answer my question, though?" he asked.

Jeremy looked confused.

"How did you think that you'd get away with it in a town this small?"

"He *didn't* think he'd get away with it." The voice from Carter's right startled him. He turned to see Frank Hines emerging from a line of trees. He half expected to see a weapon drawn, but both of the sheriff's hands were empty. "He was punishing me."

Jeremy's fear turned to panic, and he became a little boy. "I-I'm sorry, Dad," he said. "He came back to the house, and I didn't know what to do."

Frank Hines waved off his son's whimpering with a shooing flip of his hand. "I know," he said. "Your mother called me." To Carter, he said, "You must be proud of yourself."

"Not especially," Carter said. What was there to be proud of?

"You broke your big case," Hines said. "Ruined a bunch of lives. That's all in a day's work for you, isn't it?"

Something in the sheriff's tone put Carter on edge. He kept watching those hands, realizing that he'd been a fool to come out here alone. "I'm just trying to prevent an injustice."

Hines snorted a bitter laugh. "Preventing injustice. Funny, that's what I thought I was doing."

Carter recoiled. "By framing innocent kids?"

"Is that how you see Brad Dougherty, Counselor?

You see him as an innocent? He's killed two people that we know of, and he's escaped from prison. If that's your definition of innocent, then I shudder to think what guilty must look like to you."

Carter pointed at Jeremy. "There it is, Sheriff. *That's* what guilty looks like."

Hines followed Carter's finger and looked long and hard at the boy with the gun. "No," he said. "That's what stupid looks like. He made a *mistake,* for Christ's sake. He never intended to shoot anyone."

"There's a dead boy and his family to whom that makes no difference at all," Carter said.

Hines's eyes shifted back to Carter, and he smiled at a joke that only he could hear. He mocked, "To *whom* that makes no difference, huh?" The smile turned to a laugh. "Think you've got the high ground, do you? The high and *mighty* ground? Your daughter's hanging out with a murderer, and you think—"

"Brad Ward—or Dougherty, or whatever the hell his name is—didn't commit *this* murder, Sheriff. And neither did my daughter."

"Yes, he did," Hines said. "The way I see it, if they'd just stayed out of it—if Dougherty hadn't tackled my boy—there'd have been no shooting."

The point was a ridiculous one, and Carter sensed that the sheriff understood that. Carter chose not to pursue it. "Just tell me why," he said. "How could you begin to justify this charade?" He turned his head from father to son and back again. He'd take the answer from either one.

"A year from now, it would all have been over and done with," Hines said. "Everybody would have come out a winner. Dougherty would be back in prison, your daughter would be back at home, and my boy wouldn't have to pay for his stupidity with the rest of his life."

Carter was confused. "So, you never intended to arrest Nicki?"

"Of course I intended to arrest her. I had to arrest her, but the charges never would have stuck. You know as well as I do that the evidence never would have held up in court."

"It would have been plenty for an indictment," Carter said. "And with that would come thousands in legal bills, and probably imprisonment."

Hines looked unmoved. "But ultimately, she'd have walked free with a clean record."

"And Chas Delphin? You were just going to let his murder go unavenged?"

Another shrug. "He'd be dead either way. A hundred years from now, he'll still be dead. Nothing any of us can do will change that."

Carter turned to Jeremy. "*Why?*"

The boy looked up long enough to glance at his father, and then looked down again.

"Go ahead, Jeremy," Hines growled. "Tell him how this is my fault. How you did it because I'm a terrible father." When the boy was too embarrassed to answer, the sheriff went ahead on his behalf. "I'm such an asshole that I wanted him to have a baseball scholarship. Here he is, the best pitcher that this county has seen in years—hell, maybe the best pitcher they've *ever* seen—and I was such a miserable son of a bitch that I wanted him to put it to good use. Have you ever heard such cruelty?"

Carter was lost, but he sensed that it would be dangerous to interrupt.

"It worked, too. I pulled what few strings I have to pull and I got a scout to come out here and take a look at him. Jeremy got a full scholarship to UNC to pitch on their varsity team. The scout said that he might be good enough for the pros one day."

"I didn't want to go," Jeremy said. His voice was barely audible above the rain.

"Don't stop there, boy," Hines said. "Tell him all of it. Tell him about the part where you were gonna punish me."

"I didn't want your damn scholarship, Dad!" the boy shouted. "I don't want to play baseball. I *hate* baseball!"

Hines erupted. "Bullshit! That's Peter Banks talking, not you."

Jeremy rolled his eyes. "Yeah, right. That's Peter Banks." He turned to Carter. "Ask him who the *last* great baseball star of Essex was." He laughed bitterly. "Ask him about how *he* could have been a pro if he hadn't blown out his knee. He'll talk to you about that for hours. Won't you, Dad?"

"Maybe we should step in out of the rain to discuss this," Carter offered.

"Maybe you should mind your own goddamn business," Hines said.

Jeremy kept going. "Better yet, ask him how he owns this town. Get him talking about the way everybody respects him because he knew how to raise the perfect kid, and turned him into the baseball player that he could never be."

Now Carter understood Darla Sweet's fears. He watched the anger boil up into the sheriff's neck.

"You pissed on all my friends, you kicked my ass for everything I ever did wrong, and then you beat the shit out of the one friend who wasn't afraid to hang out with me."

Carter figured that had to be Peter Banks.

"That criminal was going to cost you everything."

"No, Dad! *You* cost me everything."

Hines threw his head back and launched a guffaw. "I didn't make you stupid. I didn't send you into that store."

Carter thought he might understand what was happening here. The robbery was about getting a rise out of his father. Before he had a chance to stitch too much of it together in his head, Jeremy laid it out:

"I wanted you to hurt, okay? And I wanted to be the one to hurt you."

So, he smoked pot with a friend, just days before he knew he had to pass a drug test. It was the one restriction on his scholarship. He smoked the weed to fail the test. In a twisted way, it made perfect sense.

Now, the wreckage inside the Hines house started to make sense, too.

"It wasn't enough to ruin his own life," Hines said. "He had to ruin mine, too."

"Boo hoo, Dad. How does it feel to be a *real* Hines?"

Carter took a tentative step forward. This had the feel of a confrontation about to spin out of control.

"You and your precious goddamn badge," Jeremy taunted. "Let's see how tough you are when people vote you out of office. Let's see how much of that respect is about *you*." Jeremy turned to Carter. "Do you see the beauty of it?" he asked. "I knew goddamn well that he would recognize the shirt I wore in that robbery. It was his old jersey. He had it framed, hanging in my bedroom for inspiration. And if he didn't recognize the shirt, I sure as hell knew that he would recognize my voice on the tape. And when he did, there'd be nothing he could do about it." Jeremy laughed. "In a town this size, who's gonna reelect a sheriff whose own kid robs a store? Nobody! Get it?"

Carter thought he got it, but he wanted to hear it from the kid.

"He'd never be able to arrest me. Not and keep his badge. I'd have him by the balls forever. Just by keeping my secret, he'd be a criminal himself. And with that kind of a secret over his head, I could finally get him off my back. It was beautiful. Just freaking beautiful."

"Jesus," Carter breathed.

"You disgust me," Hines said to his son.

"But not when I throw a no-hitter, right? Not when my fastball tops a hundred miles an hour and you can go hang around in the coffee shop and tell all your loser friends how I'm a chip off the old block. I only disgust you when I think for myself."

"And look what thinking for yourself gets you," Hines taunted. "Feeling smart now?"

"It would have worked!" Jeremy shouted. His voice and his face both showed desperation. "If the Quik Mart had been empty—I thought it was empty!—it would have worked. Hell, if it had been anybody else in there, it would have worked." He pointed the muzzle of the .45 at Carter, who took two steps back. "It's *his* fault it didn't work. He's the one who kept digging. "

Hines boomed, "Jeremy!"

The boy pivoted, now pointing the pistol at his father. "*It's all your fault!*" He was crying now.

As Carter watched, his heart pounding, Sheriff Hines seemed to swell, to grow taller. "You'd better use that thing, boy, or it's gonna take three hours to dig it out of your ass."

"Is that what you want?" Jeremy sobbed. "You want me to shoot you? I will, you know. I got nothing left to live for. I'll do it. I'm going to death row anyway, right? Maybe I should just shoot you both and take my chances getting away."

Carter felt the panic building in his belly. If he didn't do something to defuse all of this, someone was going to get hurt. Badly.

Hines extended his arms out to his sides, creating the largest possible target. "Then do it. Punk. Do it now. And take your time, because I sure as hell don't want you to miss your chance."

"You think I won't?" Jeremy sobbed. As his father advanced, the boy retreated, step for step.

"I think you'd better," the sheriff said, quickening his steps. "If you don't I swear to God I'll beat you to death with it."

"Stop it!" Carter shouted. This was insane. "Both of you stop it!"

But the sheriff didn't even slow down.

"Is it too late, boy? Can you do it? Do you have the guts?"

Carter found himself shadowing these two as they faced each other down. "This is madness," he said, intentionally modulating his voice. There was way too much shouting going on as it was, way too much emotion.

"Come on, boy, shoot," Hines taunted.

"I will!"

"Then do it! Now, do it!" Only fifteen feet separated the two combatants now. If Jeremy fired, his father would die.

A voice from behind Carter startled all of them. "Police officer!" Darla Sweet shouted. "Everybody freeze!"

As heads turned, Hines made his move. He lunged at his son, amid a growling roar.

Jeremy pulled the trigger and a gunshot rocked the forest. He pulled it again. With that second shot, the sheriff's brains blasted out the back of his skull. As Carter dropped to a defensive crouch, Sheriff Hines fell face-first into the sandy mulch.

Deputy Sweet yelled something, but Carter didn't catch what it was.

Jeremy didn't give her a chance to repeat it. The instant his father hit the ground, he pivoted and fired two rounds toward Darla. She dropped from sight, but Carter couldn't tell if she was hit or merely taking cover. The boy didn't waste a second putting the confusion to good use. He rocketed into the woods.

"Shit!" Carter spat. "Deputy Sweet! The sheriff's dead! Are you all right?"

She answered by bolting off into the woods after her quarry. Before he had a chance to wonder why, Carter was sprinting with her. She pointed to something on the ground, but they were past it before Carter could see what she was pointing to. "What is it?" he panted.

"His empty magazine," she said. "He reloaded."

Chapter Thirty-three

Matt Hayes couldn't escape the feeling that he'd betrayed Scotty Boyd. The look in the kid's face as Matt handed him over to the EMTs was one of pure fear. He wanted to go back to his grandmother. He was terrified that something might happen to her. Through the rapid-fire monologue, Matt had picked up that it was just Gramma and he living alone in the little house in the numbered streets. Scotty made it clear that Gramma was all he had left, and he was terrified of losing her. It was all Matt needed to know.

According to the radio reports, the next-closest police unit was nearly on the scene—he could hear the siren approaching in the distance—but the ones to follow that were a good ten to fifteen minutes away. It might not sound like a long time, but when you're in the hostage seat with a gun pointed to your head, it was an eternity.

Matt decided not to wait. The kid's story got to him.

He drove without his lights or siren. No sense upsetting people before it was necessary. He wanted to look around, get the lay of the land, so that when the cavalry did arrive, he'd have some good intel for them. He was nearly on the scene when he heard his radio call sign on the air: "Control to Trooper one two zero."

"One two zero."

"One two zero, be advised that we've received a call from number fifteen Seventh Road, claiming to be a man with two hostages. He says that if he sees any sign of a police officer, he's going to start shooting."

Matt felt his stomach muscles tighten. The stakes had just gone up a thousand percent. "One two zero's direct. I'm requesting a tac frequency for this incident." This was going to be a long operation, and unless they obtained a secondary radio channel for tactical operations, there would be so much chatter that no one would know what the hell was going on.

"Ten-four, one two zero, stand by."

Clearly, the perp was trying to establish himself as the party in control. Big mistake. Hostage-takers *never* gained control. What they never seemed to understand was no matter how long negotiations dragged on, there was only one hard and fast reality: that bad guys left the fight either in handcuffs or in body bags. There was no third option. You worked like hell to save the hostages, and you prayed that they'd get a new lease on life, but at the end of the day losing a current hostage was the preferred outcome over allowing the bad guys to snare another one.

Matt pulled his cruiser to a stop on the far side of the dune surrounding number seventeen, the house adjacent to Scotty's, taking care to stay out of sight. This part of the state was the waterside equivalent of hillbilly country. Years ago, the people who settled out here mostly made their livings as fishermen. More recently, as fishing became more difficult, the area had become a haven for people who enjoyed solitude for any number of reasons, both legal and ill. Despite having whiled away a few good summers down here, Matt couldn't imagine what attraction it held for the residents.

Daily hardships and inconveniences did instill a certain independence in people, which in turn bred intolerance for most laws that told people what they could and couldn't do in the privacy of their homes. Or stills. Or cannabis crops.

Over the past decade, thanks to raids by the FBI, DEA, and ATF, law enforcement agencies had ceded the public relations battle to the bad guys. When a badge showed up around these parts, blood pressures skyrocketed.

As Matt closed and locked his door to begin the fifty-yard trek to the dune that concealed number fifteen, he considered bringing the shotgun that stood sentry in its bracket in the front seat, or the Remington 700 .30-06 rifle that he kept in the trunk, but opted against both of them. Those were tactical weapons, and he had no intention of storming the place yet. For now, he just wanted to take a look around.

He also wanted to stay out of sight. Trenches in the sand doubled as a driveway, marking the route to the front. After a hard turn, they disappeared behind the dune. To round that corner would be to step out into the only firing lane that the perps could readily see.

Instead, Matt chose to climb the near side of the dune to get an elevated view of the property. What he saw made him smile. The shingle and tar paper shack with its steel security bars sat in the middle of two sheltering dunes that ran roughly north and south on the east and west sides of the building. Without the dunes, the tiny home would no doubt have floated away or been blown down over the years. Ironically, the same dunes that protected the property presented a huge tactical disadvantage to the people inside. They were the low point in the center of nothing but high ground, with only one avenue of escape—through that break in the dune on the westernmost side. If the perps hadn't fled already, surrender was their only viable option.

Since Brad Ward was probably shot—Scotty Boyd had been adamant that there was no way he could have missed—and the girl was reportedly so weak that she could hardly lift her head, Matt Hayes was ready to bet a month's pay that they were still inside.

Jeremy Hines had disappeared again.

For the first hundred yards, Carter had been able to keep up with Darla as they charged through the woods. Up ahead, he'd seen flashes of the boy darting in and out of their sight line. Soon, though, Carter's years behind desks began to take their toll, and Darla pulled ahead of him. As the gap widened, he lost sight of Jeremy, and now found himself struggling just to keep an eye on the uniformed deputy.

He tried to ignore the cramp under his ribs as he pressed on. If he lost sight of Darla, he could be lost out here forever.

The muddy ground sucked at his loafers as he charged through the underbrush.

Up ahead, he saw that Darla had stopped. He closed the distance in seconds.

"Why are you waiting for me?" he gasped. "He's getting away."

Darla held up her hand, gesturing for silence. "Be quiet," she hissed, and Carter pulled up short. "I don't think he's running anymore," she whispered. "I think he's hiding."

Without thinking, Carter lowered himself into a crouch, and the deputy followed suit. How could he be so stupid to fall for the same trick twice? "How does he disappear like that?" he whispered.

"He's a hunter," Darla replied. "Everybody around here is a hunter. You learn to blend in."

Carter craned his neck to take in all compass points.

"Be still," Darla hissed.

"Well, what are we supposed to do? Just wait for him to shoot first?"

"We wait for him to show himself," Darla said. "Or we just wait for the backup units to arrive."

"He likes to shoot," Carter said. He relayed the ambush the kid had set up when Carter had first started chasing him.

"He's a notoriously good shot," Darla said. "You're lucky you're here to tell the story."

Lucky, indeed. Soaked to the skin in the middle of the woods, waiting for a lunatic high schooler to take a shot at him. By that standard, what was *bad* luck?

If it weren't for his pounding heart and churning stomach, Carter might almost have felt sorry for Jeremy Hines. Carter had seen it a thousand times: Some kids on a prank break into a house or steal a car, only to have things go wrong and suddenly there's blood in the street. Nobody meant for it to happen, but intentions didn't matter anymore. There were some steps forward from which there was no step back. Prisons across the world were filled with people who had learned that lesson the hard way.

"Do you see anything?" Darla asked.

Carter shook his head. "Not a thing. The rain'll cover a lot of sounds."

"He's here," Darla said. "The woods become a big clearing and a construction site about fifty yards ahead. From there, it's wide-open spaces. He's either got to stop here or double back."

Carter felt the skin on his chest and his neck prickle. This was crazy. His job was done; he had what he needed to keep Nicki free. If he had a brain in his head, he'd be on his way to the state police or the county prosecutor to get this all cleared up, not that it would help Nicki much. Her transplant clock had ticked to zero. Jesus, when would it end?

The echoes of Jeremy's last shots still had not left his head. With his father dead, the teenager had nothing to lose by killing two more. "How good a shot is this kid?" he whispered.

Darla rose from her knees to a half-crouch, her pistol extended at arm's length, searching for a target. Carter considered it foolishly brazen to grant a larger target like that. "Good enough to compete in the junior state semifinals last year. He can part the hair on a bumblebee."

"I wonder why he didn't kill me when he had the chance," Carter mused aloud.

"How's that?"

"When I was first chasing him, he had me dead to rights, but he missed, and not by a little bit. Then, when he had me in his sights, just standing there with my fear hanging out, he didn't shoot then, either."

"I guess you're not on his list," Darla said. He could tell by her tone that she would rather watch the woods than listen to him. She was as frightened as he.

Carter didn't think that was it. Why shoot at all if you don't intend to hurt your target? He remembered the efficiency with which Jeremy dispatched his father.

Movement up ahead and to the left caught both Carter's and Darla's attention, and their heads pivoted to catch it. Jeremy Hines was making his move. He jumped from his hiding place, his throat issuing a terrible yell—a high-pitched squeal that sounded more like a wounded pig than a terrified teenager. He charged, the .45 clutched in his fist, pointed straight at them.

Darla's posture changed to a shooting stance, in which she pivoted on the balls of her feet, swinging her body in alignment with her hands. "Jeremy, freeze!" she shouted.

The boy did nothing of the sort. He raised his weapon even higher and locked his elbow.

Darla had no time to make a decision. She had to shoot now if she was going to save either one of them. "No!" she cried.

Carter understood. The kid's plan crystallized in his brain when he realized that Jeremy wasn't shooting at them—at the very millisecond that Darla Sweet's finger tightened on her trigger. Carter shoved her to the side as her weapon fired.

"Are you out of your mind?" she shrieked. She recovered her target and prepared to fire again.

She didn't understand, and Carter had no time to explain. He lunged at Jeremy, putting himself between the teenager and the deputy who would kill him.

"Janssen!" Darla yelled. "Get down! Get out of the way!"

Jeremy kept charging, shifting his aim to Carter's head. "I'll kill you!" he yelled.

Carter didn't move. If he turned out to be wrong, he was living his last five seconds on the planet.

Jeremy didn't shoot. He pulled up short, stopping mere feet before a bone-breaking collision. He whipped the gun up to eye level, to where Carter Janssen's entire worldview was limited to a half-inch muzzle in which he could see the initial lands and grooves of the rifling.

"I'll kill you!" Jeremy yelled. He was hysterical.

"Put it down!" Darla yelled. She was on her feet

now, moving around to Carter's left to get an angle on the boy. "Drop that gun or I'll shoot!"

"Darla, no!" Carter shouted. "Don't do it!"

Jeremy pivoted his weapon to Deputy Sweet, again leaving her no choice, and again driving Carter into action. This time, he tackled Jeremy, driving his shoulder into the kid's gut, and as they fell to the ground, he swore to God that he could hear the crack of Darla's bullet—not the gunshot, which came an instant later, but the crack of the bullet itself in the air—passing within inches of his head.

Jeremy hit the ground hard, and Carter landed on top of him, trying to keep control of boy's gun hand, gripping it tightly in both of his own.

"Get off me!" Jeremy grunted.

"Give me the gun," Carter demanded. "Let go!"

Darla cussed randomly, furious that there was no decent shot to take. Over and over again, she yelled, "You're crazy! You're out of your mind!"

Carter couldn't remember the last fight he'd been in, but he had a vague memory of losing it. This kid was strong, and he wriggled like a fish to get away, punching and kicking to get free. Jeremy snorted like a bull from the effort and spat out bitter curses as Carter focused every effort on keeping his gun hand under control.

Above and behind, he could hear Darla shouting at him. She screamed at him to get out of the way. She wanted to make her arrest, and if that meant killing the boy, then that was the way it would have to be.

Carter couldn't let that happen. Jeremy Hines hadn't *earned* death, and if this struggle ever stopped, he'd be able to explain it all to the deputy.

The fight ended when Carter's groin erupted in agony. Whether from a foot or a knee or a fist, he didn't know, but the kid had scored big time. A lightning bolt of pain launched deep into his belly, and he was useless. Before he knew what was happening, he was facedown on the forest floor with a mouthful of sand.

"I'm not telling you again!" Darla screamed. "Put that weapon down or I'll shoot."

From the ground, Carter shouted, "His gun is unloaded! Don't shoot!"

"Put it down!"

Christ, could she hear him? "Darla! He's unarmed! Don't shoot him!"

She was staring down the barrel of a .45. If she hesitated, she'd die. Yet, she was hearing—

"Don't listen to him!" Jeremy yelled. "This gun *is* loaded, and I swear to God I *will* shoot you. I reloaded back there. I swear to God I reloaded."

Carter saw from Darla's expression that she was beginning to see the same picture as he. "If it were true, he'd have shot you," Carter said, modulating his voice to something as close to soothing as he could muster with his guts seizing. "He left that magazine for you to find, Deputy. He wants you to think that he reloaded."

"I swear to God I'll kill you!" Jeremy screamed.

"He was never about killing anybody," Carter said. "Certainly not you or me. He could have killed me with his first shot if that's what he'd wanted to do."

Darla scowled. "But the sheriff . . ."

"Pure anger. Frustration. Terrible dumb luck." Carter let the words hang in the air. He turned his eyes toward Jeremy. "That's right, isn't it, son? You never did want to kill anyone, did you?"

Jeremy was trapped and he knew it. His face sagged and his shoulders slumped. With the pistol still in his fist, he covered his face with his hands and sobbed,

"Please kill me. Just kill me, please . . ." His words disappeared in noises of pure anguish.

"Oh, my God," Darla breathed. "He wanted me to kill him." Jeremy didn't resist as she cuffed his hands behind his back.

Carter said, "Maybe that was the plan the whole time when he left the house to go charging into the woods. Maybe he just wanted a quiet place to kill himself."

"So when he shot at me, he assumed that I would shoot back."

"Suicide by cop."

"Have a seat," Darla said as she assisted her young prisoner to the ground. After he was in place, she backpedaled a few steps and sat down on a dead fall. She looked . . . stunned.

"I didn't figure it out till the very end," Carter said, as if to soften the blow. "Are you okay?"

She indicated yes, but a part of her seemed not yet to have recovered from the shock.

"Can you help me get the word out about Nicki? The clock's ticking, and—"

Darla's eyes grew huge as she remembered. "I forgot to tell you," she said. "It was the reason I first came to the house looking for you. I know where she is."

Chapter Thirty-four

The pain in Brad's belly was a red-hot corset, ever tightening its grip. His head swam from the blood loss, and the energy consumed simply by pacing the front room left him sweaty and exhausted. Fever raged inside him. He could feel it building like a bonfire deep in his gut and his head, and the hotter it grew, the more aware he became of the steady ache of the bullet wound.

So where the hell were the cops? In his mind, he saw them surrounding the house, gathering for the assault. The drapes were pulled and the doors were locked. Beyond that, Brad couldn't think of another thing to do.

He was resigned to dying. He only hoped they'd take him out with a head shot. That was the preference of snipers, he knew. In a perfect world, snipers loved the spot over their targets' right eyebrow. An instant kill, even if it left a hell of a mess. It surprised him that the thought of never seeing another dawn brought him such a sense of peace.

Then again, maybe it wasn't so surprising. He'd seen plenty of dawns as it was, and of those he'd witnessed, precious few were the stuff of poetry. Too many mornings had bloomed sunless for him, with a view of a concrete wall. Even more had begun in homes of strangers who seemed more afraid of him than he was of them.

In the silence of the front room, he'd twice assumed Nicki to be asleep, but both times when he looked at her, she was able to offer a wan smile. "Why don't you sit down?" she asked.

"Because it hurts too much to get up again." He shook his head. "Hell of a getaway I arranged, isn't it?"

"It's been different," she said. She let a moment pass before asking, "So, what happens when they come to the door?"

"You stay low," he said. "The rest is up to them."

"Is there a way in the world that we can win?"

Brad looked at her and winced against a stab of pain. "By leaving now," he said. "I was hoping for a tidal wave or an asteroid hit to distract them, but the chances really aren't in our favor."

She didn't laugh.

"You sure you don't want a gun?" Brad asked, offering her the .22 from his waistband. The grip was smeared with blood now.

Nicki waved him off. "I won't leave, but I won't shoot, either."

"Can I ask a question?" Gramma asked from across the room.

Brad started to say no, but Nicki answered first. "Sure," she said.

"How did you end up with him?" Gramma said. "You're not violent. You're clearly sick. Did he brainwash you or something?"

Nicki took her time analyzing the vibes she was getting from Gramma. The hardness that had defined the old woman a few minutes ago was gone now. In its place was the look of a concerned grandmother. "We're just old friends," Nicki said. "I know you don't believe it, but we haven't done anything to deserve all of this." She paused as she heard her own words, then blushed. "Well, you know. Until this, with you and Scotty. He's not going to hurt you. You saw that he couldn't hurt your grandson."

The concern deepened in Gramma's eyes. "You know you can't get out of this alive, don't you?"

Brad and Nicki shared a look. "Neither one of us had much left to live for anyway," Brad said.

Everyone jumped when the phone rang. Brad shot a look to Gramma, who shrugged.

Brad picked up the receiver on the third ring and brought it to his ear. "Hello?" His tone betrayed nothing. It was nearly cheerful, in fact, as if he owned the place and this were any other day.

The voice on the other end, however, was all business. "Brad Ward?"

Brad made his voice just as serious. "Who's asking?"

"This is Commander Maury Donnelly with the North Carolina State Bureau of Investigation. I want you to release your hostage and surrender yourselves before more people get hurt."

Brad arched his eyebrows. "Well, I want world peace. Who do you think will get their wish first?"

"What's the condition of the people in there?"

"Everybody's healthy and happy," Brad said.

"I heard reports that your companion, Nicolette Janssen, is very ill and that you've been shot."

The guy was fishing for information. Clearly, they'd talked to Scotty, and now they were weighing the wisdom of believing a twelve-year-old. "It's amazing how those rumors get started, isn't it?" he said.

"Is it true or isn't it?" Donnelly pressed.

"Why don't you come on up to the front door and find out?"

"We will," Donnelly said. "Sooner or later, that's exactly what's going to happen. You can't possibly win this."

Brad laughed. "Dude, where did you get your hostage negotiation training, correspondence school? You're supposed to be telling me how we can work this out. You know, you and me. You're supposed to tell me how I can trust you. And don't forget the part where everybody else out there has an itchy trigger finger, but you can keep them calm if I just step out and give myself up."

"Sounds like you've been here before," the cop said.

"You know I have," Brad said. "Last time, I did it your way and really didn't like the outcome. This time around, I'm going for something different."

"And what is that?"

"You don't want to know."

"Yeah, I do."

Brad enjoyed this game too much sometimes. "I guess you're right. My bad. How's this: I don't want to tell you."

"Don't be foolish, Brad," For the first time, Brad could hear anger in the cop's voice. "You're talking suicide. There's no need for violence."

"I couldn't agree more. Just stay the hell away, and there won't be any."

"Listen, Brad—"

"No, *you* listen, Maury. Let's understand each other, okay? I don't have any demands, at least not yet. I don't want a million dollars or a helicopter or the release of terrorists. All I want is a few unmolested hours to think things through. Do you think you can arrange that?"

The cop fell silent for long enough for Brad to wonder if he'd hung up. When he spoke, he sounded sad. "We're not going to let you leave, son," he said. "You have to understand that. One way or another, we're going to win."

"You go ahead and think that," Brad taunted. "What would be the fun of getting away if you *let* me do it? I'd rather escape out from under your nose, like I did back in prison. In the meantime, if I see any face I don't recognize, I'm going to shoot it."

"Are you telling—"

"Have a nice day." Brad hung up the phone and yanked the plug from the wall. That should keep them guessing. There was no escape plan, of course. But if he understood anything about cops, it was the fact that they were born paranoid and stayed that way. If they *thought* he had a plan, it could only work to his benefit.

"What kind of foolishness was that?" Gramma asked. "Are you *trying* to die?"

"I'm not trying to, no," he said. "But I'm not afraid of it, either."

"I am," she said. "It's the thing I worry about most. I've watched two husbands, a daughter, and a son-in-law all die, and I'm all that Scotty has left."

The honesty of her words caught him unprepared, and the hardness of his façade faltered. "Then keep your head down when the shooting starts," he said.

"Brad," Nicki said. He could hear her breathing now, the rattling moisture in the deepest reaches of her lungs. "Let her go," she said.

He refused. "Can't do it. Won't. If I do that, there's nothing to keep the cops from blowing the house off of its foundation."

"She doesn't deserve this," Nicki said.

For the second time in thirty seconds, Brad felt a pang of real emotion. It thickened his throat and prompted him to turn away from both of them. "I don't deserve this, either," he said.

The kitchen of the Mellings' house looked more like a war room than a place to cook and eat. Scotty could tell from the looks he was getting that some of the cops didn't think he belonged there. He tried to remain as invisible as he could, even as he tried not to miss anything.

That first cop—the one he'd run into on the beach—had asked him a zillion questions before handing him off to the ambulance guys, but then, before the ambulance itself had gotten very far at all, somebody had called on the radio and told them to stop. They'd sat there for the longest time. After the EMTs put a bandage on his head, no one seemed to know what to do, so they passed the time by taking his blood pressure every other second, and by talking about everything except what was happening with Gramma.

Finally, a stream of cop cars swarmed onto the beach, and after some discussion he couldn't understand through the walls of the ambulance, a big cop with a gold badge and eagles on his collar climbed into the back and asked Scotty whether he thought he'd be up to helping the police capture the people who'd hurt him. Scotty had jumped at the chance almost before the cop had finished asking the question.

The cop's name was Maury Donnelly, but all the other cops who toadied up to him called him Commander. Scotty avoided calling him anything at all. Either way, Commander Donnelly seemed not to like anyone very much, but was nice enough to him as he explained how much Scotty could help by drawing them a map of what the inside of Gramma's house looked like.

Scotty wasn't there when they'd asked the Mellings to let them use their kitchen as a command post, but he would have loved to see it. Everybody knew that Mr. Melling brewed his own booze and grew pot under lamps in the shed out back. He must have shit his pants when he saw the cops gathering outside. In his mind, Scotty could see them all scampering to hide evidence. Trying to help them out a little, Scotty had even put a magazine over a pipe they'd forgotten to put away. He wasn't completely sure, but he'd have sworn that Commander Donnelly saw him do it, and the little smile he'd sent told Scotty that the cops weren't interested in drugs and alcohol today.

They brought Scotty into the kitchen and sat him down at the table with a piece of paper and a pencil. They asked him to draw a layout of his Gramma's house. He'd given it his best effort, but he'd never been any good at drawing pictures. After one abortive effort, they all decided to let him talk them through the layout of the house. While he described things, a cop whose name he didn't catch drew the lines on the page. The front door was here; the kitchen was there; that sort of thing. When he finished, they'd thanked him and started talking in their radios, telling people what to do.

A few minutes ago, Kathy Melling had brought him a T-shirt from her father's drawer to replace the one that the EMTs had cut off in the ambulance. It was a zillion sizes too big, and sported the silhouette of a naked woman, but Scotty was grateful for the effort. The Mellings had a window air conditioner in their kitchen, and even with all the people in the room, he was getting pretty chilly sitting in front of it.

"Hey, Scotty, can you come here?" It was Commander Donnelly, beckoning him to the table. "Make a hole for the boy," he said to the rest of his cops.

Five of them were gathered around the drawing of the house Scotty had dictated before.

"How sure are you about the placement of the furniture?" Donnelly asked.

Scotty thought it was a weird question. "Pretty sure."

"That's not good enough. I need you to be *sure.*" So much for Mr. Nice.

Scotty leaned farther into the table and looked more closely. "What do you need to know?"

"Tell us about the floor coverings," said one cop.

Responding to Scotty's look of confusion, Donnelly said, "Are there rugs or carpets on the floor?"

"There's a rug in the living room. On the floor."

"How big?"

"I don't know." Who paid attention to how big rugs were?

"Does it cover the whole floor?" Donnelly asked. "Or just the center?"

"Just the center, I guess."

"Think hard now, son. This is important. How much plain floor—floor without carpeting—is there around the outside?"

Scotty was tempted to say he didn't know, but stopped himself. He wanted to be as helpful as he could. He'd played with his soldiers on that floor a thousand times, lain on it watching television. Why couldn't he remember—

Wait a second. He could too remember. He pointed to the drawing. "The TV is on the floor. Just the floor. And about this far behind the edge of the rug." He indicated a distance of about three inches with his thumb and forefinger.

"And you think it's that way all the way around the living room?" Donnelly pressed. "Say, three feet of rug-free floor on all sides?"

Scotty closed his eyes to remember. "Yeah, about this far." This time, he used both hands to show a distance of about thirty-six inches.

"At *least* two feet," Donnelly proclaimed, turning back to the other cops.

"What are you going to do?" Scotty asked.

They weren't paying attention to him anymore.

Donnelly turned to the cop who'd first encountered Scotty on the beach. "And you're sure there's a crawl space underneath?"

Matt Hayes looked solemn. "Absolutely certain," he said.

"You realize the risk you're taking, right?" Donnelly asked. "If Ward hears you under there, he's likely to start shooting. If he fires through the floor, you're screwed."

"You're not going under the house, are you?" Scotty gasped. The thought of it horrified him.

All heads turned toward the boy as Donnelly said, "Is there something we need to know? A reason not to do that?"

"Have you seen the bugs that live under there?" Scotty said, prompting laughter from everyone but Trooper Hayes. "It's only about that high." This time, his hand marked a space of eighteen inches over the table. "I lost a soccer ball under there a week ago. No way would I crawl in there."

As one, all eyes turned to the trooper who was going to have to do just that. Matt gave a nervous chuckle. "Hey, you do what you've got to do, right?"

Chapter Thirty-five

Carter told himself to slow down even as he pushed the accelerator to the floor. With his left hand pressing the telephone against his ear, he did his best to control the speeding Volvo with his right. Between the pouring rain and the surging adrenaline, he knew he'd be lucky to arrive in Lincolntown alive. He'd been on hold for nearly five minutes now, waiting for some 911 operator to chat with her supervisor.

He knew from the tone of her voice the instant she returned to the phone that his cause here was lost. "Mr. Janssen?" she said.

"I'm here. Please don't tell me no."

"I'm afraid I have to, sir. There's just no way that I can patch you through to the command post. If you could just leave me your message, I can see to it that it's delivered."

"But I *need* to speak to the officer in charge," Carter said.

"I understand that, sir, and I've passed that along to my supervisor, but there's just no way—"

"Okay then," Carter said, surrendering to the inevitable. "Take this down. One of the people in that standoff in Lincolntown is my daughter. The commander thinks that she is guilty of a murder this afternoon, but she in fact is not. We've just found confirmation of that."

"We?"

"Deputy Darla Sweet with the Essex Sheriff's Department. She and I. The real perpetrator of the robbery at the Quik Mart was Jeremy Hines, Sheriff Frank Hines's son. He just confessed to it. So, this standoff is unnecessary."

The operator conferred with someone on her end of the line, her microphone covered. "Um, sir, we've just received news about Sheriff Hines . . ."

"That he's dead. Yes, I know. His son shot him. Terrible thing. I was there." As the words spilled out of him, Carter realized that he must sound crazy. "Look, it's a long story. All I need from the incident commander is for him to tell my daughter—Nicolette Janssen—that she's no longer a suspect in that crime."

"Sir, I can't—"

"Goddammit, that's why I need to talk to him!" It was a trait of law enforcement people everywhere to never give the impression of urgency. They were to be calm and reasonable at all times, and it was annoying as hell.

A beep in his ear alerted him to another call trying to come through. He pulled the phone away from his face far enough to see a familiar New York area code. Shit, he'd forgotten to call Dr. Cavanaugh. "I have to take this," he said to the call-taker. Without waiting for a response, he pressed the Send button and waited for the click. "Dr. Cavanaugh?"

"You're pissing me off, Mr. Janssen," he said. Carter could tell from the anger in the doctor's voice that he was finished.

"Doctor, I need more time," he said. "Not a lot, just another hour."

"Absolutely not. I'm moving to the next name on the list."

"Please don't do that." The finality of the doctor's tone felt like broken glass in Carter's chest.

"I don't know what kind of a game you think you're playing, or what makes you think you have the right to play it, but I've been very clear with you from the very beginning—"

"Listen to me," Carter said. "I've been through hell here—"

"Save it," Cavanaugh said. "I was as clear with you as I know how to be. I won't go through this again with you. I'm moving on to the next name on the list. I'm sorry. For both your daughter and you."

"Wait!" he yelled, but the line was already dead. "Shit!" He yelled the word so loudly that in the confines of the car it hurt his own ears. After all he'd gone through, he was going to lose Nicki anyway.

No. That was too simple. The stakes were too high and too many lives had already been ruined for him to fall back on fatalistic cynicism.

He'd come too far to lose the battle now. There had to be a way.

If only he could let Nicki know that she was off the hook, then she could just walk away. She could be back home tomorrow.

He needed to talk with her, one on one. But how? Even if he could get the number from directory assistance, the police would have already locked it up for negotiations. That was standard procedure in any barricade situation: the phones become a single-line connect to the command post, making it impossible for the hostage-takers to call in favors from their friends, or even to call for a pizza delivery. You had to make the bad guys one hundred percent dependent upon the good guys. Hostage negotiation was a high-stakes game that was as much mind manipulation as it was sharpshooting.

Carter had to find a way to put the transplant business behind him. What's done was done; there'd be time later to fret about the injustice. Putting the best face on it, he told himself that the negotiators now had all the time in the world, and that he himself had time to show the prosecutors that the two young people in their sights had nothing to do with the Quik Mart murders. Maybe that would take some of the itch out of the police officers' trigger fingers.

Of course, there were still the matters of the hostage-taking itself, and the outstanding warrants on Brad Ward, and the inevitable aiding and abetting charges that faced Nicolette when this was all over, but these were things that could be handled. Nicki would be alive long enough to retake her position at the end of the organ recipient list. There'd be jail time, no doubt, but with luck, Carter would be able to talk the judge into letting her receive the intravenous prostacyclin while they worked out all the details.

Nicki would be pissed, but at least she'd be alive.

The wild card here was Brad Ward. He was a desperate man with nothing to lose. Beyond the original sentence and the added time for breaking out of prison, he faced an inevitable death sentence—or, given a lenient jury, life without parole—for the killing of his fellow inmate in the joint. He had nothing to gain by surrender; faced no benefit by allowing himself to be taken alive.

It was a thought that had been nagging at Carter ever since Jeremy Hines had tried to manipulate the police into shooting him: Brad Dougherty was likely doing the exact same thing. And why not? If conditions in prison had been bad enough to commit murder and then risk death by escaping, then they were bad enough to be avoided at all costs.

With nothing left to live for, there was little room for negotiation. At the end of all the talk, it would boil down to one thing: a stranger with a badge and a gun telling a desperate kid not to die here, so he could be put to death later.

"Just kill yourself and get it over with," Carter said aloud. "Save everybody the trouble."

He felt guilty for even thinking such a thing, but then, out of nowhere, his mind grabbed on to an even more disgraceful thought.

His foot urged the accelerator even closer to the floor as he dialed a new number into his cell phone.

Matt Hayes wanted a cigarette. He *needed* a cigarette. Honest to God, he thought he'd quit for real this time, but something about the impossible tightness of the crawlspace under the house made him realize that life was too damn short and too damn dangerous to deny yourself the simple pleasures.

He lay on his back in the sand, trying his best to ignore the flies, ants, sand fleas, and God only knew what other creatures gnawed at him. As it turned out, Scotty Boyd was the smartest person in the room when it came to the wisdom of crawling under the house.

Matt had darted across the yard and approached from the living room side of the building—side two in the parlance of the police, in which the front door is always side one the others are assigned in a clockwise pattern, with side three typically being the rear. The windows were a concern, but only a minor one. The perps had closed the curtains and that cut both ways. The drapes denied snipers a view from their nest, but they likewise denied the occupants a view of what the police were doing.

On paper, his mission was a simple one. Using a powerful yet slow-turning carbide-tipped drill, Matt was to make a hole in the floor large enough to insert a tiny fiber-optic camera into the living room. He'd use the tiny monitor to position the camera, which would then beam a picture to the command post. The camera was the newest toy donated by taxpayers to the police department. A year from now, barring any unforeseen budget cuts, they expected to have an equally small microphone for audio surveillance.

Trooper Hayes had attended training for both the audio and video, but this was the first opportunity anyone from their barracks had had to use the camera in a no-shit tactical situation.

It had seemed a lot simpler in concept than it was turning out to be in practice. The biggest problem was the thickness of the flooring versus the speed of the drill. He was making progress, but it was so slow that he was beginning to feel exposed. The longer he lay here, the greater his chance of being discovered, yet he didn't dare drill any faster.

The nightmare that Matt had constructed for himself was that he would manage to drill straight into Dougherty's foot. The pissed-off gunman would then shoot through the floor, and then the folks in the command post would argue among themselves about who was man enough to climb into this dank nastiness to retrieve his bullet-riddled body.

After twenty minutes, the drill broke through. Withdrawing the bit from the hole, he unsnaked the coiled fiber-optic cable from his pocket and connected it to the transmitter box, locking it in place with a quarter turn. He rested the box in the sand and turned his head to watch the tiny monitor.

If all was right with the world, the command post would be able to see exactly what he was seeing in real time. Moving with impossible slowness and deliberation, he snaked the lens through the hole he'd drilled, praying that no one inside would glance in the wrong direction and see it.

From here on out, it was all about patience. And a little bit of luck.

Scotty jumped out of his seat, grunting against the pain in his head. "That's it!" he yelled, pointing. "That's her. That's Gramma."

Donnelly motioned for the boy to settle down, and they all leaned in closer to the little television monitor on the kitchen table. The angle on the picture was an odd one, and the panoramic lens distorted everything, but they clearly were looking at the inside of a small house. They could see three people. An older woman— Scotty's Gramma—sat stiff and tall in a chair on the left. Her posture suggested that her wrists might be bound to the arms of her seat.

"They tied up my gramma," Scotty said, his voice dripping with contempt.

No one seemed particularly bothered.

"Is that Nicolette Janssen there on the couch?" someone asked, pointing to the woman on the right-hand side of the screen.

Eyes turned to Scotty. "That's the sick girl," he said. "The guy is Brad. He's the one I shot."

From this worm's-eye view, they could see not only the two women, but also the short hallway that led to the bedrooms beyond them, and the edge of the door to the kitchen.

"You dictated a pretty good picture, Scotty," Donnelly said. Scotty felt himself blush.

A cop touched the dark spot on the front of Brad's T-shirt. "Looks like he's bleeding."

"I knew it," Scotty said.

Donnelly seemed annoyed. "If he believes he's finished, we're in a hell of a lot of trouble here," he said. "There's not an animal in the world that's not most dangerous when it's cornered and hurt." He turned to a young dark-skinned cop that everyone called Muhammad. "Call the teams and verify that all assets are in position."

Muhammad talked into his radio. A moment later, he reported, "When Hayes gets back to his post, they'll be all set. Two three-man entry teams, two sniper teams."

"Good," Donnelly said. "Tell them to get comfortable. We're in no hurry."

Chapter Thirty-six

A soaked trooper—his name tag read P. EVANOW—stood at Carter's car window against a backdrop of yellow barricade tape that blocked all access to the beach road. "You have to turn around, sir. There's a hostage situation in progress."

Carter showed his badge and credentials. "I am a district attorney, and I have information that the incident commander needs to know."

Trooper Evanow was unimpressed. "I'm sure that badge means something in New York, but right here, it means that you still have to move along."

Carter felt his face flush as his mind raced. How could—

His cell phone rang, and Carter snatched it from the seat where he'd left it. "Janssen," he said.

A familiar voice said, "Carter, this is Warren Michaels. You were right, June Parker does have a cell phone. I have the number right here."

Brad gave in to the need to sit. His belly was getting hotter all the time.

"How are you feeling?" Nicki asked him.

"Like somebody's barbecuing chicken in my gut."

Between the thick clouds, the setting sun, and the pulled drapes, it could have been midnight inside the Parker home. Out there somewhere, people were planning their deaths.

"Do you keep hearing noises?" Nicki asked.

"There's a friggin' army out there," Brad said. "But we've got time. I don't think they'll make their move till the wee hours. They'll hold out as long as they can." He tried to sound like the authority. Certainly, that's how it went down when they arrested him before. Then, they waited till four in the morning and took him out of a sound sleep.

"Why prolong the inevitable?" Gramma asked.

"You're a hundred years old," Brad snapped. "Why do *you* prolong the inevitable by getting up in the morning?"

"Brad!" Nicki gasped.

Gramma's tone was smooth as cream. "I need to be alive for that little boy you brutalized."

Brad's laugh came with a lot of pain. "Yeah, I brutalized *him*. He's got a boo-boo on his head and I've got a hole drilled through me."

Nicki decided to try again. "Brad?"

"I'm not letting her go," he said for the thousandth time.

"But she didn't—"

"—do anything to deserve this." Brad finished the sentence for her.

"But you can't be willing for her to get hurt." Nicki said this as a statement of fact. "Think how you'd feel if that happened."

"That won't be a problem if she does what she's told and keeps her head down at the end."

"But—"

"Nicki, please. I don't want to go through all of this again. I'm tired and I hurt. I know what I'm doing, okay?" He added with a smile, "Not that you can tell by looking."

"If I get killed," Gramma said, "you'll both be the murderers that you claim not to be."

Brad shifted in his chair, wincing against the belly spikes. "I already *am* the murderer that Nicki claims not to be. She's innocent of everything but hanging around with me."

"Unless you count kidnapping," Nicki said.

"You had nothing to do with that, either," Brad snapped. "You hear that, Granny?"

The new tone to his voice seemed to startle Gramma.

"You remember that, okay? All of this—everything bad that has happened here—has been my doing. Nicki wanted to call the police from the very beginning. None of this is what she'd signed on for."

"Then let her go, too," Gramma said. "If she's innocent, it's the thing to do. It's the reasonable—"

A high-pitched synthesized Bach fugue cut her off. The sound startled them all.

"Cell phone," Nicki said.

They shifted their eyes to Gramma. She nodded toward the bag perched on top of the television. "In my purse."

"You expecting a phone call?" Brad asked.

"I only have it for emergencies," Gramma said. "I don't think I've ever gotten a call on it."

"Gee, who do you think it's for?" Brad asked, clearly knowing the answer. The arms of the kitchen chair popped as he pressed against them to raise himself to his feet. He hobbled over to the purse, pulled out a cheap featureless cell phone, and pressed the Send button. "Yeah?"

Donnelly jumped as if someone had nailed him with a cattle prod. "What the hell's he doing?" A second later, it was obvious. "Cell phone! Where the hell did he get a cell phone? Goddammit, why didn't someone think to jam that!"

Carter's heart froze as a man's voice answered, "Yeah?" He worked hard to keep his voice soft. "Is this Brad?"

"Who wants to know?"

"This is Carter Janssen. Nicolette's father."

"She hates to be called that."

"I know," Carter said, holding his head just so, thankful for the good signal and not wanting to risk it. "I rarely call her that, actually. Usually it's Nicki. Is she there?"

"Yeah, she's here. I don't know that she'll want to talk to you."

"How about you, Brad?" Carter said. "Are you willing to talk to me?" Carter imagined himself as a fisherman, luring his prey oh-so-gently toward the hook. If he pushed too hard, he'd lose him before he had a chance to present his proposal.

"She's here of her own free will," Brad said. The words sounded rehearsed.

"I know. But things have changed, Brad. They know who the real killer is from the Quik Mart. It's a kid named Jeremy Hines, the sheriff's boy, and he's in custody." He decided not to mention the sheriff's murder.

"So?"

Carter scowled. It was obvious, wasn't it? "So Nicki has nothing to run from anymore." He paused to let the words sink in. "She needs to know that. Will you let me speak to her?"

Brad's tone got softer as he said, "Maybe she doesn't want to."

"Give her the chance. Please. Just let me talk to her for a few minutes."

"How do I know this isn't some sort of a trap? You could be making all of this up."

"You're not getting it, Brad. Nicki doesn't have to worry about traps. She's free and clear, and she needs to know that." Another pause, just a second or two. "There's also a way out for you, Brad. There's a way to turn all of this into something good."

Carter could hear voices on the other end of the phone, but they were not directed at him. One of them belonged to Nicki. "Brad?" Carter said. "Are you there?"

"Who is it?" Nicki asked.

"The police want to talk to you," Brad lied, holding out the phone to Nicki. "I told them I didn't think you'd want to."

"What do they want?"

"To talk you into giving up and leaving me here."

"Tell them to forget it. I'm staying."

Commander Donnelly pounded the table with his fist, making everyone jump. Suddenly, Scotty didn't want to be there anymore. "Can we trace that call?" he asked the room.

"Once we know the number for the cell phone, we can."

"Find it," Donnelly barked. He turned to Scotty. "How about you? Do you know your grandmother's cell phone number?"

The boy's eyes widened. "We were never allowed to use it. She just kept it for emergencies. I don't think I ever heard it ring, even."

Donnelly kicked a chair across the room. "Dammit!"

"Why did you just lie to her?" Carter shouted. He couldn't believe it. In all the permutations Carter had run through his mind, this was one he'd never considered. "Why did you tell her that you're talking to the police?"

"She asked who I was talking to."

"Listen to me, Brad. Don't do this. Please don't do this. I know where you're coming from, I think. You don't want to be alone. Not now, not at a time like this. I can respect that, but listen to me, okay? Just listen to me and promise that you won't hang up."

"You've got one minute."

"Okay," Carter said. "Okay, good." His brain raced to pull all the pieces together. "There's no easy way to do this, Brad, so I'm just going to lay it out on the line for you. You have to believe me when I tell you it's the truth: In the time since I last talked with Nicki on the phone—what was that, four hours ago?—another set of heart and lungs have come and gone. I got the page a couple of hours ago, and when the doctor found out what was happening, he knocked Nicki off the list. The first time was their fault, and they stepped up to the plate to make it right. This second time we were the ones who fumbled the ball, and now Nicki's only immediate hope for survival has evaporated."

"And you want to blame me for that?" Brad said.

Yes, he wanted to blame him. He wanted to blame Brad for every goddamn thing that had gone wrong these past two days and kick the shit out of him for it, but what was the point? "I'm beyond casting blame," he said. "Nicki's a big girl and she makes her own decisions. They're not always the brightest, but at least they're hers. None of that changes the fact that she's been knocked back to the end of the recipient list. That's done and can't be undone."

"So, why are you telling me?" Brad asked.

Surely, he could see where this was going. Carter closed his eyes, praying that God would one day forgive him for he was about to propose. "Nicki's blood type makes her the so-called universal recipient. That means that she can take donated organs from just about anyone." He waited to hear something from Brad. "Are you there?"

"Yeah, I'm here. What's your point?"

Shit, he was going to make Carter actually say the words, wasn't he? "Brad, when I see the world from your perspective, it's a damned unfriendly place. If you give yourself up, you'll never see the outside of a prison again, not for your whole life."

"That ain't gonna happen," Brad said, forcing a laugh.

"I don't blame you," Carter said. "But it doesn't have to come to that. You can end it all right now. You've got a gun, and you know that one way or another your life is over, so why don't you make it for the good of everyone?"

"What the *hell* are you suggesting?" The sudden burst of anger told Carter that Brad had already answered his own question.

"A bullet through your head," Carter said. He couldn't be any more direct than that. "That's all it would take. Leave a note there saying that you want your organs to go to Nicki, and the world can be right again. You could die doing something good, Brad. You could make—"

The line went dead.

"No, don't!" Carter yelled, but it was too late. When he redialed the number it was no surprise that Brad had turned the telephone off. Slamming the steering wheel in frustrated fury, Carter marched back to the cop at the roadblock.

"Look, officer," he said. He produced his prosecutor's badge again. "I'll say this once more, and you'll either listen, or I swear I will have every one of your tax returns from now until doomsday audited, and I'll pull every string I can to ruin your career. And all of that's just a backup in case I can't get an indictment for criminal neglect if something happens to my daughter. I *need* to speak to the officer in charge of this incident, and I need to speak to him now."

When he saw the color drain from Trooper Evanow's face, Carter knew that he'd broken through to the young cop.

The sudden anger startled Nicki. "Brad, what is it? What did they want?"

"Nothing," he said, but a different kind of heat in his eyes told Nicki differently.

"What was the big explosion about?"

"Nothing, okay? It was about nothing." He fiddled with the phone, then barked at Gramma, "How the hell do you turn this goddamn thing off?"

Gramma pointed with a nod. "The upper left-hand button."

Brad pushed the button and the phone made a sound like a whistling bomb as it turned off. He dropped it back into her purse and paced the living room, holding his side tightly.

He limped over to stand in front of Nicki and gestured to Gramma. "If I let her go, will you promise to go with her?"

"Not a chance. We made a deal. We're sticking together till the end."

"I don't want you getting hurt."

"Till the *end*, Brad. We've gotten this far together, we can see it all the way through. I'm not going. I love you."

The scowl lines deepened as he looked at her, and she tried to cheer him with a soft smile.

"I'm not going," she said again.

Brad looked like he wanted to say something but couldn't bring himself to speak the words. He stomped the floor and rattled something in his gut that made him fold at the waist. "Shit!"

"What is wrong with you, Brad?"

He made himself stand straight, despite the pain. "Not a thing," he grunted. "Not a goddamn thing."

Nicki watched as he drew his Leatherman and limped toward Gramma.

Trooper Hayes had transitioned to his role as tactical sniper, and he wondered if it was possible to have worse conditions. A new wave of pelting rain had rolled in, pounding him and his team. Matt and his spotter, Luis Martinez, a close friend since the Academy, lay ridiculously close to each other atop the dune at the rear of the house—side three—each taking advantage of the limited cover provided by the jungle-camouflaged tarp they'd stretched overhead. While the true purpose of the tarp was to protect their equipment, they were nonetheless grateful for a little cover.

"Are we having fun yet?" Matt grumbled.

"Just remember that this adrenaline rush is what SWAT is all about," Luis drawled, his tone heavy with irony. "Want me to take over on the trigger for a while?"

Both the spotter and the shooter were equally trained as marksmen. If this had been a more intense standoff, a switch might have been in order. As it was, with the windows closed, and no one appearing to be in any kind of a hurry, stress hadn't become an issue. "Nah," he said. "I'm fine."

"He said he wouldn't be taken alive," Luis said. "What's your bet?"

"I bet it's easier to talk about than do," Matt said. "I give it even odds."

"Assault units, get ready!" The voice in their earpieces startled them both. "Perp's got a knife and he's moving for the old woman." The warning came from Muhammad Dali, the Voice of God for this operation, the one who passed along the orders from Commander Donnelly. Matt pressed his cheek to the stock of his rifle, but kept both eyes open, focusing past the scope to the side of the house that was his responsibility. Luis, meanwhile, settled into the eyepieces of his tripod-mounted binocular spotting scope. All they needed was a target and an order to take it out. Matt felt ashamed by the thrill he felt at the thought of his first kill.

"It's getting damn dark out here," Luis observed. "Why don't they fire up the lights?"

Matt didn't bother to answer. Below and to his right, he could see the side-three entry team on the far side of the dune, gathering for their assault. He knew without looking that a similar team was assembling on side one. It occurred to Matt that with this flimsy sticks-and-paper construction, people better choose their targets carefully and shoot straight. The walls wouldn't stop a BB.

The rain and the unpleasantness of the sand meant nothing. Nothing existed but the mission. If the balloon went up, Matt's orders were clear: take any shot necessary to keep the perpetrators from harming the hostage, or from getting away. One way or another, these assholes wouldn't kill again.

Chapter Thirty-seven

Brad was six feet away from Gramma when a motor sputtered to life outside the house and the blackness beyond the curtains erupted in the brilliant white light of two noontimes.

"What's happening?" Nicki gasped.

"Generator," Brad said. "They don't want us slipping out when they can't see. Plus, blinding us gives them even more advantage."

Gramma seemed not to notice the lights and the noise. All she saw was the knife in Brad's hand. "W-what are you going to do?"

"Not what you're worried about," he said. "Relax."

The old woman's eyes grew huge as she realized what his intentions were. "Are you letting me go?"

"If you fight me or bite me or try to punch me, or even just mildly piss me off, I'm going to cut your throat," he said. He let the words settle on her. "But otherwise, yes, I'm letting you go." Leaning down closer to her, he could see the tears welling in her eyes.

As he reached for the cord that bound her hands, it almost looked as if he was kissing her cheek as he whispered, "When you get out there, you tell them not

to rush the place, you understand? You tell them that
we need some time. You tell them that if I see a face—
if I *think* I see a face—I'm going to shoot it. Do you
understand that?"

"Yes," Gramma said. "Yes, I understand perfectly."

"You tell them that this isn't about you or about me
or about Nicki. You tell them that the reason I'm letting you go is because I don't want your grandkid to
end up without anyone. I've been there, and it sucks."
He felt his throat thicken as he said those words, and
he got to the business of slipping the blade between
Gramma's flesh and the rope that held her right wrist
in place. The cord cut easily and fell to the floor. "Remember what I told you about lashing out at me."

"I-I remember," she stammered. She didn't move.

When the second rope was cut, he helped her stand.
The effort made the room spin. When she was on her
feet, he moved close again, and whispered even more
softly than before, "I've got one more thing I want you
to tell them when you get outside . . ."

Muhammad couldn't contain the enthusiasm in his
voice as he shouted, "They're coming out! He's releasing the grandmother! He's releasing her!" Matt smiled.
Muhammad's voice could not have been pitched higher
if he was doing play-by-play. There were some other
voices in the background, and then the young cop was
all business again. "Side one assault team, get ready,"
he said.

It wasn't Matt's side of the building, and protocol
required that he not be distracted from his quadrant of
responsibility, but this kind of drama was hard to resist. He watched as the sergeant in charge of the side
one assault team stepped partially out into the open

from behind his dune, as two other team members took
up positions behind the dead Bronco. He could see
right away that the release itself would be blocked
from his view by the peak of the roof.

He returned his eyes to the back door and settled in
again. "Well, that changes a lot of things," he told
Luis.

It was the noblest, most stupid thing Brad had ever
done. As he opened the door for the old woman and
ushered her out, he saw beyond the glare of the lights
that the SWAT guys were moving up to receive her.
Watching her walk out to them, he couldn't help but
admire her spirit. Conscious of her audience, Gramma
straightened herself and walked with as much dignity
as she could muster out toward the lights. When she
reached the truck, two black-clad gunmen darted out
and dragged her back to cover.

Brad closed the door. "Well, it shouldn't be long
now," he said.

Nicki smiled at him over the back of the sofa. "Thank
you," she said. "It was the right thing."

"Then how come it felt so stupid?"

"Don't you see?" she said. "We just bought ourselves all the time in the world. Without her, there's no
reason to storm the place anymore."

Brad couldn't contain the grunt as he lifted Nicki's
feet and helped himself to the end of the sofa, where he
put her feet back down on his lap. "Let's hope you're
right," he said. "Because from where I sit, they've got
no reason not to shoot us both dead."

* * *

Scotty bolted out of the Mellings' front door before anyone could stop him and jumped from the stoop into the sand, where he sprinted around the corner toward the bright lights that marked his house. Somebody yelled for him to stop, but then somebody else said, "Let him go."

His head hurt from the effort, and he felt a little dizzy, but that was okay. He wanted to see his Gramma. He *needed* to see her.

There she was.

At first, he saw just a cluster of cops, backlit against the floodlights, but then, in the middle of them, he saw her. She looked stronger and taller than he remembered, and pretty pissed. He could tell from her body language that she was tired of being pushed around by these cops, and he told himself that maybe it was because she was at least half as anxious to see him as he was to see her.

They must have said something about Scotty on the radio, because he was still fifty yards away when she looked up, staring right at him, and muscled her way through the cops to head his way.

They met somewhere in between, and Scotty felt the air leave his lungs as Gramma enveloped him in a huge bear hug. He realized out of nowhere that he was crying, and while he didn't know why, he knew that he couldn't stop. No one had ever looked as beautiful as Gramma did in that moment.

"I'd never leave you, sweetie," she whispered, so close to his ear that he could feel her breath on his cheek. "Never in a million years."

Scotty tried to say something, but his voice wouldn't work. It probably would have been something lame anyway.

A black-clad cop cleared his throat and placed his hand on Gramma's shoulder. "Pardon me," he said, "but they need to talk to you in the command post."

Scotty let Gramma hold his hand as they walked back to the Mellings' house and stepped inside. He didn't even let go when other people could see.

The mood in the command post had lightened. All heads turned as they entered.

"Maury Donnelly," the commander said, stepping forward and offering his hand. "We're very glad to see you, Mrs. Parker. Are you hurt?"

Gramma shook her head. "No, I'm fine, but that boy in there, Brad, he wanted me to be sure to give you a message as soon as I saw you. He meant what he said before: if he sees a face, he'll shoot it. I think he's serious. And he also said if you try to rush the building, he'll shoot the girl."

Those were the first words Carter heard as Trooper Evanow ushered him into the room.

Brad fiddled with the pistol in his lap, turning it over, checking the action to make sure it worked. He dropped out the magazine and checked the gauge on the back. Ten rounds left. Nine more than he probably needed.

"You still planning to shoot it out with them?" Nicki asked.

"Only if they start it," Brad said. He grunted against a stab of pain that lit up his right side.

For the first time—miraculously, foolishly, she realized, because all the signs had been there from the beginning—she saw that he was seriously suicidal. In her heart of hearts, she'd allowed herself to believe that it had just been tough talk, driven by his desire to come off as a hard-ass. "So, you're seriously trying to die?"

Brad gave her a wry look. "I'm seriously trying to get away, actually, but we seem to have run out of options. I'm not going back to prison."

"So you're going to *die* instead?"

"It's not so bad. You said so yourself."

Nicki struggled to a sitting position, and her head spun from the effort. "But you have a *choice*," she said. "Do you know what I'd give to have a choice to stay alive?"

"I won't go back. I'd *rather* be dead."

"Living is always better than dying."

"Oh, come on, Nicki, open your eyes. I've been raped. I've been beaten till I couldn't stand."

"Tell somebody, then."

He wanted to laugh, but it hurt too much to try. "You mean walk down to the warden's office, like you'd walk down to the principal's office, and just tell him that you want Zippo transferred to a different table in the cafeteria? The guards *know,* Nicki. They know every goddamn thing, and half of them make money on the deal. To report another inmate, you have to give names. You give names, and somebody'll slip into your cell and cut your nuts off. Or cut your gut open so you can hold your intestines in your hand. Those assholes get away with what they get away with *because* the guards know. Because they *enjoy* it. Don't tell me that living's better than dying. Not until you know what you're talking about."

Nicki hated the fear and sadness she saw in Brad's face. "Then why didn't you just kill yourself?" she asked. "Why did you go through the effort to escape if life has no meaning?"

"*Had*," Brad said, emphasizing the past tense. "Life *had* meaning as long as I had a plan to get out of there. Now, that's gone. It's all gone. Everything."

"So, the solution is to get yourself killed by the very people you hate the most? Why involve so many people? If that's your only solution, why not just do it yourself?"

"I guess I'm just too much of a pussy." He wished that the subject had never come up. There was no way to make her understand.

"Oh, now there's an epitaph," Nicki scoffed. "'Too much of a pussy to do himself in.' Very classy. The history books will be impressed."

"Are you kidding? Christ on a crutch, we won't get within a hundred yards of making the history books. We're nobody."

"I don't believe that."

"How *is* that view from your glass house? If life is so valuable, why aren't you back in New York with your father and his doctor friends, hooked up to your hormone pumps?"

Nicki felt her chest rattle as the airflow faltered. It took an enormous effort, but she swung her feet to the floor and leaned in closer to him, so close that she had difficulty focusing on his features. "Because for me, it doesn't matter. For me, no matter what happens, life is over. For you, there's a chance."

"Jesus, I told you—"

"That prison sucks. Yeah, okay. Then maybe you shouldn't have killed those people. Maybe you should have chosen your friends better. Maybe, maybe, maybe." She took no pleasure in watching her words hurt him. "On the other hand, maybe you're the one who's destined to make a difference in prison. I don't know, maybe there's some arsonist who you won't meet for another five years whose life is going to be turned around because he met *you*. Maybe *you're* the only one who can tell him the magic thing that will make life livable for *him*."

Brad smirked. "A prison savior, right?" He laughed.

"Yes, exactly," Nicki said, animated. "Why not? It's possible. You saved me, why can't you save someone else?"

He made a circular motion with his head to take in the whole room. "You call this being saved?"

"You know what I mean. You know how important you were to me when I was hurting. This isn't your fault, Brad. It isn't my fault, either. It's just the way things turned out. Believe me, I've learned how to rationalize my way through shit that makes no sense."

"You think I haven't? You think that I haven't waded through my dung heap of a life and tried to figure out what went wrong? My list is a hell of a lot longer than yours."

"But killing yourself is not the answer! If you do that, I'll have nothing. I'll have nobody."

Brad opened his mouth to argue, but then he stopped. He looked away.

Nicki cupped his chin with her fingers and turned his face to her. "I love you, Brad. Even if I found a miracle cure and lived to be eighty years old, I'll never love anyone as much again. I know that. You were there for me. You've always been there for me. I'll never leave you. If you let them take you to prison, I promise I'll visit. I'll move there if I have to, but you'll never be completely alone."

Brad felt the pressure of tears arrive in a rush, too fast to stop them. A sob escaped with the sound of a cough, and as he pressed his hands to his eyes to stem the tide, he realized that it was useless. Nicki pulled him into her arms and nestled his face in the soft spot between her neck and shoulder the way her mother used to hold her to make childhood pains go away.

He trembled under her touch as fear and sadness poured from him. The strength and humor were gone, leaving a terrified shell of the fallen God she adored. As she pulled him closer and felt the heat of him on her shoulder, she realized that this was the moment she'd been dreaming of. They were together alone, just the two of them, their souls bonded in an intimacy that transcended any of the carnal fumblings of the night before.

Still, she wished that she had made love to him. She'd deferred to fear and confusion, and now she hated herself for not releasing the white-knuckled grip she held clenched on her life. She'd turned her back on her one chance to make him truly happy, and now the chance was gone forever.

"I'm here," she whispered. "I love you so much." She rubbed his back, feeling the tautness of his muscles beneath his T-shirt, ignoring the stickiness of his blood.

"I'm so sorry," Brad choked, not lifting his head. "I'm so, so sorry."

She petted his hair. "It's okay," she whispered. "It will all be okay."

Brad pushed himself away and swiped at his eyes. "Promise me you'll leave me here," he said.

"Brad—"

"No. You don't understand. There's a way for you to live. There's a way for you to live for both of us."

"What are you talking about?"

He paused long enough to control his breathing. "That wasn't the police on the phone," he said. "It was your father."

Nicki scowled. "But you said—"

"I know what I said. I'm sorry. I was pissed and I lied. But now I'm telling you. They've found the real killer from the Quik Mart. You don't have to hide anymore. You don't have to be a part of this at all. You can walk out of here and go right home."

"Home to what?" She felt light-headed. The news he delivered seemed too large for her to process.

"Your future," Brad said. "Any future. Whatever you've got. You don't need to be here anymore."

"But you're here," she said. How could there be anything more?

"Come on," he said, holding out his hand. "I'll walk you out."

Nicki pulled her hand away and retreated to the far end of the sofa. "And then what?"

"And then . . . whatever."

Something was going unsaid and it scared her. Her father had done something. She could feel it. He'd worked some sort of a deal. "What did he say to you?"

"Huh?"

"My father. What did he say to you?"

"I just told you."

Nicki was unconvinced. "No. No way. You said I could live for both of us. What did he tell you to do?"

Brad tried to settle her down. "Come on, Nicki, there's nothing—"

"I don't want them," she said. "I don't want your lungs. Don't even consider it." The thought sickened her.

He looked surprised that she'd put it together so quickly. "Look, Nicki, it's more complicated than you think."

"No."

"Listen to me, okay?"

"No."

"I owe you this."

She looked at him as if he'd grown a new head. "You *owe* me? God, what are we, vampires?"

Brad reached for her, but his gut snatched him back. "You don't understand," he grunted. "It really is my fault. That's the rest of what your father told me. Another set of donor organs came available today, but because you're with me, they took them back. You lost another chance at life because of me."

"No."

"Yes. What, you think I'm making this up?"

Nicki took a deep breath. She had a lot to say. "It's not because of you. That's what I keep trying to tell you. It's because of me. I'm doing exactly what I chose to do. You gave me God only knows how many chances to walk away, and I said no to all of them. I won't let you shoulder the burden of this. It's not fair."

Brad was close to begging. "But you're a better person than I am, Nicki. You're kinder. You care more. You deserve the chance."

"You're not spare parts, Brad! I won't let you force them to shoot you down."

"Then I'll do it myself," Brad said. He raised the pistol to his temple and closed his eyes.

Chapter Thirty-eight

Carter told the story of Nicki's innocence as quickly as he could, but Commander Donnelly seemed unmoved.

"We need official confirmation, you realize," he said.

Carter understood. "Should be easy enough. Just a phone call away. But I need to get the information to my daughter, so she can know that she's off the hook for the murders."

"I would if I could, but Dougherty yanked the phone out of the wall, and ever since your call, he's turned off the cell phone."

Carter acknowledged the rebuke and let it go. "How about a loudspeaker?" he asked.

"So you *were* the one on the phone," Donnelly said. That had been a test, apparently. "What did you talk about?"

"I told him what I just told you. But he wouldn't let me speak with Nicki."

"I don't buy it," Donnelly said. "We were watching it all right here. He got pretty damned agitated."

Carter was too ashamed of himself to repeat the suggested suicide. "He's a volatile guy, I suppose. Plus, I probably wasn't as diplomatic as I might have been."

Donnelly's scowl said he wasn't buying, but as he opened his mouth to say more, the crowd around the kitchen table erupted with excitement.

"Uh-oh," someone said. "This doesn't look good."

Carter followed the commander to the peer at the monitor. Nicki and Brad were yelling at each other.

"They were just sitting and hugging and this happened," a cop explained.

They watched as Brad struggled to his feet and became even more animated, gesticulating wildly. He looked like he might be crying.

Donnelly said, "Muhammad, tell all units to stand ready. Looks like things are getting emotional."

The radio operator did as he was told.

Carter couldn't take his eyes off the screen. His stomach churned from anxiety, and he wanted to look away, but he couldn't. "Please don't let anything happen to her," he prayed.

Things seemed to settle down again, and then Brad made them all jump when he raised the pistol from his lap and pressed it against his head.

Nicki lunged from the sofa. "No!"

Brad stiff-armed her and spun away, landing on his knees on the floor. His stomach muscles tightened to compensate, launching a spear of agony that shot all the way up to his jaw. He hoped that Nicki wouldn't watch.

"Brad, don't! Please, please don't do this!"

Brad clamped his eyes tighter and willed his finger to find the trigger. Just a little pressure. Not much at all. He could make this work, and when he was done, nothing else would ever matter again.

It was a *good* thing, he told himself. It was the *right* thing.

"Brad, *please,*" Nicki begged. She dropped to the floor to be closer to him. "Not today. Not here. You can always do it later if things get too bad."

He heard the words, but he tried to push them from his brain. They were meaningless. Nicki didn't understand the stakes. She didn't understand that this was the one time when he could do this and it would actually *mean* something. Sure, she could talk about turning down the donation of his organs—she could say that to his face, and maybe even mean it in her heart as she was saying it, but when it was all done, she'd come to her senses. He knew she would.

Just a little bit of pressure. That's all it would take. His hand trembled, and he felt tears on his cheeks. Just a little more . . .

Nicki kissed him. With his eyes closed, he didn't see it coming, but at the instant a bullet should have been leaving the muzzle of his pistol, he felt her lips on his.

"Then take me, too," she said. "One bullet and we'll go together."

Brad opened his eyes. Nicki's face was too close for him to see it clearly, but he recognized the look in her eyes. It was her kind look, her loving look. The look that made his stomach flip even before there'd been a hole drilled through it.

"I love you," she whispered.

Brad closed his eyes again. He didn't want to hear those words. He wanted to do this and get it over with.

If she didn't have the good sense to get out of the way, then that wasn't his problem.

"I love you," she repeated, and kissed him again. A surge of energy shot through his body; it was a feeling he'd never experienced. A chill, maybe, but something better. Something more intimate.

Pulling the pistol away from his ear, he wrapped his arms around Nicki and gave himself up to her kiss. A new passion welled from his soul, filling his chest and then his head. It was a wonderful feeling, a liberating feeling. It was as if the darkness parted and revealed for him a glimpse of what the world was supposed to be. He let the pistol slide to the floor.

Grasping her face in his hands, he looked into her eyes, and all the pain and the fear were gone.

Then something on the floor behind her caught his attention.

Nicki sensed that something was wrong. "What is it?" she asked, following his eye line.

Brad scowled as he tried to make sense of a piece of black spaghetti on the floor. Snatching the gun back into his hand, he rose to his knees and moved in for a closer look. He had to get within two feet before he understood. "It's a goddamn camera," he said, his voice leaden with disbelief. "They've been watching everything we do!"

The Mellings' kitchen erupted in noise. "Oh shit!" someone shouted. "We're made. He sees the camera."

The last thing they saw in the television screen before it went blank was the enormous muzzle of Brad's pistol.

* * *

To his left, Trooper Matt Hayes saw Luis fumbling for the transmit button on his portable radio. Before he could get to it, someone else on the channel yelled, "Shots fired! Shots fired! All units report status."

While Luis announced to the world that the side-three sniper team was unhurt, Matt settled in behind his scope to do business. It wouldn't be long now.

Nicki screamed, thinking Brad had gone through with the suicide. Even when her brain had reconciled with her eyes, and she realized that Brad was still alive, she didn't comprehend what had just happened.

Brad's fury had returned. "Those bastards!" he yelled. "They've been *watching* us!" He thought of the cops who'd been standing outside when he opened the door to release Gramma, and now he understood how they knew to be there; why they seemed so calm when the door opened up.

"Goddammit!" he yelled, and he fired a shot into the ceiling.

Nicki rose to settle him down, but as she tried, the room tilted sideways. "Come on, baby, don't—"

A new sound from outside startled them, and as they turned, the curtains jumped as the front window broke. A smoking canister sailed into the room, skipping across the floor in two quick hops before settling against the wall closest to them. Nicki felt her lungs close, and she had the sensation that someone had poured ground glass into her eyes.

Just like that, someone had stolen all the air.

"Tear gas," Brad growled, and despite his wound, he darted to the corner where the smoking canister lay, picked it up, and hurled it back toward the window.

The canister was hot—like a pot on the stove is hot—and he yelled and cursed as the skin on his palm blistered. "Shit!"

The hole in his belly made his throw an awkward, ugly thing. The canister barely made it as far as the window before it got hung up in the curtains and fell to the floor.

"Close your eyes!" he yelled. He pulled his T-shirt over his head and off, handing it to Nicki. "Breathe through this," he said, and he pressed it against her face.

Nicki didn't respond, couldn't respond as the gas inflamed her sinuses and throat. She felt consciousness slipping. They needed to get out of there. To stay was to die, if not by the onslaught of bullets, then by suffocation. She remembered her doctor telling her to be careful around cigarette smoke and other pollutants. He told her that she'd be more sensitive than others.

Brad knew they had to go. The siege was over now. He'd never even considered the use of tear gas as the first wave of their assault. It had never even occurred to him that he wouldn't have a chance to shoot it out with a team of armed men swarming in through the front and back doors simultaneously. How foolish he'd been for *not* thinking about it. From the cops' perspective, it was immeasurably safer to have their prey come to them than the other way around.

But Nicki wasn't walking anywhere. She wasn't *crawling* anywhere. With barely enough strength to stand a few minutes ago, she looked hardly alive now, every breath an exercise in torture. He knew how bad it was for himself; he couldn't imagine the agony she was having to endure.

"We're getting you out of here," he said.

Blood spilled from his belly wound now, cascading down his leg under his trousers, painting a meandering crimson line down onto the carpet. He dreaded the thought of what was coming as he kneeled in front of Nicki, preparing to hoist her onto his shoulder to carry her outside. "Just a little more," he said, and to give himself the use of both hands, he let Ben Maestri's pistol fall to the carpet.

The front wall erupted in flame. Brad guessed that the tear gas canister had heated the fabric of the drapes to its ignition point, and once ignited, the fire spread as if fed by gasoline. Flames leaped from the floor to the ceiling in the front of the room, and from there, they spread across the ceiling, igniting everything in their path.

Brad had never seen anything like it. In the time it took for him to wonder at the speed of the fire's spread, the temperature in the room shot from merely stifling in the summer heat to untenable, radiating from the front wall and the ceiling. Brad pulled Nicki down onto the floor, where the temperature was survivable, but the concentration of gas the greatest.

Sputtering and choking to grab a breath of air, Brad vomited, but paid it no mind. They had to get out of the house. Now. And the front door was no longer an option.

Nicki had gone completely limp, as inanimate as a dress-up doll, incapable of aiding her own rescue. Brad tied his T-shirt around her nose and mouth, hoping to filter out some of the rancid atmosphere, and then wrapped his right arm around her chest, under her arms—a hold that he vaguely remembered from a YMCA water rescue course. Crawling on his wounded side, he began to drag her across the carpet toward the kitchen and its door to freedom. It was an agonizing, impossibly slow journey.

After fifteen seconds yielded only a few feet of distance, it occurred to him that he faced a far more grue-some death than he'd ever imagined.

Carter felt his sanity slipping. They'd been *so close* to a peaceful resolution. Brad had put his gun down, for God's sake! Now that the command post had been blinded, a violent outcome was guaranteed. Through the garbled mess of the radio traffic, he heard excited cries of shots fired, and here in the tiny kitchen, every-one was shouting orders at once.

One urgent cry cut through the commotion like a torpedo through water: "Team one to command, we've got heavy fire showing in the front of the building."

Carter jumped at the words. "What does that mean?" he asked the room. When no one answered, he grabbed Donnelly's arm. "What kind of fire? Are people shoot-ing?"

"No," Donnelly said. "The building's on fire." He turned back to his team at the table. "Alert fire and res-cue. Have them start units this way."

"Wait." Carter pulled him back. "Nicki's lungs can't take that kind of assault. Are you getting them out?"

Donnelly's look was cold and unreadable. "We'll do what we can if they surrender, but we're cops, not firefighters. I'm sorry."

"But they'll die in there."

Trooper Hayes couldn't believe the speed with which the fire grew. At first, there was only the white mist of the gas canister, but then, out of nowhere, it seemed, the smoke turned black and started to roll out of the far side of the building. After he heard the sound of break-ing glass, all hell broke loose. Literally. A fireball rolled out of the front of the building and into the air, igniting the roof in the process.

All in less than a minute.

His earpiece popped as someone broke squelch. "Team one to team three, the front of the building is impassible. If they make a move, it'll be on your side. Keep your eyes open."

"Shouldn't we at least try and rescue them?" Luis asked.

"They promised to shoot anyone they saw," Matt said. "They're the ones who set the rules, not us." *They're dead,* Matt thought. Or if they weren't, they would be in another couple of minutes. At least the old woman and the boy were safe.

Brad moved like an inchworm on his side, each cycle of arms and knees taking him only a foot and a half and lighting an even hotter fire in his belly. He yelled out against the pain, if only to fight off his own approaching wave of unconsciousness.

Finally, he reached the kitchen. He kicked open the swinging door and heaved himself and Nicki across the threshold onto the cool tile floor. The atmosphere in here was better than it had been in the front room, at least a hundred degrees cooler, and the air was nearly breathable.

But it was getting bad quickly. Looking back toward the living room, he saw the roiling cloud of black smoke pushing through the opened kitchen door. He kicked it shut again, but it was too late. Through swollen, teary eyes, he watched in horror as the killing cloud rolled across the ceiling and banked toward the floor. Beside him, Nicki stirred, barking out a horrid, pain-racked cough.

"We're close," he rasped. "Hang in there. We're close."

Without the friction of the carpet, it was easier going. He dragged her to the back door and smiled. Just a few feet separated them now from a breath of air. They'd step outside, and the miserably thick summer air would taste like honey. Like life.

He reached up, turned the knob, and pulled.

Shit! The key was on top of the goddamn refrigerator.

Carter couldn't take it anymore. Nobody even noticed when he strode out of the Mellings' kitchen and into the night. The rain had stopped. Overhead, the moon was trying to force its way through the clouds.

Disoriented at first, Carter stepped down off the tiny stoop into the lumpy assortment of sand and grass that masqueraded for a lawn in this part of the world, and walked a half-dozen paces to the left. As soon as he cleared the side of the Mellings' house, there was no missing the scene of the standoff.

In the distance lay a patch of light brighter than noon, projecting up toward the heavens from behind a dune. In the center of the shaft of light, a plume of black smoke climbed toward the sky. "Oh, my God," he breathed.

"They won't let you go down there," said a voice from the darkness to his right.

Carter turned to see an old woman and a young boy sitting together in the sand. They were just silhouettes, but he could make out enough detail to see that the boy had a bandage on his head.

"It's my house and they wouldn't let me go," the boy clarified.

Carter felt an inexplicable rush of emotion as he saw these two. "I'm sorry," he said.

"Are you Carter Janssen?" the old woman asked.

"I am."

"Then I have something very sad to tell you. That's a very mixed-up boy in there, that Brad. He's going to die tonight."

Carter felt a cold fist grip his insides. *Please just let him die alone,* he didn't say.

"I'm June Parker, by the way." She reached around the boy to extend her hand. "This is my grandson, Scotty Boyd."

Carter shook the woman's hand and then Scotty's.

She continued, "Before he released me, that Brad told me to tell you something when I saw you. He said that his guts were yours to do with what you want. He said he wanted them to go to Nicki, and that I'd have to be a witness to make that happen. Does that make sense to you?"

"Yes, it does." Carter felt like a ghoul.

"There's something else," Gramma said. "He said that nothing comes for free. That you owe him a favor."

Carter waved her off. "Not now. Tell me about it later."

"No, it has to be now," she insisted. "He said it was very important, and if I don't pass it along now, I'll forget some details."

Carter sighed. He didn't want this. He didn't need this. But he listened.

It took less than a minute.

The smoke in the kitchen had banked down to less than four feet above the floor. Against the backdrop of the white light outside, the smoke layer might as well have been constructed with a straight edge, so sharp was the dividing line between life and death. With the smoke came unbelievable heat as the ravenous flames burned through the flimsy kitchen door and raced along the ceiling, consuming everything in their path.

Somewhere in that inferno lay the key to the dead bolt, placed so diligently and proudly on top of the refrigerator.

Keeping his head as low as he could, Brad slapped around the top of the refrigerator, hoping to feel the key. It had to be there somewhere. It *had* to be.

And there it was, farther back than he'd thought, and as his fingertip hit it, he could just barely make out the sound of the key sliding across the top of the fridge toward the back. "No!" he shouted, but there was nothing to do. He heard the unmistakable sound of the key falling off the far edge of the refrigerator, tumbling down through the tubing and wiring before coming to rest on the floor.

Brad hammered the refrigerator door with his fist. "Goddammit!"

"Brad?" Nicki rasped.

"Right here." He joined Nicki on the floor near the door. Across the room, all of ten feet away, the entire doorjamb leading to the living room seethed with fire.

"A window," Nicki said. She tried to raise herself to a sitting position.

"Bars, remember?" To keep out home invaders, he thought wryly. Or maybe just to ensure they never left alive.

Think, Brad told himself. There was always a way. The thought of breaking down the door was too much to contemplate, not only because of the agony, but because of the futility of it. He remembered the size of the dead bolt, the sturdiness of the door. That wasn't even in play.

And the chances of rescue were zip. *If I see a face I'll shoot it.* Great call there. So, what was the choice? Surely, there had to be something.

Of course! But he'd left it on the floor in the other room.

Chapter Thirty-nine

Pressing himself into the unyielding floor in an effort to get away from the searing heat of the fire that roiled above him, Brad crawled back through the flaming doorjamb, out into the living room. He needed his pistol.

Before the fire had started, the distance between the kitchen and the front room had seemed like nothing at all, just a few feet. But now, as he felt the skin on his back wrinkling like old parchment, and the stench of burning hair mixed with the rest of the horrific olfactory assaults, it felt as if he were crawling the length of a swimming pool.

Please let it be there, he prayed. As if it could have wandered off on its own.

There it was, right where he thought, and thank God for it. Seconds meant everything in this heat. His clock had ticked down to nothing, and he still had to make it back to the kitchen. The pain of the fire on his back eclipsed the pain of his bullet wound.

The terror of burning to death had eclipsed his fear of living.

* * *

Nicki was dying. Of this, she was one hundred percent certain. And as she watched Brad crawl back into the inferno that was the living room, she knew that she would die alone. Even as the panic welled up, she realized the bitter irony in the prayer she offered up to God to allow her to die of asphyxia before the fire could get to her.

For the past nine months, ever since she'd first gotten her terrible prognosis, she'd dreaded the slow suffocation that would eventually take her. Now, as she lay on her back, helpless to move, watching the fire roll across the ceiling of the kitchen, she saw suffocation as a fine alternative to immolation.

Once Brad disappeared back into the burning living room, Nicki started counting. She arbitrarily decided that twenty seconds was all the time he could have in there and survive. She counted aloud, so Brad could hear her and zero in on the sound of her voice. "One and two and three and four and . . ." Ten to get in, ten to get out. Anyone can do anything, she figured, for ten seconds.

When she got to twelve, she started to worry for real. At eighteen, she knew it was over. Brad was dead, had to be. Incinerated in his effort to save her. Despite that, she found herself awash in an odd sense of calm. Even if she could have mustered the strength or the wind for a scream, she wasn't sure that she'd have tried. Soon, they'd be dead together, forever. Maybe that was the whole purpose of this terrible trick God had played on them. The fire would speed their peaceful, eternal reunion in Heaven. And it would be Heaven, too. If she and Brad were together, how could it be anything but?

"Nicki! Are you still there?"

It was Brad! "I'm here!" she rasped. She could barely hear herself.

He touched her leg. "We're outta here."

He had eight .40 caliber rounds in his gun, and there wasn't a lock in the world to resist that kind of attack. The smoke in the kitchen had banked down impossibly low, until the doorknob was the last thing visible before the air became a deadly cloud. "Cover your ears," he said, and he took aim.

Matt Hayes saw the back door jump as the bullets ripped through the wood. In the sharpness of the floodlights, he could see every detail as chips of wood flew from the door and its jamb.

Next to him, Luis yelled into his radio, "Shots fired! Shots fired on side three. We're taking fire."

"No, we're not," Matt said, but his spotter wasn't listening. From what Matt could see, the perps were trying to shoot themselves out of an inferno.

Carter jumped as he heard five, then six, then seven sharp reports. "No," he breathed. He took off, sprinting toward Nicki and Brad, leaving their victims behind.

Even in the reduced visibility, Brad could see the bullets chewing the woodwork around the doorknob. In the close confines of the tiny kitchen, the noise of the gunshots was stunning, each of them carrying a percussive force that he could feel in his chest. After the first two shots, his eardrums caved in to the assault and the shots became bolts of pain masked by a thick silence.

He'd deafened himself and he didn't care.

He fired seven shots before he kicked at the door with the sole of his foot. It flew open, and then was sucked closed again as the voracious blaze gulped at the new supply of fresh air and doubled in intensity. Brad dropped to the floor in a futile attempt to escape the excruciating heat.

He rolled to his back and kicked at the door again. This time, it stayed open. He grabbed Nicki's hand and pulled her toward the door. Just five or six feet more, and it would be all over.

Trooper Hayes watched the back door fly open not once, but twice. To his left, Luis announced on the radio that the perps were on their way out the back door, and down below, he could see assault team three readying for battle.

Matt gripped his rifle tighter to his shoulder and got ready.

Then, there they were: the boy dragging the girl, who might as well have been dead for all she was moving. And the boy had a gun.

"Freeze!" The chorus arose from eight armed men positioned all around the perimeter of the back of the house. "Put the gun down! Now! Drop that weapon, and get on the ground!"

At first, the boy didn't respond. He just stumbled out of the door and into the brightly lit night, dragging the girl behind him. Then he saw the police.

Through his ten-power scope, Matt could see the panic when it arrived on the boy's face.

"I said, put your weapon down!" someone yelled again.

Instead, the boy hoisted the girl up by her armpits as a shield and pressed his gun to her temple. The moment he denied a shot to the ground team, Matt Hayes knew that it would all come down to him.

And at that moment, he knew that the boy would die.

The air smelled and tasted even better than Brad had hoped. They'd made it! No other thought fluttered in his mind. He was alive, and Nicki was alive, and that was all that mattered.

Crouching in the doorway, still agonized by the radiating heat of the fire, he looked down at Nicki and gave her one of the smiles he knew she loved so much.

She didn't smile back. Instead, her face was all twisted in a mask of emotion. She looked as if she were shouting something at him, but he couldn't make out any words.

When he saw the cops, all the relief and all the happiness evaporated, leaving only the certainty that they were going to gun him down. Seeing the skirmish line in front of him, and the half-dozen rifle barrels pointed at his chest, he knew that he'd entered the final minute of his life. One way or the other, they were taking him down.

Confused, but oddly calm, his mind replayed the words of Carter Janssen. There really was a way to make this whole disaster something more meaningful. But with all those guns, he had to make sure they hit the right target.

"I'm sorry," he said to Nicki, and then he hoisted her up by her armpits to use her as a human shield.

Leaving only a head shot.

Nicki couldn't move. Paralyzed by fear and unable to breathe, her screams sounded like moans, raspy, throaty, inaudible trifles that were swallowed by the cacophony of the fire and the confusion. When he smiled at her, clearly proud of himself for making the rescue, and relieved to be safe once again, she tried to manufacture words that would tell him to put his gun down. "The gun!" she rasped. "They'll see the gun! They'll shoot you!"

Brad didn't seem to get it.

And then he did. Nicki saw him reach a decision, saw his expression change when he settled on a plan. When he apologized and then hauled her up, she knew what the plan was.

"No! No, please don't!" Tapping a reservoir of strength somewhere deep in her soul, beyond the limits of her scorched and tortured lungs, she lashed out at him, kicking and wriggling and doing everything she could to make it impossible for the police to shoot. "Don't shoot!" she wheezed.

"Nicki, stop it!" Brad grunted. "Let me do this."

She felt his grip slipping.

Trooper Hayes waited for an opportunity. The girl was screaming for mercy, screaming to get away from the asshole who held her, but in all her frantic movement, the sight picture became so scrambled that he couldn't take a shot.

"Take him out," Luis whispered. "Jesus, take a shot."

"I don't *have* a shot," Matt hissed.

But then he did. Just like that, out of nowhere, the girl dropped out of the sight picture, and there was Brad Dougherty, a perfect target.

Matt centered the reticle and squeezed the trigger.

Nicki saw the bullet tear a hole in Brad's chest. He made a barking sound as he shuffled a little two-step backward before somebody unplugged the power cord that kept him standing and he sat down hard, his legs folding beneath him.

"Oh, shit," he said, and he fell sideways onto her, his shoulders and head landing on her lap.

"Brad!" she cried. "Oh, my God, Brad!" His blood flowed hot and with impossible speed, soaking her legs and her shorts and her shirt as she hugged him tightly to her breast. "Don't die," she begged.

Brad lifted his arms in an effort to return the embrace, but they didn't work. "It hurts, Nicki," he said. "Oh, Jesus, it really hurts bad." As he spoke, bloody bubbles formed at his nose and mouth. Nicki wiped them away, leaving crimson smears on his face.

Behind her, she was aware of a lot of shouting, and of people running toward her, but she didn't care what they were saying.

"I'm so sorry," Brad said. "Please don't hate me."

"I *love* you!" she sobbed. "I'll always love you."

Somebody placed their hands on Nicki's shoulders and she shook them away. "Keep your hands off of me!" she shrieked. There, she'd found her voice again.

"You're under arrest," the voice said, and hands gripped her forearms, trying to pull them behind her back. But they were slick with blood and the officer had a hard time keeping hold. In the background, she heard somebody discussing a helluva lung shot.

Nicki pulled Brad tighter. "Wait for me, okay?" she sobbed. "Promise you'll wait."

Brad managed a smile. For just an instant, the mask of agony dissolved away and he shined brightly for her one more time.

Then the light in his eyes turned dark.

When they yanked Nicki to her feet, Brad spun away from her and landed face-first in the sand.

Chapter Forty

It was one of those springs when the grass never got a chance to dry. Despite the brilliant blue sky, the sod was so waterlogged it felt freshly planted. The time was long gone when Carter worried about the wetness seeping through the stitching of his Italian loafers. There were a lot of things he didn't worry about anymore. So much had changed.

Cemeteries, for example. Until a couple of years ago, he'd thought of these vast gardens of the dead as grisly, awful places. Now, he took a certain solace in visiting them.

He'd purposely parked a good distance away from the row he was looking for. He'd discovered that the walk gave him time to prepare himself for the meeting, and to decompress afterward. As always, he dressed as if the funeral were today.

On this April day, Carter marveled at the paradox of so much life teeming in a place set aside for the dead. Birds had rediscovered their voices after the long, bleak winter, and the flowers seemed somehow more vibrant here. The beauty of the place made it all the more comforting.

It was a beautiful gravesite, nestled into the shadow of a stout oak, and just a few feet away from a thicket of honeysuckle that filled the air with the perfume that for Carter defined the arrival of spring. He was pleased to see that the scar of the new grave had largely grown over, and delighted that someone had recently filled the little flower pot with freshly cut tulips, Nicki's favorite flower.

As he stooped to brush grass clippings away from the nameplate, a wave of emotion sneaked up on him and he had to clench his jaw to fight it away.

"Don't you miss headstones?" a lady's voice asked.

Carter jerked his head up to see Gisela Hines sitting on a concrete bench, watching. She wore a flower-print dress that screamed springtime. "Mrs. Hines," Carter said, rising to his feet. "I didn't see you there."

Her expression betrayed neither cheer nor sadness. "A graveyard looks too much like a golf course without the stones," she said.

Carter had never thought of that. "I don't know. Without the headstones, it's a more peaceful place to visit. Less intimidating."

"I just wish we could have written a final message to him," Gisela said. She looked and sounded like a woman who had wept until there were no tears left. "I could have told him one more time that we loved him."

Carter resisted the urge to offer up a platitude. Instead, he went back to the task of sweeping the grass clippings off Jeremy Hines's marker. Silence was probably best now anyway. Words did not exist that could console her loss.

As Carter dug a blade of grass out of the carved dates on the plaque, he prayed that Jeremy's young soul had found the peace he'd sought in taking his own life. The deputies swore that they'd left him alone for only a couple of minutes, but it was all he'd needed to hang himself in his cell.

"How are you holding up?" Carter asked. He eyed the spot on the bench next to Gisela, and she moved to make room for him.

"I'm lonely," she said. "It's sweet of you to visit."

Carter blushed. He didn't know how to respond.

"Do you ever wonder how you could have made things different?" Gisela asked. "I lay awake some nights—every night, really—wondering if things would have been different if I'd left Frank before Jeremy became so angry. I wonder if there weren't signs that I could have read, or if maybe there were signs I did read but chose to ignore. Do you do that?"

"I try not to," he said. "I think that's a road to insanity. The clock only spins forward, you know? If you don't move on when a chapter closes, I think you're doomed."

Gisela weighed that. It wasn't anything she hadn't thought of on her own. "It's hard to do."

"There's nothing harder in the world."

Gisela said softly, "How is Nicolette?"

Carter's expression softened. "She's doing okay," he said. "The antirejection drugs seem to be working well, and there's no sign that the disease has returned." He turned to look at Gisela and waited for their gazes to meet. "Jeremy's heart and lungs are strong." His voice caught and he cleared his throat. "I can't tell you how grateful—"

Gisela placed her hand on Carter's leg and squeezed. "You already have," she said. "Many, many times over. He simply didn't need them anymore, and under the circumstances, well . . ." She drilled a look straight through Carter. "They're not Jeremy's anymore. They belong to Nicolette, and please don't ever refer to them that way again."

Carter's eyes reddened as the wave of emotion sucker punched him again. He dared not attempt to speak.

A quarter mile away as the crow flies, Nicki stood in the shade of a dogwood looking at the marker her father had bought as a peace offering. At her request, it read,

BRAD WARD DOUGHERTY
His Smile Lit My World

"You hate it, don't you?" she said. "It's way too corny and it would have pissed you off." She sniffed and cleared her throat. "Well, tough. I'm making the decisions now."

In another month, it would be a year since their trip together into hell, yet this was the first chance she'd had to visit and see his grave. It was as pretty as a place like this could be, peaceful and spooky all at the same time. Having spoken to Brad daily in her head, she felt silly speaking aloud to a patch of grass.

He knew all about her long stay in the hospital after the fire, and he knew that she'd sold him out by signing papers laying all of the blame for the carjacking and kidnapping at his feet. By doing so, and with the help of testimony from Scotty and his grandmother, all the charges against her had been dropped. That would have made Brad happy.

Then came the transplants, out of the blue. She'd just recovered from her fire-related injuries when word came that she was being leapfrogged up the recipient list. She didn't understand all the details, but she got the sense that her dad knew who the donor was. He wouldn't tell, of course, and even if he would, she didn't think she wanted to hear. The procedure went flawlessly. The difference to her health was immeasurable. She felt young again. She still had drugs to take—they would be a part of her life forever—but the frequency of visits to the hospital was decreasing, and for the first time since she could remember, the doctors were smiling and delivering good news.

Secretly, Nicki suspected that Brad had pulled some strings in Heaven to make it all happen. If anyone in the world could charm the likes of Saint Peter, it would be him.

"I brought you a present," she said to Brad. Stooping low and balancing herself to keep from kneeling in the wet grass, she pulled the little vase from the marker and set it upright. "No, they're not flowers. Sorry about that, but you never were much of a flower type. I brought you something to read instead."

She reached into her jacket pocket and pulled out a carefully folded page from the *Michigan City News*.

"I can't take any credit for this," she explained. "This one is all Daddy. The journal you told Mrs. Parker about was still there. He won't let me read it, but he said that he had you pegged wrong. Those were his words: pegged wrong. That's the equivalent of God admitting that gnats were a mistake.

"Whatever you wrote pissed off the right people. Daddy leaned on the prosecutor out there to file charges for what happened to you. They didn't want to at first because you weren't there to testify, and they were worried that prisoners would be too scared to testify against each other. Then Daddy suggested that they forget about the inmates, and go after that one guard,

Lucas somebody." She looked at the article, trying to find the name.

"Lucas Georgen," said her father's voice from behind.

She jumped and put her hand on her heart, a gesture that first startled him and then made him smile. "What are you doing, Daddy?"

"Sorry. I haven't been listening, I promise. Just that last part. Lucas Georgen, rapist scumbag. We had no trouble at all getting people to spill their guts about him."

Nicki was shocked to see that he was talking to the grave, too. "Anyway," she said, "he got twenty years."

Carter paid silent respects to Brad, then he turned his gaze to Nicki. "How are you holding up?"

Nicki took a deep breath and blew it out with a dramatic flair. "Everything's working fine."

"That's not really what I meant," he said. He nodded toward the grave. "How are you *holding up*?"

That answer took some thought. "Okay, I think. I only cried once." Nicki spindled the newspaper article and tapped it into the vase. "I try to tell myself that this is the only time he's ever really been happy."

"I tell myself that about you, sometimes," Carter mused.

Nicki didn't reply. What was there to say?

"Well, I didn't mean to intrude," Carter said, stepping back. "Take your time. I'll be—"

"It was the sweetest thing," Nicki said, interrupting. She saw his look of confusion. "What you did. The marker, the stuff with the prosecution in Michigan, all of it. It was sweet."

Her words disarmed him. He looked at the ground.

"I thought I'd try being a good father for a change," he mumbled.

"It's hard to do when you've got a crappy kid to deal with," she said.

Overhead, a cloud passed in front of the sun, blurring the edges of shadows. Carter cleared his throat again. "Well, I'll give you some time alone with Brad."

"I don't need it," she said, standing and brushing her pants legs straight. "He's not here. Not really." She tapped her chest with her finger. "He's here."

Carter cocked his head. "You sure? It's likely to be a long time before we come back this way."

"This is all the past," Nicki said. "I'm tired of the past. Now that I've got a future, I thought I'd try living for it."

As Nicki reached out to hold her father's hand, the sun emerged in a breathtaking starburst of light. The entire universe seemed to be smiling.

Don't miss John Gilstrap's next compelling
Jonathan Grave thriller

Final Target

Coming from Kensington in Summer 2017

Keep reading to enjoy a sample excerpt . . .

Chapter One

Jonathan Grave heard the sounds of ongoing torture a full minute before he arrived on the scene. An approach like this in the middle of the night through the tangled mass of the Mexican jungle was an exercise in patience. He was outnumbered and outgunned, so his only advantage was surprise. Well, that and marksmanship. And night vision.

Ahead of him, and too far away to be seen through the undergrowth, his teammate and dear friend Brian Van De Muelebroecke (aka Boxers) was likewise closing in on the source of the atrocity.

The last few yards, the last few minutes, were always the most difficult. Until now, the hostage's suffering had been an academic exercise, something talked about in briefings. But hearing the agonized cries above the cacophony of the moving foliage and screeching critters of this humidity factory made it all very real. The sense of urgency tempted Jonathan to move faster than that which was prudent. And prudence made the difference between life and death.

The slow pace of his approach was killing Jonathan. It was 02:15, the night was blacker than black, and that victim who no doubt was praying for death had no idea that he was mere minutes away from relief. All that had to happen was for Jonathan and Boxers to get into position, read the situation for what it was, and then execute the rescue plan. There was nothing terribly elegant about it. They would move in, kill the bad guys who didn't run away, and they'd pluck their precious cargo—their PC, a DEA agent named Harry Dawkins—to safety. There was a bit of yada yada built into the details, but those were the basics. If past was precedent, the torturers were cartel henchmen.

But first, Jonathan had to get to the PC, and get eyes on the situation, and he had thousands of years of human evolution working against him. As a species, humans don't face many natural predators, and as a result, we don't pay close attention to the danger signs that surround us. Until darkness falls.

When vision becomes limited, other senses pick up the slack, particularly hearing. As he moved through the tangle of undergrowth and overgrowth, Jonathan was hyperaware of the noises he made. A breaking twig, or the rattle of battle gear, would rise above the natural noises of the environment and alert his prey that something was out of the ordinary. They wouldn't know necessarily what the sound was, but they would be aware of *something*.

Alerted prey was dangerous prey, and Jonathan's two-man team did not have the manpower necessary to cope with too many departures from the plan.

Another scream split the night, this time with a slurred plea to stop. "I already told you everything I know," Dawkins said in heavily accented Spanish. The words sounded slurred. "I don't know anything more."

In time, the magnified light of his night vision goggles, NVGs, began to flare with the light of electric lanterns. "I have eyes on the clearing," Boxers' voice said in his right ear. He was barely whispering, but he was audible. "They're yanking the PC's teeth. We need to go hot soon."

Jonathan responded by pressing the transmit button on his ballistic vest to break squelch a single time. There was no need for an audible answer. By their own SOPs, one click meant yes, two meant no.

As if to emphasize the horror, another scream rattled the night.

Jonathan pressed a second transmit button on his vest, activating the radio transceiver in his left ear, the one dedicated to the channel that linked him to his DEA masters. The transceiver in his right ear was reserved for the team he actually trusted. "Air One," he said over the radio. "Are you set for exfil?"

"I'm at a high orbit," a voice replied. "Awaiting instructions." The voice belonged to a guy named Potter, whom Jonathan didn't know, and that bothered the hell out of him. The Airedale was cruising the heavens in a Little Bird helicopter that would pluck them from one of three predetermined exfiltration points. He was a gift from the United States Drug Enforcement Administration as an off-the-record contribution to their own employee's rescue. For reasons that apparently made sense to the folks who plied their trade from offices on Pennsylvania Avenue, this op was too sensitive to assign an FBI or even a US military rescue team, yet somehow it could support a government-paid pilot, and that inconsistency bothered Jonathan. A lot. It was possible, of course, that Potter was every bit as freelance as Jonathan, but that thought wasn't exactly comforting. All too often, freelancers' loyalty was as susceptible to high bidders as their skills were.

"Be advised that we will be going hot soon," Jonathan whispered.

"Affirm. Copy that you're going hot soon. Tell me what you want and I'll be there."

Jonathan keyed the other mike. "Big Guy, are you already in position?"

Boxers broke squelch once. *Yes*.

Jonathan replayed Dawkins's plea in his head. *I already told you everything I know.* The fact that the PC had revealed information—even if it wasn't everything he knew—meant that Jonathan and Boxers were too late to prevent all the damage they had hoped to. Maybe if DEA hadn't been so slow on the draw, or if the US government in general had reacted faster with resources already owned by Uncle Sam, the bad guys wouldn't know *anything*.

The bud in Jonathan's left ear popped. "Team Alpha, this is Overwatch. Over."

"Go ahead, Overwatch," Jonathan replied. He thought the "over" suffix was stupid, a throwback to outdated radio protocols.

"We have thermal signatures on Alpha One and Alpha Two, and we show you approaching a cluster of uniform sierras from roughly the northwest and southeast."

Somewhere in the United States, Overwatch—no doubt a teenager judging from his voice—was watching a computer screen with a live view from a satellite a couple hundred miles overhead. As Jonathan wiped a dribble of sweat from his eyes, he wondered if the teenager was wearing a wrap of some kind to keep warm in the air conditioning. "Uniform sierra" was what big boys wrapped in Snoopy blankets called unknown subjects.

"That would be us, Overwatch," Jonathan whispered. He and Boxers had attached transponders to their kit to make them discernible to eyes in the sky. Even in a crowd, they'd be the only two guys flashing here-I-am signals to the satellite.

"Be advised that we count a total of eight uniform sierras in the immediate area. One of them will be your PC. Consider all the others to be hostile."

In his right ear, Boxers whispered, "Sentries and torturers are hostile. Check. Moron."

Jonathan suppressed a chuckle as he switched his NVGs from light enhancement to thermal mode and scanned his surroundings. It wasn't his preferred setting for a firefight because of the loss of visual acuity, but in a jungle environment, even with the advantage of infrared illumination gear, the thick vegetation provided too many shadows to hide in. "How far are the nearest unfriendlies from our locations?" he asked on the government net.

A few seconds passed in silence. "They appear to have set up sentries on the perimeter," Overwatch said. "Alpha One, you should have one on your left about twenty yards out, call it your eleven o'clock, and then another at your one, one-thirty, about the same distance. Alpha Two, you are right between two of them at your nine and three. Call it fifteen yards to nine and thirty to three. The others are clustered around a light source in the middle. I believe it's an electric lantern."

Jonathan, Alpha One, found each of the targets nearest to him via their heat signature, and then switched back to light enhancement. Now that he knew where they were, they were easy to see. The concern, always, were the ones you didn't see.

As if reading his mind, Venice (Ven-EE-chay) Alexander, aka Mother Hen, spoke through the transceiver in his right ear. "I concur with Overwatch," she said. The government masters didn't know that Venice could independently tap into the same signal that they were using for imagery. She was *that good* at the business of taming electrons. He liked having that second set of eyes. While he knew no reason why Uncle Sam would try to jam him up, there was some history of that, and he knew that Venice always had his best interests at heart.

On the local net, Jonathan whispered, "Ready, Big Guy?"

"On your go," Boxers replied.

Jonathan raised his suppressed 4.6 millimeter MP7 rifle up to high-ready and pressed the extended butt-stock into the soft spot of his shoulder. He verified with his thumb that the selector switch was set to full-auto and settled the infrared laser sight on the first target's head. He pressed his transmit button with fingers of his left hand and whispered, "Four, three, two . . ."

There was no need to finish the count—it was the syntax that mattered. At the silent *zero*, he pressed the trigger and sent a two-round burst into the sentry's brain. Confident of the kill, he pivoted left and shot his second target before he had a chance to react. Two down.

From somewhere in the unseen corners of the jungle, two more bursts rattled the night, and Jonathan knew without asking that the body count had jumped to four.

Time to move.

Jonathan glided swiftly through the undergrowth, rifle up and ready, closing in on the light source. They were ten seconds into the fight now, plenty of time for the bad guys to react. If their weapons were on them and they were trained, they would be ready to fight back.

An AK boomed through the night, followed by others, but Jonathan heard no rounds pass nearby. Strike the training concern. Soldiers fired at targets, thugs fired at fear. Barring the lucky shot, the shooters were just wasting ammunition.

Jonathan didn't slow, even as the rate of fire increased. His NVGs danced with muzzle flashes. The war was now fifteen seconds old, the element of surprise was gone, and that left only skill and marksmanship.

Three feet behind every muzzle flash there resided a shooter. Jonathan killed two more with as many shots.

And then there was silence.

"Status," Jonathan said over the local net.

"Nice shooting, Tex," Boxers said through a faked southern drawl. "I got three."

"That makes seven." With luck, number eight would be their PC. "Mother Hen?"

Before Venice could respond, the teenager said, "Alpha Team, Overwatch, I show all targets down. Nice shooting."

Jonathan didn't bother to acknowledge the transmission.

"I concur," Venice said. She could hear the teenager, but the teenager could not hear her. Of the two opinions, only one mattered.

Jonathan closed the distance to the center of the clearing. A naked middle-aged man sat bound to a stout wooden chair, his hands and face smeared with blood, but still alive. Dead men surrounded him like spokes of a wheel. This would be their PC, Harry Dawkins, and he looked terrified.

"Harry Dawkins?" Jonathan asked.

The man just stared. He was dysfunctional, beyond fear.

"Hey, Dawkins!" Boxers boomed from the other side of the clearing. At just south of seven feet tall and well north of two hundred and fifty pounds, Boxers was a huge man with a huge voice that could change the weather when he wanted it to.

The victim jumped. "Yes!" he shouted. "I'm Harry Dawkins."

As Jonathan moved closer, he saw that most of the man's teeth had been removed, and with all the blood, it was hard to verify his identity from the picture they'd been given. "What's your mother's maiden name?" Jonathan asked.

The guy wasn't patching it together.

"Focus," Jonathan said. "We're the good guys. We're here to take you home. But first we need to know your mother's maiden name. We need to confirm your identity."

"B-Baxter," he said. The hard consonant brought a spray of blood.

Jonathan pressed both transmit buttons simultaneously. "PC is secure," he said. Then he stooped closer to Dawkins so he could look him straight in the eye. He rocked his NVGs out of the way so the man could see his eyes. Dawkins hadn't earned the right to see Jonathan's face, so the balaclava stayed in place. "This is over, Mr. Dawkins," he said. "We're going to get you out of here."

Boxers busied himself with the task of checking the kidnappers' bodies for identification and making sure they were dead.

The kidnappers had tied Dawkins to the chair at his wrists, biceps, thighs, and ankles using coarse rope that reminded Jonathan of the twine he used to tie up newspapers for recycling. The knots were tight and they'd all been in place long enough to cause significant swelling of his hands and feet. Several of Dawkins's fingernails were missing.

Jonathan loathed torture. He looked at the bodies at his feet and wished that he could wake the bastards up to kill them again.

"Listen to me, Harry," Jonathan instructed. "We're going to need your help to do our jobs right, understand? I'm going to cut you loose, but then you're going to have to work hard to walk on your own." It was good news that the torturers hadn't made it to his feet yet.

Jonathan pulled his KA-BAR knife from its scabbard on his left shoulder, and slipped its seven-inch razor-sharp blade carefully into the hair-width spaces between rope, skin, and wood. He started with the biceps, then moved to the thighs. The ankles were next, followed last by the hands. Dawkins seemed cooperative enough, but you never knew how panic or joy were going to affect people. The edge on the KA-BAR was far too sharp to have arms flailing too early.

"Who are you?" Dawkins asked.

Jonathan ignored the question. A truthful answer was too complicated, and it didn't matter. Dawkins surely understood that leaving this spot was better than staying, regardless of who the rescuer was.

"Listen to me, Harry," Jonathan said before cutting the final ropes. "Are you listening to me?"

Dawkins nodded.

"I need verbal answers," Jonathan said. After this kind of ordeal, torture victims retreated into dark places, and audible answers were an important way to show that they'd returned to some corner of reality.

"I hear you," Dawkins said.

"Good. I'm about to cut your arms free. You need to remain still while I do that. I could shave a bear bald with the edge on this blade, and I don't need you cutting either one of us up with a lot of flailing. Are we clear?"

Dawkins nodded, then seemed to understand the error of his silent answer. "Yes, I understand."

"Good," Jonathan said. "This is almost over." Those were easy words to say, but they were not true. There was a whole lot of real estate to cover before they were airborne again and even more before they were truly out of danger.

The ropes fell away easily, and in seconds, Harry Dawkins was free of his bonds. Deep red stripes marked the locations of the ropes. The man made no effort to move.

"Do you think you can stand?" Jonathan asked. He

offered a silent prayer with the question. He and Boxers were capable of carrying the PC to the exfil location if they had to, but it was way at the bottom of his list of preferred options. He glanced behind him to see Boxers continuing his search of the torturers' pockets, pausing at each body long enough to take fingerprints that would be transmitted back to Venice for identification. Uncle Sam had not asked him for that information, but if a request came, Jonathan would consider it.

"I think I can," Dawkins said. Leaning hard on his arms for support, he rose to his feet like a man twice his reported age of forty-three. He wobbled there for a second or two, then took a tentative step forward. He didn't fall, but it was unnerving to watch.

"How long have you been tied to that chair?" Jonathan asked.

"Too long," Dawkins said with a wry chuckle. "Since last night."

Jonathan worked the math. Twenty-four hours without moving, and now walking on swollen feet and light-headed from emotional trauma, if not from blood loss.

"Scorpion, Mother Hen." Venice's voice crackled in his right ear. "Emergency traffic."

Air One beat her to it: "Break, break, break. Alpha Team, you have three—no, four victor-bravo uniform sierras approaching from the northwest." Vehicle-borne unknown subjects.

"If that means there are four vehicles approaching your location, I concur," Venice said. She didn't like being upstaged.

Jonathan pressed both transmit buttons simultaneously. "I copy. Keep me informed." He turned to Boxers, who had heard the same radio traffic and was already on his way over. Jonathan opened a Velcro flap on his thigh and withdrew a map. He pulled his NVGs back into place and clicked his IR flashlight so he could read. "Hey, Big Guy, pull a pair of boots off one of our sleeping friends and give them to the PC. The jungle is a bitch on bare feet."

"What's happening?" Dawkins asked.

Jonathan ignored him. According to the map—and to the satellite images he'd studied in the spin-up to this operation—the closest point of the nearest road was a dogleg about three-quarters of a mile from where they stood.

"Alpha Team, Overwatch," the teenager said from under his blanky. "The vehicles have stopped and the uniform sierras are debarking. I count eight men in total, and all are armed. Stand by for map coordinates."

Jonathan wrote down the minutes and seconds of longitude and latitude, and knew from just eyeballing that the bad guys had stopped at the dogleg.

"Air One, Alpha," Jonathan said to the Little Bird pilot. "Are the bad guys walking or running?"

"I'd call it strolling. Over."

"So, they're not reinforcements," Boxers said, reading Jonathan's mind. He handed a pair of worn and bloody tennis shoes to Dawkins.

"I'm guessing shift change," Jonathan said.

"What, people are coming?" Dawkins had just connected the dots, and panic started to bloom.

Jonathan placed a hand on Dawkins's chest to calm him down. "Take it easy," he said. "We've got this. Put those on your feet and be ready to walk in thirty seconds." To Boxers, he said, "Let's douse the lights. No sense giving them a homing beacon." It was a matter of turning off switches, not exactly a big challenge.

With the lights out, Dawkins's world turned black. "I can't see anything," he said. His voice was getting squeaky.

"Shoes," Jonathan snapped. "You need to trust us. We're not going to leave you, but when it's time to go, you're going to need to move fast and keep a hand on me. I won't let you get lost or hurt."

"Are we gonna fight them?" Boxers asked. Ever the fan of a good firefight, his tone was hopeful as Dawkins's was dreadful.

Jonathan pressed his transmit button. "Air One, Alpha. Give me the bad guys' distance and trajectory. Also, are they carrying lights?"

"I show them approximately three hundred meters to your northeast, still closing at a casual pace. They have white light sources. I'm guessing from their heat signatures that they're flashlights, but I can't be certain."

Jonathan started to acknowledge the information when the pilot broke squelch again.

"Alpha, Air One. Before you ask, I cannot engage from the air. This is not a US government operation."

Jonathan and Boxers looked at each other. With the four-tube NVG arrays in place, Boxers looked like a huge creature from a *Star Wars* movie.

"What the hell?" Big Guy said. "Where did that come from?"

Jonathan had no idea. The last thing he wanted was an overzealous chopper driver shooting up the jungle from overhead. He'd spent too many missions receiving air support from the best in the business to trust his life to an amateur.

Jonathan didn't want to take a defensive position and have a shoot-out with a bunch of unknowns. It wasn't the risk so much as it was the loss of time. In a shoot-out, it's easy to identify the people you've killed, and if the wounded are screamers, they're easy, too. It's the ones who are smart enough to wait you out who you have to worry about. When he was doing this shit for Uncle Sam, he could remove all doubt by calling in a strike from a Hellfire missile. At times like this, he missed those days.

Waiting out a sandbagger could take hours, and their ride home—the Little Bird—didn't have hours' worth of fuel.

"We're going to skirt them," Jonathan announced.

Boxers waited for the rest.

Jonathan shared his map with Big Guy and traced the routes with his finger. "The bad guys are coming in from here, from our two o'clock, a direct line from their vehicles, which are here." He pointed to the dog-leg. "We'll head due north, then double back when we hit the road. If we time it right, we'll be on our way in their truck before they even find this slice of Hell."

"We're gonna pass awfully close," Boxers observed.

"Fifty, sixty yards, probably," Jonathan said. "We'll just go quiet as they pass."

"And if they engage?"

"We engage back."

"And we're doing all of this with a naked blind man in tow," Boxers said.

"Hey," Dawkins snapped. "I'm right here."

"No offense," Boxers grumbled.

"Let's go," Jonathan said. He moved over to Harry,

taking care to make noise in his approach so he wouldn't startle the guy. "Hold your hand out, Harry," he said.

The PC hesitated, but did as he was told.

"I'm going to take your hand," Jonathan said as he did just that, "and put it here in one of my PALS loops."

"Your what?"

"They're attachment straps for pouches and other stuff," Jonathan explained. "Stuff you don't need to worry about. You think of them as finger rings."

Dawkins yelped as he fitted his wounded fingertips through the tight elastic. "Hurts like shit."

"Better than dyin'," Boxers observed.

No response. None was needed.

"Okay, here we go," Jonathan said, and they started off into the night. He keyed both mikes simultaneously and relayed their plans. "I want to know if anybody wanders off or drifts toward us. My intent is not to engage. But more important than that is not walking into an ambush."

"I copy," the Overwatch teenager said. "I'll let you know if I see anything."

For three, maybe four minutes, they moved as quietly as they could through the thick underbrush. The approaching bad guys were so noisy and clueless that Jonathan's team could have been whistling and not be noticed. Then, like flipping a switch, all that talking and jabbering stopped. The beams turned in their direction, painting the jungle with a swirling pattern of lights and shadows.

Jonathan and Boxers took a knee, and Dawkins followed.

"What's happening?" Dawkins whispered.

"Shh," Jonathan hissed.

The bud in his right ear popped. "Break, break, break," Venice said. "The other team seems to be turning in your direction."

Jonathan's stomach knotted. This was wrong. Why would they do that? It was almost as if they'd been informed of Jonathan's presence.

He keyed the mike to the Little Bird. "Air One, Alpha," he whispered. "How are we doing?"

"Alpha, Air One, you're doing fine," the pilot said in his left ear. "You're close to the approaching hazard, but they are staying to their course."

"That's a lie!" Venice declared in his right ear. "They're closing on you."

"Overwatch, do you concur?" Jonathan asked. But apparently the teenager had taken a soda break.

"Scorpion, Mother Hen" Venice said. "I smell a trap."

"So it looks like we're going to have a gunfight after all," Boxers said with a chuckle on the local net. "Maybe two if the dickhead in the sky is trying to get us hurt."